Adam J Shardlow is a
Guardian and The Idler. In his spare time (which he
never has) he enjoys spending time with his
invisible dog, Marlowe.

the
missing

ADAM J. SHARDLOW

Libros
INTERNATIONAL

ISBN 978-1-905988-53-2

Cover by Julia D Higginson

Published by Libros International

www.librosinternational.com

Printed and bound in Great Britain by
CPI Antony Rowe, Chippenham and Eastbourne

Acknowledgements

Thanks to Helen, Ben and Stuart for believing, Maureen for questioning and WA, CM and NG for the inspiration.

To Helen, for everything, thank you.

The Missing

His stare penetrated deep within, his eyes burning like desert fire while he conjured winds that whipped a suffocating blanket of burnished sand into the air. He created a mirage from dislocated heat shimmers that confused all I saw and made me speak out of turn. It was a gaze that appeared to judge and weigh my response, examining its substance and validation against all that I had said before. If I was found lacking he would ignore my inebriated ramblings and mark me a fool; his only act, to smile, white teeth standing out against ebony skin, bone against scorched crust. A slight shake of his head would seal the pronouncement; and he would turn away from temptation, leaving me none the wiser.

But he did not take that path. He must have seen some pitiful longing in my face, greedy thoughts traceable in my speech that forced him to act, to evaluate my hidden meaning as a request. He sought out an unseen desire, a naked ambition, and that made him choose the darker path. This road leads through the forest that should be shunned, a place of dark aspirations and unspoken longings that ought not to be acknowledged, a tangled world that exists on the edge of reality. It is a mirror world, distorted and yet the same. A land twisted out of recognition and yet still containing the kernel of reality. The place we yearn for as children. Jealously guarded by adult ogres who, not permitted to enter themselves, would hide this secret garden away forever.

If only he had chosen differently and never listened to the most selfish of hearts doused in bitter recriminations. Some thoughts are better left unsaid.

My mouth talked, my mind wandered, structure and meaning were lost. I knew what I was trying to say but the words came out half formed, disfigured; mutant vowels and stillborn sounds. Yet he listened. He could have ignored me like all the others, but he picked his way through the crowd with intent and he chose the seat next to mine.

Did he buy me a drink and help me on the way to drunkenness? Did he encourage and cajole me into my current state, leading me on with a beckoning finger, tugging and pulling at my shirt, muttering sweet nothings in my ear? If he did I cannot remember and thus find myself unable to condemn him outright. It was always my own failings that stirred his loins and will remain forever so.

He played on my suffering by listening, by acting as the catalyst in the foaming mire that was spat forth. He preyed on what I was asking, succour to my dreams, tempting my fate. He opened the door, slid back the panel and showed me what was hidden in the mirror world.

One

The bar was noisy. It had swollen with people until overflowing, fit to burst like the vein-shattered stomach of a profane indulger. Light and noise spilt from the open door onto the hot pavement, briefly lighting up the queue of stragglers who peered between the smoke-woven heads into the perspiration-sweet interior. Inside, bodies pressed hard against one another, eyes bulging, narrow stares from the strong, wary glances of the timid. Shoulders barged and pushed at the crowds, levering a way into the throng between the sweat-stung bodies, naked flesh prickled with heat, warm to the touch of a lover, cold to a trespasser.

Lights skirted over the crowd. Beams of scarlet and violet probing into the drab interior, searchlights licking the flesh of dancers, reflecting yellowed eyes and pale skin, the flash of jewellery or an imitation watch, the glint of a gold tooth, fashion-conscious shades worn pushed back onto heads columned the light back into the heavens. Pulsing blue strobes beat out a devil rhythm while a glitter ball shed a waterfall of starlight across the room, turning it into a miniature cosmos. This club was primitive, sexual, heated, wet, slippery, cruel, intoxicating – a place of magic waiting to happen.

Two muscled skinheads stood at the door, watching those that entered, eyeing up the girls and entertaining thoughts of violence with any customer who even considered making eye contact. They acted as if they owned the bar. It was their 'patch' they would have said if they had spoken, but apart from the odd mention of football or a line to a partially dressed girl, they remained silent. They were the sentinels of the bar; a Gog and Magog of their own imaginings, gatekeepers who ruled with polite contempt over all the entrances and exits. They had power and they would abuse it.

They knew who to stop and who to let in; the pimps, the dealers, the whores, the wise guys and sneaks, the petty thieves and carjackers, all were ushered through with a nod of recognition. They looked the other way and eyed those coming down the street from the centre of the city. The innocent, the young, the unaware, they were ushered in with a helping hand, pushed inside, the doors slamming as they entered. These were fodder, sustenance in a booming economy of crime. Lambs to the slaughter.

Gog and Magog guarded the entrance to Hades on the lookout for the cocksure and pissed. Troublemakers who would shoot back remarks before they realised where they were. Baseball cap-wearing men, tooled up and too stupid to appreciate they were out of their league. Little fish that would shout and scream, talk tough and flash about a blade but would break all too easily when the crowd turned ugly. It was this they guarded and protected. Fights had to be contained, the offending parties taken out back and taught about real respect and fear. Knuckledusters and sovereign rings used to hammer home the truth that they were not wanted here. Nothing was allowed to get out of hand or spill out onto the street in case it drew attention from the police, the last people invited to the party.

They arrived in a small group, jeans riding low on insubstantial hips, trainer laces undone and T-shirts stained. They would be watched as they moved down the dimly lit street, kicking a can of cheap cider out in front, cigarettes lit for gesticulation. They were always loud, poor imitation ghetto talk punctuated with "fuck, fuck, fuck." Eyes rolling and shaved heads, faces set into a scowl of hate.

They reached the door and stuck out pimple-covered chins, a

top lip sneer with a downy moustache as Magog turned to address them.

"Not tonight, lads…we're full."

The tallest – the one wearing the thickest gold chain – eyed the man mountain and risked talking back.

"Fuck ya, we just saw others go in."

Gog turned to assist his brother-in-service. His soulless countenance settled on the boy and he said in the same commanding voice, "We don't allow trainers. It's not that sort of club. Try the Palais on the Main Road."

"Fuck off, you fucking retard; we don't go to no skank club. Let us in."

He spat the words out full of venom and hate, perhaps not yet understanding his fate. The rest of the collection sniggered or took turns to gob on the floor in an attempt to look hard. Snorting up a rheumy mess that pearled on the pavement like bird shit. They didn't want to have to walk back up the street, a walk of shame with their backs to the giants, but at the same time they didn't want to face off against the bouncers, to risk a heavy bone-deep beating.

As they reassessed their options two more men came down the street; they stumbled slightly, talking in the hushed tones of those who don't want to admit their current state of inebriation. One was tall and lanky, sandy hair left to flutter around a thin face with a disarming smile that all too often broke out into an exaggerated grin. He wore jeans that had seen better days and a shirt that had never experienced a hot iron. He walked with the gait of a reanimated scarecrow, all knees and elbows moving to a tune of his own devising.

His friend, who lagged behind, was better dressed and proportioned. He seemed hesitant, hugging the wall as if he would melt into the shadows given the first opportunity. He did not want to be here, not in this part of town; he wanted to retreat to the safety of the streets he knew, back to the crowds and the music, back to bars with imported beer and zinc table tops. But he moved after his friend and reached the crowded entrance.

The city thugs turned and stared down the new couple as they approached, daring either man to push to the front while their own business was still outstanding, but Gog had already seen the men and made his decision. An arm, thick and hard with steroid muscle, pulled the crowd into two, forming a path.

"What the fuck yer think yer doing? We're here first," screamed their leader, but he seemed unable to move from behind the arm which formed a tattooed barricade.

"All right, gentlemen – this way," Magog added whilst holding open the door.

The scarecrow man walked forward, grinning at the snarling baseball caps.

"Fucking twat," they shouted.

"Yeah, guess I won't see you inside, yer skank," he retorted.

The other guest made no eye contact. He stared ahead of him and followed his friend inside. The door closed behind them; locking out the city, locking out the thugs, the giants and any chance of escape.

It was the fifth bar of the evening and Nick Stewart was starting to feel ill. He had been permitted to begin on his usual beer but Munch soon insisted they move onto harder drinks and had come back from one bar with two dark green concoctions that had tasted sweet and salty at the same time – a drink that felt light on the tongue but burned the oesophagus as it slid down like out-of-date cough mixture. They went by the name of Head Bangers, though Nick was more worried about the effect they seemed to be having on his stomach lining, making him feel nauseous, the delicate skin burnt.

After that it was round after round of cheap shots. "Two for the price of one," beamed Munch. Double the damage, double the headache in the morning, double the amount of vomit he would have to evacuate into the toilet or onto the side of the street. He could not drink like this; it was not what his body was made for and already he was lagging behind his friend.

But Munch would not hear no for an answer; this was his way of being a friend, his way of helping, understanding, finding a solution to a problem. He really did believe that salvation could be found in the gritty dregs at the bottom of a glass, and if you got to the bottom and found nothing – well, oblivion worked just as well.

At first Nick had been in agreement. He had wanted to drink; he craved some kind of escape, to take his mind off recent events, and who better than Munch who never appeared to have a rational thought in his head and lived in a fantasy world of his own making. Spending time with him, being brainless, not caring, shifting the inconsequential delights of male desire was what he needed. But as usual Munch had got carried away; his natural exuberance and lack of any self-control took over, forcing their small party from the glittering fashion bars of the Lace Market, through to the cheap and nasty mega-pubs of The Square, and now this place, a hidden bar with no name or identity, a place where they did not belong, at the wrong end of the city.

They had not known such a place existed when the evening began, but news had filtered through the arcane pub scene that Munch was more than a part of. He heard it confirmed from a girl with dreadlocks and numerous piercings in her top lip, building his excitement until this was the only place he wanted to be. With his mind made up he was off, his desire suddenly cemented to try somewhere fresh, somewhere unknown, a place that snarled danger and excitement, with the added possibility of sex with someone new.

Munch returned from the bar with a tray containing shot glasses and an entire bottle of tequila, a puss-coloured worm suspended in the urine yellow liquor.

"Man, you can buy entire bottles in this place. Ain't that cool? What a shit hot place."

Nick looked up from the bottle as it was poured with undue care by Munch into the two glasses. He watched the gyrating crowd, the barely clad women with black and white skin exposed, the men in low-cut jeans and vests, tattoos flexing as they bumped and ground their pricks into their partners' arses. The room resembled some cheap underground bar in Latin America and felt just as hot – not the crowded room in Nottingham on a Friday night that it was in reality.

Also, since entering, Nick had had the feeling that he was being watched. That the dancers were in some way disapproving of his entrance into their world and so they were studying him. Ready to pounce, like wild animals watching their prey. He felt vulnerable and miscast. A voice in his head kept repeating that he should leave, that all would be fine if he just got out and went home. He ignored it.

Munch finished off the first of his tequila hits with an exaggerated flourish of the hand.

"Ahhh, that's good," he pronounced, drawing out the last syllable until it turned into a contented sigh.

"Come on, drink."

He pointed at the glass that sat before Nick.

"More where that came from."

Nick picked up the glass and sniffed. It smelt chemical, like toxic fire. Across the rim he could make out Munch in blurred contrast, egging him on. His lips touched the sharp glass, a greasy texture that burnt his dry lips. The glass was tipped back with a snap of the neck and the tequila slipped into his throat. It was rough, like drinking petrol, and left a stinging slug trail down into his stomach. He felt tears prick at his eyeballs but it stayed down. He dropped his head back and looked at Munch who grinned again.

"Good one, yer bastard."

The glasses were refilled and the game started.

Nick soon forgot where he was, the trepidation he had felt on entering the bar, the sensation of being watched, fear melting into acceptance and then inebriated delight. The dancing pack merged into a being with many arms, legs and stomachs, a moving, oscillating primal creature that pulsated to music that no longer seemed to be a deafening hip hop but something ancient, a beat that moved and tugged and led. The sound of shifting sands and a wind that howled from forgotten places.

The lights heightened the experience, drawing him out of the mundane and into a new world. Stars and meteors rushed past him, while the rings of a planet beamed overhead sending him reeling to the rainbow at the end of the world. Balls of radiance slammed against his body, illuminated from behind by a path of flame, yet they exited without leaving a scar. Energy entered his weary body. He felt alive, dangerous, exhilarated.

Munch moved into the vacant seat at his side as the music increased in tempo.

"So what did she say?"

The conversation went back to this evening, the reason for him being out, why he was drinking.

"What could she say? I laid it all out to her. I need to sell the flat. I need the money so I can quit work and act. It's my flat...why can't I do what I want with it? It's not hers, she moved in with me. That's all I said, I laid it out straight."

Another shot was dropped into the gullet, more fire to the flames that burned out of control.

"It's the only way I'm going to get on with my life. I mean, things were going well and then I had to put it all on hold, what with Mum..."

More drink, glasses clinking in a mock toast. Munch nodding in agreement, pushing him on.

"Girls, they don't understand, man, never understand us. Never have. Think they own us and can control us, but no way. That's why the Munch Man will never settle down."

The bottle was grabbed and Munch took a long swig, a burp of air escaping from the neck as he passed it over. Nick followed suit. He could feel the worm tickling at his gums, which was accompanied with an encouraging chant from his friend.

"That's right…open wide."

The bug slipped inside and disappeared accompanied with a cheer and clapping hands from his friend. The creature was swallowed; it crept down and through him, his body acting as a mausoleum as the worm's nutrients and life were absorbed into him.

He passed the bottle back and stood up slowly. The room twisted and span, arched and stretched. It bulged unexplained in the middle and strayed away into nothingness at the edge. He turned to look down at Munch who was refilling the glasses again.

"Going to the shitter," he mumbled as a wave of nausea washed over him.

His mate waved him away.

"Yeah, have one for me."

Nick turned and made for a small gap between the twisting, lurching dancers. Faces loomed close. Eyes narrow and accusing, wide pupils and long lashes all looking at him. Some smirked and laughed. He could feel it inside him, the laughter and scorn building up and spilling out into the faces of those around him. He felt ridiculous; he knew he looked drunk, a lurching, staggering mess. He laughed with them. Ha, ha, bloody ha.

A black girl – young with a wide mouth and ruby lips – smiled, her face stretching open like a preying shark. She wiped the sweat from between her breasts and placed her fingers to his mouth. He tasted salt and desire. He tried to grin back at her, a leer of suggestion, but she was whisked away by a thickset woman who pushed him back with a scowl and a look of palpable distaste.

He moved for the far wall and searched for the toilet. Slipping through a poster-covered door he let it swing shut behind him, leaving the music to become a dull thud, the footsteps of some lumbering hell creature passing through the void. He turned to face the toilet, staggered and slipped on the wet floor. His world pitched forward and briefly hung in front of him before he landed face first on the ground, his forehead smacking hard against the dirt encrusted tiles, sounding like a smashed fruit. He bit deep into his top lip, his bottom teeth cleaving into the flesh.

"Shit."

He got back to his feet as quickly as possible, slipping again in the mess of the floor. The smell of disinfectant and faeces adhered to his mouth, to his face; it was in his hair. His shirt was wet with piss.

He rushed over to the sink and ran the taps. Pushing cold water across his face, he looked up into the cracked and silvering mirror. He had split his lip and blood dripped down his chin and onto his white shirt. He touched gingerly at a spot above his right eye. It felt tender, bruised, already the blue of rotting liver.

He splashed at his face with more water and tried unsuccessfully to clean his shirt. He knew that he looked awful, that there was nothing to salvage and that his dignity still lay on the piss-covered floor, but he was too drunk to care.

Having gone to the urinal he made his way back to Munch as quickly as he could without looking too hard at the faces that stared and laughed. He had decided to leave; it was time to get out, the damage for the night already done. He realised he could not get any lower. He wanted sleep and a shower; he wanted to wash away his shame and forget about this evening.

There was a thin black man with a pointed goatee sitting in his seat, while a fat woman cuddled up to Munch, who grinned and giggled while pointing at the two new bottles of tequila on the table. Seeing him standing over them the woman inserted a slug-like tongue into Munch's ear, slipping it deep into the cavity of his head.

His friend looked up.

"Fuck, what happened?"

He looked concerned and moved forward, pushing at the woman in irritation, his hand barely covering one of her enormous breasts.

Nick sat down heavily, the cheap leather couch with its lost stuffing bruising his arse.

"I slipped in the toilet."

His lower back was starting to feel tight as well. He knew tomorrow he would ache and already felt miserable for himself.

The thin black man, all eyes and pock-marked cheeks sat woven into a smoke shroud created from a smouldering black cheroot, turned to address him.

"You want me to slap the bitch that did that to yer, man?" His brow was knitted as if in concern but Nick realised he was being made fun of; he was the butt of a joke, the pretext for laughter. The furrowed cross-hatching disappeared to be replaced with a smirk and laughing eyes that seemed to smoulder and burn like hot coals.

"It was no one. I just slipped."

Nick stood again as Munch and the fat woman joined in the laughter, a laugh at his expense.

"I'm going."

"Ah come on, man. Sit down and have a drink with us."

The black man leaned forward and started to pour drinks into the empty glasses.

"Yeah, sit down, Nick, you're spoiling the view."

He sat down reluctantly but turned away from the continuing laughter. He watched the dancers. A man held a woman tight as he tilted her backwards, her short skirt riding up her gleaming thighs to reveal an almost non-existent G-string, her buttocks lustrous white and smooth.

"You'd like a lady like that?" enquired the guest as he handed over a drink.

"A lady to show off dancing, maybe to take home and make love to? She is a sweet honey, yes?"

He spoke with an accent, a drawl that made every word sound languid yet concise. There was no street talk, just a soft lilting voice that even in the clamour of the club floated and teased its way into Nick's thoughts. It was a voice born of waves, a becalmed ocean that lapped lazily against his mind, sand dunes cresting on the horizon.

"I've already got one," he mumbled almost apologetically.

"Then where is this fine lady? Why ain't she with you tonight?"

Nick found himself warming to the man, who smelled of wood smoke and something sweeter - a candy herb, liquorice - that intoxicated the senses. He wanted to trust this man, to talk to him about his current problems. Here was someone who would listen and no doubt give good counsel, a man who had lived, a man who had dined out on life and was prepared to share his mind.

"We argued. I said some things I shouldn't have done about her not helping out enough…about her stopping me from going where I want to go."

"And where is it you want to go?"

"Nowhere in particular. I just want to give up my job. I think I can make it as an actor. I'm not the best but I think I've got some talent. I need time to prepare and rehearse and I can't if I still have to go to my day job. I just feel…" He trailed off. He was frustrated, of that he was certain, but there was something more.

"You just feel she ain't helping you. That she's holding you back. Yes?"

"Kind of. It would just be so much easier if it was just me I had to worry about, not her as well. Do you know what I mean?"

He nodded and smiled. To Nick's eyes he looked wise; deep inside that slender frame there was great respect for people and their problems. Nick knew that this man had suffered at the hands of others. It gave him a gravitas not witnessed in all men. But he also scared Nick, his foreignness, his appeal, his eyes that never strayed from Nick's own; they were invitations to somewhere unseen, mirrors that concealed a hidden world.

"I understand. Sometimes you wish it was just you, then you wouldn't have to do no work nor do those living things that stop a man from following his dreams. Men should be allowed to follow their dreams, whatever they are, whoever they are. Sometimes yer wish you could magic all the problems away."

Nick agreed. At last here was someone who understood. Someone who really knew what was going on in his own mind, the reason he felt so frustrated, so alone, the feeling that he was living someone else's life when he had never been given the chance to live his own.

"I just want to have a crack at doing something I know I'm good at. People like me never get the chance. I just wish things were different."

Again the man smiled. His eyes widened as he grinned and nodded his head. "Good," was all he said as his eyes flashed with flame and the music increased its tempo.

There was a metallic taste in the air, the tang of cordite or ash that struck the back of his throat, making Nick gulp in air. A shiver of electricity passed through him as he looked around, convinced a fire had broken out, but the dancers remained where they were, swaying and moving, dark silhouettes against the sunset lights, a desert dance between shifting dunes. He turned back to his spiritual companion but the chair was vacant.

Saturday 15th June, 2002

Deborah was sitting cross-legged in front of her small portable television when she saw the pair she wanted on 'Top of the Pops'. She knew straightaway that they were right, perfect in every detail. The teenage star wiggled her butt whilst wearing them low on the hips, set off with a silver belt and a large copper clasp. As the repetitive beat and Latin rhythms played out, she would shake and grind, her stomach muscles flexing as her piercing rocked suggestively from side to side. Chantelle would sing the evocative lyrics, winking at the audience to highlight just what she meant.

"I wanna be your bi-atch,

I want you to be my slave."

And Deborah would pretend, out of sight of her parents, that it was she that was singing, and mimic Chantelle's every move in a stage made up of her bed and an audience of stuffed toys and dolls.

The jeans were tight, frayed around the waistband and with several well-placed rips on the thighs. At first Deborah thought Chantelle must have had them specially made for her, but then she read an interview with the star in a magazine where she mentioned that the jeans had been bought off the shelf. They were a pair of 'Bangles', designer wear that Chantelle had lent her name and image to and Deborah was desperate to own an exact match.

She had been pestering her mum since last weekend. She needed new jeans anyway as her current pair were starting to look a little half-mast and she had worn a hole in the left knee from playing in the field. Mum had said she could have a pair if they weren't too expensive but now, she claimed, she wasn't free to go into town and buy them for her. She said she was too busy as they were having friends around for dinner and she needed to get on with the cooking.

Deborah had sulked about the house all day. She tried to make it look as if her life depended on getting those new jeans. She shuffled with an exaggerated gait from the lounge into the kitchen where she sat and huffed at the dining table, her face set in rigid dejection. Mum ignored her and busied herself in the kitchen.

"It's no good looking like that, Debs, I'm too busy today. We'll go next weekend after your swimming lesson," said Mum as she checked the heat in the oven and wondered why it was not getting hot enough.

"But you said last weekend I could get them on Saturday – today's Saturday."

"I know, but now I'm busy."

The door to the kitchen opened and a muddy brother walked in and grinned on seeing Deborah's miserable face. Her father followed, looked at the chaos in the kitchen and sighed.

"Don't go any further," screamed Mum on seeing the state of her youngest, Jonathon. "I've just cleaned up in here and I don't want mud tramping all through the house. Take your shoes off right there…and you, Michael."

Jonathon flopped down onto the floor and pulled at his football boots, the laces thick with soil. Michael slipped his shoes off quickly and looked over at his daughter.

"What's the matter with long face over there?"

Mum let out a noise of irritation before answering.

"She's moaning about those bloody jeans and getting under my feet."

"No I'm not," moaned Deborah, though she knew it was the truth.

"What's the problem then?" asked Dad.

"I'm just bored and…"

Her voice trailed off at the end of the sentence; she could not think what else to say that did not make it sound as if she were whinging. It was true that she was bored, but that was only because she had been looking forward to going into town. She liked town on a Saturday, it was always busy and crowded and she could normally persuade Mum to buy her something, even if it was only a burger.

Michael turned to his wife. He knew that he would be considered 'under her feet' as well if he stayed in the kitchen and now that Jonathon had finished his football training he had nothing to do until later that evening. He had watched the big England match at lunch and wanted to see the highlights of Ferdinand's header but knew that would annoy his wife even more.

"I could take you in to town if you want?"

He watched as Deb's face lit up the way only the face of a child could.

"If your mum doesn't mind?" he added and gave her a wink.

Mum was sieving out flour into a large bowl, trying her best to ignore everyone.

"I don't care what you do, just do it out of the kitchen."

Deborah got up from the table and ran upstairs shouting over her shoulder, "I'll just get ready, Dad."

Michael looked down at his son in his muddy shorts and stained top.

"Do you want to come?" he asked, but in truth he already knew the answer.

"Nah", said the boy, getting up and kicking his boots into the cloakroom. "I'm gonna play on the computer."

Michael could hear the kids running around upstairs as he put his shoes back on. He looked over at his wife who was now cutting up some vegetable that he could not identify.

"Were you going to buy her the jeans?"

He didn't want to get into trouble if he did get them; his wife had a cunning streak to her and could be using tonight's party as a way of getting out of the purchase. Both the women in his life were a bit devious in the way they would manipulate events.

"She needs some new ones, but only get them if they're not too expensive. She'll grow out of them in six months."

"I could put them on the credit card."

Everything seemed to be bought on credit at the moment. No matter how much he paid off the balance it never seemed to decrease. He would probably have to start doing some of the later shifts on the buses; they paid a little better than the daytime ones.

"Whatever," replied his wife as she hacked at a carrot.

As the rain had started up again Michael decided to take the car. It would mean he would have to pay for parking but at least they would stay dry and they could get home quickly if necessary.

Debs sat in the passenger seat and sang along to some tape she had insisted he put on. Every now and again he caught the odd lyric that sounded a little sordid but he was sure Debs didn't know what those words really meant. He caught his daughter looking in a compact mirror and applying some lipstick. She had insisted on adding some glitter eyeshadow that he thought made her look like a clown. She was growing up fast – too fast, he thought. She was already wearing a bra and he knew it wouldn't be too long before he had two women at the mercy of their menstrual cycles in the house.

"You gonna park in Victoria car park?" she asked while tracing a raindrop across the passenger window and leaving a smudge mark.

He wanted to park down by the river because it was a bit cheaper but then they would get wet on the trek into town. Better to be on the safe side.

"Yeah, if we can get in."

There were only a few cars in the queue for the shopping centre. The World Cup match replays would have started by now so the majority of men would have rushed home to watch it or were still in the pubs from the earlier game, all thoughts of going home obliterated by booze. They waited ten minutes before some obliging shoppers – their car packed with new purchases – left, and they were let inside. Even with the rain and the game they were almost on the bottom floor before they could find a place to park.

He let Debs lead the way as he wasn't sure where the shop she was talking about was located. He followed her as she weaved her way between the cars and made her way to the lifts. He didn't really like coming into Nottingham and normally left his wife to walk around the shops at the weekend. If he needed anything he would ask her to pick it up for him. Debs was running ahead, looking back over her shoulder to make him move faster. God, he wished she would stop wearing quite such revealing clothes. It was not that warm outside and he noticed for the first time that under her coat she was wearing some kind of crop top.

"Is that all you had to wear?" he asked as he got close to her.

Debs held the door open for him and looked down at her exposed midriff.

"Why, what's wrong with it?"

He started to form a sentence about her not showing her body off quite so much but changed his mind. If her mum thought it was OK then who was he to argue?

"You'll catch a cold."

Was he getting old? No, not yet, he still had plenty of years ahead of him. He just felt tired, that was the problem. They had ended up with a family slightly earlier than expected when Janet had got pregnant; it was a bit of a mistake but not an issue, not for him at least. Money had been tight, really tight, for the first few years but now that Jonathon was at school they were getting it together at last. Certainly Janet didn't seem to resent her predicament as much as she used to.

They got into the lift and started to move up from the basement to the ground floor.

"It stinks in here," said Debs, screwing up her nose at the distinct smell of urine.

The shopping centre had recently had a refit, its 1970s concrete hidden behind glass and tall green plants. Unfortunately the extent of the makeover had not extended to the car park and the lifts which were still used by the local drunks as a place to sleep. Trying not to come into contact with the walls of the moving toilet, Michael held his child close until the doors opened and the light and music of 'The Victoria Shopping Centre' was revealed.

He manoeuvred Debs through the crowd of harried faces that surged forward. He could feel the press of their bodies against him, the rub of synthetic materials that shrieked and sighed.

They found themselves in an oasis of plants and mirrors. From hidden speakers dull music was playing – a soothing undersea sensation to help calm the consumers as they took part in their shopping event. The reflections of people moving were bounced onto the eye so that it appeared they were standing inside a giant crystal filled with expressionless faces and gaudy sale signs.

Debs pointed off down the main precinct and pulled Michael in that direction. He found it hard to get his bearings inside this place so allowed his daughter to take the lead as she seemed to know where they were heading.

Everywhere there were people moving ceaselessly from one shop to another. Michael could not understand how the same individuals could come to this place every week, looking in the same shops and following the same dull route. It was as if they were on some never-ending Saturday pilgrimage to the gods of retail.

"Where are we going?" Michael asked his daughter as she propelled him forward.

"It's just up here. There's a special offer on at Jeans Genie."

Michael knew that normally Debs would be stopping off at every clothes shop along the way, plus pulling her mum into the record shops, but today she made straight for the pair of jeans. She must really want them. He hoped they were not too expensive. He made a mental note to insist she buy something cheaper if they were over thirty pounds.

They reached the shop which was full of teenagers browsing through acres of denim as shop assistants not much older than the kids attempted to keep everything orderly.

Debs made straight for a large display in the centre that was topped by a large cardboard cut-out of a woman posing seductively. Michael noticed her belly button had a large fake ruby in it. He now realised why his daughter had insisted on wearing that top and eye shadow. Averting his eyes from the arresting image he turned his attention back to Debs who was clawing at a pile of jeans.

"Do you know what size to get?" he asked as she held a pair against her legs.

He had forgotten to ask his wife what size she needed. He knew the measurements were different for girls; they didn't use inches but were always going on about numbers. He knew his wife was always happy when she got into clothes that were a size twelve and moaned when it was a size fourteen. Debs was about half the size of his wife so was she a six?

"These should fit," replied Debs, holding a pair up triumphantly.

"Are you sure?"

Michael took hold of the garment. The material felt thin and it was cut ragged around the waist, plus there were a couple of purpose made slashes at the top of the legs. They were not very practical and would probably fall to bits in the tumble-drier. He looked for a price tag, which was hidden inside. The price shocked him – a penny under fifty quid. How could a pair of kid's jeans cost so much? He could probably buy himself two pairs for that price. Plus these already had holes in them.

Debs smiled up at him, her eyes dancing with the chance of owning a bit of Chantelle. She wanted those jeans as if her life depended upon them. She would be able to show them off to her friends – and then there was the school disco coming up where they were allowed to wear whatever they wanted.

"You'll have to try them on. I'm not buying them unless they fit you."

He didn't want to have to come back again next Saturday and swap them. He looked around the shop.

"There are some changing rooms over there."

He handed her the jeans and pushed his daughter through the crowds towards the women's room. At the curtained entrance an attendant with an artificial smile acted like a robot repeating the same questions to all who came up to her.

"How many garments?" asked the girl, chewing gum and fiddling with a pile of coloured tags.

"Just one," said Debs and held her hand out.

She was given a blue chitty with a raised number one and the curtain was pulled aside for her to enter. She stepped forward and then turned back towards Michael.

"Wait there, Dad; I want you to be the first to see me in them."

She grinned mischievously before turning, the curtain swinging back to block her from view.

Michael turned and looked at the mêlée within the shop. Perhaps he could persuade Debs to buy a cheaper pair. He spotted a sale rack and sidled over to take a closer look. A couple of teenage boys were looking through the garments but they gave way to Michael as he approached. He looked through the smaller sizes and found a pair that was about right. They were darker in colour and the material was a lot thicker, so he guessed they would probably last longer. They didn't have any of the rips and tears of the others but in Michael's eyes they actually looked new as opposed to well worn like the ones she wanted.

He checked the price. The fifty pound sticker was half obscured with a new price of twenty. That was more like it. He wondered if he would be able to persuade Debs to try them on.

He moved back to the changing room and waited outside while trying not to look at the curtain. He didn't want anyone to think that he was taking time out to peek into the women's changing areas. He checked his watch. If he got Debs the pair she wanted he might be able to make it back to watch the last ten minutes of the repeated game. He would get a bollocking from Janet but what else was new?

Where was she? She should have got the jeans on by now and been out here pirouetting in front of him. Two women came out of the changing rooms together. He strained his neck to look round them for any sight of his daughter. The assistant on the outside of the curtain gave him a funny look. He smiled at her and returned to passing the time.

Two minutes later he approached the assistant.

"Could you check my daughter please? She went in five minutes ago to try on some jeans. She's about this high," he placed his hand at his chest height, "with brown hair, about shoulder height. Her name's Deborah."

The woman looked him up and down, her eyes screwing up as she scrutinized him.

"In the changing rooms?"

"Yeah, you gave her a blue tag and she took some jeans inside."

Doubt played on her plain features.

"About five minutes ago," he added and smiled to reassure her.

The girl turned and disappeared behind the curtain, tutting loudly as she left.

Where did they get them? He didn't consider himself very well educated – in fact he flunked out of school at fifteen – but he had basic common sense. Most of the young people he seemed to come into contact with today didn't seem to have anything between their ears. He hoped Deborah grew up better than that. She was not brilliant at school but they had both tried to encourage her. Education was important now.

The girl came back.

"There's no girl in there," she said dismissively.

He was starting to feel a little impatient. It was like this when he did the school buses for the kids at the local secondary school. Eventually they would wind him up a little too far.

"She's in there. I watched her go in myself. You even served her. Now go and look again."

He didn't want to sound condescending but he knew that's how it came out.

He could tell the girl wanted to tell him to piss off, but she went back into the changing room without a word. He could hear her making a play of calling his daughter's name in a stupid voice expressly designed to taunt him.

Michael pulled open the curtain and stepped inside. The girl turned round to face him, determination in her eyes.

"Get out. This is for women only."

He ignored her.

"Deborah, stop messing about. Debs, where are you?"

The girl advanced on him and grabbed at the top of his arm as he pulled at one of the cubicle doors. It was empty. A female voice shouted out angrily from the back of another cubicle.

"Get out! Get out!"

There were six available spaces; two were taken up with women in different stages of undress. The other four were empty. Michael moved up and down between the cubicles calling out his daughter's name.

A security guard stepped in from the shop floor.

"What's going on, Jayne?"

"This man's trying to get in and see the women. Call the police."

"I'm just after my daughter."

Michael didn't mean it, but he was angry so his voice came out louder than he intended. It sounded shrill and concerned.

"His daughter never came in. He's lying, he's a pervert."

He shrugged the girl off and pushed his way past the security guard and back out into the shop. He looked around. She must have come out when he was looking at the sale rack. He shouted out her name.

"Deborah!"

Shoppers looked up at the red-faced man, distracted from what they were doing.

"Deborah!"

He couldn't see her anywhere. She was desperate to get a pair of those jeans, so she would never have left the shop and she knew not to talk to strangers. Why was the place so busy? He started to push and shove his way through the hordes of people who had all stopped to gawp at him.

"Deborah...Deborah!"

He kept calling out her name waiting for a reply. None came.

"Excuse me, sir..."

The security guard took hold of him, using a firm grip. Determined fingers bit into the flesh of his wrist.

"I'm after my daughter," replied Michael pushing at the burly guard.

Michael was strong but the guard was big and he seemed single-minded in his intent.

"I really must insist, sir. The police are on their way."

Michael pushed at a woman who blocked his view of the shop floor; she fell to the ground in a heap of plastic carrier bags.

"Deborah! Where are you?" He turned to the guard. "Help me find my daughter, she was in the dressing room."

"Yes, sir. If you come with me to the office."

Office? Why did he have to go to the office? Deborah was out here, in the shop somewhere. Why was no one helping?

"Has anyone seen my daughter?"

Blank faces stared at him. A man shouted something obscene as he helped his wife to her feet. Teenagers laughed, embarrassed at the display.

Two uniformed officers pushed their way through and nodded to the guard. They grabbed Michael by the arms and forced him towards the back of the shop.

He tried to stop them. He wanted to stay down here and look for Deborah but they moved him on with ease. He was pushed out of the shop floor and into a small office. The door was slammed shut. He was forced to sit in a chair.

"What's going on?" asked the first officer, a tall thin man with a Seventies-style moustache.

"My daughter, I'm after my daughter. She's gone missing."

Michael was breathing hard. Fighting against the security guard and policemen had taken its toll on him.

"One of the girls said he was trying to get into the changing rooms. His daughter never went in there," accused the security guard standing by the door to stop any attempt at an escape.

"Debs went in there. I saw her."

"Debs, is that the girl's name? What does she look like?" The policeman turned to his younger colleague. "See if we can put out a call on the tannoy."

"Her name's Deborah Wade, she's only thirteen. She was wearing a short white top that showed off her tummy and a pair of jeans with a hole in the knee. I think she was wearing her trainers.

She must have wandered out of the shop."

The description came out in a jumble. Why didn't he keep a photo of her in his wallet? They would be able to find her quicker with a photo.

The second policeman took the name and left the room. There was still quite a commotion going on outside.

"Did you see the girl?" the remaining officer asked the security guard.

"No. I saw him come in the shop and play with the kids' rack. We get a few dodgy people coming in and hanging around the changing rooms. Jayne said he was loitering outside while holding onto to a pair of girl's trousers. No young girl ever went in or came out."

"She did. I saw her."

Michael could feel tears prick at his eyes. He fought them back. He didn't want to cry in front of these men. Where could she have gone?

The policeman turned back to Michael.

"Do you have anyone we can ring, sir? Someone who could give us more details? Her mother, for example?"

He thought of his wife patiently sorting out the details for tonight's dinner. The slight panic she always felt as she tried to make everything perfect for the guests, to set the right tone and ambience. She would drop everything and have to come into town – she would blame Michael.

He gave the officer his mobile with the number for home flashing up on the screen. The officer took it and pressed the dial button.

"I really should be outside looking for Debs. She'll be worried on her own."

The police officer smiled but didn't reply. The security guard looked at the floor.

"Hello, Mrs Wade?"

Michael could hear the minuscule tinny voice on the other end of the phone make an affirmative noise.

"No need to be alarmed, madam. I'm PC Brown and I'm with your husband. We're looking for your daughter, Deborah."

There was a loud commotion on the line. The distance and microphone distorted the sound. Michael thought it sounded like a cartoon character speaking, a puppet mouse.

The policeman nodded, a confused look crossing his face.

"Could you come down to 'The Victoria Shopping Centre', to the Jeans Genie shop? Ask for PC Brown."

He handed the phone back to Michael.

"She's angry, isn't she?" He knew she would be and regretted the whole coming into town business. He should have just stayed at home.

The police officer looked over at the security guard and then back at Michael. He stood upright and pushed his shoulders back.

"She's coming down to get you, sir. She also says you don't have a daughter."

The others he could understand, but it was his wife's refusal to admit that Deborah existed that hurt the most. She had arrived with darkness clouding her face and now looked at him with a view of disgusted concern. He could tell she felt sorry for him, having a breakdown in front of people at the local shopping centre, running and screaming around a shop while people laughed at him. He was like a confused animal, his eyes wide with uncomprehending fright. He knew that she found his belief in a young teenage girl more disturbing because of the connotations. She wanted to know why he was fantasising about young girls. Even if he did claim she was his daughter. She had spoken to the police officers, her voice loud so that he could hear. She said she had read the papers, she said she knew all about people like that, hanging around changing rooms. She turned to face him and he felt ashamed as she told him it was perverted, desperate and sordid.

He had thought at first that it was part of an elaborate television programme. One of those that was on early on ITV. Everyone playing along to make him look stupid, while viewers laughed into their fish suppers at his expense, but the realisation was much darker and it swept over him like a sickening tsunami, leaving him bereft and broken.

What he didn't understand was, had he imagined Deborah and because of that was now insane? Or by waking up from his dream had he been insane and was now cured? Or even worse, was this now the dream and somewhere his poor little Deborah was waiting for him, calling out for her father, all alone and afraid in the dark?

Two

He left Munch to carry on drinking in the bar, not because he wanted to go home any more – in truth he was not sure he would be that welcome at home – but because he felt quite light-headed and giddy, like a small child who had eaten too many sweets and was suffering from an overdose of sugar. He had drunk his fill, his body was saturated, already he could smell it leaching from his pores; he simply could not face drinking anything else. He felt bloated from the wear and tear of the evening, the last round of tequila having made him feel sick. Tomorrow he would pay the price, but for now, breathing in the warm air of the evening, he felt alive. It was a strange sensation, his body ragged and pained while his mind had been left unsullied. He actually thought he was clear-headed, but then he remembered the red-eye gleam of the black mystery man and he realised his mind was definitely drink-fogged.

He had staggered out of the bar in a hurry, not one hundred per cent sure he would make it to the door without being sick. The two bouncers, back in their respective niches adjacent to the entrance, nodded at him as he tripped into the street. The capped chav boys had long ago left to find better sport, but it seemed not too far as a cry came from the drunks across the street alerting him to their tormenting presence.

He watched, swaying in the lit doorway, the man-mountains towering above him as the boys happy-slapped a tramp whose face was already bleeding from an earlier punch. The tramp went down as one boy kneed him in the balls, covering his head with a hand that still clutched a can of extra strong lager. The boys now took it in turns to kick at him, turning his head into a bloody pulp. It was a sick game; a pack of rabid animals attacking the weak and defenceless, easy sport for the horde, something to help pass the night in the violent city.

Nick looked round at the two bouncers but they ignored him. They had no desire to interfere. No wish to end up a victim of crime if one of the lads pulled a blade or even worse in a police van having to explain why they had dismembered and mutilated a group of ASBO teenagers. Nick thought about intervening but knew it was useless. Nottingham was not cut out for social obligation and niceties; it was dirty and violent and would rather spit in your eye than hold out a helping hand. People always walked by on the other side of the street for fear of what would happen if they dared interfere.

It was still humid; the streets which warmed to melting during the day gave off tar heat he could feel through his trainers. His jeans felt damp at the knees where he had fallen to the toilet floor and he noticed his shirt was stained from the night's excesses, already displaying sweat rings around the armpits, plus there was blood down the front.

This summer had been unusually hot, the weathermen standing before a map of a UK that glowed an unearthly desert red without any clouds to hide it. They spoke knowledgeably about the coming rains and storms that would help to cool the country, but the weather never appeared to make landfall. Instead the television stations showed images from parks and gardens, arid and dry, water pumps in some suburban streets and rows of flowers and plants wilting in the harsh Sahara-style sun. There seemed to be no let-up and so the country and city simmered towards boiling point.

Not wishing to incur the wrath of the thugs across the street, he turned and made his way back towards the city. He departed to the sound of laughter from the boys as they slowly dribbled the can of extra strong lager onto the head of the tramp who lay unmoving in the gutter, his blood mixing with the amber liquid and pooling on the double yellow lines.

The streets grew light as the neon from the closing bars and pubs spilled out into the night. An ambulance, its lights flashing and siren whooping to clear a path, rushed away from him as modified hatchback cars with chrome spinners and exaggerated exhausts rushed the traffic lights in a daring circuit race on the ugly inner-city ring road.

It very rarely seemed to quieten down in the city centre even in the winter, but the heat was making it too hard to sleep and so forced people out into the night. This in its turn had resulted in an increase in time to commit crime for those who spent their hours in the dark, and a universal feeling of possible threat in all the others. The Evening Post, the local paper, would report daily on those mugged, the upsurge in drive-by shootings, the abducted girls that had gone missing and presumed raped, plus the continual war that was going on between two local gangs that would always leave at least one body on the weekend streets. The city was coming apart at the seams. The police, unable to control it through lack of resources or desire, had in the main retreated back to their stations to await the onset of winter and quieter times.

Once across the dual lanes of the main road Nick turned to his left and threaded his way through the cobbled streets of the Lace Market. He had been fortunate; with the money from his mother's death he had been able to purchase a small flat in the close mediaeval lanes that had become a property developer's wet dream. Even with all the crime, property prices in Nottingham had gone through the roof, forcing more and more people into the sort of areas which only five years ago they would never have considered visiting, never mind living in.

His mother's death from cancer had allowed him to get a step up. A lucky break some might say, but he saw it more as a poor conciliatory prize. He hated the way the money had come his way and would have much preferred to have her back, but it had given him a financial breathing space and the chance to pursue his acting. Something he would never have had the chance to do without her death. She had given him the spark of a new life through her own demise.

He had invested his money in a small flat in the heart of the area. It was a run-down building that needed lots of work. As the area became popular with the young wealthy and the other buildings were renovated, teased and pressed into service as luxury apartments, he watched the value of his mouldy flat rise quickly in the nine months he had lived there. He realised, not for the first time, that perhaps it was time to cash in and use the equity to carry on with his dream.

He crossed into a warren of streets, little more than pedestrian paths, passed several parked BMWs which tomorrow would display broken windows and spray-painted obscenities about their owners, and made for his building's front door.

All was quiet and dark. A street lamp which he could never remember working hung uselessly from a wall bracket. The downstairs windows were covered with iron bars thickly smeared with black paint and pigeon shit while the brickwork still displayed the soot that had scarred it from a hundred years before; water damage was evident in the mortar. The building exuded neglect and was a cyst on the area. It merely existed as a project for some future developer, a gold mine for those with the inclination and deep pockets.

The lobby area was pure gloom and ruin. The main strip light was broken, having been smashed the month before and never replaced, but even in the daytime little light made its way into the scruffy interior. Nick was forced to hold a hand out in front of him and wave it about pathetically while shuffling his feet an inch at a time as if he were an invalid. The last shot of tequila was starting to take effect and, with little to focus his wandering eyes upon, it was becoming difficult to retain any semblance of balance. Stumbling forward he hit the edge of the first step awkwardly, causing a big toe to bend backwards inside his shoe. He shot back from the stairs and flapped about like a winged bird while swearing and stamping his foot. On his second attempt he waited until his left hand found the banister, which he grabbed firmly to steady his swaying form. Two deep breaths were sucked in to counteract the feeling of sick that scorched the very back of his throat before he resumed and attempted a slow ascent.

Reaching a landing, he moved outwards until he made contact with a wall and a timer switch. A sickly yellow light spilled across the stairs, lighting up the hard-wearing carpet that had still managed to fray where too many feet had trodden. The stark decoration reflected the meagre light back at him, showing scuff marks, and against one wall, damp. Someone had attempted to brighten this communal area with a picture, but the frame was already coming loose and the print of a girl on a beach had not been set straight, causing it to billow into one corner, distorting her body, turning her into a carnival freak.

The timer was ticking, counting down until the area was plunged into darkness once again. Nick turned and staggered for the next set of stairs but something caught his attention, forcing him to look upwards. He swayed as if blown by some unfelt breeze before shaking his head to dispel the image of someone who was perhaps never there looking over the banister. Had he seen a person or was his mind still playing tricks on him, the alcohol turning shadows into ghosts?

The next flight was somewhat easier with the light on. The steps with the frayed carpet caused a problem, but once negotiated he was almost home and dry. At the final bend the light switched off. He swore under his breath. Almost home, only to be thwarted by a timer switch. The next light switch was above him on the landing next to his flat's door. In the dark he bent forward, assuming the position of an animal, his weight spread between stocky shoulders and thick knees. He took the final few stairs on all fours. They felt gritty under his fingertips and something wet was laced into the weave. Wiping a hand down his jeans he left a brown smear. He continued swearing until he reached the last step.

Swaying at the top he leaned forward in exaggeration, righting himself against a possible fall backwards down the staircase. Knowledge that such a tumble would hurt even in his current state made him push forward and stagger to the door. Keys were fumbled from a pocket; caught up with his wallet and loose change. Pulling them out caused a scatter of coins to erupt onto the floor; they bounced and slewed across the carpet. Several fell the long drop back down to the floor below. The sound echoed up in the darkness.

He bent in exaggeration, grunting with the effort, in imitation of an old man, though it caused him no discomfort. A hand ran around the carpet like a large naked spider on a leash, feeling for the coins. On all fours he resembled a stunned cow, pawing at the floor before slaughter.

He grunted when he was hit in the side and toppled to the floor, a leg giving way first. His chin rubbed along the carpet, which had been expertly designed to give carpet burns. There was a hefty whack to his right shoulder that came out of nowhere; he lay dazed until anger welled up within him and he hissed as quietly as possible at his invisible attacker.

"Watch out, I'm on the fucking floor, you moron."

He got slowly to his feet and felt around him, arms waving in the darkness. No one answered, nor could he hear anyone's tread on the steps. He moved back in surprise, convinced that someone was just beyond his grasp, someone who mocked him in this sate of inebriation. He collided with the wall and turned the light switch on with an elbow. The hallway was empty. He looked over the banister and maybe someone descended but it could just as well have been a confusion of darkness and parallel banisters morphing into his attacker's fictional shape. This building hid much within its shadows that it was unwilling to give up. It was a house of decay and gloom, filled with unclaimed sounds and hidden voices. At times the whole place made Nick feel uneasy, as if he was being watched from the dark corners and lonely hallways. He was quick to dismiss it as too much drink.

Bending down again, he picked up the remainder of the loose money before letting himself inside his flat.

In the bedroom, he tiptoed carefully, afraid to wake the other occupant. He ripped himself from his clothes and eased himself onto the bed. His chin hurt and his knee felt as if it was swelling, plus he realised he had a headache; but all this faded as sleep took over, leaving him to dream of a black man covered in tattoos with eyes that glowed a deep hell red.

The human body is between fifty and sixty per cent water and it relies on this liquid to keep actions fluid and the body working. It is for this reason that nutritionists state a person should drink plenty of liquid every day to maintain a healthy lifestyle. Lack of water to the brain causes it to dehydrate; this along with by-products produced by the body's liver can cause a person to feel sick, produce sweat, and the head to ache. Specialists call it Veisalgia, but it is more commonly known as a hangover.

Nick's skull felt as if something external was applying pressure to his temples; an unseen implement that pushed against the sensitive thin skin at a point either side of his eyes. It hurt. It was not a sharp piercing pain, more a slow and consistent build-up that would eventually result in the sides of his head caving in and his brain shutting down, leaving the remnants to leach out of the hole created, like human guacamole.

He was lying on his front, right arm stretched out high and resting against the headboard. His shoulders were twisted, leaving the left arm to point downwards and carefully cup his testicles; even in the worst excesses of drink his mind had unconsciously protected the soft parts of the body's anatomy. He also had a semi-hard-on, but whatever had caused such arousal was now lost in the fog of sleep. Legs were stretched out in opposite directions, knees up and ankles flexed. To any bystander his profile resembled a man frozen in the act of sprinting, but this was an athleticism that never got any further than the bedroom. Muscles moved with difficulty as he slowly awoke from whatever night callisthenics he had been indulging in.

The bedclothes had been pushed aside, the sweat that built up from having a duck down duvet covering him in the heat of August too much to stand. Having slept in the same position for some hours the sheet below his body felt damp and stank of stale beer; it also looked to sleep-encrusted eyes to have been stained yellow, as if he had sweated out last night's binge of booze and curry and created a debauched Turin shroud.

Nick moved tentatively, bones cracking in appreciation as muscles were stretched. Tendons in his right calf at the point the muscle joined the back of the knee were locked, sending waves of shock to an already suffering brain. He tried to remember what the muscle was called but it hurt too much to consider. Bending double, he grabbed and massaged it until the heat subsided.

Though not fully awake, he was able to start piecing together the world around him. He knew he was home, in his own bed and alone. The pain having subsided from his cramping muscles, he rolled onto his back and stretched less forcefully than before, the cool of the new part of the bed acting as the catalyst to fully open his eyes.

He could hear the sound of cars passing on the street below, accompanied by the movement of feet and the shouts of parents as the population of the suburbs moved in for another Saturday's tour of duty around the shops of Nottingham. The flat, while not on a main road, was above a cobbled cut-through used by many to get into the city centre from the bus stop at the bottom of the hill. The cars were part of the queue that by this time in the morning would be snaking around the block waiting to get into a car park. One car out, one car in – an hour of sitting, windows open to let out some of the fake leather heat, engines murmuring, filling the air with a petroleum blanket that blocked out the oxygen, just so that little Ant'ney or Sooze could be bought a new game for their Playstation or get their weekly visit to a McBurger for fat and fries.

The curtains billowed as a rare gust of air blew through the open top window. It filled the room before it vacated the space, leaving the thin material to settle back into its usual folds and creases, a small gap remaining where they did not join completely. A jet of light struck out across the bed, heating his legs where it made contact. The sun was already bright and almost at its zenith. The flat would get full sun for another eight hours until it dipped behind the tall Victorian buildings that made up the Lace Market. The rooms heated slowly until they felt as if all the air had been sucked out and replaced with scorched sand, making any constant or prolonged movement unbearable. The red bricks retained their heat well into the night; in some places they resembled hard baked breads, each flat turned slowly into a giant furnace. The apartment was the yang to the building's yin, the public passageways all damp and cold while the flat acted as a mini oven.

The sun highlighted that the room, in all its uniform creaminess, was neat and clean, apart from the dishevelled pile of clothes that lay thrown on the chair, the remainder scattered on the floor, where Nick had stripped them off the previous night. He was an intrusion into this well ordered space. The Habitat 'less is more' look jarred with his faded jeans, dark crumpled shirt and black underwear; his mere presence polluted the ordered image.

Though it was his bedroom Nick had never cared for its decoration, and considered it merely a place to sleep. The only other use for a bed, as far as he could ascertain, was as a desirable piece of equipment for sex. It had instead the spirit of a woman's room. The orderly wardrobe with the door shut tight, hiding the shoe rack with paired-up high heels, a box of tissues placed neatly in front of the mirror. Nick's clothes were hidden away in a chest of drawers, an unsightly mess of similar T-shirts, odd socks and several packets of unwanted gift handkerchiefs. The only other presence in the room was the jumble of watch and coins that sat on top of a book, both of which rested next to the radio alarm clock on his bedside table. It had not always been like that. When he had first moved in he had lived out of a suitcase, not bothering to buy a wardrobe until Natalie arrived and set up home.

She had started with the bathroom, the leaving behind of a toothbrush which was slowly added to until she had colonised all available space. Toiletries had appeared, boxes of tampons and bottles of unguents designed to strip away whole layers of skin. Boots were left on the bedroom floor, then a small pile of clothes, jeans and summer tops that were just as quickly replaced by a petite suitcase before an attack was made on the wardrobe and full annexation was achieved. The front room sofa sprouted coordinated cushions and the kitchen crockery actually matched; finally pictures in frames were adorning the walls and Nick knew that he was beaten.

He didn't remember switching off the alarm clock; though in last night's intoxicated state he might have done it before falling onto the mattress, the small part of him that was not lost to alcohol having the foresight to understand that he would not want waking at seven-thirty in the morning. The only other explanation was that Natalie had turned it off when she got up.

His hand snaked over and felt the other side of the bed. There was a slight dip in the mattress caused by the frequent presence of another body, the springs having given slightly from being pressed down. The space was empty; but as he slid the hand over the cotton sheet a slight smell of perfume wafted upwards. Lavender – Natalie's smell.

She must have got up earlier that morning and left him to wallow in headache-infused sleep. He strained to listen for the familiar sound of her step in the kitchen, or perhaps the sound of water gushing from the shower. All was silent. If she was in, she was quietly reading somewhere; more likely she had gone out, having had no desire to speak to him after last night's tantrum.

Last night – the details came back with force – the reason he had gone out, the reason he had got so inebriated. The frustration of the last few months had poured out of him, as if an internal dam had been breached. His moods had swung ever lower over the last couple of weeks. He had taken to sitting in front of the television ignoring her conversation, hating himself for what he was doing. He knew he often suffered from bouts of depression but this was something worse – it seemed a wave of pure mood had crashed about his shoulders and dragged him deep below the water to the very bottom of a cold, dark ocean. At times like this – Natalie, friends, family, work, his lack of progression in life, the city, the news – everything it seemed was designed to press upon his fragile skeleton and crush him below fate's heavy heel.

He just needed that one slight jibe, that one fateful criticism to prick at his already low self-confidence to release the flood waters, and Natalie had provided it with a single remark.

"We don't have fun anymore."

The phrase left her lips and wounded him like a spear in the side. The accusation was horrendous. 'You' – meaning him – don't have any fun anymore, would have been acceptable because he was willing to castigate myself. He was not having any fun, and he did not deserve any fun at this current time. He knew finally what the term 'wretched' meant – it was how he felt every day the phone was silent and the casting calls never came.

It was the – 'we don't have fun' – that meant his actions were now impinging on her. His state was now affecting them both; therefore all their problems were caused by him. That was more than he wanted to admit and so he had roared at her like an injured lion.

He had ranted and raved in an attempt to prove a point; he wanted to show that he could have fun, that he was fun; the word had been created to describe him perfectly. He could have fun with or without her. She was the only reason he was like this. He left the flat, he slammed the door. He went to meet Munch and he drank a ridiculous amount of alcohol.

This morning Nick had expected an argument. He had expected recriminations. Natalie was hot-headed and she could bare a grudge. He had thought she would use the advantage of his hangover to extract an apology. An apology, he realised, she deserved. Last night he had been in the wrong, he knew that now; he was taking his own frustrations out on the one thing in his life that was perfect.

Nick knew that he was no good at arguing. He was not able to convey what it was he wanted to say. It always sounded perfect in his head, a slice of pure logic that no one in their right mind would dare to refute. He could see himself delivering his part of the dialogue, each sentence perfectly balanced, lean and trimmed. It would leave the other person speechless, unable to counter, left on the back foot with a resigned look creeping into their eyes. But when he said it, when he opened his mouth, that perfect sentence would vanish, pulled away on some drifting breath of air and instead, what came out would sound stupid, puerile or of such unimportance Natalie would more often than not refuse to allow him to finish.

Last night he realised he had said many stupid things. He wanted to know why she couldn't go out and earn more money so that he could stay home instead of carrying on with his crap job when he should be preparing for the next role or audition. Why did she have to be so reliant on him, why was he the one that was always giving, never receiving? Petty frustrations that were the root of all evil, but they had been building for some time.

Natalie had cried – embarrassed, alarmed, angry – she was all of them at once, and it was Nick who had made her feel that way. He had made her feel small and insignificant, which had never been his intention. In retaliation, his faults were laid out one by one – how he was too needy, too pig-headed, too prone to crazy highs and desperate lows, always thinking that he was in the right. He was arrogant, sexist, and never listened to her; she had been happy until she met him.

Nick could deal with that, but the thing that took him over the top was the argument that he was the reason she never had fun. It inferred that he was dull, never open to anything new or exciting, a sedentary beast that was slowly dragging her down into his pit of ordinariness, a boy in man's clothes, unwilling to meet her exacting demands.

He had left the flat. Grabbed keys and wallet and walked out. If she wanted to accuse him of never having any fun then he would show her how much fun he could have. Nick went out, met Munch in a bar and they drank until the whole world made sense. They made jokes about loose women and talked about sport. They shouted and screamed, made stupid noises when attractive girls came into view. They marched around town like their lives depended on getting as much liquor down their throats as possible. They visited bad clubs where they were ten or fifteen years older than everyone else and danced atrociously as close to the scantily clad girls as they dared. They had curry and were sick in the street and got into an argument with a man twice their collective size, until finally sodden with alcohol, he had ended up somewhere dark and grimy and...and his memory was a blank after that.

Once he had wallowed in self-pity and denial and realised how stupid he was being, he had stumbled into the bedroom early in the morning, reeking of sweat and vomit. He had ignored Natalie's naked sleeping figure and had fallen onto the bed into a comatose sleep.

He pulled himself upright and swung his legs around in a slow movement until he sat on the edge of the bed. He had to resist the urge to retch, knowing that if he started he would never finish, plus it would never come out of the cream rug that covered the stripped floorboards. Sucking in enough warm air to steady his stomach he eventually stood upright and stretched once more.

Leaving the fug of his bed behind, he entered the bathroom and stood over the toilet. Not bothering to lift the seat, piss jettisoned out hotter than he expected, stinging the end of his now flaccid cock. Urine splashed onto the seat and he made a mental note to clean it up later or else face yet another bone of contention. He moved to the sink and turned on the taps. Yesterday he had not bothered to shave, it being a dress down day at work, so his cheeks showed a good dark shadow of bristles. He could not face having to shave today either.

He threw some cool water over his face and ruffled his hair until it looked respectable. He still looked tired, with large dark bags under his eyes, but he certainly looked better than he was expecting for someone who had imbibed quite so much. He noticed he had a split lip. He tried to recall how it happened. Perhaps in the argument with the big man he had been punched, but he couldn't remember being hit, then again he couldn't remember much of last night. His knees felt bruised as well.

Deciding that this was probably the best he was going to look, he left to get dressed. Showering could be left until tonight when Nick was due to take Natalie out for dinner. At least then it might have some restorative effect. He slipped into some clean pants, socks and T-shirt, but stuck to last night's jeans. Finally dressed, he pulled back the curtains and looked down onto the street below.

Light glared off the pavement and the air shimmered. It was another hot day. At this time of year, late on in August, the weather should be turning, rain clouds coming in and cooling the evenings. This was an Indian summer and it seemed to have been going on forever. Women walked around the streets in little more than bikini tops, their stomachs on show whether they were firm and trim or sticking out over their hipster jeans. The men would already be in the pubs, sitting with bare chests, tattoos the colour of peacocks on full display. They would watch the women saunter past, marking those they fancied. The city felt as if it were on some continual summer holiday and the children had been let out of school forever, but the heat was starting to take its toll and tempers were frayed. Too much of a good thing mixed with alcohol made the city feel like a ticking bomb.

Nick needed a drink. He moved down to the kitchen and turned on the tap, letting the water drain out until it was cool. He drank back an entire glass and followed it with another, then with an enormous belch. He felt better.

Natalie was nowhere to be seen – she was out in the heat. He looked about and spotted his mobile thrown on top of the couch. He had not taken it with him last night. A spiteful measure that made sure she would be unable to ring him and ask what time he would be coming home and whether he had finished sulking or not. She always simmered down quicker than he did; she was first to scream and always cried, but her mood swung back to normality just as quickly. Nick supposed it had something to do with her European upbringing – all that emotion allowed to run riot. Her origins were still noticeable in her slight Italian accent, her devotion to everything sartorial and the way in which she could take the contents of his fridge and create a decent meal.

No messages had been left on the phone and he dallied over whether or not to ring her. On the verge of pressing the connect button, he changed his mind. Let her stew a little longer. Let her worry about him for once.

He wrote a text instead.

What time u back?

Dinner is @ 8.30!

He normally finished with a couple of kisses, double capital X's representing a smacker right on her lips. He didn't bother this time. The phone beeped to let him know the text had been sent.

The rest of the day was free for him to do as he pleased. He could go out and do a bit of shopping – there were one or two items he needed and he couldn't trust Natalie to buy the right products. However the act of going outside with a headache and joining the throng of people as they moved through the square, past the Council House and the small rubbish-strewn street that led up to the Victoria Centre, left him feeling nauseous. The shops themselves would be heaving with people going on mad spending frenzies, the sun having brought out a carefree attitude to money and their bank balances. The only other option would be to stay inside, turn on the fan they had bought last week and perhaps read the script that had come in the post. To try once more to make a character out of the jumble of words and ideas created by a writer he had never heard of.

He was sure that this was the root of all his evils, the continual frustration that no matter how hard he worked, he never seemed to improve or grow as an actor. He'd had some early success, appearing on the stage in local productions, a walk-on part in a BBC soap and the odd advert, but he had now had nothing for six months. No acting work at all. Every time he put himself forward he was rejected out of hand. No one wanted him and doors were routinely slammed in his face. It was the reason he'd had to go back to an office job, a lackey to his old friend Munch.

He had considered quitting, but then had no idea what else he would do. Apart from spending more time in the pub or watching TV he had no further ambitions in life. He wanted to act, he wanted to be on stage, see his face on the television. It made him feel different, as if his life meant something, it made him believe he was something other than just normal. It made life worthwhile. He knew he could act, he could go through the bare bones skill of pretending as well as anybody else, but he also felt that he had that quality which set him apart from all the other actors: he had presence, character; he had star potential.

This lack of work, this frustration, was the reason he had not been receptive to Natalie recently, why his mood had darkened. It was a millstone around his neck that was dragging him down, but no matter how hard he tried, he seemed unable to remove it. He was getting desperate and had recently started putting himself forward for anything that came along, any hackneyed piece of writing, even local adverts. He just wanted to get back out there, see his name on something, anything.

He looked down at the script; it was for a television show. He had been asked to audition for one of the heavies in the hour-long pilot. He really wanted to put himself up for the lead, but they needed a name for that part and he was still a nobody. Nick did not feel like a heavy. He should be a hero, not a crook. He thought of the bouncers he saw around Nottingham, all gold chains and necks bulging thick with veins and bunched up muscles, and how they scrutinised who got in and who stayed out, the threat of a beating if anyone stood out of line. He remembered the couple from the previous night, looming characters that welled up inside his mind as if they were characters out of some fairy tale, giants who seek out boys and girls to grind down to make their bread. It made him shudder. He was not one of those people. He was too small and slim for a start.

He threw the script to one side and chose instead to watch a film on television, diversion tactics that would allow him to nod off if required, stimulation that would not risk further pain to his aching brain.

Two hours later as the credits crawled across the television screen and he had drunk his way through a four-pack of Coke in the hope the caffeine and sugar would ease his plight, he still had not received a text back from Natalie. He decided it was perhaps time to send another before sitting down to have a mid-afternoon snack.

Where are U? XX

He sent the kisses this time, just so she understood that he considered what had happened the night before as water under the bridge. If she was still a little angry with him he wanted her to simmer down in time for tonight's meal.

They were going out to celebrate a year's anniversary. A year since they had met in the Cookie Club. Nick – propping up the bar and thinking of going home, her – dancing sensually to the music, swaying backwards and forwards in a tight top that showed off her figure. He had been watching her for half an hour, mesmerized by the snake-like movements that contorted her body. Realising there was not a chance in hell she would be interested in the pasty-looking nobody at the bar who was even being ignored by his own mate, he had turned his back to the dance floor and concentrated on downing his pint.

She came over and wiggled into the pocket gap by his side. Her breasts briefly pushing past his arm had felt warm and firm. She leaned in over the sticky table top and was quickly surrounded by two members of staff, attentive to her every need. She pointed at a sparking mineral water, accepted the bottle and pushed in a straw which she had been offered before turning back to look out over the dance floor.

Nick had stood stock-still, wishing with all his heart that he had the audacity to try and talk to her but knowing deep down he would never be able to summon up the courage. Girls like this were never interested in the likes of him. He would often try the actor story when he flirted but the women soon ignored him when he could not mention a film he had worked on and instead spoke enthusiastically about a Pot Noodle advert.

It was not that he was ugly or in any way a turn-off, it was just that he was safe. Women could tell that he was reliable, a nice person who would look after his girlfriend and care about her feelings. It was obvious that this girl didn't go out with 'nice' boys; she was interested in thrills, men with muscles, fast cars and fat wallets no doubt.

She caught his eye and spoke. So intent had he been on attempting to be cool and nonchalant he missed what she said and had to ask her to repeat it.

"I said is this place always busy?"

She leaned in towards him this time so that he could hear her as a song by The Jam started and the dancers were joined by a load of blokes doing poor imitations of Paul Weller. He scanned the frantic heap of humanity as they crushed onto the small space and tried desperately to think of something witty as a riposte.

"Pretty much."

Not the greatest of chat-up lines.

"It's a cool place. I like it."

A slight accent made her appear at once sophisticated and alluring. Words like 'cool' never sounded out of place in Natalie's repertoire of responses. Used in his own East Midlands English it always sounded false, a term that was out of touch with the white kids and false-Bronx with the black.

"I don't come here often, but yeah, it's not bad. Better than a lot of the other places."

He tried to think of a question, one to keep her interested, keep her next to him while he summoned up the courage to ask whether or not she wanted another drink.

"Is this your first time here?"

She nodded in time with the music and smiled to indicate yes.

"First time in Nottingham or just here?"

She shook her head, curly black hair snaking past her elfin face.

"I've been in Nottingham a while. First time here, though."

She finished the last of her water, the straw making a slurping noise as she sucked up the dregs. It made her giggle. It was now or never.

"Can I get you another drink?"

He tried to make it sound as innocent as possible. A new friend asking a kind question, all salacious ideas removed far from thought.

"No thanks. I've got to go."

Struck out on his first attempt, he was already resigned to the reply having heard it so many times before.

She leaned in closer and grabbed the lapel of his leather jacket as she was pushed from behind.

"You can come with me if you want."

And that was how they met, Natalie taking all the initiative and Nick being led out of the club by a small but warm hand. Out into the electric lit evening to a selection of underground bars he never knew existed. Getting steadily drunk and more ambitious, he started to feel good about himself, he got more daring, his responses better timed and delivered with wit and charm. She had smiled and laughed at him; he had joined her on the dance floor, anxious about onlookers at first and then, as he moved to the music, giving it all up as she rubbed herself against him while others looked on with envy in their eyes. He had been the king of the castle that night, on top form, pulling his usual monosyllabic mood-struck personality up to a new height. It was as if a new man had been hatched from deep within.

She had invited him back to her shared house where they had sat on the sofa discussing everything from favourite films to world politics. They had kissed and fooled around until he fell asleep on her living room floor early in the morning. His only regret was that Munch never got to see him leave with the most attractive girl in the club.

Nick checked the time; it was getting late and he had still not heard from Natalie. Accepting that he would have to bite the bullet, he decided to ring. The call went straight to her answerphone. She had her mobile turned off. At least that explained why she had not got back in touch. She was teaching him a lesson, turning her mobile off put him at a disadvantage, leaving him to guess at her movements and worry whether she would even turn up for tonight's dinner. She was probably taking an afternoon drink somewhere, laughing at him as he fretted over what to do next.

He needed a walk. Get out for some exercise and then, if he bumped into her, he could decide on the best course of action. Slipping into some light shoes he went out, leaving the windows open.

Nick moved through the Lace Market. Once an industrial town, Nottingham had been a Victorian powerhouse producing lace for a once wealthy Empire. This had allowed the city to make money and gain a little bit of commercial power and the Lace Market was a reminder of that past age. The area was dominated by large red-brick factories that crowded in on small cobbled streets, the bottom of the buildings roped off by black iron railings, the doors large and imposing. Like most cities, the industry had long gone and the area renovated and re-used. The powerhouses had been cut and spliced into individual units that sold for the sort of money that would have been enough to build an entire factory from nothing a hundred years ago.

Some of the apartments had porters or intercom phones, hidden parking spaces underground and, if you could afford it, a view. Everyone shopped at Habitat or Ikea, so they all had the same uniform furniture - leather couches, plasma televisions and the latest gadgets. The Joneses had come in from the suburbs.

Passing quickly the crest of the hill, Nick passed an area dominated by the old St Mary's church, a mediaeval sandstone building that sat up high on its own little hill punctured with old graves that lay at oblique angles. Some of the gravestones lined the narrow alleyways around the church as if they were slowly leaking away from the graveyard, extending death over the city as those buried attempted to increase their property rights.

Old shop fronts and offices had given way to wine bars and eateries to service the ever expanding population. All day brunches and wheat beer. The whole area now dedicated to the pastimes and debauchery of the trendy set. Even one of the churches had given up trying to save souls and had become a large bar and restaurant. The only building that remained underused was Nick's own, a rotting set of flats converted when the area was cheap, and now due a makeover.

Leaving the Lace Market, he walked downhill from High Pavement, passed quickly through Middle Pavement and reached Low Pavement. When Nottingham decides on a naming convention it sticks to it. This was Nottingham proper. The city centre looked like every other city centre in Britain. The same shops, the same cafés, the same post-war architecture. The same glazed look on the kids and parents as they meander from one purchasing experience to another, exactly like they did last week, and precisely like they would do again next week. The same litter crammed into over-spilling bins, the same fat and disease-filled pigeons pecking at the remains of a fast food lunch.

Nick knew that Natalie only went to certain higher priced shops; those that didn't project the right image were ignored, leaving her with a set route around the city centre. The only reason she would be around this area would be to purchase some essentials from the Marks and Spencer's Food Hall, or perhaps some sensible knickers for that certain time of the month.

Not wanting to join the crush of people buying their pre-mashed potatoes or julienne carrots he moved up towards the Old Market Square while attempting to place another phone call. Still her mobile bleeped back at him with a hopelessly lost sound. He was starting to get annoyed. The crime did not warrant the punishment she was inflicting.

The Square was the nominated centre of the city, the place in which all streets collided. Recently renovated, the large open space of granite – hard and unwelcoming with all greenery and plant life surgically removed – was known affectionately by the locals as 'Slab Square' due to the monstrous grey uniform style in which it had been originally built. The renovations had not improved matters. At one end stood the Council House, constructed to resemble a reduced-in-stature St Paul's Cathedral.

It housed a few specialist shops and acted as a designated meeting point for thousands of flustered first daters. Two stone lion statues sat at the base of the building acting as the unofficial guardians of the square. They looked pissed off, as if being used as a courting couch for teenagers and those on their first date was not their desired intention. They looked ignoble, defeated by crime and grime.

Nick moved past the sunbathing couples and the kids using the area as a makeshift skateboard park and entered the cool interior of the building. Underneath the ornately decorated ceiling he pressed his face against the glass of the shop fronts, scanning for any sight of Natalie. The shops were for the most part empty, the crowds preferring to loiter outside in the sun. The bored shop staff clocked him from behind their counters as he looked inside like an unsuccessful Peeping Tom. None of them returned his forced smile.

If he was being honest with himself he knew he could not really expect to just stumble across Natalie. Nottingham is not a big city but it was always busy and at the weekend it swelled its population with families from the suburbs. Natalie could be anywhere, and he realised he could have passed her twenty times on the street and not have been able to see her due to the crush of rushing bodies. It was a fruitless task and one he was not enjoying in the heat. Sweat already stained his T-shirt and the back of his neck felt raw from the sun. He should have stayed at home and waited for her to make an appearance.

He left and trailed back through the town, picking up a Saturday paper that screamed with the headline 'The Missing Man Strikes Again'. More crime with little chance of resolution. He added a large bottle of coke to his purchases before heading back to the flat. He would just have to wait it out.

By eight in the evening Nick was starting to worry. Dinner was booked for eight thirty and there was no time for Natalie to come back and get ready in time for them to go out. He rang the restaurant and cancelled before trying Natalie's phone for the fifth time in an hour. It still returned the same monotonous beeping, the sound challenging him to do something about it, a sound of defiance.

He was at a loss as to what to do. His inaction infuriated him but he had already racked his brain for some way out of the impasse, all to no avail. He could feel his humour lowering; dark clouds hovering at the back of his mind waiting to blow in and release a deluge of grey rain, shifting his mood to gloom. He tried to change his approach, to think positively. The last thing he needed right now was one of his crushing lows coming in, reducing him to a bleating child.

After this length of time he was sure she could not be out on her own and must have met up with some friends. He tried to remember the names of the girls she went out with. There was a Becky or Bex, who she might have worked with in some capacity, and another girl called Kris, but he had no way of contacting them. Nick had never met any of them in person, preferring to go out with Munch or with Natalie as a couple. He had no numbers to ring to ask if Natalie was with them and could not remember any surnames, so he could not even look them up in the phone book. Even if he did have a name, most people just used their mobile phones and never bothered with a landline. He returned to the couch and sat down heavily. He turned the television back on, the roar of Saturday night's bland shows washing over him in the semi-darkness. Outside on the street he could hear a siren start up. He tried his best to ignore it.

He must have fallen asleep waiting for her. The television was still on, a documentary about a military coup. He got up slowly and stretched tired muscles that had cramped again before moving over to the television and snapping it off. The time was 11.20 in the evening. He listened to the sounds of the flat to see if he could hear any noise from a second occupant. It was almost silent, just the usual banging and gurgling from the old pipes, the creak of the walls settling from the day's heat and, if he listened carefully, the sound of footsteps. They seemed to be coming from the hall outside his door; they were laboured and certainly not the dainty treads of his girlfriend. He assumed it was his next-door neighbour, a horrifically ugly old geriatric who Nick was convinced was half senile. He had no desire to speak to the man and listened until he heard a door slam. A car revved on the street, its exhaust backfiring noisily.

He supposed that Natalie could already be in the flat. Tucked up in bed and sleeping soundly. Perhaps she had already come in and, not wanting to wake him, had slipped into bed where she would already be dreaming. But he knew this was a lie. He was trying to calm himself, afraid now of the possibilities, the truth that was slowly dawning. The flat felt cold and alien, a dark place where only unhappiness could be attained. It no longer felt like his; the whole world felt in some way unfamiliar, as if he were living in an altered state.

Moving down the hall, Nick's feet made a slapping sound on the wooden floor. He approached the front door with caution. It stood closed with the chain hanging limp. Natalie always put the chain on and bolted the door. No matter how tipsy she was, no matter how much she had partied, she always locked the door behind her and could not sleep if he ever forgot to do it.

She was scared of the night, terrified of the dark, and had always wanted to lock the world out. She admitted to him once that, as a child, she had been for counselling due to bad nightmares, dreams about a shadow that would come in the night and carry her far away from home, never to be seen again. He had told her not to be so stupid, that such things didn't exist, but he had locked the door anyway.

He turned and entered the bedroom, hoping she would be there, hoping she would be curled up on her side having forgotten about the chain for the first time ever. Let her be there, please, please, please, he almost prayed. He didn't know who it was to, but he kept reciting it over and over in his mind, a mantra 'just let her be there, let her be there'. He wanted to close his eyes as the bed came into view, to hide away from what he knew would be the reality.

He noted the valance and then the corner of the mattress. There were no clothes thrown on the chair in the corner. But Natalie was neat; she would have put her things away in the wardrobe. He could now see the bottom third of the bed. There were no legs, no feet with painted toenails sticking out at awkward angles. She could be curled up. Despite the heat of the night she could have bent herself up into a tight ball; she always did that.

The sheets lay in a crumpled mess. Still stuck in the same mountains and valleys where he had left them when he had risen that morning. He could see half the bed. He moved faster, pushing himself into the room.

It was empty.

He looked around, as if expecting her to be in some other part of the bedroom, a ridiculous action – but it delayed the inevitable. The room was tiny and there was nowhere she could have hidden. She was not a practical joke kind of person and climbing inside the wardrobe was not something she would even consider.

Nick felt sick; he could feel his heart beating inside his ribcage, action that made up for his unmoving mind, which felt like an echoing cavern. What should he do now? Should he be ringing the police? Is this the time to involve them? She had not even been gone twenty-four hours and the fact they had argued would probably mean the police would not be interested. He tried to imagine the call and every time the officer on the other end of the line either laughed or told him sternly that it was a waste of their time.

He went back out to the living room and sat down to consider possible events. After running through a number of horrid scenarios he decided to be sensible. Two possible situations loomed large in his imagination: either she had met with an accident and was in hospital, or she was staying with a friend and teaching him a lesson. Any other possible explanation was too horrible to even consider in depth for now.

He tried her mobile number again. It was still switched off. If she was at the hospital and had been hit by a car then the staff would have rung him. The home number was in her mobile. But what if the mobile had broken on impact, what if there was no way to contact him? What if she was unconscious and her mobile out of action – they would have no way of knowing who she was or how to contact her family. He could feel the panic rising, clouding his judgement. She would have had her purse with her and in that she carried bank and credit cards, and they would have her name on. She could be identified, but what if they had been stolen? A thousand permutations of an unfolding drama played themselves out in his mind until he screamed out at them to stop. His voice rang out, shattering the silence of the flat.

He picked up the phone and a copy of the local directory and thumbed through until he got to the section for hospitals. There were a couple in Nottingham but only one that would take accidents. The Queen's Medical Centre was a large modern building on the outskirts of the city centre. He dialled the number quickly and sat listening to the options available. He chose general enquiries and, after having sat through some tinny hold music, was put through to a rushed-sounding woman.

"QMC, how can I help?"

She didn't sound like she really wanted to help in any way and that any phone calls were simply an annoyance.

"I'm looking for my girlfriend. She hasn't come home. I think she might have had an accident."

The woman made a sound as if she was tutting, as if the accident was in some inexplicable way Nick's fault.

"I'll put you through. Hold on."

The phone went briefly dead, only to be followed by the sound of several pips and someone else picking up.

"A&E."

The woman had been replaced by a man with a West Indian drawl.

Nick repeated his request.

"What's her name?"

"Natalie, Natalie Hope – but I don't know if she is in there, just that she might be, perhaps. I don't know."

Nick realised he was starting to sound confused and was unsure if he was making much sense, but the man seemed unfazed. He repeated her name several times as he searched through a database. Nick could hear his fingers expertly tapping away at a computer keyboard.

"I've got no Natalie Hope, but it's Saturday night. Not every one gets identified until later on, some not until tomorrow. Let me take down some details."

He asked for a description, starting off with the basics like height (about five six), hair colour (dark and curly – a natural curl that she hated as it ruined any design she had in mind), weight (Nick had no idea but knew she was small, not fat, but not skinny either). Distinguishing marks (she had a mole on her lower back, just to the left of her spine. He liked to watch it going up and down when they were having sex – he didn't tell this to the receptionist). She also had a tattoo on her inner thigh of a serpent with small wings.

"What's your name, sir?"

"Nick Stuart – I live in Nottingham so could come down if it helps."

"We've got enough people hanging around here; if she turns up, Mr Stuart, we'll give you a call. What number can we get you on?"

He gave out a mobile number in case he had to leave the flat. The man thanked Nick for his time and hung up.

Nick felt empty and, for the first time in his life, completely useless. He didn't know what to do. Would it be better to go out and search the streets or should he stay in and wait on the off chance? It was dark outside and nearing midnight, but the streets of Nottingham would still be in full swing. The bars would be packed to bursting and some of the better clubs would only just be opening.

He reconsidered; perhaps he was being too hasty. She could still be out, dancing the night away, oblivious to his frantic thoughts. She could be round at a friend's house, eating takeaway pizza and sipping wine. Having a good time, ignorant of his worry and concern. But he knew that was not like her; she always let him know where she was.

Nick was aware that when he went out, it was only his mobile that kept him in touch with Natalie. If it was not for that little piece of technology she would have no idea where he could be, what bar he was in or whether he was round at Munch's playing on his Xbox.

He started to feel better, less anxious. He decided he had been overreacting.

He grabbed a bag of crisps from the kitchen and turned the TV back on. He would sit and wait for the call from the hospital which would tell him that she had not been admitted and some time later tonight or perhaps tomorrow morning Natalie would crash into the flat and they would laugh at how stupid he had been. He would apologise and they would make love.

The phone rang an hour and half later, making Nick jump as he dozed on the settee. He wiped the dribble from the side of his mouth as he picked up the receiver. He was expecting it to be Natalie, her voice quiet with the realisation of the trauma she had put him through. It wasn't her.

"Mr Stuart?"

He swung his legs round and concentrated on the voice that sounded official. A deep tone, full of knowledge that it wanted to impart, but at the same time understanding the damage and intrusion it was about to cause; respectable and commanding, the sort of voice that, as an actor, Nick would have very much liked to cultivate.

"We have a young lady down here that matches your

description. She passed out in a bar and has not yet regained consciousness."

"Shit – is she OK?"

This made sense. Nick could deal with this situation. At last there was an answer to the mystery.

"It's too early to say. She's being CAT scanned at the moment – you should come down."

He sounded concerned, the implication that Nick should come down sooner rather than later. Time was an issue.

"Ask for a Dr Mati when you get here."

Nick moved quickly, grabbing his mobile phone and running for the door. He stopped in the hallway. Natalie would need things for when she came round. He went into the bedroom and opened up her wardrobe with the intention of packing some underwear and clean clothes.

It was empty.

Where before it had contained a selection of garments, some hanging limp from coat hangers while others were neatly folded on shelves, it was now completely devoid of anything but a thin trace of dust. Nick stood for a moment before the open wardrobe, as if by will alone he could make everything return, that he could magic the shelves full and complete his task.

He closed the doors slowly. Not at first believing his own eyes, he needed to check again. He opened the doors a second time but they remained resolutely bare. This he had not expected. He felt a chill pass through him as realisation dawned.

He moved quickly to the bathroom and pulled open the top drawers of the cabinet. Again they were empty of any contents and for the first time he noted that her shampoo and razor were missing from the side of the bath.

She had left him.

He was alone.

While he had lain immobile in his drunken state she had packed a suitcase and left, stolen away into the night without even having the decency to let him know. He imagined her tiptoeing around him as he snored and farted, collecting together her life before looking down at his slumbering form and perhaps blowing him a kiss for old times' sake.

She had let herself out and gone clubbing, perhaps to celebrate the fact that he was no longer a part of her life, enjoying her new won freedom – so much so that she had drunk herself into a condition of collapse.

He thought about leaving her where she was. Leaving her to make her own mistakes, to explain to the doctors and nurses how she came to such a sad state of affairs. She deserved it, if not for the leaving but for putting him through a day of hell; she deserved to be punished for her actions. But then would it not be better to be by her bedside when she awoke, what better way to chastise her, to make her feel regret at what she had dared do to him?

He would go down to the hospital and play the victim; the honest, loving boyfriend, ill-treated and used yet still coming to help her in her desperate hour of need. He was a knight, prepared to help the lowly poor girl; he would reek of chivalry in her presence, while she smelt of sick and hospital disinfectant.

Leaving the lights of the flat on to dissuade burglars, he stepped out into the dank hallway and locked the door behind him. He turned to descend, but noticed the door to the flat across from his was open; a thin blue light was cast outwards as if from a television left to white noise. Nick knew the single man of indeterminate age that lived there by sight and reputation, but he had never really spoken to him; he didn't even know his name. The neighbour always looked strange; he hugged the shadows of the building, preferring to stay out of the light. He shunned the other residents, and never had any visitors. He hid behind his door and only descended the stairs when he knew it was all clear. He was like a hermit or a vampire who only stepped out at night. Nick had decided early on that he was best not bothering the man. If he wanted to be private then that was his choice. As far as neighbours went it could be a lot worse. At least the guy was quiet. However, feeling virtuous, he decided to help the man out and alert him to this lack of security.

He moved over to the door and was preparing to knock when it was forcefully slammed in his face, causing Nick to rap his knuckles against the cracked and flaking wood. He let out an involuntary gasp of pain and snatched the bruised hand back to his chest.

The door was reopened and the man thrust his head out. He didn't seem to be wearing much in the way of clothing, his eyes were red rimmed and sore. Nick noticed for the first time that he didn't seem to have any eyelashes and a form of alopecia was affecting his scalp. Nick stepped away from the unsettling emaciated white image.

"What the fuck yer want?"

Even from this distance Nick could smell the man's breath, which reminded him of rotting meat – it was the stench of the abattoir. It looked as if his neighbour was falling to bits, decaying as he stood up in his Y-fronts. While his thin body was in the main hairless, what little hair he had on his head was plastered to his skull with its own grease. His hands and feet were too big for his limbs, and down the inside of his thighs, noticeable due to his state of undress, were thick pink welts. He didn't seem at all shy about his lack of clothes and didn't bother to shield himself behind the door.

"Sorry, I just wanted to let you know you'd left your front door open. I didn't mean to intrude."

The man looked at his door as if it had offended him by not closing on its own accord thus saving him from this confrontation, before returning to Nick.

"What yer doing sneaking around in the dark?"

Nick didn't want to get into a conversation. Sometimes it was best not to talk to your neighbours. You could choose your friends; you can't choose who you live next to. He wanted to return to the days when the man ignored him.

"I live opposite. I was just going out."

Nick turned to leave.

"I know who you are."

His voice was softer now, almost apologetic, with perhaps just a hint of accusation in it. He said it as if Nick was some kind of criminal, a man on the run from the police, a deviant.

"It's a bit late to be going out, innit? Mind you, I don't know how anyone sleeps in this heat. I can't remember the last time I closed my eyes."

Nick turned.

"I'm going to the hospital. My girlfriend's been in an accident." He didn't know why he had to tell this man about his actions, it just came out. It was as good an excuse as any to be leaving his flat so early in the morning.

"Girlfriend? Thought yer were a queer."

He closed the door abruptly, leaving Nick alone in the gloom.

Down on the street Nick hailed a black cab as quickly as he could. The Asian taxi driver tried to engage him in conversation, talking about how Nick was his only sober fare of the night, but Nick tried his best to ignore the man and eventually he got the hint and went quiet.

He was dropped off outside the dirty foyer of Accident and Emergency. He had just enough money to pay the fare but was unable to add a tip that didn't insult the driver, who gave him a pissed-off look in return. There was little Nick could do about it.

He entered through the sliding doors. It was busy as patients enjoyed the warm air and smoked a cigarette before returning to the cooler, chlorine-infused wards. He pushed his way past the elderly and infirm who sat in wheelchairs while chatting amiably with the Salvation Army officer on duty, and made his way over to the reception. Nick was surprised at how busy it was, the early hour having no meaning here. Time stood still in the hospital;

whether it was day or night it was always time to help patients.

"I'm here to meet with a Dr Mati," he told the receptionist.

Without even looking up she asked his name before instructing him to take a seat and to wait. Nick looked around but soon realised there were no free seats available, so he opted to loiter by an understocked vending machine.

Groups of people sat around the badly lit interior with bored expressions painted across their faces. This was a place to be endured, to get through with the minimum of fuss and with hope unscathed. No one wanted to be here. Somewhere far off he could hear a person weeping. A small number of patients had blood dripping from ugly head wounds which they attempted to stay with large bundles of toilet paper, their friends scowling, annoyed they had to end their evening in such dull surroundings.

A well built man with a Middle Eastern complexion, short cropped black hair and large black-rimmed glasses that said trendy but intelligent approached. Nick thought at first he was going to ask for change to get a coffee, but he introduced himself as Dr Mati.

"Sorry, I was expecting a man in a white coat."

He nodded and grinned wide.

"I don't normally bother wearing one on busy nights; it's the only way to make it through reception without being mauled."

He indicated that Nick should follow. They moved down a number of passageways, their feet squeaking on the polished rubber floor.

"Do you know if it's Natalie or not?" Nick asked, hoping that it was her and that she had not yet woken up. He wanted his moment of triumph; he wanted to be looking down on her as she lay swaddled in the bed sheets, feeling hopeless and bruised. Another thought struck him – what if this was her way of making a cry for help? Perhaps she had been planning to teach him a lesson, only she had drunk too much and ended up here? Perhaps he had been in the wrong all along.

"We were hoping you'd tell us that. She's taken some tablets, not sure what but probably a mix of GHB and Ecstasy, and is still out for the count. It was touch and go for a while but we have her on a respirator. Has she been taking drugs long?"

A cold wave of numbing horror washed over Nick as Mati made his comments. As far as he knew Natalie had never shown any interest in drugs; she only drank occasionally and then it was only a little white wine. She loved to party but got high through her own sheer exuberance. She didn't need artificial stimulants. What in hell's name was she doing?

"She doesn't do drugs."

He nodded.

"Well, this time she overdosed," he said as if Nick's statement meant nothing.

They reached a ward and were shown through into a separate room. It was dark.

"The police will want to talk to her when she comes around. They'll need a statement from her and from you."

He motioned at the body that lay in a bed, propped up against three thick pillows.

"I have the description you gave us, five six, curly dark hair, mole..."

"And the tattoo?"

Nick interrupted as he moved over to take a look, anxious not to make a noise even though he knew the sleep was induced and she was not going to wake.

"Tattoo?"

Dark hair had been scraped back from her face and tied up on top of her head. It was covered with a blue plastic hat similar to those found in hotel showers. A transparent mask was clamped to her face obscuring it from view but helping her to breathe. Her features were not distinct until Nick was standing over her.

The respirator made a sighing noise as it moved up and down by Nick's side. A gentle whisper of help to those with dependent lungs. He looked down. The covers had been pulled up and over her chest, her clothes replaced with a hospital gown.

Nick shook his head in the dark, it was a slight movement but enough so that Mati could see.

"Is everything all right, Mr Stuart?"

Nick felt the lack of sensation in his body replaced with the anger and despair of earlier. This was someone else's mess. Something Nick would not have to deal with.

"It's not her," he said, turning to leave the room.

Dr Mati caught up with him as he moved back down the corridor heading for the reception. Nick wanted to get outside and suck in clean air; the night would be warm but it would not be polluted by the ill and dying, the oxygen inside coated with germs that even now he could taste at the back of his throat.

"Well, that's good news for you."

Mati's voice was calm, matter-of-fact. He seemed relieved but only slightly. It was still a patient he would have to identify, paperwork he would have to file.

Nick stopped walking and turned to Mati.

"Will she be all right?"

He felt somehow concerned for the woman who slept on without any of her family knowing where she was, not knowing that she lay in hospital, good drugs being pumped into her to expel the bad. A girl with no name or identity – mere lost luggage until she was claimed.

"She'll be fine. Someone will notice she's missing before too long."

The word 'missing' made Nick wince.

"And I'm sure your girlfriend will turn up. People normally do," he continued, oblivious to the look of pain that crossed Nick's features.

Nick made his way outside. He stood for a moment in the foyer and let the cool breeze from the air conditioning blow over him, cooling his skin until small welts appeared. Natalie had left him.

Of this he was certain. It was no longer a game, she was not teaching him a lesson, waiting in the wings, out of view until he had repented of his sins, ready to make her entrance and surprise him. She had instead tired of his moaning and left him for good.

He felt alone. He watched as friends and families cluttered the pavement and spilled out into the hot night. Some laughed, happy that their ordeal was over with, while others wept for a loved one left behind, a relation who would perhaps be dead in the morning.

He had no one. There were only two people in the world that even knew he existed, one was his father and the other was Munch. At this time of night only one would be awake. He flicked open his mobile and waited for it to connect.

"All right, mate?"

Munch sounded as if he was out again. His hangover having worn off, he would have noted the tang of Saturday night in the air and disappeared into the city. Nick didn't want to join him but he wanted to know that someone somewhere at least knew who he was.

"No. I'm still hung over and Natalie has left me. She's cleaned out her things and just gone."

There was a muffled commotion on the other end of the phone, voices and the sound of crushed bodies that went quiet as Munch slipped outside and onto the street.

"Sorry, couldn't hear you in there. Who's left you?"

"Natalie. She's gone. I don't know where, but she's cleared out."

There was an intake of breath before Munch replied. He sounded confused.

"Natalie who?"

Nick knew that Munch was always ready for a joke, a quick one-liner or a wind-up that could last all night, but tonight he was not in the mood. His voice must have come over as sharp as he told his friend to stop mucking about.

"No, mate, I'm not messing. I don't know who you're on about."

Thursday 27th October, 2005

Her cheekbones were high but the skin sagged from them, forming small droops around the mouth. Had the skin always been like that? She could remember a time when her cheeks were taut and the only marks on her face were two little dimples that would appear when she smiled. Also she noted that the skin used to be a nice pale cream with just a hint of strawberry evident when she was hot, but now there were funny little marks there, coffee-coloured blemishes that had spread slowly from deep within the tissue. The magazine she read said they were liver spots. Why were they called that? She didn't like liver.

The eyes still had somewhat of a youthful gleam about them, the whites were only marred in one place by a small pink vein that ran out from the corner of her eye, tapering until it disappeared near the iris. Her eyelashes were long, and though she was not wearing any mascara at the moment, as she had the oven to clean, they still stood out proud and were clearly noticeable.

She wore her hair up today, a bundled knot on the back of her head that was held in place with a scrunchie. She was thinking of getting it cut. She didn't think long hair suited middle-aged women. Perhaps if she had it snipped to about shoulder-length it would be a little more manageable. Mind you, there was still that infuriating kink at the front that no matter what she did, it always gave her hair a lopsided look, as if it was about to teeter and fall off her head all together.

Her breasts looked quite firm but she was wearing one of her better bras. She cupped them and pushed them upwards. Perhaps they were an inch lower than when she was young but what can you expect? Gravity will eventually take its toll on anything bigger than a C cup.

All in all she thought she didn't look too bad. She turned and tried a side profile. Juliet, their daughter, had been lucky to get her looks and not her father's. If she had her time over again she would not mind being a model. It must be better than working in a sandwich factory. Sitting on your bum all day getting margarine stuck between your fingers and splashes of mustard on your shoes. She bet models didn't come home smelling of cheddar with tomato pips stuck to their jeans.

Being a model she would have spent her life visiting exotic places, gone to Paris and Rome, America even. She had always wanted to see the Empire State Building. They would probably have asked her to advertise perfume in ornate bottles made from green glass while she wore a giant ball gown. Or her face would be used to market an expensive but feminine drink which she would sip in a famous bar while men admired her from afar. She had to admit that would have been better than the one week they normally spent in Skegness when the factories closed for summer.

She let out a sigh as her mind ran away from her. She knew she shouldn't spend her time thinking about what might have been. It was pointless; she should think about the future and be thankful for what she had – a loving daughter, who was a real beauty, and Terry, who was faithful and kind. It could have been a lot worse. The woman down the road had to have a restraining order placed on her husband who beat her up and stole all her money so that he could get drunk. What kind of life was that? Working yourself to the bone just so your money could be poured down the drain, plus you end up with a broken jaw for daring to say anything.

Think about the future and what could be, not the past. That was the way forward. There was always light at the end of the tunnel. And what did her future hold for her today? She had an appointment at the doctors to talk about her 'woman's problem' and she still had the oven to clean.

She returned to the kitchen and grabbed the can of 'Mr Squeaky Klean' she had placed on the draining board next to her rubber gloves and an industrial scrubber. The oven was all ready to go. She had placed newspaper on the floor to catch the dirt and got a cushion for her knees from the patio furniture. She didn't really feel up to the task; she'd had a bad night. She had not slept as she felt too hot; burning up like a furnace, and then she had bled quite heavily even though it wasn't the right time. That meant she had to wake Terry and get him out of bed. While she went to the toilet he had stripped the bed, changed the plastic on her side and remade it. He was asleep by the time she came back.

She had felt tired and a little weak this morning but Terry had got up early and made breakfast for Juliet and a strong cup of tea for her. He'd told her to stay in bed while he fixed a packed lunch for himself and his daughter – a job she always did in the morning while they got ready for school and work.

She had watched a bit of telly in bed and eventually got up about nine. She had felt better after her rest, but now she felt tired again. Perhaps she should have a sleep before she went to the doctor's this afternoon? But she was not sure she had the time. It depended on how long the job in hand took to finish.

As she bent down to start on the work she heard the letterbox clatter and the sound of envelopes tumbling to the floor. Ignoring them, she covered the door in thick foam and listened to the bubbles pop and hiss as they got to work on the grease. Satisfied she had coated the entire door she decided to let the foam do its work and shuffled out to the front of the house.

They were the usual collection: a selection of bills from the gas company and a clothing catalogue, a flyer for cheap pizza and a new dry cleaning shop. The only addition to the paltry selection was the letter she had been waiting for from Juliet's school.

She tore it open and looked at the list of scores the teachers had decided that Juliet would be expected to make in this year's mock exams. They were not very good. A collection of low grades, some of which were barely pass marks. Juliet had told her mum not to expect any miracles, but one teacher had also put down a straight fail, which seemed a little unfair. It was not that she was lazy or did not try, but Juliet, as beautiful and as perfect as she was in her mother's eyes, was just not cut out for the academic world. She had scored a C grade for art, which was encouraging as her daughter enjoyed art and she seemed to like the teacher.

Juliet did not have a good attention span; she found reading anything longer than a magazine article tedious and very rarely made it through a half-hour TV show. School was one long effort for her, and her mother knew that even if she willed herself to listen to every word the teacher said, at the end of class her daughter could rarely remember what the lesson had been about. She wished that Juliet had been born to better parents or perhaps in a better area of the country. She wished she could give so much more to her daughter but felt hopeless. What was it that temp worker had said to her at work? "Some people were just born in the wrong place" – that's how she felt about her daughter; she was born to the wrong family, in the wrong part of the country, perhaps even at the wrong time.

She hoped today went well, for her daughter's sake, she did not want the girl to be disappointed. Juliet wanted to build up what she called her 'portfolio' and a photographer was interested in Juliet for a publicity calendar shoot. She had already been selected by the local paper as Miss Spring twice and had her picture in it, plus the photos she had got her cousin to take had turned out well. This was a real opportunity. This could really make something of her girl. It was that or face the daily grind of the factory floor or the dull reality of a shop girl.

Maybe she could be her daughter's manager and help her through the difficult stage of starting a career. She used to cut Juliet's hair and often helped her to put on make-up before she went out to a disco. That way she could chaperone her daughter and keep her on the straight and narrow, and probably get some trips abroad in at the same time. She wondered if she should get some of those expensive magazines from the corner shop, the ones with all the models wearing luxurious clothes in glossy photographs. She made a mental note to pick some up after she had been to the doctor's. But for now she had the oven door to finish.

In the end she bought three magazines, two more than she had planned. They cost over ten pounds but she was in such a bad mood she didn't care. She had almost run home from the doctors and now sat looking at the pictures while having a strong cup of tea and a packet of crisps she had bought for Terry's lunch but he had forgotten to take.

In truth she knew what the doctor was going to say. She had always known in the back of her mind, but she was still shocked when he suggested it. A hysterectomy would be her best bet – that's how he phrased it – best bet. As if it was something that could win her a small fortune if she chose well.

She also knew that she would go ahead with the operation. She could not stand any more of these hot flushes, headaches and bleeds. Hormones and tablets seemed to have no effect and she wanted to be finished with the whole thing. She hated being a slave to her own body, particularly as it reminded her of the steady decline she faced as she aged. It was not fair; she had once been as beautiful and trim as Juliet. Now she didn't want to see herself naked and Terry barely glanced at her when she stripped down.

She flipped through the rest of the magazine. The pictures of healthy skinny women made her feel sick. She threw the magazine down and drank her tea instead.

Hearing the back door open, she pushed herself out of the seat and headed for the kitchen.

Juliet stood by the window drinking a glass of water she had poured direct from the tap. Her head was back and her throat bobbed as the drink slipped down her long neck. She drank the entire glass in long thirsty gulps and finished by letting out a long sigh.

"Were you thirsty?"

"It helps the skin, keeps it hydrated and pure-looking," Juliet replied while searching through her bag for a brush. "Will you help me get ready for my interview? Dad won't be late, will he?"

"Of course not."

And he wouldn't be. She had made sure that he knew his daughter had pinned all her hopes on this interview. She knew that the last thing he wanted was to upset his Juliet and so she had nagged him for days ensuring he would remember the date and the time of the appointment. She let it be known that upsetting Juliet would have the worse result of disappointing his wife.

"Have you decided what you're going to wear?"

Juliet combed at her long brassy locks.

"The grey pinstripe suit. It looks professional, I think. Like I know what I'm doing."

"Good idea. I've already got it out of the wardrobe and run the roller over it to get rid of any fluff. I hung it on the back of your door. You'd better get showered."

Juliet smiled, her little white teeth in two perfect rows parted slightly between her waxy lips. Mum sometimes knew her better than she knew herself.

Upstairs she laid out all the products required for her shower. She had two types of shampoo. One introduced body and bounce to her hair while the other made her scalp healthy. The conditioner she used made the hair soft but still allowed it to contain a subtle flexibility. She had recently bought an exfoliating rub for her body and used this all over. She wasn't really sure what that was meant to do but she liked the gritty feeling. It was like washing in pink sand.

She was careful shaving her legs, not wanting to leave any cuts as she planned to show them off with some heels. Her legs were one of her best features, being long and thin and, since her time at the parlour, a nice shade of milk chocolate.

Her mum came in while she was finishing off with a cooler shower to lower the pink glow of her body.

"There are some warm towels here," she said from the other side of the curtain.

"Thanks."

Juliet turned the shower off and shook herself to get rid of the excess water.

An arm snaked around the curtain and handed her a small towel to wrap her wet hair. Her mum departed while Juliet got out of the shower and started to pat herself dry, using little dabbing motions, not rubbing vigorously as that was bad for the skin. She then applied baby oil just like it said in the magazines.

Checking herself in the full-length mirror for any body hairs that looked out of place she decided she was pretty much perfect.

In her bedroom Mum had already plugged in the hairdryer and attached the large diffuser. Her make-up case was open and several items had been taken out and lined up on the melamine top.

Now in a dressing gown for warmth, she methodically massaged her scalp. Downstairs she could hear her dad's voice. He must have returned while she was in the shower. She felt relieved that he was home, as she desperately wanted him to take her. The bus would have messed up her appearance and given her less time to get ready.

She treated her hair with the yellow oil that cost fifty pounds for a tiny tube. Juliet didn't think it actually made any difference but her mum had decided it would be a good investment and so she used it as the instructions insisted. Finally, she put the hairdryer on a low setting and performed the laborious task of drying while ensuring it didn't frizz.

Half an hour later she was finished.

Checking the time she dressed quickly. She chose the big pants, which helped flatten her stomach – not that she needed any help, but it also ensured that she didn't have a visible panty line. She put on the matching balcony bra. She got down the new crème brûlée coloured blouse from which her mum had carefully removed the shop tags. She put it on and checked her cleavage in the mirror. Just right, she thought – a hint of breast but nothing that could be considered tarty. If she was going to be a model she wanted to be a Crawford not a Page 3. She put on the suit and high heels that strapped around her tiny ankles. Again she checked herself in the mirror, adding and subtracting jewellery. She eventually decided upon a small silver crucifix and two rings – one on each hand.

A shout came from downstairs.

"Juliet! We should make a move."

Dad would be worried about the amount of traffic on the road as it was still rush hour. He always liked to leave plenty of time so that she was never late.

"Coming."

Giving her reflection one last inspection, she grabbed her portfolio and set off for the appointment.

In the kitchen her mother gave her the once-over, pulling and tugging at her jacket to ensure it fit perfectly. She moved her daughter from side to side, twisting her around by her hips before feeling satisfied.

"Beautiful, you look beautiful. They'd be foolish not to give you the job. Isn't that right, Terry?"

Dad looked at her and smiled.

"You sure you don't want anything to eat before you go?"

"No, Mum, I'll eat when I get back."

In the car she asked her dad what chance he thought she had. Mum was good at all the cooing and preparation, but Juliet believed she sometimes lived in a fantasy world when it came to the reality of modelling. Juliet knew there would be a lot of competition for this role and her dad would give her a more down-to-earth answer.

"You'll be fine, love; just don't be disappointed if things don't work out. There'll be plenty of other opportunities. Remember, me and your mum are behind you all the way."

He never took his eyes off the road as he spoke.

"I know, Dad."

She looked down at her portfolio and got out the sheet of paper on which she had written the details. The man on the phone had sounded young but kind, reassuring her that she was perfect, just what he was looking for. He had given her the specific time of 5.30pm; she had assured him she would be on time. This was to be an interview only and they should be finished by six. If they both agreed they could work together he would plan a shoot for next week.

She was really hopeful this was her break. It sounded as if he was eager to work with her but she worried that the photos he wanted were going to be too revealing. It might scare her mum and dad. Swimsuits she would do, even a bikini, but nothing topless.

They were nearing the studio situated above a hairdresser's on the main road. Terry eyed the road nervously. It was snarled up with traffic as people pulled over to quickly visit the shops on their way home, plus there was a zebra crossing halfway down that caused all the cars to bunch up.

"It looks busy," he muttered to his daughter.

"Stop here." She indicated a space by the side of the road. "It's only round the corner, and it looks better if I don't turn up with my dad."

Juliet hoped he had not taken that the wrong way. She was not embarrassed by her parents; far from it, she loved spending time with both of them. She just didn't want the photographer to see her and think that she was still a child.

"Your mum said I was to take you to the door so your hair doesn't get messed up."

"I'll be fine, it's not very windy. We'll tell Mum you took me all the way."

She opened the door and slipped out, trying the new 'descending from a car' turn she had been practising for when she was invited to a red carpet event.

"Good luck, dear."

She gave him the thumbs up and grinned.

The street was busy but she had several minutes to spare. She weaved her way through the crowds, crossed the road carefully and made for the studio. Arriving at the door she checked the nameplate 'Kristoph – Photos by Design', and rang the bell. The voice of a young man answered.

"Hi, it's Juliet Bryson – I'm here for my appointment."

The door buzzed and she pushed it open. Inside, she followed the wooden stairs up to the landing. Two large doors stood facing one another. She chose the one indicated by another sign and entered. It was abnormally dark inside.

Terry waited. He listened to the radio. Old songs from when he was a teenager, wearing a leather jacket and driving a motorcycle. He sang the half remembered words or made them up when he needed to fill in the gaps. His voice was soft, an audible whisper, a breathy morass.

Large pats of rain started a slow beat on the roof of the car. He leaned forward and looked up into the grey sky. Bruised clouds flexed and knotted as the water was squeezed from them. He could see the individual drops all falling down towards him. He leaned back as the people passing the car hurried up, desperate to get home. Switching the channel on the radio he found the news and listened. The troubles of the world filled the car but his mind was on his daughter. She should be finished by now. He hoped the photographer was not being difficult or demanding. He didn't understand – why did his daughter want to go into such an unpredictable profession? She should find herself a job in a shop or small office. Work her way up the ladder. After a few years she could relax; companies became dependent on you after that length of time, especially if you were the only person who knew how to do certain jobs. That's how he had stayed so long in the factory. It was not that he particularly enjoyed the job; he didn't feel any emotion about it at all. It was just work. It was what you did Monday to Friday, the space between the weekends and holidays. He was not the fastest or the cleverest but as he had been at the factory the longest he just knew what to do in every eventuality.

Kids had it too hard now, too much choice on offer for their undeveloped brains to deal with. No wonder some of them went off the tracks and took drugs. How can you live not knowing what was going to happen to you next year, the year after, in ten years' time? He had always known.

He checked his watch. She was twenty minutes late. He would give it another ten minutes and then he would go and look for her. He didn't want to turn up just as she was finishing and risk embarrassing his daughter.

Juliet was suited to modelling. She was beautiful, of that he was certain. He knew that all parents thought their children were attractive, even those who were quite plain or downright ugly, but this was more than parental blindness. She had classic looks, well proportioned limbs, none of that awkwardness that a lot of children seemed to suffer from, as if they were borrowing a body that they had not yet got used to. He could detect a little bit of himself in her features – she had his eyes. They were the same shape, the same hazel with flecks of green, and she had his hair colouring. Her mum's eyes were quite small and a not very interesting mud colour.

Juliet had always enjoyed being the centre of attention. He remembered watching her in a school nativity. She had not played Mary – that was too small a part for her. She had been an angel. A celestial creature made of light and tinfoil that had descended from heaven to inform and help the mere mortals. Acting the part of a creature of God did not come easy to a seven-year-old, but she had played it with all seriousness. Since then she had gone on to do ballet and dance, where she perfected her poise and the graceful way she had of holding her body, which in turn had led her to being photographed for the paper.

He knew that if they lived in London or somewhere down south she would probably get plenty of work, but up here models were not really in demand. Margaret was always saying they should move south, but he had never fancied it. They could barely make ends meet as it was and moving to a more expensive part of the country would just be foolish. Besides he had always lived here. This was their place.

He grabbed his jacket from the back seat and eased himself out of the car. Outside he wrapped himself up, protection from the inclement weather. He locked the car and followed the path his daughter had taken.

The high street was now clear. Rush hour was over. The shops were shutting up for the night. The only reason people would come out now would be to get fish and chips or a takeaway from the Chinese. He moved down the street and crossed at the zebra crossing. He could still see the lights on at the hairdresser's. He passed the window. It had steamed up a little. Inside, loud music played as two young girls swept up the day's debris from the floor.

He moved to the side and looked for a bell on the large green door. There was nothing. He had expected a nameplate, some kind of advertisement to the world that a photographer resided here and was available for weddings, portraits and any other work – but there was nothing.

He tried knocking. The door was old, made of thick heavy wood with only a tiny window in the top half. His knuckles hurt after only an ineffectual rapping. He tried looking through the window but it was too dark to see anything.

He turned back to the hairdresser's and banged on the window. The girls looked up, one of them jumped as if caught in an uncompromising position.

"We're closed," they mouthed above the noise and returned to their sweepings.

He knocked again and indicated for them to go to the door. They looked at him warily but finally one of them approached and slid back the bolts.

"Sorry, we're closed. You'll have to come back tomorrow," said the girl, only opening the door a crack.

"I'm trying to see the photographer upstairs. There's no bell."

She turned to look at her friend who had stopped to turn down the music.

"Do you know what he means?" she asked.

The girl shrugged and dropped her bottom lip.

She turned back to Terry.

"There is no photographer upstairs."

She shut the door.

He took a step back and looked at the premises. Had he got the right address? He was sure he had. He looked up and down the street, concerned that his Juliet needed him.

He went to the nearest phone box and dug out the contact address that his wife had written down for him. A duplicate of the details Juliet carried. He rang the number carefully. The phone piped and squeaked but no connection was made and after a few seconds the noise was replaced by the sound of a continuous purr, as if a cat had answered. The number did not exist.

He stepped back out into the rain. Fat drops had given way to a steadier downpour. His instincts told him something was seriously wrong. Where was his sweet Juliet?

Later, the police sat them down in the too warm living room and explained everything to them in as calm a manner as possible. The police were angry with them for wasting their time; the Brysons were angry with the police for giving up the search for Juliet so quickly.

The police had responded to the call from Terry quickly and efficiently (young girls going missing was the sort of crime that needed a quick response as they held too many possibilities for bad PR exposure). They had descended on the studio but when it was opened up, the rooms were found to be empty. The landlord claimed the space had not been let in over a year and the girls from the hairdresser's said they had never heard of anyone working above them.

The phone number was checked and found to be dead and when Terry tried to show the police the advert that Juliet had ripped out of the paper, he found instead an advertisement for a new pet shop that had never been there before.

The police widened their search (as the first twenty-four were considered critical) and were just about to announce the largest manhunt in the history of the county when a young detective went to Juliet's school. He met with a well-informed headmistress who claimed they did not have a student called Juliet Bryson studying at the school, and what's more they never had.

Now the police checked all their sources. The local newspaper stated that the girl they had as Miss Spring was a girl by the name of Alice Monks. The friends and neighbours on the Brysons' street assured the police that the couple did not have a child, indeed it had often been remarked upon that they were unfortunately childless as it seemed like they would make good parents. Work colleagues said the same, and when the local births and deaths register was checked, no one of that name had ever been born.

What Margaret wanted to know was who had come into their house and redecorated Juliet's room, removed her posters and clothes, and replaced the photos of her in the family album with pictures of just the two of them. She was confused and angry and when she attempted to explain herself to the police the words came out garbled, the kind policewoman looking at her as if she were slightly mad. She tried to push a school report onto them, her daughter's report, received only that morning in the post, but the envelope contained a bank statement and no report was ever found.

It didn't make any sense; Juliet could not just vanish, that wasn't possible. Her daughter was real, she had spoken to her several hours ago, but she couldn't explain this to the police, to Terry, to anyone. She had cried until no more tears fell and her eyes hurt, she had been sick twice and collapsed in a dead faint, it felt as if someone had reached inside and cut a piece of her away, a part of her own body that she needed to survive.

She took to her bed and the doctors were called. They analysed her and concluded she was in a fragile state of mind due to a bad experience in hospital fifteen years before when her womb was removed. They thought that perhaps she had invented a child to compensate. Slipping in and out of a lucid state, she kept muttering to herself that it was all her fault.

Terry just felt numb. He apologised to the police and to his friends. Even though they pleaded with him to stay, he resigned from his job. He shut the outside world away and refused to answer the phone calls that in time dwindled and stopped. He never went to the pub anymore or called in at the bookie's. He never went to the corner shop to pick up a paper. All he wanted to do was hide from the memories he had in his head of a beautiful young girl with red hair and long legs. He went and sat in the rain; at least the rain felt good.

Three

He had been willing to ignore Munch, putting his sick joke down to his inability to understand personal boundaries and to make light of everything. It was that or the equally likely possibility that Munch was drinking too much and it was starting to affect his short- and long-term memory.

They had always been friends, having met in their first year of comprehensive school. Neither had been part of the football team, the music club, the drama society, the D&D geeks, or the trendies, so they had formed their own clique of two that revolved around listening to music, watching films and trying to find shopkeepers who would sell them beer without the production of their obviously faked IDs. As school morphed into college and college into work, as others moved to new towns and started new lives, Munch and Nick remained. They had little desire to go anywhere else and apart from the odd holiday to Spain, neither had lived away from Nottingham. Nick could not remember a time that Munch had not been present in his life, but even after such a lasting friendship Nick knew that Munch was at heart an idiot, or if that was too harsh, he was at least missing those few bits of grey matter that went into making a fully rounded person. He had no understanding of emotions or human conduct, and as Munch got older it became increasingly difficult to get a serious answer out of him.

He realised that Munch was not perhaps the most reliable person to talk to in the circumstances. Nick wanted to speak to someone he could trust. Someone who would listen and be constructive, a person who would not scoff but would consider him sane and be prepared to let him finish his tale, as bizarre as it was sounding at the moment.

He had not been to bed, unable to sleep in the heat of the night. The quietness of the flat and the empty feeling it was suddenly emanating made him feel nervous. The place no longer felt like their home. It was as if he had wandered into someone else's life, similar to his own but lacking the crucial element of Natalie. The flat felt like a stage set awaiting the return of its actors. For the first time he felt like a stranger in his own life.

He had made a methodical search of the flat as soon as he got back from the hospital, convinced that she could not have taken everything she owned and got it out of the flat without him waking. But there was nothing left, and even more intriguing was the fact that the two suitcases they used for any weekends away were still under the bed. This had led Nick to the conclusion that a 'friend' must have helped her leave, an idea he found disturbing and somewhat reprehensible.

His mind whirring, he had watched as the sun slipped into the clear sky and at the earliest opportunity rang his father. Charles Stuart lived in the next county, having moved there ten months ago when his wife, Nick's mother, died after a long battle with cancer. Nick saw him as practical person, not one to break down when troubles occurred. They had all been devastated by the death, but it had been expected. Once she was no longer with them Charles seemed to say a goodbye and then alter his life accordingly. He had moved to Lincolnshire a week after his wife's death. He sold the family home and most of the contents, claiming it held too many memories and that he wanted a fresh start. He bought a dog and a small house on the outskirts of a village. He had, as far as Nick and his sister knew, never been a pet kind of person, but he doted on the animal and took her everywhere with him. She was a large golden Labrador, a little porky around the middle, but with a good temperament. He named her Tess – Nick's mum's name had been Elizabeth. Friends called her Bess.

Nick knew his father would already be up; he had always been an early riser, even before he bought the dog, preferring to get outside and breathe what he termed 'real air'. He hated to be closeted inside, and was as ready to roam as Tess. Looking back on it, Nick realised there was a lot of the canine in his father; they were a good match.

The phone was picked up after only three rings. Nick could hear Tess barking in the background.

"Charlie Stuart."

On first meeting him, many thought his father too formal, too reserved and closed off, but Nick knew he wasn't really like that. He had always been a doting family man; it was just that he was a bit old-fashioned, a bit stuck in his ways. He had spent the last thirty years working for the university and now acted as a consultant to small businesses. His motto that he always used to repeat to Nick and Wendy as children was 'If you're going to do something, do it properly'. This became his mantra, and wife, son and daughter would chant it back at him the moment he opened his mouth. He always smiled and laughed out loud at their cheek.

"Hi, Dad. It's Nick."

Nick could still hear Tess in the background; her loud bark would puncture most of the conservation as if she wanted to add her own thoughts to the discussion.

"Quiet, Tess! How are you, Nick?"

Nick felt depressed, worried, confused, completely at a loss as to what had happened in his life – but they were not the sort of emotions his dad expected a conversation to open with. You could build up to problems but never open with them. There was a strict hierarchy to phone calls with his father.

"Not too bad."

"Good. I was over your neck of the woods earlier this week at some conference… Wednesday, I think it was. I expect you were at work."

Charlie understood that his son was not really cut out for the nine to five; that his heart lay elsewhere. In truth, if Charles had his time over again he would have preferred to do more than applied mechanics. He always fancied himself as a sailor, charting a course around the world and sailing it single-handedly, not that he had ever told his son as much. But he knew he should at least attempt to encourage Nick and admitting to his own fanciful dreams was not going to help the situation. Nick would often be given job adverts his dad had cut out from the local paper, work he thought Nick would be capable of. He even offered to help him apply for them. Charles knew that his son could do so much more, and that trying to kick-start a career as an actor was not a sensible option. He hoped his son would realise that a person had to be sensible once they reached a certain age and that going after dreams more often than not ended in disillusionment. He was also aware that his son never bothered to apply for any of the posts and threw the clippings out the first opportunity he got.

Wendy – as she liked to point out to her older brother by showing off her house, her car, her family – was a great success in marketing, with more degrees and letters after her name than there were in the alphabet. She thought of him as a waster and tried whenever possible to tell him to get a proper job. But Nick was happy doing little jobs and picking up the cash once a month; it filled the void, paid the bills and allowed him to wait until he earned enough from acting to give it all up.

He'd had such high hopes when he had started out, and had originally thought that by his early thirties he could claim 'actor' as his designated role in life, but it seemed that things were never that simple. He had not received the formal training that so many of the younger actors seemed to possess, nor did he 'know' people in the business, which seemed to guarantee so many instant placements. He just wasn't that lucky in life. He was one of life's workers. He knew he would get there; it would just take time.

"Erm, yeah, work's kind of slow at the moment."

He paused.

"Dad, I've got a bit of a problem."

"What's the matter?"

It sounded as if his father was eating something.

"Natalie's gone missing."

He went quiet for a moment, the munching sound ceasing as he mulled over the statement.

"Natalie?"

Nick could feel his heart quicken and the sensation of panic rising up from his stomach. His father knew who Natalie was, he had met her countless times, they got on together, they had a shared interest in holidays, food and wine. There was no need for him to name check her like this.

"Nat...my Natalie. She's left me."

"Remind me. Is she someone you work with?"

Nick had to sit down. He moved over to the dining table and sat heavily on a chair. He was unsure how to continue. How could he tell his father that his girlfriend who he had shared his entire life with had been expunged completely from his life, had disappeared without trace?

He chose to ignore his father's lack of knowledge and pressed on.

"I woke up yesterday morning and she was gone. She wasn't in the flat and her mobile's turned off. She's moved everything out while I was asleep."

"Oh, I didn't know someone had moved in with you. Did you have a row or something? A falling out?"

"Sort of."

Nick thought about his parents' relationship and how they had never argued, not once, or at least never while he was in earshot. They had been a perfect couple, both taking the role of mother, father, wife, husband and lover seriously. They were devoted to each other and to raising their small family.

"Dad, you've met Natalie lots of times. You say she reminds you of Mum when she was young. Why can't you remember her; why can't anyone remember her?"

His voice came out in a strangled howl, a pitiful cry of frustration.

"My God, Nick, what's the matter? I've probably just forgotten who she is – my mind isn't what it used to be. This Natalie has probably gone to blow off steam, that's all. She'll be back."

Charles went silent while thinking of the best possible advice he could give his incoherent and troubled son. Nick imagined him staring down at Tess as she looked up at him with her large chestnut eyes, her tail beating against the back of the sofa.

"How about I come over for lunch? Does that pub near you still let dogs in?"

Nick was relieved; he wanted to see him. He wanted to see a reassuring face. He needed someone to take charge and advise him on the way forward.

"Yes. That'd be good, Dad."

Charles spoke of a number of errands he had to run first, so they agreed to meet at about one o'clock. This would allow Nick to make a visit to the police. He had not mentioned it to his father, not wanting to cause any alarm. He knew how his father thought, how concerned he would be about his own son. He was worried that mentioning the police would only distress him further.

Nick looked out on the street below the window. The shadows were long and empty of life, deep grooves of darkness that cut into the sandstone and brick of the building facades, the sun not yet high enough to intrude. The party people had all gone home or were asleep in a stranger's bed, their night and energy spent. The sirens, a background beat he had got used to hearing in the city, were silent for once. He could hear a pigeon cooing – its tune soft and mournful as it woke early to scavenge on the vomit and greasy chip wrappers left over from last night – but that was the only sound. It was a moment of peace rarely felt in the city. Even the usual rasps and moans of the building – a place that creaked and reeked of age and disappointment glossed over with thick cream paint – was for once silent. Eerily so, thought Nick, as if it were holding its breath, hiding from sight and scared of being caught.

He felt numb as realisation started to spread and the sun moved into the sky. Something was seriously wrong and yet he felt incapable of doing anything about it. It was as if he had been stung by something toxic and the poison had crept through his blood and arteries, resulting in all ability being drawn from his limbs. It was if he had been paralyzed by the oddity of the situation.

Natalie was gone. Gone to the point that no one apart from himself seemed capable of remembering her; she had been wiped from the memories of the two people he trusted as easily and as definitely as turning out a light. They had no recollection of her existence at all. If they could not remember who she was, what then of everyone else that knew her? Her family, her friends, her work colleagues – he could not believe that anyone could simply cease to be. It was against logic. Some mistake had been made. An empty void colonised a space within the flat – a place that was reserved for her. He had now moved beyond concern to outright fear. Something bad was happening.

Nick had already decided that he would go to the police station as soon as it was light. He knew that they would more than likely send him away, but he needed to go for his own peace of mind. It was what would be expected of him and he needed – no, wanted – to speak to a person of authority who would tell him what to do. He felt like a lost child, who needed desperately to see a parent rushing forward to claim him. Instead he felt as if he were stuck between strangers who asked questions for which he could find no answers.

The first rays of sunlight hit the windows of the building opposite and reflected the sun back into the flat, briefly outlining the room behind him. A movement in the glass caught his eye – a shimmer of white, flashing like a fish caught on a hook. He saw the outline of a forehead and two dark sockets, the flare of a pale face. Nick turned quickly, half expecting to see her standing in the middle of the room, having returned from the hidden place to beg his forgiveness.

The room was empty. He looked around, attempting to work out what had cast the ghost impression on his consciousness, what tangle of light and shadow had deceived him. He looked back to the window but the movement was gone. He worried that he was losing his mind as he took a last drink of cool black coffee.

It was almost peaceful out on the street. Sunday mornings still felt different from the rest of the week; even with the shops now open and all day drinking. For Nick they retained the reverence of youth, in many ways still sacred, the hope of false redemption. Certainly he had always enjoyed his Sundays, not in any religious 'communing with God' way, but the peace, relaxation, thick Sunday paper and fried breakfast he always insisted on. It was a time to relax and kick back, wind down after a long week at work while at the same time building up the impetus for what was approaching. It was a form of religion he had created that just happened to share its sabbath.

Nick liked to sit back on the couch, a bit of music playing in the background, the windows open with a light breeze tugging at the curtains and Natalie in her tight sleeping shorts, normally teasing him about a hangover. Later, he would sit and read through his latest part – practise, acting muscles flexing, getting ready for whatever audition he had later in the week. It was the only day that he could just get on with the acting work and even if suffering from the night before, he could still get more done on a Sunday afternoon than in all the other stolen moments of the week. It was the one day that he felt like an actor, with all the hopes and dreams that he had for leaving his temporary job and acting full-time being but a shallow breath away. Now he worried that he would never get those Sundays back; they would seem somewhat hollow since Natalie's disappearance. She was part of their make-up, they were meant to be family days, loving days, hugging days. Even though it gave him even more time to rehearse, he knew he wouldn't be able to face it until he found her.

He passed through the Square; a number of the shops were getting ready for the day ahead. The bars and cafés, some of which would have only been shut for a few hours, were being cleaned, the pavements outside hosed down; small tables were put out for the sun worshippers. Past the library, leaving the commercial centre behind, he walked up Derby Road, the shops finally petering out to be replaced by grand Victorian villas that had long ago been turned into cramped and squalid flats. Originally it had been a mainly student area, but now the students were slowly being pushed out as the developers turned it into yet another commune for those who already owned everything.

The road stretched upward for about a quarter of a mile until it reached a plateau. At a set of traffic lights sat a small wooden police station that looked strangely out of place next to all the red brick. It nestled amidst old-fashioned grandeur, but the building looked as if it would be more at home in a discoloured seaside postcard. It was the quaint wooden shack on the beach or the headquarters for the local bowls team, not a police station.

Nick crossed the road and entered. It was quiet inside. A small hatch in one wall was closed with a sheet of thick tarnished plastic. The remaining walls were taken up with pin boards that were adorned with fliers warning the community to look out for car thieves, pickpockets, scam artists, unscrupulous door-to-door salesmen, kids in gangs, kids in 'hoodies', the effects of alcohol, drugs, knives, gun crime and fire works. There were leaflets to be taken away about credit card fraud, internet swindles and mail deception, plus several posters warning about how to avoid catching bird flu. They blew listlessly in the warm breeze as the door behind him closed.

He was the only person waiting. Bending down to look through the small hatch into the office beyond, he could see two police officers engaged in an early morning cup of tea, biscuit at the ready and a read of the day's newspapers their only concern. Nick knocked on the partition. One of the officers looked up at the sudden disorder and quickly removed his feet from the top of the desk. He turned and looked at his colleague as if in need of help with the interruption. He got out of his chair slowly, as if it pained him, before turning and moving towards Nick.

The hatch was at an odd height, roughly level with Nick's chest. As the plastic was pulled back he had to bend to look through and then cock his head back to look up at the policeman, who refused to bend forward.

"Good morning, sir. How can I help?"

Nick had a good view up his nose; his nostrils filled with dark curly hair that had been allowed to get out of hand. He had biscuit crumbs around the corners of his mouth.

"My girlfriend has gone missing."

The officer nodded as if to say that Nick was indeed correct.

"When did she disappear, sir?"

"Yesterday. She wasn't at home when I woke and she never came back. I think something might have happened to her."

"Yesterday?"

He at last bent down to look at Nick and almost made it to eye level before stopping somewhat higher.

"We can't really refer to a person as 'missing' until they have been gone for at least forty-eight hours."

A pained expression crossed Nick's face, causing the officer – who had up to that point been gruff and business-like in his manner due his dislike of the early shift – to change track, if only to get rid of the nuisance and get back to his crossword quicker.

"She probably had too much to drink last night and crashed at a friend's. Hot weather and these new drinking laws are causing us all sorts of problems. Roll on winter, eh?"

"Her mobile's turned off. She never turns it off."

He shrugged before answering. "Perhaps the battery's dead. Most people who have gone on a bit of a bender tend to be crap at phoning the people who are worried; probably scared you'll shout at her for being stupid. She'll turn up."

"What about the percentage who haven't gone on a bender?"

He paused and took a deep breath. The police officer was not prepared at such an early time in the morning to get into a heated debate with a member of the public.

"You'll have to come back, sir."

He closed the hatch as Nick straightened up. He could have guessed that their answer would be terse and to the point, but Nick had expected some kind of response. A form to fill out would have made him feel less apprehensive. But he knew that if everyone who went missing for twenty-four hours was investigated, the police would be besieged with work. It was logical that some sort of time frame would need to be put on cases. But he also knew that this was different. Something kept telling him that it was partly his fault that she was gone and that she would not return. He kept getting small flashes back to the night he went out. He was with Munch, they were drinking and then…and then he couldn't remember. It felt like someone had removed part of his memory. There was a hole where the 'then' should have been. Instead of darkness or missing time, the hole in his mind appeared to be filled with hot sand that slid and shifted, making it impossible for him to judge what was real; instead, everything slipped off into nothingness.

He left the station but vowed to come back. He had not mentioned that her possessions were also missing, as he knew the officer would just smirk and then offer that as the reason why she had gone. He also did not want to say that two people in close relationships with her had inexplicably forgotten that she ever existed in the first place.

Without anything else to do but wait for his father, Nick went back to the flat and tidied up. He actually dusted and mopped the wooden floor, something he had not done for months. He just wanted to keep busy, but his mind kept returning to Natalie and the night she had disappeared.

His father turned up ten minutes early, which was about normal for him. Nick buzzed him into the flat while at the same time ensuring his mobile was fully charged in case she rang. They met out on the landing. Tess sat scratching at something on her stomach while they greeted each other and got the general part of the conversation out of the way. The pub that Charles liked was traditional, with horse brasses, warm beer and pork scratchings sold in little clear bags. It was the only old pub left in the city that Nick knew of, all the others having become wine bars or Belgian beer houses. The only time Nick ever went to this pub was in the presence of his father. It had become their allotted meeting place, a clubhouse of their very own, the Stuart family wigwam and den.

Nick returned from the bar carrying two pints of bitter and a dog bowl full of water on a tray. Charles sat looking through the menu while deciding what to have. He looked up as his beer was put down in front of him.

"You look tired."

He said it with concern evident in his voice.

"I didn't sleep well last night," Nick admitted. "I'm not sure what to do. Something strange is going on."

His father looked perplexed.

"You don't remember Natalie at all, do you? Natalie Hope? She's been living with me for about six months; she was from Italy, from Le Marche. Does this ring any bells with you?"

Charles shook his head.

"No, no it doesn't. Perhaps it's me. I'm getting older…things happen to us as we age."

"It's not you. You haven't had any other memory lapses, have you? You still remember where you live, who I am, who you are. Munch can't remember her either."

"Now him I do remember. How could anyone forget that gawky chap with those big ears."

Charles took a drink before changing the subject.

"You look like you've been in the wars."

He looked at his son's mouth as he said it, making Nick put his hand up to the scab that had formed across his lip. It stung as he touched it, triggering a memory. He remembered a toilet, a dirty smelly bathroom he hadn't wanted to be in. There had been water and, being drunk, he had slipped and fell. His face had crunched into the floor and pain and blood had followed.

His hand left his face and touched the contours of his head. There was a point on his scalp hidden amongst his hair that felt tender. He had banged his head, hard. He remembered now. The details flooded back. He had fallen and when he had gone back out, Munch had laughed; Munch and his friends. New people. A woman, large-breasted, who giggled and licked at his friend's ear, biting at the lobe as if she were attempting to feed upon him. There had been someone else as well…

"I fell over."

"Have you rung this Natalie's parents, her friends, anyone else who knows her?"

Nick had been expecting this and it was the one stumbling block in his being able to admit to himself that he was not going mad.

"I haven't got any of their numbers. I don't even know where Natalie's parents live."

Natalie had never talked about her family. It was if that part of her life was in some way closed off, a 'no-go' territory. Having just lost his mum, Nick had not really been that interested in happy families and had never had the decency to ask. He had switched off that element of his own life, declaring his family of no importance to either of them, and if he could not talk about his family – Mum and Dad as a parental unit – then he was not that keen to hear about anyone else's. He had no idea where Natalie's parents lived, what they looked like, if they were even alive. They could have been in Italy or the UK. Thinking about it in his current position, it dawned on him that most of Natalie's private life was a closed book. He had been happy just being with her, just the two of them. History, family, and all the baggage that came with them, none of that mattered to him – to them.

Charles looked confused. He found this all a bit strange. He and Elizabeth had known everything about each other. They spent all their time together, they visited each other's families, became good friends with both sets; they took part in each other's hobbies and pastimes. They had been inseparable, right up until the end. Charles had done everything he could for her; he had loved everything about her, even when her body started to fail, forcing him to nurse her like a fragile child.

"You've never even talked to them on the phone?" he asked.

Nick shook his head. "Not once."

"Well, you'll have to find out the details. They deserve to know."

"Everything's gone. There's no way to get in touch."

"Well, check for friends. She's probably just staying with one of them. Nick – how can you live with someone and not know their parents?"

Nick could feel himself starting to get a little defensive. He didn't want to have to shout down his father but he felt as if he were being backed into a corner. He felt the walls at his sides closing, suffocating him, trapping him away from any chance of escape.

"It just never came up. It's never been a problem."

"Is that why you've never introduced us?"

"You've met."

Charles shook his head and laughed.

"I think that knock on the head has sent you a little screwy. You know you can get a little…" He stopped as if choosing the next word carefully; he seemed to Nick to be running through his entire gamut. "…a little excited sometimes. Perhaps a trip to the doctor would be more appropriate?"

Nick stood up and looked down at his father. He didn't want to be mocked; he'd had enough of that from Munch. He had expected so much more from his own blood.

"It's you who's got the problem, you and fucking Munch."

He started to shout. He hadn't meant to, never having raised his voice to his father before, but this was too much.

"She's real. I'm not making this up. I have a whole set of memories about this woman, what she smells like, how she wears her hair, what chocolate she likes. I didn't just invent her overnight. I didn't."

"All right, Nick, for Christ's sake, sit down."

Several people looked over from the bar, raising eyebrows at the commotion. Nick looked back at them, defying anyone to kick up a rumpus. They looked away and Nick sat.

"Jesus, what's got into you?"

"I just thought you'd be able to help, that's all."

"OK, just calm down. I'll help you find her, don't worry."

He put the menu down on the table that he had been gripping during the outburst, his knuckles tight and balled as if arthritic or painful.

"I'll have the beef roll."

Nick got up and ordered some food at the bar before returning to his father and the problem.

"What else can I do?"

"You've checked the hospitals, that sort of thing?"

Nick nodded.

"You'll have to tell the police."

"I went this morning. They say they can't do anything for forty-eight hours."

His father nodded as if that made sense to him.

"Then it's a waiting game."

He had spent the evening unable to sleep. He would get out of bed, every half-hour, sheets cold and uninhabitable, and check the flat for movement. He wandered from room to room like some wraith subjected to a damned life, nothing more than a grey face at the window that scanned the empty lane for any sign of Natalie. The street lamps doused the scene in the colour of rust; the church looked as if it had been built from amber. Twice he was convinced he heard laughter outside the door, though it sounded male rather than the light tones of a woman. He snatched at the handle and opened it wide, anxious to catch whoever was taunting him. It was nothing. The hall remained dark, with many places to hide, noises from the floors below radiating upwards, scratching from the hollow walls, while pipes hollered and screamed. He had never noticed how old the place felt, almost ancient. Hidden histories that needed to be spoken lay dormant within.

Eventually he had fallen into a fitful sleep in which he dreamed of a tent in a desert. The tent was black, in stark contrast to the silver sands that blew and lashed at his face. He stood some way off, watching the flag fluttering above whip and snake in the breeze. The desert was otherwise empty, a harsh lonely land.

With little else to do he walked towards the entrance of the tent, but never seemed to get any closer. The sands shifted under his feet, his weight pushing him further and further down with each step. He was sinking. Soon the sand was higher than his knees and he was unable to propel himself forward. He stopped, exhausted, the tent further away than ever. But still he continued to sink deeper, his waist slipping below the fine sands.

He tried to shout out for help but his voice was taken up and hidden in the wide open spaces. He started to struggle, desperate to get loose, but that only speeded up the process; his chest disappeared into the cool earth. He looked towards the tent and thought he saw movement, someone staring out, two pinpricks of amber light that could have been eyes, but already the sands were claiming his neck.

He called again but his mouth filled with the taste of the desert. It ran inside him, choking him, filling his nose and throat. He attempted to push upwards but the strain was too much and he collapsed backwards into darkness, slipping down into the draining sands, choking on earth, crushed by nature.

On Monday morning Nick phoned work and claimed he was sick. Munch answered the phone. Every time Nick needed money he would go back to Munch who would hire him as it gave him someone to talk to and relieved the monotony of actually having to work. Even though he was a manager, Munch was even less committed to the job than Nick, preferring to give his work to someone else whenever possible.

Always scruffy with two days' growth of beard and dirty blonde hair that would not lie flat, Munch had a way of worming his way into people's lives and once on the family couch he was impossible to budge. He was, Nick realised with shame, becoming his equivalent of Tess, the only plus being Munch didn't have to go outside to shit.

Nick didn't give him any specifics. After the disturbed phone call from the hospital he decided against discussing Natalie. Instead he claimed a stomach bug and left it at that.

"Blinder on Friday – couldn't get up till after three."

Nick agreed that he had felt equally as bad and thought of his cut lip and the bump nestling in his hairline.

"Munch, about that night. We went somewhere new and I slipped in the toilet and cracked my head. You thought it was funny."

"Yeah, yeah, you're right. What was it called? There were a bunch of real twats outside. I didn't think they were going to let us in at first, seemed to be some kind of black man's haunt."

"I went for a piss and when I came back you were with some woman. A big girl with huge tits; she had some friends with her, I think."

"Did I? Shit...I must have been well pissed. I don't like the fat ones."

"She seemed to like you. Try to think back."

From down the telephone line he could hear Munch strain as he asked his friend to attempt a feat akin to thinking. There was silence as the cogs shifted into gear, and a lot of shallow breathing.

"Yeah, I think you're right. Fuck, she was ugly."

Munch was all for expressing himself at every opportunity he got. He was not a devotee of political correctness either. How he stayed in a job at all without offending half of his colleagues was a mystery to anyone who met him.

"Forgetting the girl for a moment, who else was with her?"

"I don't know. They just came over and opened a bottle. Never seen them before."

Nick had a sudden image of a man buying large bottles of tequila that he placed on the table and offered to the people around him. He had sat quietly, relaxed in the raucous surroundings. It was as if there was an ocean of calm around him, a bubble of slowed time. He had refilled the glasses lazily, his eyes watching, judging and smiling. They had all drunk but he, he had nursed the same drink all night. The memory was stilted though, cracked, a film seen as if distorted through water or across a scratched convex screen.

"You didn't get a name or a phone number?"

"No. Why, you interested? Do you want to meet up for a bit of riding the ripples?"

"No. It's probably nothing anyway."

Nick finished the call quickly and sat for a moment, drawing mental and physical energy for what he knew had to be completed today.

He had decided to return to the police station. This felt like the only course of action open to him. He needed to offload the guilt he felt at her disappearance onto someone who could make a physical difference. The police had never known Natalie so would be able to give impartial advice, whereas he was not convinced his father really believed what he was saying. There had been a look in his eye that had resembled pity, or at least concern. The last thing that Nick wanted to feel was judged.

There was a different officer stationed at the reception from his previous visit. She was taking down details from a large Iranian woman who didn't speak much English. Attempting to help with the handicap, the pair had developed a routine of acting out what it was they were both trying to say, while the other watched and nodded if it was believed to be correct. It was a slow and tiresome routine that made a mockery of the crime.

Nick stood behind the large darkly-veiled woman who smelt of spice and sweat. It was still hot outside and like him she must have walked uphill from the city centre. By her side were two inadequate shopping bags stuffed with vegetables, green stems and leaves overhanging and wilting. She appeared to be reporting an incident whereby someone had overcharged her, refusing to return any change from a twenty-pound note. She kept letting out a low wail and pointing with beautifully manicured nails at the collection of coins on the reception, beating her breast and mopping at her brow. The police officer was trying to be sympathetic and tactful, while at the same time admitting there was little that the police could do, by holding up her hands and miming a giant shrug followed by a shake of the head. It was comical in its simplicity and if he had felt in a better mood Nick might have laughed, but instead he stood resolute behind her, willing her to give up and give him access to the policewoman. Eventually the Iranian lady got the message, picked up her bags and shuffled out, muttering to herself what Nick imagined to be curses upon the person who had dared to overcharge her.

The policewoman smiled as if in some discomfort as he came close to the window and assumed the impractical position demanded by the design of the reception. He bent down low and looked up at her.

"How can I help?" she asked.

Walking up the hill Nick had prepared a little speech, mulling it over in his head until he felt he could get it off pat without sounding too confused or too much like a victim. He wanted them to understand the urgency of the situation, to look beyond the obvious and understand that he was now no longer just concerned that something had happened to Natalie but was convinced there was reason for them to act, something other that demanded their attention. He also did not want to suffer the embarrassment of sounding ever so slightly mad.

Something else was also starting to gnaw at him. He felt that this disappearance was somehow his own fault – not just the now somewhat trivial argument – but the idea that he was in some way complicit in her vanishing. Something had happened that he was responsible for, of that he was positive. He just couldn't remember what it was.

"I came in yesterday to report that my girlfriend's gone missing, but was told there was nothing you could do until forty-eight hours had passed. It's now forty-eight hours, give or take an hour."

She nodded, which encouraged Nick immensely. He felt as if he was getting somewhere at last and a proper hunt for Natalie could begin in earnest. He hoped that a team of police would be called out and the countryside and waste ground around Nottingham would be combed for evidence.

"What incident number do you have?"

"Incident number?"

"When you came in yesterday you would have been given an incident number so that we can keep track of who's been in and when."

He shook his head. "I wasn't given any number."

She paused. Her lips pursed, displaying a slight downy moustache. Nick felt chastised; he was being treated as if he had done something wrong, a naughty schoolchild in front of the matron, with all his indiscretions laid bare.

"You came into this police station yesterday?"

He nodded.

"And reported a missing person? But you were not given any incident number?"

He nodded again and added a smile in the hope of placating her.

"I wasn't given one because it was not over forty-eight hours."

"Which officer did you speak to?"

"I don't know – a tall one. He had dark hair and quite a big...nose."

"What was his name, sir? Or his number?"

Nick's voice became quiet. The officer was belittling him with her interrogation. She was probably not going to be as helpful as he had at first thought.

"I didn't get his name...or number."

She let out a long, steam-train-coming-into-a-station sigh. This was obviously going to be more work than she had expected and she wished for the days of the Iranian woman. Fumbling through a number of multi-coloured forms, she stopped at a pale green sheet, changed her mind and threw a pink one at him.

"We take missing people very seriously, particularly young women, what with that 'Missing Man' on the loose. If you've seen the news you'll know that three have vanished in the last month. Sit down and fill this out. Someone will be with you as soon as they can."

She pointed to a row of plastic chairs against the pinboard wall.

Nick remembered the headline from the paper; he had not paid much attention but there had been a report on the local news a week earlier. Young women, out on the town laughing and drinking with friends, had been snatched, often within earshot of their mates, and made to vanish into the night. There were no witnesses and, so it seemed at the moment, little evidence of how the crimes were executed or why the girls had been chosen. They called the abductor 'The Missing Man', Nick assumed more out of sensationalism than in praise of his invisibility.

"Can I have a pen?"

She picked up a biro that was missing its top, the end chewed and ragged.

"Make sure you give it back."

Nick assumed working with criminals had made her slightly distrustful of everyone, an offered pen an opportunity for theft. He smiled again, a look that promised that he would not steal her dog-eared cheap biro and would attempt in all his dealings to stay on her good side.

The form was simple: name, address, telephone, mobile et cetera for the person making the statement, plus a number of tick boxes that reduced in severity depending on the crime you were reporting. Murder, rape, violent attack, burglary, assault, and somewhere near the bottom, 'missing person'. He ticked the box, wondering if the amount of time you waited for an interview was dependent on the seriousness of the crime or whether it was a first come, first served operation.

Nick finished writing out the form by signing and dating it. There was a number in the corner of the page which he assumed was the incident number; he made a note of it in his mobile. As he stood to hand the form back the reception door opened and a policeman in wire-framed glasses shoved his head into the waiting room and beckoned Nick to follow. Nick made sure he returned the precious biro to its owner before he did so.

He was taken to a small room containing nothing more than a desk and a couple of chairs. It was beyond sparse, with no windows and a florescent strip light caged into the ceiling. It reminded Nick of his pod at work. It had a similar sort of smell, old coffee and heated plastic giving a depressing feel to a place. It was an environment full of tension and loss.

He sat, and the officer, who looked a little overweight to be of any use in a chase situation, sat down opposite. He took off his hat to reveal a shock of silver hair. He was much older than Nick had at first taken him for, but now, uncrowned, his age was evident from the bulbous nose decorated with broken veins and the pair of cheap glasses hiding bloodshot, tired eyes.

He coughed to clear his throat before speaking. There was the unmistakable smell of roll-up tobacco on his breath.

"Do you have a form?" he asked in a broad local accent.

Nick handed the pink paperwork over. The officer took hold of it, pushed his glasses up to the bridge of his nose and scrutinised the work.

"Nice handwriting."

Nick remained silent.

"Now, Mr Stuart, you're reporting the disappearance of one..." he peered down at the report again,"...one Miss Natalie Hope of Apartment 8, 145 Hollowstone, the place in which you also reside?"

Nick nodded and took a deep breath, ready to tell his story once more. "I woke up Saturday morning and she had already left the flat. She never came home. I've tried ringing her to get in contact but her mobile is turned off and she never turns her mobile off. I think something's happened to her."

He looked sympathetic, tired but sympathetic.

"Has she ever disappeared before? Does she do it regularly?"

"No. She's never done anything remotely like this. She goes out a lot with her mates, without me, but she always comes home. She always *has* come home."

The officer nodded as if this was a good answer, the right answer.

"Was she out the night in question with her friends?"

"I don't think so. I'd gone out early with a mate. She was in bed when I got back."

He pulled out a large pad of paper and started to take some notes.

"You are sure she was in the bed when you came home on Friday night?"

"It was more like Saturday morning when I got in. I was a bit wasted, but I'm sure she was there."

Nick thought back to the night he arrived home, drunk and sweating. He was almost positive she was in the bed when he got home, but he had not checked. It was just that the room felt occupied. Rooms change when someone else inhabits them, they feel lived in and that was the feeling he had that night. All he had to do was reach out and touch her, but he hadn't. He had turned his back and fallen asleep. He had left her alone on her side of the bed.

"These friends of hers, what are their names?"

This was the bit Nick had been dreading, the bit where his story started to sound implausible, slightly too disjointed to be convincing. A mess of half-remembered facts and misheard conversations told to him as he watched the television. How can a man live with someone for six months and not know their friends? Not know what they do on a Friday night? Or where they go?

"One's called Bex – I don't know her surname – and a Krissy. I'm not sure of her other name either."

He wrote down the details and circled the names.

"Do you have an address for them, a telephone number?"

He shook his head. "No. I don't really know them. I've never even met them."

The police officer sucked on his teeth before changing tack.

"OK. What about the places she frequents, certain bars, clubs, that sort of thing?"

"Sometimes we go to the Cookie Club, and Shaw's in Hockley. When we first met she took me to several basement bars, little out of the way places, but recently we've been staying in a lot. I've been rehearsing – I'm an actor – or we've just been going to places that we know."

"Can you give me a list? If she went out it'll help us to draw up a pattern of her movements. That's if anyone's seen her, or even remembers her. Nottingham's a busy place on a Friday night."

Nick took the offer of his pen which he noted was as dog-eared as the previous one and started to write a list of places that he knew Natalie would frequent. He wrote down several bars, a couple of cafés she sometimes ate lunch in, and the name of a nightclub. He also listed the shops she normally visited but could only think of three possibilities, his memory of clothing boutiques being quite limited.

"The addresses are just rough estimates. I'm not sure of all the street names."

The officer accepted the list and folded it neatly.

"OK, so what about her parents?"

Nick shook his head, hoping the police officer would drop the question. It was meant to be resignation, a sign that perhaps they were dead or forgotten. The police officer's eyes narrowed in response.

"What do you mean by that?"

"I don't know them. We've never met. Natalie is part Italian on her mother's side, but I don't know if they live here or in Italy."

"At least give me their names. I can run a check."

"I'm not sure what they are."

The police officer started to look a little mystified; his temples were starting to twitch, a vein was now noticeable and throbbing in his neck. His eyes remained narrowed with confusion.

"How long have you been together?"

"Just under six months; she moved in with me soon after we met."

"And you've never seen her family and you don't know any of her friends? Are you even sure she was your girlfriend?"

He said it with a wry smile but the jibe gored painfully. Nick answered, anger flaming inside of him.

"What do you mean by that?"

"Nothing. Calm down. You must have heard her speak on the phone to her parents; did she talk in Italian or English? She must have mentioned the odd name to you – Giuseppe or something."

Nick ignored the joke and instead tried to summon an image of Natalie on the phone. He thought of her sitting on the edge of the sofa, legs bent up under her chin with just her feet sticking out as she flexed her toes backwards and forwards. He tried to remember who it was she was talking to. It never sounded like a call to a parent; most the time it was in English but now and again she spoke the odd word in Italian. They normally sounded like swear words.

Reconsidering, Nick thought it strange that she had never mentioned her family. Most girls he had known spent half their lives on the phone to family and friends but she was different, she hardly ever used it to call anyone. He guessed she was just trying to be sensitive because his own mother was dead. He had noticed it was the sort of thing people did, not talk about their own family in case he broke down crying in front of them. They thought they were being sympathetic but all it did was remind him even more that she was not around.

"I don't think she ever spoke to them."

"But they are alive?"

"I think so." He thought again. "To be honest, I've no idea."

The officer let out a grunt of discouragement, turned the page of his notebook and eased down a new piece of paper.

"What about work?"

The police officer's eyebrows slowly rose as Nick remained silent, a cantilever bridge expanding to let through the ship of disbelief.

"She works in marketing, advertising – something arty."

"And the company would be called?"

Nick wanted to help him, he really did, but once again his mind drew a blank. He had always found his own temporary jobs desperately dull. In the main they had been office-based IT roles, hardly fighter pilot material, so he had never bothered talking about them. If anyone asked he would shake his head and instead talk of his acting. Nick assumed everyone else felt the same about what they did; for him these jobs were just a means to an end. He knew Munch was not bothered about his career and though his father had worked all his life at the university, he very rarely spoke about it. It was acting that inspired Nick. He could talk about that for hours and would – if anyone showed the slightest interest.

"She has to go away every once in while on business, just a couple of days here and there."

"You don't know the company, do you?"

Nick looked sheepish.

"I've got to have something to go on; otherwise there's nowhere to begin. I suggest you go back home and hunt through her stuff. Look for telephone numbers, credit card bills, pay slips – anything that will give us a clue. And when we find her I suggest you ask some questions and get some answers."

Nick didn't want to add further to the police's problems but there had been no other chance for him to broach the issue.

"She took everything with her."

The officer stopped writing and very slowly closed his notebook before throwing it on the table in irritation.

"You telling me she's moved out?"

"She took her things, but now she's vanished. No one has seen her and I'm worried."

"Have you ever heard of wasting police time? It can cost you big bucks, mister. You do appreciate that someone who moves out is not necessarily classed as a missing person. Perhaps she doesn't want you to find her."

He understood perfectly. In many ways the police officer was right. He had always been so mesmerised by Natalie, her natural beauty, her good demeanour, her sexy tight body and willing sexual technique that he had kind of forgotten the essentials. He had never really found out about *her* – her wants and needs, her hopes and fears. The reasons she was the person she was. What was it that shaped her, who was important to her, who were the people she cared for and could never be without? Was he her first love, or merely the most recent in a long line? Had she only lately come to Nottingham? Or had she lived here for years? He didn't know the very basics of who she was and what made her tick. He realised for the first time that he had been spending his life with someone he didn't really know at all.

"You must be able to do something?" he asked. "I don't want to beg but I will. I really think something's happened to her. I know it sounds like a lover's tiff but I'm scared."

The officer pursed his lips as he scrutinised Nick.

"All I can do is send out details to the local hospitals and to officers on the streets. That reminds me, I'll need a photo. A picture always works better than a description."

Nick fumbled for his phone. At last he had something worthwhile. His mobile had a built-in camera and the first thing he had done when he had got it was take a photo of Natalie. She had been laughing at the time; they had been messing around in the kitchen. He had been thwacking the elastic of her shorts, pulling them halfway down her bum, exposing her. He remembered they had ended up having sex on the kitchen table.

He tried to pull up the picture but the file was empty. All the other photos seemed to be available still but that single one had vanished. It had been deleted. The phone never left his side. It would be impossible for someone to gain access. He snapped the phone shut.

"I did have one but I must have deleted it."

"A phone photo's no good anyway. Have you got anything else?"

"I'm not sure I have."

"You're not making this easy for us, are you. Incidentally, what were you doing on the night in question? You understand we have to ask? You said you were out drinking; where did you go?"

"Lots of places, pubs, many outside of the town centre, away from all of the kids."

"And you were out with your friend the whole time?"

"Yes."

"And you didn't speak to your girlfriend the entire evening or have any contact with her?"

"No."

Nick knew what he was thinking, where he was trying to lead the questioning.

"I was out, she was home. That's it. Sometime in the morning she vanished. Anything else you want to know?"

"What's your friend's name, just for the record?"

Nick gave it, along with Munch's home address and mobile number. The police officer diligently noted the details in his book.

"I'll pass your details over, but I have a feeling they are going to laugh in my face when they read this report."

The officer put a hand into his breast pocket and handed Nick a business card with his details professionally made up including a badge number and full name. PC James Woodruff. Nick thanked him.

"I'm just here to make arrangements, a detective will be appointed. They'll probably want to come round and see you."

Nick stood ready to leave. "Of course."

The officer smiled as he stood up, his face stretching into a hundred shatter lines. Smiling really didn't suit him.

"I'm sure she's not far away, Mr Stuart. She's probably just lying low, giving you the runaround."

Nick smiled at the kind gesture but said nothing. He left, determined to get home and tear the place apart. He knew now he had been stupid. If Natalie was anywhere the clues would be in the flat. She must have left something behind, something that would prove to the doubters that she was real and in danger. That would be half the mystery over. Then the police would take the story a little more seriously and start combing the parks and waste ground for her, in case…he didn't want to think about 'in case'.

Nick was sweating by the time he made it back; it was still hot out on the street and busier than normal as people left work early or like him took a fake sick day. Inside it was cooler, chilling the sweat that dribbled unpleasantly down the back of his shirt. The stairwell leading up to the flat was always cold. Nick assumed it was caused by the thick old walls and dark bricks, plus the shoddy work the builders had done in the decades-old refurbishment.

As he reached the landing his neighbour opened his door and smiled sickly at him. A thin piece of skin the colour of vellum hung from his forehead, as if he was in the process of being stripped down like old wallpaper.

"I wanted to say sorry for last night. Caught me at a bad time."

Nick opened his own door.

"Sure. No problem."

"Good. I didn't want you thinking I was getting at you, eh. Just don't like people snooping around."

"Whatever."

Nick shut his door behind him, locking the awful sight outside. He waited until he heard the neighbour's door squeal on dry hinges, finally clicking to a close. It took a surprisingly long time, as if the man was waiting for Nick to come back out.

First port of call was the bedroom. There was a selection of shoe boxes stacked on top of the wardrobe. He pulled them down and threw them onto the bed. The first one was empty. The second, a large box which had contained some expensive walking boots he had bought, their name embossed onto the lid, held nothing but tissue paper. The third was half full of greeting cards.

He tipped them out, spreading the images of snowy Christmas scenes, holiday postcards and birthdays long gone across the duvet. He started to search through, looking for the one that Natalie would have given him. She had sent him a Valentine's Day card earlier in the year, a romantic poem stencilled on the front against a black and white image from a time long past. He had sent her a dirty limerick in return. There should be a birthday card as well, one containing a rude remark. Though the cards made him slow down and remember past events, he soon noted that Natalie's were missing.

He gave up and instead moved around the room, pulling open drawers. The one by her side of the bed held a bit of loose change, a taxi driver's card and a packet of mints. The two in the chest of drawers were filled with some of his clothes, the others were empty.

He moved into the front room. There was a large dresser that ran down one side of the flat. It was full of little drawers and cupboards. He pulled them out one by one. There were coasters, old magazines, boxes of matches, dried-up pens and loose photos that he quickly remembered having taken on a holiday before he had known Natalie. There was a selection of vases in the large cupboard that he had inherited from his grandmother, some spare batteries, elastic bands, a BT phone book and the Yellow Pages, a selection of DVDs and CDs (all of which were his), a tablecloth and a selection of tea towels. In the last drawer he pulled out a pile of bills, all neatly folded and arranged in date order. Something he would never have bothered to do.

He grabbed them and sat down at the coffee table. They were mainly utility bills with a few internet offers and credit card statements mixed in. They were all in Nick's name. Not one of them was addressed to Natalie.

He started to get desperate and went to the bathroom. Natalie had kept shelves of lotions and potions, cream for this and that, strange implements lined up as if for some intricate keyhole surgery, as well as the usual shampoo and conditioners (three different types), tampons and panty liners. Now all he could find was a bottle of antidepressants, but these had been bought over the counter by him, plus his own razor and toothbrush.

It was the same story in the kitchen. In one drawer he found a collection of old bus tickets, receipts and matchboxes picked up in bars, but again it only contained items he had put in.

Back in the bedroom he looked under the bed, behind the chest of drawers; he even popped the hatch of the small loft area. They were all empty. How could someone leave so little of themselves in a place? How could someone not make an impact on their surroundings? Leave no lasting imprint? He was everywhere in the flat, the sum of a thousand odds and ends; he had shed all his recent life events into the place like a discarded snake skin – but Natalie, she was more like a ghost.

He was starting to feel bad again, initial optimism dwindling and leaving him spent. Had Natalie moved out her personal items over the last week? Taking her time, having planned the whole event until the argument became the catalyst for her final withdrawal? She seemed to have orchestrated a complete and utter vacation of his life. A cold and tactical retreat rather than the emotional wrench of having to go through any crying and wailing, which he knew he was bound to do. She had decided to slip out quietly. Discreet and secretive, he imagined her furtively leaving every morning on the pretence of going to work when in reality she was moving out little bits of her life, packed away in the large black bag she used for work. He also knew that this was so unlike the woman he had lived with. She was not devious; she was, apart from his father, perhaps the most honest person he knew.

Without anything to prove she was real, Nick now felt that the police would simply ignore him. He would be regarded as nothing more than a crackpot, a weaver of stories who, through his own inability to tell what was real and imagined, had created a woman, a perfect woman to share his miserable life with.

He moved back to the living room and resumed his position at the window. Perhaps he was going mad, perhaps Natalie had never existed and he had created her to keep him company. His life had certainly been going through turmoil recently. The dark moods that were prone to grab at him two or three times a year seemed to be becoming more frequent since the death of his mother. Her demise had hurt; perhaps it had left a scar in his mind that he had not been aware of previously. It was strange that Natalie had entered his life shortly after he had lost his mother. Had she been a replacement? A phantom lover created to heal the void? Perhaps his reaction to her death, the removal of the person who gave birth to him, was to disappear into a world of his own making and there hide out, lost forever to the real world.

But then would he not have been lost to his father and friends as well? They had all acted as if he was fine; the evidence to the contrary was the mention of Natalie. It seemed that she had been removed completely from their lives but for him, echoes of her still reverberated in this space, in this life. He could summon up an image of her with ease, her whole personality filling in the gaps.

Had he been mad and the bump on the head returned him to some kind of normality? Or was it that the bump that had created this disillusion and now he was experiencing the creation of a person who in truth never existed?

He turned away from the window and glanced down. He noticed that the floor was looking dusty again, though he had only cleaned it yesterday. He went to the kitchen and retrieved the dustpan and brush.

Getting down on his knees he started to sweep at the floor. Pushing the brush underneath the settee he felt it hit something hard. An object skidded out across the bare floorboards and came to rest by his side. He picked it up.

It was a familiar small black book. One he kept for use as a memory aid. Birthdays, anniversaries, telephone numbers, shopping lists – anything that if he had to rely on his own recollection would soon be forgotten. He normally kept it in the inside pocket of his work suit but due to the hot weather he had not bothered wearing one recently. It must have slipped out and been kicked under the settee.

He flicked through the pages. They were full of a random collection of scribblings and lists. His sister's changing home telephone number and address, his mother's old car registration number used when he applied for insurance, his own national insurance code, a list of websites for ordering flowers.

He stopped.

The reason that he had ordered the flowers was as a present for Natalie. The only time he had bought flowers for someone that didn't involve their death. He had been at work and had decided to do something spontaneous. He had listed the websites on his PC, deliberated over the price of a nice bunch and a cheaper spray. He had in the end checked the delivery times for different shops in Nottingham and ordered a bouquet from a shop that could deliver later on the same day.

He had placed the order at a shop off the Square, a collection of roses and some exotic cream-coloured flower that had left orange blobs of pollen on his shirt cuff. They had been delivered to Natalie's work. She had come home beaming, proud to be called out of a meeting and able to return cradling a gift that demonstrated love, her colleagues cooing and gurgling over the typed card.

She had cooked him a special dinner that night. They had rented a DVD and sat in each other's arms, taking it in turns to eat from the small bucket of ice cream they shared.

The memory was warm and full of love, too detailed to be the creation of a disturbed mind but also proof at last that he had not fashioned Natalie from nothing. She was no longer a phantom created by a damaged mind over the last few months.

He flicked on further through the little book. There were many telephone numbers, some attached to names, others simply ringed to show their importance. He could not remember what they had all been for but knew that some of them were related to Natalie. One was a number she had asked him to write down because she didn't have any paper when out one night. There was also an address that meant nothing to him in green pen, in Natalie's familiar loopy handwriting.

Finally he had something tangible that could be shown to the police, some hard evidence that proved she existed and had been a very real part of his life.

His mobile phone began to ring, returning his mind to the here and now.

His first thought was that it was going to be Natalie, but a number – one he did not recognize – was flashing on the screen. He answered.

"Could I speak to Mr Stuart, please?" said a soft female voice.

To Nick the accent sounded strange, well educated, but the intonation was not Standard English or local dialect. She sounded foreign.

"That's me," he replied as he sank down on the couch.

"My name's Detective Bonita Beltran. I've been assigned to look into the disappearance of Natalie Hope. I was wondering if I could come and meet with you."

She sounded professional and courteous, nothing like how he had expected a police detective to speak. She sounded more like a doctor, someone who cared but was also paid to be in the position of giving bad news.

They fixed a time for later in the day. She was coming into Nottingham around four in the afternoon and asked him to get together anything that might shed light on the disappearance for when she arrived. To box them up, she said. He looked at the single small black book; it looked almost insignificant where he had placed it on the coffee table. He would only need a very small box.

Nick decided to give up any further search and instead wait for the police. He attempted to watch television in a bid to ease the boredom, but his eyes kept wandering back to the book. He picked it up and started to leaf through the pages again. He rarely looked at it normally; he'd got into the bad habit of writing things in it, purging his mind, and then never looking in it again. He still managed to miss everyone's birthday even with the dates captured inside. It was meant to serve a purpose and nothing more, but now it was his only link to Natalie and that made it priceless.

The police would want to take it away so that they could attempt to decipher the clues that it might hold to her disappearance, so he used the time wisely and made a note of any details that he thought might be worthwhile. He moved his way through the old memories that the book held, noting the places that acted as tantalising links to Natalie.

Nick's mobile rang again; he thought it would be the policewoman but it was his dad ringing to see if Natalie had turned up. He told him the police were on their way over to talk.

"Police? Is it wise including them just yet? As far as you know this Natalie might have simply left you. Perhaps she doesn't want to be found."

He didn't like the way his father had used the term 'this Natalie', as if she was no one of importance. It hurt especially as they had always liked each other so much. Plus it was the second time someone had proposed the idea that she didn't want to be found.

"The authorities need to know. If she wants to be left alone when found, then fine. I'll respect that wish. I just need to know she is OK."

"Do you want me to come over? I might be of help."

Nick declined, but was encouraged that his father seemed to be concerned about the loss, even though he had no memory of the woman.

The knock at the door made him jump. With no music on in the flat it was possible to hear the cranky old lift coming up the shaft before announcing its arrival with a discreet buzzing sound followed by the cage doors scraping open. Otherwise the sound of feet on the thin carpet and concrete steps echoing up the arterial staircase would announce the arrival of anyone not using the lift. For such a heavy-set building it was full of the sounds of shuffling people and faintly muffled voices announcing the presence of hidden occupants. The lives of people played out in echoes through the rumbling pipes, a flushing lavatory, a washing machine hitting a spin cycle, the cries of a woman reaching orgasm and that same woman crying late at night. Even when Nick was convinced the flats were empty the building belied their presence. They became audio spooks, poltergeists that shared in his life.

Detective Beltran must have used the unlit staircase. He opened the door. He was not sure what he had been expecting; he hadn't any preconceived ideas of what a detective for the British police should look like. The voice on the other end of the phone had sounded feminine yet at the same time strong and authoritative. It was reassuring, but he had not put a face to that voice. He realised the name might have given it away but he had not been intuitive enough to notice.

She smiled briefly as he opened the door, her mouth wide with teeth pearly white against ebony skin. She was tall, a little taller than Nick in her sensible heels. She had quite broad shoulders, though these were enhanced by the sharp dark grey suit she wore. Her hair was cut short and close to her head, which made her eyes appear large and diverting.

"Mr Stuart?"

She took a hesitant step forward. He could smell coconut oil and soap.

He stepped back from the door and let her enter.

"Thanks for coming," he said as she passed and moved down the hall without Nick having to show her the way.

Once in the living room she sat on the sofa before taking a large note pad out of her bag and unclipping a pen.

"Would you like a cup of tea or something?"

Nick didn't know if having the police in your house was the same as builders or plumbers who seemed to live off a diet of tea and biscuits and would refuse to work unless able to gorge on an endless supply.

"Sorry, I haven't got time."

She indicated toward the seat opposite her. Nick sat down in a lazy chair, good for reading the paper in but not so good for perching on the edge of. He slipped back into it so that the detective was looking down on him.

"PC Woodruff gave me the file and his notes from the interview. There's not a lot to be going on with." She paused and looked down at her book. "Not a lot at all."

Nick shuffled forward in the chair. He didn't feel comfortable.

"We haven't been together long. It was all a bit of a whirlwind."

"It says here you've been together about six months."

She had an accent; it had been eroded perhaps by having been in the UK for some time. He had thought at first – due to her colour – it was West Indian, but now realised it was a mixture of places and ended up sounding a sort of British-Australian. She must have spent time living elsewhere, as her sentences had the unnerving habit of rising at the end, as if everything was a question, which in her line of work was probably convenient.

Nick felt he had to stand. He felt like a schoolkid in the chair.

"I know it sounds a bit…"

He searched for the least damning of terms.

"A bit…unusual, but we never got around to doing all that family and couple stuff."

"You were still in the first flush of love, you might say."

He wouldn't have said that, but it seemed to fit, a linguistic lifeline thrown out to help.

"If you like. We just spent time together in the flat, being with each other. The rest of our time was quite separate."

"If it was all so sudden, what's stopped her from having a change of heart, moving on to the next lover boy?"

He had never heard anyone use the expression 'lover boy' before. It sounded derisive coming from her. He had a feeling he was being mocked.

"She might well have done, and if that's the case then fine. But to move out over the space of several hours and take everything with her while I slept just doesn't seem right. She's not like that."

Beltran nodded as if agreeing but contradicted it with her response.

"Not impulsive? Yet she moved in with you after only a few days. I'd say that was impulsive, wouldn't you?"

Nick was beginning to find her tone offensive. It sounded as if she thought he was a waste of her time, that she had more important work to be getting on with, as if Nick was merely an afterthought in her busy day. He had been neatly added into her schedule and she wanted to be done with him as soon as possible.

"She would have a left a note. Something to say it was over. She wouldn't have just left. Are you going to do anything or am I just wasting my time?"

He sounded determined for the first time. The last couple of days had knocked him for six but now the police were involved he craved some solution to the problem.

"As far as I see it, a person has gone missing. I've reported it and now I'd like someone to do something about it. You might be right, perhaps she has left me, perhaps she has just wandered off; I don't care. I'd prefer that to something bad having happened to her."

He thought for a second she'd tell him to shut up and stop acting like a whinging cretin. Making her dislike him this early into an investigation was probably not going to help matters, but he wanted to assert himself. Perhaps she thought the reason Natalie had left him was because he was a useless boyfriend, or that he'd cheated on her or because he hit her, or made her do stuff she wasn't partial to. To Nick, Beltran looked like the sort of woman who didn't like men too much.

"You're right, I'm sorry. It's been a bit of a bad day. My daughter's been acting up. I'm on the way to her school now for a meeting with the headmaster."

She stood up and creased down her trousers. She unbuttoned her jacket and removed it, laying it neatly onto the couch.

"Right, if you'll show me around the flat. I think the bedroom first."

He moved slowly around the place with Beltran in tow. She made encouraging noises about the place. She liked the layout and the modern décor. He thought at one point she was going to enquire as to whether she could buy it, but in the end he realised she was trying to work out how much he was worth, probably calculating whether Natalie was some kind of gold-digger, the sort of woman who had merely moved in to move out with access to a joint account and silverware hidden in her bag.

Beltran opened the odd drawer with his permission and looked inside. There was nothing there, or at least nothing that Nick had noted. She stared at the space before closing it again, as if the mere absence of her clothes and her life would help solve the case. She acted as if she had seen too many Sherlock Holmes films and he half expected her to bend, pick a hair from the floor and announce the answer to the mystery based on its placement. But instead she just looked, nodded and then closed the drawer.

As there was not much to see they ended up back in the living room. Beltran had made a few notes as they walked. He was not able to read what they said.

"Do you have a photo?" she asked, having sat back down.

"No, I never took any. I don't have a camera, apart from the one on my phone."

"It's going to be difficult without a photo. I could get an artist's impression made but they're not normally as good for triggering a response from the public. Did you find anything that would be of use to us?"

"There's this."

He reached down and picked the black book off the table. He held it out towards Beltran.

"Her diary? Yes, that will be good."

"It's not hers. It's mine. I use it for writing down anything of use."

She opened the book and flicked through it.

"Why would we need your notebook?"

"I just thought it might be useful. There are several numbers inside which she dictated to me. I don't know how, but perhaps they'll lead to something."

He grabbed the book back and indicated the correct pages to her.

"Look, here and here. That's her handwriting, not mine."

"And this is all you have?"

"There's nothing else. I've looked everywhere. The place, as you've seen, has been cleaned out. She took everything that was hers with her."

The suspicious look on her face deepened, causing Nick to continue.

"The flat's mine, all the bills are in my name. She never got any post, or if she did it's been thrown away. I've never seen her with a cheque book; she always paid for stuff in cash. Whatever personal papers she had must be with her."

Beltran put down her notes and sighed as if she were tired.

"It's a little bit strange, don't you think?"

Nick shrugged in a non-committal way but he knew it was strange and he felt cheated because of it.

"Natalie either went to great lengths to walk out on you knowing that you'd never be able to find her again, in which case she's probably been keeping things from you, or something else has happened."

"Like what?"

He asked the question but Nick wasn't sure he wanted to know the answer.

Beltran returned the shrug.

"It's early days."

Nick knew what she wanted to say and he blurted it out before she got up to leave.

"You're talking about the 'Missing Man', aren't you? Could she be one of his victims?"

Nick didn't like the term victim. To his ears it sounded as if she was already dead, a body dumped by the side of the road or rotting in a shallow grave.

"I doubt it; it's not his way – to abduct from an apartment. He's always snatched girls from busy streets in the city centre, girls who have normally drunk too much and don't even realise they're being abducted until it's too late. It would be a complete change of tack for him to sneak into someone's flat, abduct someone and then decide to clean the place out."

"But you said it was girls he abducted – that matches."

"I suppose."

She left it at that. A small agreement but nothing more, nothing concrete. Beltran departed after another half an hour of inconsequential questioning. She gave him a card and her number should he think of anything. She stressed the 'anything', as if the case depended on it.

Bonita stood in the corridor; the lack of light made it hard to see the shabby interior which smelt of mould and damp. Nick Stuart's flat had been pleasant enough, the decoration modern and clean, but the communal area of the block was a mess. It was old and decrepit and in desperate need of refurbishment. There was water damage creeping out of the brickwork and few of the common lights worked. The central stairwell felt tired, like an old lady near the end of her life, a place that wanted so desperately to die but was forced to cling on to a ragged resemblance of being, still sheltering the few offspring that relied so heavily upon her.

She moved in the darkness over to a light switch that could just be seen standing out against the yellowed wallpaper. She depressed the button and the light flickered on above her head. It was a large florescent bulb, the sort used in factories and schools, but perhaps due to its age, it gave off a meagre orange glow that dimmed and flexed as the power fluctuated. She could hear a distinct ticking sound as the switch counted down the seconds before it would plunge her back into the half-light.

There was a set of stairs running down at one end of the passage; the banister surrounding them looked old and unstable, the carpet running down into the gloom, thin and threadbare with the concrete obvious below. At the alternate end of the corridor was a lift. Bonita had tried to board it on arrival but had been alarmed at the water that dripped continuously from the overhead hatch. She had quickly decided to walk the few flights to the top.

This floor was the last in the building, a small landing that jutted out across the main area with only enough space for a couple of flats; the final two apartments before the roof. There were three doors, one to each flat and a fire escape, protected with a thick chain and padlock. A fire and safety issue she would have to report to the building's owner.

Bonita risked a peek over the banister and counted nine flights of stairs leading down to where a shaft of sunlight came in from the street. She quickly calculated that Natalie would have had to make several trips up and down to have got everything out. Assuming she was travelling light, that still would have taken some time. In the dark she would not have rushed for fear of crashing over the side and plummeting into the void.

As if in anticipation of the falling body, a shadow pierced the sun-flecked entrance and a bald head appeared, before vanishing. It was replaced by the sound of the lift mechanism which started to whirl and grunt. She could hear the turbine screech and the cable rasping as the cage descended. It made a ridiculous amount of noise, which late at night would drum around the empty building, probably waking several of the residents, perhaps even a drunk Nick Stuart. Bonita decided that if Natalie had left the building she had used the stairs.

The lift briefly stopped in the lobby allowing a passenger to board before it started an ascent. The lights turned themselves out with a fizz, forcing Bonita to return and switch them back on. There were a few strange marks on the carpet which had caught her eye. Small brown stains that were not at first discernible, but as her sight had grown used to the flickering light, she had been aware of six spots in the middle of the hallway that could be blood. She knew that they could also be a myriad of other liquids but they were worth noting.

Nick had been right to mention the 'Missing Man'; he had abducted three girls in the city over the summer months of which she had first-hand knowledge as her husband, also a detective, had been investigating. No bodies had been found, but in these sorts of cases they normally took a while to bob back to the surface of the river Trent.

She bent down to get a better look at the marks as the lift door opened and someone stepped out onto the landing. Hands grabbed her shoulder and spun her around as a bony finger pressed hard into her left breast.

"What the fuck yer doing snooping around outside my place, yer black bitch?"

She grabbed at the offending finger and pushed it backwards; forcing the arm away from her, bending it back towards the small man.

He swore heavily before attempting to snatch the hand back. She held on, well aware that if necessary she could break his scrawny little finger with ease.

"I'll call the fucking cops, yer bitch!"

He fell to his knees; the carrier bag he had been holding crashed to the floor, its contents spilling out.

"I am the police, you odious little man."

He looked up at her, an expression of fear and contempt mingling as she gave his finger another sharp jab backwards before letting it go. He would be of little problem to her, one swift kick would bring him down and she was more than prepared to defend herself if required. Past experience had taught her to fight back.

He cradled his hand to his chest, nursing it before he looked up again.

"You nearly broke my finger."

He said it as a statement rather than an objection to the pain.

"Then you shouldn't poke it where it's not wanted."

She got out her identification and flashed it at the male specimen who she had at first glance assumed to be a pensioner but now realised was much younger, only hidden below a serious skin complaint.

"Your neighbour, Mr Stuart, has reported his girlfriend missing. You wouldn't have seen her, would you?"

The man grabbed at his plastic bag and refilled it with the spilled goods that looked to Bonita like hardware supplies.

"Never seen the girl. I thought he lived alone or he was some kinda poof."

Bonita bent down and passed him a round of masking tape which he snatched at and returned to its place in his bag.

"You have an interesting way of expressing yourself, mister."

He stood up and hurried over to his front door; his hands shook as he took out his keys.

"How I express myself is no business of yours. I never seen no girl and I told him so as well. Now leave me alone, I've got nothing else to say."

He slipped inside his flat, the door slamming shut behind him.

"He's a bit odd, isn't he?"

The detective turned to face Nick Stuart standing in his open doorway, obviously alerted by the sound.

"Just a bit. Takes all sorts, I suppose. I assume you and him don't have a neighbourly relationship?"

"Not really."

She pointed down to the floor at the spots.

"Any idea what those marks are?"

He craned his neck and peered over.

"Don't know. Can't say I've ever noticed them before, but then I usually don't bother with the light. What do you think they are?"

Beltran stood and sighed. She'd be late to get her daughter now.

"Probably nothing. I'll let myself out."

She decided against the lift and made for the stairs, Nick Stuart's door closing as she reached the first landing. The altercation at least managed to clear up one issue. Any undue noise that Natalie made on the night of her disappearance would have been enough for someone to have heard the commotion, even from behind their locked doors.

Could they be spots of blood? Nick had returned to the corridor moments after Beltran had left. He now squatted over them, peering intently at the six round splashes. He touched the ground tentatively. They were dry and felt no different from any other area of the carpet. They appeared to be quite old, but how long they had been there was impossible to tell. He had told the truth, he had never noticed them before, but then the carpet was so old, so marked and scuffed, that he tried his best to avoid looking down.

He knew what Beltran was hinting at. They could be blood, Natalie's blood. But by the same rationale they could be splashes of blood from any of the tenants, or perhaps even contractors working in the building. They were small and inconsequential, the sort of marks that might be left from a small cut or nosebleed, certainly nothing to get too concerned about. They might not even turn out to be blood at all and could just as likely be spilt coffee that had aged to the colour of rust.

Nick stood. For a brief moment he felt a chill run through his body. The implication of the marks perhaps indicating some past violent incident? Or was it the sensation of being watched? He looked up at his neighbour's door. The spy hole in the door formed an iris that appeared briefly to blink back at him. He thought he heard a sound from behind it, the noise of someone stepping lightly, backing away from the door.

He turned and moved back into his flat. He wanted to make some phone calls. The numbers he had copied down from his notebook were weighing heavily on his mind. He needed to feel useful and wasn't sure that Beltran would place the necessary urgency on them. He wanted to do a bit of investigating himself. He now realised he had not known Natalie well enough; he had thought he understood what made her tick, what she was capable of, but that idea had been nullified. The fact that he knew so little about her unnerved him as much as the disappearance. The Natalie he knew was becoming less substantial, she was becoming a memory and he had nothing left to enforce the mental images he held of her. By not being the person he had assumed, she had become an enigma; she was more complex, had more facets than he had deemed it necessary to acknowledge.

She had purposefully not told him about whole episodes of her life, not deeply held secrets but the mundane aspects of her life; the sort of things that should come up in normal conversation. They were the aspects of her person that you would conceivably tell strangers at a bus stop if you happened to get into conversation, so equally, they were the things you told your boyfriend. She had been purposefully blinding him as to who she was.

He knew nothing of her life before she had met him, and that was wrong. It was a flaw in their relationship and he felt cheated knowing that the police would probably turn up more about who she was than he currently understood. He wanted to make sure that nothing untoward fish-tailed into view, nothing that would come back to haunt him. If there was some big secret in her life then he wanted to know what it was before the police returned to mock and laugh at him.

He had to begin slowly. He knew his own limitations; he was useless at retaining facts unless they were of significant importance to him and the only items that fell into that category were his encyclopaedic knowledge of Hollywood cinema and aspects of his acting. He tended to work on the principle of throwing information at his brain and seeing what stuck, assuming that if it did stick it was probably of some kind of importance. Munch was always saying that Nick was one of the cleverest people he had ever known, but then Munch believed anyone who watched BBC2 must have a doctorate and be a member of Mensa.

With no better evidence he started with the first of the phone numbers that had been written down in Natalie's handwriting. He picked up the phone and dialled quickly.

The number connected after a few rings, to be replaced with what sounded at first like the inside of a busy shop or office.

"Guy's Hair. How can I help?"

It was a hairdressing salon, a place Natalie must have visited regularly as her hair was nearly always perfect.

Nick had not prepared a speech and was at first a little unsure what to ask. The girl who answered probably spoke to hundreds of people a week – the chance of her remembering one individual would be remote at best.

"Hello?"

The girl sounded busy and impatient.

"Hi, I'm ringing on behalf of my girlfriend…"

"What's her name?"

The girl interrupted him before he could continue, but in the background he heard the familiar tap of nails on a keyboard.

"Natalie Hope."

There was more typing and then a small wait before the girl continued.

"Yeah, she used Jacob last time but he's left. Does she have a particular stylist in mind or should I just book her in for the most convenient time?"

"You have a record of her last appointment?"

"Yes, sir. Two months ago. To be honest she should be coming in more regularly than that. What time does she want?"

He hung up the phone before things got confusing.

Nick's heart beat faster. She did exist. There were records of her going about her life. Little snippets of information and data that recorded her in action. A Natalie Hope had been and had her hair cut at the salon two months ago, which meant he could not have imagined her. It was too much of a coincidence that there were two girls with the same name.

He rang the next number, excited at the possibilities. It was dead. The number must have been disconnected or written down wrongly in the first place.

There were only two numbers left. He tried the third, hoping the remainder were not dead ends as well.

"JJP Media. How can I help?"

It was a switchboard. The name also rang a bell with Nick. Was not JJP the company that Natalie had worked for? And if it was, would she still be employed by them? Just because she had run out on him didn't mean that she would have left her entire old life behind. She would still need money and for that she needed a job.

"Could I speak to Natalie Hope?"

"We don't have anyone by that name working here. What is it concerning and I'll put you in touch with the right person?"

He felt his hope for a reunion dashed.

"Have you never had anyone there by that name? She gave me this number."

"No, sorry, no one I know of anyway. Is it to do with one of our contracts or are you merely enquiring about services?"

Nick really didn't see the point of getting into a discussion about the company; it would not help and he was almost at the point of hanging up when a thought occurred to him.

"Do you have a Bex working for you?"

There was a slight intake of breath at the other end of the phone.

"I'm Becky Barker. Who is this?"

Her tone of voice was suspicious, as if the woman thought she was being set up for a crank call. Nick imagined she was already looking around the office for the potential candidate who would pull such a stunt.

"Are you the only Becky in the place?"

This could be the breakthrough he needed. The friend from work – but again it sounded as if she had never heard of Natalie.

"Yes…" She drew the answer out, weary now of what she was likely to be giving away.

"And you don't know a Natalie Hope. I'm her boyfriend. I'm trying to find her."

"I don't think I can help. I've never heard of anyone called that."

"She's Italian, curly dark hair. She's gone missing. If you know where she is and you're covering for her, that's fine. But, just let me know she's OK, that's all I care about."

"Look, I'm sorry but I think you have the wrong number. I don't know anyone by that name."

She sounded impatient now, his pleading starting to alarm her. He could tell she wanted to hang up.

"Are you sure? You can tell her I'm sorry we argued. It was stupid of me."

"OK, bye…"

The phone went dead.

She sat in the car outside the school. The engine was running, leaving the air conditioning to circulate inside the cabin. The leather was still warm; she could feel it sticking to her skin, moulding to her body through the thin fabric of her shirt. She checked the time; she was five minutes late. She figured she could take another five before she had to cross the threshold and enter the school, before she must resume the duty of motherhood and put her professional image on hold. Five minutes before she re-entered the world where she lost all control, all authority.

Her life seemed to be ruled by her daughter at the moment, a daughter who would not listen to reason and insisted on causing trouble. She had expected the relationship to get easier as the girl grew older, not become the game of tug-of-war it seemed to be currently. She felt as if she spent more time in school than her daughter did and having to explain to the headmaster why Abeni had not arrived that morning, standing in front of him as he eyeballed her over the desk was embarrassing. No, it was worse than that, it was degrading.

She picked up the file and notebook from the passenger seat and opened it to the page where she had taken down notes from Nick Stuart. She reread them, taking satisfaction in the fact that this was one area in which she had full control and respect. As a detective she had earned a high opinion fast, as a black female police officer from a country on the other side of the world who spoke with a funny accent – she'd had no choice. She had clawed her way up the ladder, but she knew she was good at what she did. It had taken some time, but she had eventually proved it to the force; she had spent a week in hospital but earned her detective badge. If only Abeni had the same high opinion of her that they did.

Bonita often thought of her past life, her time spent as the only black cop in the Wellington force and as one of its few female officers. It seemed like it belonged to another time. For three years she had attempted to make the most of her unique position but she was obviously not *pakeha* and she was never easily accepted by the Maori. She had always felt like somewhere in between, stuck in her own third position.

Her parents had decided to move out to New Zealand in the late sixties, leaving Nottingham behind while Bonita was still young enough not to have made any friends. They had been attracted to a country still youthful and devoid of the crowds that were making inner-city life laborious and uncomfortable. If she cast her mind back she could still remember the movement of the boat, the constant rocking; sometimes comforting while at others violent and angry. They had in the main been welcomed in the country but none of them had ever felt at home.

Bonita had never thought about becoming a police officer. After school she knew she did not want to carry on with learning, yet she wanted something other than working in a shop or a typing pool. She had been surprised when the police accepted her, having assumed she would end up working at the hospital as a nurse. It seemed her boss was enlightened and wanted to have an ethnically diverse force before the idea was even touted in the mainstream consciousness. As he had said at the time, she was 'the first nigger to apply, so the job was hers'.

After the death of her father, her mother had wanted to move back to the UK to be with the dwindling remains of her family. With no one left in the country and having never found a suitable man, Bonita decided to follow. She had a good reference from her boss and on reaching Nottingham found a force desperate for good honest hard-working coppers. The racism was more overt, the crime was more prominent and a good deal more violent but Bonita liked it; she at last felt at home. She thought it was ironic that she had found a home in the very place her parents had been so desperate to leave.

Within two years she met Miles Borrail, a detective from Scotland who had also made the city his home; they married and had Abeni two years later. It was almost a perfect life. She had kept her name for identification purposes. The force only needed one Detective Borrail, besides which Bonita Borrail sounded slightly odd, even worse than Bonita Beltran. Too much alliteration, too much of a culture clash; she wanted to hold on to what little identity she felt she had left.

There was a sullen knock on the car window which made her jump. Abeni looked in at her mother, her face stuck in her usual insolent pout. Bonita sighed and got out, eyeing her daughter with disappointment.

Miles kept saying that she needed better discipline, a harsher regime, and that she was mixing with the wrong crowd, but apart from keeping her inside indefinitely Bonita could think of nothing that would help. Working the shifts between them augmented the problem. While they were often on completely separate schedules there was always some period of time that resulted in both of them being out of the house. Then they had to rely on Bonita's Maman – her own mother – to look after her, and Abeni could run rings around her.

"What are you looking so sulky about?"

"Nothing!" Abeni spat the words out and lowered her eyes to the pavement.

Bonita closed the car door and locked it while making sure nothing was on show.

"And where were you this morning?"

Abeni sucked her teeth but said nothing in return.

"I asked you a question."

"I's was nowhere."

"It's 'I was nowhere', not I's. And you were somewhere, just not where you were meant to be. You'll be grounded for this. Maman will stay in and look after you."

The girl looked up, her face screwed up in scorn.

"That ain't fair. I's don't wanna spend no time with her. She spends all her time going on with those stupid stories of hers, even when I'm watching Neighbours."

"Well, you're going to be the perfect trapped audience for her. I'll get her to tell you some of the real long ones. Now shall we go up to see the headmaster before we both get a bad name for ourselves?"

Abeni blew a bubble of gum which splattered against her lips as a reply.

Monday 8th May 1989

He had, at first, been annoyed that the client had kept him waiting for the document. Due to their sluggish attitude it meant he had to work late and miss the six o'clock train he had been hoping to catch. He always got his work completed on time; it was expected of him, it was what the client paid for, but he was always hampered by having to rely on other people. If he could eliminate other people from the equation then his life would be so much easier, as he always liked to say, 'Hell is other people'. But Rebecca would always point out to him that as a solicitor his work was 'other people'; without them he would have very little else to do.

He was the James in Harrow, Peter and James, a practice just off Fleet Street. He did not mind being the third name, the last in the group. As he saw it, the name Harrow was easier for clients to remember and so Toby (his colleague, who the name belonged to) always got the first enquiries and the dissatisfied clients who rang to speak to the company. When they had started the practice they had toyed with the idea of calling themselves Harrow, James and Peter but they agreed that the name sounded like a children's entertainment trio (was there not a set of children's books called James and Peter? He seemed to remember Rebecca reading a book with that name to his young nephew). So they finally decided on the current name and that suited him fine. He didn't feel like third fiddle and knew that his colleagues never thought of him as such.

Now that he was out of the office he felt better. It was too stuffy in there on a day like this. Even with the windows open the building did not allow for a good circulation of air and when he did get a decent gust it always smelt of car fumes; it suffocated, as if all the oxygen had been removed. With a bit of luck he would be able to make it home in time to sit out in the garden before it got dark. He imagined himself relaxing in the wicker patio furniture they had recently purchased, with a cool gin and tonic in hand and the day's papers to read.

He left as soon as he had completed the paperwork and made

his way through the city, heading for Charing Cross. Sometimes if the weather was bad or he simply could not be bothered to walk he would get a taxi. Rebecca kept telling him he should stroll to work, as he needed the exercise (he liked his food, in fact he considered himself something of the *gourmet*; Rebecca told him he was a *gourmand*) but today the weather was nice and he decided to make use of the half an hour before his train left to take some air.

He passed people sitting outside cafés and bars, making the most of the unusually good weather. He could smell suntan lotion (or was it some exotic drink that was being mixed?) The streets resembled a scene from a Parisian postcard, flower baskets had been put up to beautify the area, though the marigolds had not been watered for some time and were looking a little tired of life.

He checked the time on his watch and increased his speed accordingly. He did not want to miss this train. He started to feel quite hot and could feel his shirt sticking to his lower back. He wanted to take his jacket off but worried that people would be able to see the large sweat rings that were probably visible under his armpits. He started to breathe hard. Rebecca was right, he needed to get fit. He wondered whether he should buy an exercise bike.

Entering the station, prickly heat stabbing at the back of his neck and with his knees feeling unsteady, he moved towards the platform where he could see the train already waiting. He hated being late and though there remained five minutes before the train pulled out, he worried that it would be gone before he made it on board.

Finally he reached a door and pulled at the handle. It opened and he stepped up and into the carriage. It was old rolling stock, the sort that still had small hard seats. The first carriage was full. A man eyed him over the top of his paper, as if warning him away from already claimed territory.

Lawrence moved down the train past the collection of middle

management types reading the large papers, and the shop workers whose noses were buried in magazines or tabloids. He made his way to the door at the end and pushed his way into the second carriage. That was busy too. He had not expected so many people on the later train; the sun must have brought them all out for drinks after work. He passed a group of youths, male and female, entwined in each other's arms. They took it in turns at heavy petting (he had heard someone use the term 'snogging' on the television), they wore shorts and had their legs thrust out on top of a vacant seat. He hoped to God that it was not the only unoccupied place on the train.

He pushed through to the third carriage as the train gave a jolt. He could hear the engine at the front start to rev and whine. He hoped he could find a seat before it pulled out of the station. He found trying to walk on a moving train particularly difficult. He had once fallen on a woman while travelling on one of the fast-moving trains and in his haste to get off her had inadvertently grabbed at her breast. Just the thought of the embarrassing incident made his face flush.

He reached the final carriage and spied a pair of vacant seats about halfway along. At last, he thought, somewhere to sit. He pushed himself forward and gratefully sat down. Secretly he wished he had taken a taxi; he would have got here a lot earlier and been able to ensure himself a place to sit and would not feel so hot and uncomfortable. He hoped he didn't smell. He breathed in close to his body, trying to smell any sweat. It seemed to be fine.

Lawrence sat back and closed his eyes. He listened to his own breathing. It sounded laboured and he thought he heard a funny rattle at the end as if a pea were stuck in his throat and vibrated as he sucked in and expelled air. Could you become asthmatic with age? He hoped not.

Stretching out, he felt the engine tug at the train and pull the carriages forward. He would be home soon, sitting in the garden.

Rebecca would get him a drink and he would tell her about his day. He wondered if she would come to the train station to meet him. On certain days, if time permitted she would wait for him and greet him as he stepped down to the platform. He always felt like a conquering hero when she did that, a returning solider from the war, whose one true love had waited all that time for her man, both of them counting the days until they would be united and the horrors left behind. Rebecca had something of that era about her. In fact he often thought about her wearing floral print dresses, her hair done up tightly on her head, which was strange because she normally wore jeans and a white blouse. They would walk back arm in arm from the station, back to their Edwardian brick house, the one that Rebecca had lovingly restored and turned from a mere house into a home, their home, a place where they would feel safe and protected. Rebecca would probably have made something nice for dinner; he hoped for a nice steak but knew it would more likely be a salad, unless she made a prawn cocktail with some of those little frozen prawns. He liked them, he liked the rose sauce the best; the mayonnaise and tomato paste made a thick sweet taste. He did not really care for the lettuce it came on nor the brown bread, but he ate them anyway or else Rebecca would give him a lecture about his diet.

Later they would watch television together, snuggle up on the expensive antique sofa they had bought from a shop in Brighton. The news – or a documentary – was his favourite, something informative or about animals. He liked natural history programmes best, he did not like being out in nature but liked to watch it up close from the comfort of his living room.

He wondered about whether to buy a dog or not. Rebecca was at home all day so she could walk it. He would quite like a small Jack Russell or similar, something small but loving that would perhaps join them on the bed at night even though he knew Rebecca would more than likely make it sleep downstairs in its own basket. He would have to buy a tartan blanket for the basket.

He heard himself snore, a deep fart of a noise just on the edge of consciousness. He opened his eyes. He did not want to fall asleep and miss his stop. He looked around at the rest of the carriage hoping that no one was laughing at his snoring. It was empty.

He checked his watch. There was still fifteen minutes before the due arrival time for Haywards Heath. He could not remember the train stopping since they had left the station. He must have dropped off briefly. He hoped he had not made too much noise in his sleep. He checked for his wallet to make sure no one had stolen it while he had been dozing.

It was strange that everyone sitting in his carriage had got off so early into the journey. Perhaps they had all been on their way to the same venue. For the first time he noticed that though the train was still moving and moving quite fast, he could no longer hear the engine. In truth he could not hear anything.

Rebecca checked the time of the large grandfather clock in the hall against her wristwatch. It was keeping good time. The watchmaker in the village was obviously better than she had given him credit for. She moved through into the living room. The room was clean and smelt of the summer flowers she had bought from the florist and supplemented with ones from the garden. She should have been working on the manuscript the publishers had sent through but it had been such a beautiful day she had never got around to sitting at her desk. Instead she had found that all those little jobs she had been meaning to do took up all the morning and most of the afternoon. Mind you, the place now looked lovely, the surfaces practically sparkled. She had spent the rest of the day preparing a dinner for that evening. She had cooked some chicken, let it cool and made a nice salad, plus she had put a bottle of wine in the fridge. She had also bought a Black Forest Gateau but would wait until Lawrence had eaten before bringing it to the table. She could almost imagine his face when he saw it. It was a bit naughty but at her insistence he had been trying really hard recently to lose some of that extra weight, so it would be a nice surprise.

She checked the time again. If she left now she should just be able to make it to the station on time. It was a shame he had to work late, but the meal would make up for it.

She closed the French windows that led out onto the patio and locked them carefully just in case. She thought about taking a jacket but decided it was too warm.

Walking down the street she watched the neighbourhood with a critical eye. They had found the house five years ago and she had lavished all her care and attention on the property and on the area. She was a member of several community groups that had been set up to ensure the area maintained its beauty and charm. She was rigorous in her appraisal of her neighbours' property and would pull anyone up if they allowed their property to fall into disrepair. It was the same editorial scrutiny she would use to ensure the council did not fall behind in their duties as well. However, today the neighbourhood looked almost perfect.

She reached the station just as the train was pulling in. Hands snaked out of open windows and pulled at the handles. The doors swung open one by one and people alighted onto the platform. They appeared tired and started to shuffle towards her. She looked between the breaks in the crowd for the familiar sight of Lawrence moving towards her. She could not see him, so she stretched onto her tiptoes. The crowd milled about her; a young lad jostled her back to a standing position. He muttered a brief apology before he too was swept away.

They started to thin out. She could hear the doors of the train being slammed shut, the sound echoing off the Victorian concourse. The engine revved its motor and sent up a plume of dark smoke before it started to move. Still there was no sight of Lawrence. She moved away from the platform's edge so that she could see across the thinning crowd. The remaining people moved slower, they were the elderly who took their time in getting down from the train or the young, who didn't have any particular place to go and all the time in the world to get there.

Lawrence was not among them. He was not on the train. She felt cheated. She had been so looking forward to seeing him. She sometimes got a feeling like a young excited child when she saw him, even though they had been married for fifteen years, but today he was missing.

He must have got stuck at work, but it was strange he had not telephoned to say he would not make the next train as well, as he normally always called ahead.

She left the platform and headed home as quickly as she could. Reaching the house she opened the door and went straight for the phone. She knew the number without looking it up as she often phoned Lawrence while he was at work, to check on him and see how the day was progressing.

The line clicked and went straight to the answerphone. A chirrupy female voice apologised that they were closed but gave the opening hours for the following week. There was something a little odd about the message and she had to listen to it twice before she realised what it was.

"This is Harrow and Peter Solicitors. I'm afraid no one is available to take your call at this time. Our opening hours are Monday to Friday, 8.30am to 5.00pm. Please leave a message after the beep and we will return your call at the earliest opportunity."

Rebecca let the beep sound but did not know what to say. She replaced the handset. She moved into living room and sat down on the couch.

Twice she had heard them quite distinctly state the name of the company. Lawrence's name was missing. How strange. Perhaps the voice recording was not working correctly and was skipping his name like a record that has a small scratch.

She was sure he would be on the next train which was due in

forty-five minutes. Perhaps she had simply misheard him and he had always intended to get the later train, or he had said the wrong time. He often said the wrong thing when his mind was on his work.

For the first time she looked up at her surroundings. It was the living room she had left only twenty minutes ago to walk to the station but now it was somehow different. Less perfect, more lived in. She noticed the rug was in need of a good clean though she was sure she had vacuumed it that morning.

The wedding picture on the mantelpiece was missing. She stood and moved over. In its place was a picture of herself in front of the Taj Mahal. She could not remember ever going to the Taj Mahal. Where was the wedding picture? The two of them side by side, her in the beautiful white satin dress that had been specially made and Lawrence in his bottle blue suit. They had been sitting under white honeysuckle. It was one of her most prized possessions.

In fact where were all the pictures of Lawrence? Someone had been in the house while she was out and rather than robbing the place they had simply removed all the pictures of Lawrence and her and replaced them. The picture of them in the Lake District had been swapped for a drawing by Michelangelo; the picture of Lawrence holding up the Leaning Tower of Pisa was now a picture of Rebecca looking out over Rome. The whole room had been changed.

She backed out of the living room and into the hall. The pictures that ran along the side of the stairs were also different. She followed them up. In the bedroom she noticed that the brass alarm clock that Lawrence set for 6.30 every morning was gone. His whole bedside area was empty and the new book she had bought him only last week was no longer there.

She went over to the wardrobe and opened the doors. Her clothes were all lined up, largest items to the left, smallest to the right. All the clothes hangers faced the same way. The whole wardrobe was used up, but Lawrence's clothes were gone. There were none left.

She stepped back and sat on the bed. He was gone, removed from existence. This was not what she had wanted. She had been joking. He had understood it was just a whimsical throwaway line. She had never wanted it, not really. This was a joke surely.

The phone rang. She jumped at the shrill sound it made. She moved downstairs quickly. It must be Lawrence ringing to say where he was. She grabbed at the receiver.

"Hello, is that you, Lawrence?" she garbled down the phone.

"No it's me, Claire." A friend from the local council. "Who's Lawrence?"

Four

He felt a bit ridiculous. Dressed in his dark clothes he was concerned that people were watching him, mistrustful of the man who tried unsuccessfully to blend with the thin shadows cast by the door pillars. He had been standing in the same spot for half an hour, watching the office across the street with intent. Nothing had happened. Few people visited and even fewer departed, but it was now almost lunchtime and that, he hoped, would make all the difference.

It had only taken a quick check on the internet to find out where the offices of JJP Media were. He had left home just before lunch and staked out the building, walking past its entrance a number of times to ensure he had the correct office. There was an intercom on the door where visitors had to announce their presence. He knew any attempt to get hold of Becky by that means would result in failure, so instead he had decided to wait, his sunglasses covering his eyes and, he hoped, blurring his features enough so that he could not be recognized, as he played the part of home-made spy.

A young woman had come out after only five minutes into his wait. He had no idea if it was Becky so he had waited until she got near the corner of the street before he called out her name.

"Hey, Becky."

She had ignored him. It was not much of a test but it was better than nothing.

As chimes rang out from council offices announcing noon, the doors to the office opened and a woman came out arm in arm with a young man. They moved down the stairs talking animatedly before turning away from Nick and moving down the street. He was not sure how many people worked in the office so dared not risk going after them only to find out he had been mistaken. Instead he would have to try out his vocal test again.

"Becky," he shouted down the street before stepping back into the shadows.

This time the girl stopped and turned. Both she and the man stared long and hard back up the street, back towards the door they had just exited before both laughed, turned and continued their lunchtime stroll.

Nick stepped out into the sun and started to follow them. They were heading for the large shopping centre. As they neared, the crowds start to swell, forcing Nick to get closer or risk losing her in the growing swarm of plastic bags, stretch T-shirts and baseball caps. Once through the glass doors, the space opened up, displaying a selection of shops on each side and a water clock in garish shades of turquoise and gold that was ignored by the kids and adults and used instead as a makeshift seat or a convenient meeting point.

He thought at first of attempting to walk straight up to the woman, explaining his situation and asking her outright what she knew about Natalie. However, with the man in tow it was going to be a little more difficult. The last thing he wanted to do was antagonise someone and cause a scene. He wanted Becky to be cooperative and he was unsure whether a direct approach could be justified.

They had unlinked arms but still walked shoulder to shoulder, pointing out objects of interest in the shop windows. It seemed to be a small excursion from work, a lunchtime distraction, making it clear to Nick that he had about fifty minutes in which to make his move or leave it until the end of the day and follow her home, an idea that unnerved him.

The couple disappeared into a women's clothes shop. Nick followed. He was now unsure what to do. It was a big store and at first he affected an interest in the racked-up dresses, but then thought this would look somewhat amiss and stood for a moment with his back against a glass mirror. Eventually he tried to look like a man searching for his partner, while at the same time keeping his eye on the pair of shoppers.

They at last split up. Becky moved over to a rack, chose an item she liked and held the white top against her. She twisted backwards and forwards as she examined herself in a mirror. Her friend was rummaging through a sale bin of oversized belts with gusto, his arms half submerged in the fake snakeskin.

This was his chance.

He stepped forward and tapped her on the shoulder.

"Becky?"

She turned to face him and smiled, expecting a familiar face. Her look faltered on seeing Nick.

"Yes?"

"We spoke on the phone. I'm looking for Natalie."

She didn't respond straightaway, as if what he was saying was hard for her to understand. They stood, both staring at one another for a moment. The knowledge of unfamiliarity caused an embarrassing silence that desperately needed to be filled.

"I don't know anyone by that name. I told you that on the phone."

He thought she would shout and scream, perhaps call over her friend to get rid of him, but instead she was calm. Her voice remained quiet and she looked him straight in the eye. She was being brave, he could tell; but the fact she had not flinched reassured him and he pressed her further.

"You used to work with her; you were friends. You'd go drinking with her."

"Used to work with her?" She paused, as if thinking back on some distant memory that had been lost, a half remembered story of a past event.

"She was at work on Friday; three days ago. You can't have forgotten her."

"I didn't know we were on the pull?"

Her colleague had sauntered over, two belts clasped in one chubby paw. He held the other one out to Nick flaccidly, as he looked him up and down. He obviously liked what he saw and smiled almost coquettishly.

"I'm Johnny, pleased to meet you."

Nick grabbed at the hand and shook it quickly before looking back at Becky. She was biting her bottom lip as if in deep concentration but she looked more confused than ever. Something was niggling at her, a thread of memory that, if pulled on, threatened to disentangle her whole mind; an event so crucial it would upset her very belief in existence.

"You do know her, don't you? I can see it in your eyes."

"Know who?" replied Johnny who was starting to get on Nick's nerves with his sudden appearance.

"I don't know…that name…after you rang I thought about it and it's like I did know someone, but for the life of me I can't remember who. It's like they've been knocked out of my head, like when you have an accident."

"Can you remember what she looked like?"

"Will someone tell me who we're talking about?" moaned Johnny, causing Nick to hold up his hand to silence him.

"Johnny, give me some time, will you? I'll meet you outside," added Becky.

The man raised his eyes and gave a comical sigh before grumbling something under his breath and wiggling out of the shop.

"I keep trying to think of her, but all I get is a headache. I know the name means something but I don't know what."

Nick nodded in sympathy. Natalie had been erased, but residual amounts of her seemed still to exist with those who had cared for and knew her the best. A shadow that hid in the back of the mind that was tricked into view with the mention of a name or the smell of perfume, a buried memory waiting to rise, if only assistance was forthcoming.

He worried that as time slipped by without Natalie's return he would end up losing more and more of her, that she would become a faint whisper until he became like everyone else and she would no longer exist for him at all, all memory and belief that she had ever been flesh and blood forgotten and abandoned.

"I don't think I can help you."

Nick understood. She had tried her best but there was nothing to return. In a few days she probably wouldn't even remember the name of Natalie Hope; her face would not cause an echo, her smell trigger no recollection of time past.

He gave Becky his phone number just in case, scribbling it on a piece of paper, but he knew she wouldn't call. She wouldn't look at the phone number again until she came to wash her clothes and it slipped out of the pocket. A piece of debris that would be screwed up and thrown in the bin, all memory of what it symbolised long forgotten.

There were police on the landing when he got back home. Two guys in white overalls were photographing the dark marks on the carpet, a heavy arc light above them buzzing and revealing the area in all its extreme ugliness. They both flashed badges as he made it to the top of stairs, but only one finished a phone call with 'he's back'. They watched him intently as he placed his key in the door and opened it for them to enter. They didn't speak, and at first he expected them to simply step over the threshold as if it were their given right to enter his property. Instead, they turned away and started to talk in quiet voices while examining the floor. Nick noticed for the first time an unmistakable whiff of bleach, an alien smell in such dingy surroundings. It was faint but evident, lingering in the background with the smell of dust and ingrained dirt. Perhaps the landlord had at last made an abortive effort to clean the building or else it was entrenched into the unblemished white suits the officers wore. They looked more akin to scientists than the police, biologists on the hunt for some strange new microbe or disease. They would probably find several within the carpet weave of the hallway.

Having been ignored, Nick left them to it but a knock on his door came moments later. Beltran towered over a small man with little hair and round glasses who smiled nervously. Nick opened the door wide to let them in, noticing at the same time that the two overall-wearing officers seemed to be picking at the carpet with tweezers.

"Don't lock the door, Mr Stuart," commented Beltran as she moved down the hall. "They'll need to come in here after they finish."

In the living room the small man perched on the edge of the sofa. He accepted a cup of tea, which he proceeded to drink in small almost bird-like sips. The man turned out to be an artist. While Nick and Beltran spoke he would interject with questions of his own about how Natalie looked, before returning to his sketchbook where he scratched away at the surface humming to himself and frowning.

"So you have a hair appointment that she went to three months ago and her friend who has worked with her every day for longer than you've known her but now can't remember what she looks like."

Nick agreed. "I know; something strange is going on. It's more than the fact she's gone missing now; something else has happened. My dad's met her plenty of times and Munch knows what she is like, but both seem to have forgotten her. It's like their minds have been zapped and all the memories removed. She's being removed from history, which explains why all her things have gone as well."

"Really," Beltran's voice was full of scorn. "So why is it that you can remember her and no one else can?"

"I don't know. I know her the best, I love her. Perhaps it takes longer for it to work."

Beltran stood up and shook her head in disbelief. "What's *it*, Nick?"

"You know, the…the magic." He hated himself for saying it the moment it left his mouth. It was stupid and puerile. There was no magic in the world and anyone who thought so was deluding themselves. It was the sort of comment a child would make and the look on Beltran's face made him feel infantile.

"You never mentioned this in your initial interview, Mr Stuart. I think you'll find it pretty difficult for anyone to track her down if, as you say, she has been removed from history."

To Nick it sounded as if she was almost laughing. It certainly appeared that she did not want to take the case much further.

"But she did exist. My memory and the hair appointment prove that."

"The hair appointment could be for anyone called Natalie Hope – the name is common enough. And as for you, have you ever thought of seeing a professional?"

"I don't think you're taking this very seriously. A woman's life could be at risk."

"Really? What makes you say that? You say she's missing, but there appears to be no reason to suspect she's in danger. Is there?"

Beltran's implication was obvious.

"Unless of course that turns out to be her blood on the carpet outside your front door. Then, perhaps, we have a case."

Nick let the taunt hit home and went silent. His face burned hot from embarrassment and anger.

"I've finished."

The fat bird artist removed his glasses and placed them into the top pocket of his jacket before turning his study around for them all to see.

"Well, Mr Stuart? Any good?"

Nick crossed the room and picked up the picture. He traced the pencil drawing with his finger. Her chin was perhaps a little too pronounced and he had styled her as if stepping out of a 1950s advertisement, but it was a pretty good likeness. A very good likeness.

"It's good," was all that he could say as tears welled and his throat went dry.

His Natalie existed again, if only on paper. He had a picture of her at last that was sharper than the dying mental image he was holding on to with such passion.

The artist nodded and held out his hand to receive the picture back.

"Could you make me a copy?" Nick asked, his eyes staying on the image as he passed it over.

The small man looked over at Beltran who nodded.

"I'll make a copy this afternoon and send it over to you."

"Thank you."

There was a knock at the door and the two forensic officers stepped in. Their white paper overalls crackled and snapped as they moved about.

"We've finished outside and we'd like to begin in here now, ma'am."

Beltran made introductions and explained that it was a routine search; they were looking for anything that could help. The smallest piece of evidence that could fall behind drawers, hide in the cracks between floorboards, skin mixed in with the hidden dust. The secreted evidence of a life lived.

The officers carried between them a metal container about the size of a large briefcase. One of them pulled in a large vacuum cleaner wrapped in plastic. It looked as if they were prepared to fight some viral outbreak that had somehow got loose in the flats.

"Natalie was pretty paranoid when it came to cleaning. I doubt you'll find much." Nick spoke to Beltran by way of conversation but she simply shrugged.

While the police made themselves busy around the flat, Nick made coffee for them all; he even put some biscuits on a plate. It was as if he were having family over for tea rather than the possible start of a murder investigation. It was the sort of thing his mother would have done when she was alive: calmly made tea and provided food while the entire world went to hell.

Beltran watched the team as they lifted up cushions and vacuumed at the back of cupboards. The aftershave bottles and deodorant sprays were dusted for fingerprints and the kitchen bin emptied into black sacks. The skirting boards were dusted and the windows sprayed with moisture to reveal finger and hand prints; photos were taken of the flat from every conceivable angle and the bed doused in ultraviolet light that returned too many bodily fluid stains for Nick's liking.

Beltran came over as Nick poured out a mug of coffee for her and handed it over.

"We'll need your fingerprints to eliminate you from the scene."

He looked down at his hand and folded them closed into neat fists.

"OK. It feels kind of strange. I imagine the neighbours think I've killed her, what with you lot here."

Beltran gave Nick a hard stare but said nothing. He realised it was a stupid thing to say and coloured up again as the full implications hit home.

"It's just routine. We have so little to go on and it seems to be getting less and less with each passing hour."

"As long as you're looking, that's the main thing."

To Nick, Beltran's constantly calm voice was becoming tiresome. It still sounded to him as if she were not really bothered about Natalie, that her disappearance was not strange or unusual and that it was him who needed to be protected, from himself if anyone.

The artist excused himself and left the flat as one of the forensic officers moved over and interrupted.

"Can we have a word, ma'am?"

Beltran moved to leave with the officer. "We're doing our best, Nick," she added just as she moved away

They walked down to the end of the room and started to speak in low voices. Nick noticed the officer had a large white disc in his hand. He presented it to Beltran, using it to back up what he was explaining. Beltran looked concerned and took hold of the white circle. She held it up to the light; her eyes narrowed as she scanned its surface.

She looked over at Nick, made some mental calculation and excused the officer.

"Have you found something?" he asked.

"No. Quite the reverse."

She placed the disc on the table.

"This is a filter from the industrial vacuum. We use it to capture small particles in the air. It sucks them in and once captured they are displayed here for analysis."

Nick nodded that he understood.

"Normally in a flat of this size it would be clogged with hair and skin. What colour hair has Natalie got?"

She addressed Nick but she remained looking at the empty filter.

"Dark, almost black. She always wore it long. You know this. I told you."

"I just wanted to hear you say it again. What do you see on the filter?"

He looked at the circle that was covered in a selection of body debris and dust particles, some of which were stuck in the thin weave.

"Hair, black bits and nail clippings."

She sighed. "Any long black hairs?"

He looked again but had to shake his head. There was nothing like Natalie's hair, only his own short and thin strands.

"That's the problem. We always leave a trace of ourselves. We found plenty of your hair but none of Natalie's. Not one filament."

"What does that mean?"

"It either means Natalie cleans impossibly well or..." She let the thought hang in the air. "Have you had anyone in to clean this place? Professionals? Since she went missing?"

"No. What are you trying to say?"

"I think you need to speak with a doctor."

Nick examined Beltran's set jaw; her teeth clamped shut, her eyes for the first time unable to look him in the face. She looked down, away from Nick, it were as if she were ashamed of making eye contact.

"I feel fine."

She looked up at this statement.

"Mr Stuart...Nick, I don't think Natalie has been here for a long time. I think you're just having problems dealing with these facts – and that's where a doctor comes in. We've swept this place clean and there is no trace of her. Her things aren't here, her friends don't know her, and you can't supply us with a picture. I think this was just your way of making a cry for help."

The words stung. They hurt more than if Natalie's mangled body had been laid at his feet. A corpse the police could deal with, that was tangible. But Natalie was too complex an issue. They didn't know where or how to begin.

"So she's a complete figment of my imagination. Why...why would I do that? It doesn't make sense."

"I'm not saying she doesn't exist, just that she left you a long time ago."

"That's fucking ridiculous. She was here Friday night and last week and the week before that. She lives here."

Nick took a step towards Beltran. He wasn't sure what he planned to do but he wanted to grab and shake this woman who doubted him until she realised he was telling the truth.

Beltran pushed hard. She was strong. Her knuckles bruised his flesh.

"Christ, Nick. Don't be an idiot."

The command made him sit like an obedient dog.

Beltran looked over at the other officers who were advancing on Nick. She was in control. No need for the handcuffs. They stopped and moved away while keeping an eye on the discussion.

"I understand what you're going through, but I don't think this is really a police matter. I'm sorry."

They were giving up.

"You can't do this. I need your help."

She shrugged the accusation off.

"Speak to a doctor."

Nick watched as they began to pack away their equipment, too dumbfounded to say anything in return. He had come so far. After so many false starts he had finally managed to prove to the doubters that she was real, only for it all to crumble to dust before his very eyes.

The phone started to ring. He still jumped every time its high-pitched drill split the quiet of the apartment. He still always hoped it was Natalie and that this had all been a huge mistake. He picked up the receiver and listened, afraid to say anything that would scare her away.

"Nick?"

It was a man's voice, one that rarely rang him while sounding quite so cheerful. It was his agent, a failed actor with ideas above his station who had moved sideways in the industry in the hope of staying fed. He was not the sort of person that Nick wanted to speak to right now.

The agent launched into his patter, his voice shrill and loud, echoing around the inside of Nick's skull causing him to wince. At first he was unable to take in what the man was saying, wanting nothing more than to put the phone down and bring the intrusion to a swift conclusion. He had no time for this, for the first time ever here was an event that made all others pale into insignificance.

Finally the sheer exuberance his agent radiated forced him to listen.

"Good news, Nick. The actor they had cast to play Jason in the 'Crime Season' pilot has only gone and fallen off his horse. The director went back and checked the audition tapes and out of the blue he wants to know if you would be interested in the lead."

And then Nick remembered. It all came flooding back, with crystal, ice-cold clarity. He had been sitting in a dingy bar talking to a man with fire in his eyes and dark trouble in his soul. The lights in the room started to arc and flex as if he were back in the disco. Bodies distorted and lengthened as if pulled, reality slipping through the floor. The phone fell from his fingers and crashed to the floor, accompanied by the concerned cry of the caller.

He sat awkwardly as a wave of emotion thrust up from his stomach. He felt sick, physically ill. His knees felt weak and the room cold, even though his face felt flushed and hot. He had to fight for air, but a pain built and seized hold of his chest. It hurt deep inside. He could feel air going inside but it didn't seem to do any good. It was as if the world had been filled with a gas he could not breathe, or else he was stuck deep underwater.

Beltran's face appeared from nowhere. It loomed up in front of him. Her voice sounded concerned but indistinct.

"Nick? Are you all right?"

He collapsed forward onto all fours, shaking like an animal, shaking so violently he started to choke. He could see a pair of sensible dark shoes in front of his face, but they moved out of shot and were replaced with flashing lights that danced and sparkled like fireworks going off in the night sky. And then he was sinking through sand. He was back in the dream as his face disappeared into the darkness, his nose and mouth full of the shifting white granules that stopped the air. He fought against them, but each movement dragged him further and further down, into the darkness, into nothing.

Nick woke up in an ambulance. A mask had been stuck to his face. It smelt of sick. His stomach felt as if a hot rock had been placed inside it while his throat burned with a prickling heat. Acrid saliva pooled on his tongue, forcing him to spit or risk gagging on the mess. His weak hands fumbled with the mask, which felt as if it were welded to his face with sweat. A hand reached down and slapped his feeble fingers away. The oxygen was pumped into him; it was cold frigid air that stung with its purity. At last the mask was prised away, the oxygen replaced with the muggy warmth inside the ambulance, as hands, insistent in their intent, moved his head to the right. They were clever fingers; they knew he had to be sick again.

The puke was clear but smelt like the inside of a rotting carcass. Strings of snot and mucus ran out of his nostrils as well as his mouth. Something damp was pressed to his face. Nick thought of his dad and how when he was young he would clean his face by licking his handkerchief and rubbing at the offending mark. It was rough but effective. The stranger's hands felt like that.

The mask was replaced and Nick moved his own head back. He stared up at the ceiling. He felt cocooned, safe, lying on his back in silence. No, there was noise, but it was far away. Muffled behind cotton wool walls, and he was swaying from side to side, a cradle rocking. It felt good.

It now seemed conclusive. She had reviewed all the data that had come in from the different government agencies that dealt with border crossings and not one of them could prove that a Natalie Hope had ever entered the UK within the last ten years. True, their data capture techniques were very rarely accurate, and information had a habit of getting misplaced, but the only people they had matching that name with a similar birthday were either of the wrong nationality or the wrong age. The net had been spread wide and nothing had snagged.

There was also no match on the name Natalie Hope working for

JJP Marketing earning money and paying taxes in the Nottingham city area. Natalie did not exist. She was a figment of the imagination, a ghost, a fantasy woman. And yet…and yet Bonita felt that there was a case to be investigated. She couldn't accept the truth as Nick saw it; that way madness lay. A crime might not have been committed, but there was something, some nugget that kept pulling her back to re-examine the details.

It reminded her of the past, a dim echo from all that business with the Wheen girl. Her first and only mistake since taking over as Detective in Charge; the first cross against her name. She had made up for it since, but it still felt sore, a rough wound that had never fully healed.

Nick Stewart was taking it badly. He really believed in this ghost woman, which again had resonance with the Wheen case, though she could not see how the cases could be related. It was just too unlikely. Besides, the victims – if they ever existed – were completely unalike.

Nick was still out cold. She had looked through his wallet with its couple of bank cards and old receipts nestled inside. Nothing incriminating, but again nothing to point to the existence of a loved one gone missing. She looked at his phone. Once she had skimmed past his friend Munch and the name of his agent, most of the numbers seemed to relate to fast food joints. For someone of his age he was a bit of a loner. She rang the only other number listed.

Nick must have drifted back to sleep for when he awoke he was somewhere new. There was noise. A horrid cacophony of television sets turned down low while people muttered over the top. Electronic machines beeped and burped while trolley wheels yelped on rubber floors. A whole world of activity was taking place but it was hidden from him behind a lurid curtain made up of bands of yellow suns and deformed turquoise birds.

Sunlight was entering the window, splashing a rectangle of

yellow heat across the bed. His right arm, outside of the bed covers, felt hot where the light was encountered. A drip had been pushed in deep under the skin causing it to discolour and throb. He liked the pain; it made him realise he was still alive.

Someone was sitting at the end of the bed looking at him from over a clipboard. His first thought was that it was Natalie, the image too blurred to make out. But then he remembered and the image shifted and coalesced. The figure came closer and peered down. He felt small. The face was familiar. Short cropped hair and bad coffee breath. The man grinned, displaying a set of almost perfect but yellow teeth.

"Yes, I thought I recognised you. Feeling better?"

The curtain behind him twitched and parted as Dr Mati stepped to his side to make way for the next act. Detective Beltran stepped inside the bright shielded world while handing over one of the two Styrofoam cups she was carrying. She acknowledged that Nick was awake but addressed herself to the man in the white coat who Nick had finally realised was the doctor who had rung him about the girl that was not Natalie.

"How is he?"

She almost sounded concerned.

Doctor Mati struck the back of his biro harshly and wrote something on a pad of paper before answering.

"Delayed shock. The body stores everything up and just tries to act as if it's business as usual. Only later does the victim pay the price. Not so common in women for some reason. I've met him before."

They knew Nick was awake, but they spoke about him as if he were still unconscious. He was their specimen. A tadpole in a jar to be watched by excited children until bored when they would flush him down the toilet or leave to float belly up and dead.

"He came in a few nights ago. We thought we had his girlfriend in the hospital but it was a case of mistaken identity. The girl, she died. We've still got the body."

Beltran moved forward and bent down to Nick's eye level.

"How are you feeling?"

Nick wanted to say that he felt like shit, that he felt hollowed out, an empty vessel. He didn't want to cry in front of a policewoman, but large wet tears pricked at his eyes and slid fully acknowledged down his cheeks. He felt wretched, as if darkness, anguish, hate and all the pain of the world had been poured into him all at once. He didn't want to speak; he didn't want anything other than to be left alone to nurse this horror. He had felt like this before, after his mother died, but he had always had the solitude of home to hide out in. Now he was on public display and he resented the audience.

"I've called your father. He's on his way. He sounds nice."

Doctor Mati started to back out of the curtain. It wrapped around his body and shrouded him, giving him large colourful wings. He briefly resembled a camp vampire.

"I've got my other patients to see. I'll leave you two together."

Beltran called over her shoulder as the doctor vanished beyond the curtain and into the ward.

"I'll talk with you before I leave."

She looked back down at Nick and sniffed.

"Quite a scare you gave me. I wouldn't have thought you the type for fainting."

Nick noticed for the first time that she had a scar above her left eye that must run onto her eyelid. She put a hand up to rub at it as he stared, uncomfortable underneath his scrutiny. Her hand was also marked. She looked at the back of her hand and then back at Nick.

"Hit and run. Someone I was investigating caught me with my guard down. I was left in a ditch for two days until someone found me."

Nick's voice croaked. It sounded scratched.

"Where?"

"Just outside the city, along the side of a busy dual carriageway.

People kept passing for so long and yet no one saw me. It was like I was invisible. I almost died."

"Did they catch the driver?"

"No. Never." Her voice sounded bitter.

She reached down to the floor and picked up her bag, retrieving a red notebook. "I want to speak to your neighbours and your dad when he gets here."

He interrupted, the memories of the last few days resurfacing like a lurid dream half glimpsed. "I remembered something."

Nick needed something to drink. His mouth was dry, his lips sticking to his gums. He made a move for the jug of water by the bed but was stopped by Beltran. She pushed him gently back and took over. Pouring the water into a small paper cup, she helped him to sit up before passing him the drink. The water was hospital warm in Nick's mouth and tasted of antiseptic.

"Whatever it is, it can wait."

Nick could hear his dad's voice somewhere in the ward. He was being loud, concern for his son overriding his normally gentle demeanour. Beltran noticed the recognition on Nick's face and pulled the curtain to one side, revealing them both to the world.

His father rushed over. He was wearing a pyjama shirt that had been hastily tucked into a pair of green cords. He looked old, like a man shuffling around a retirement home. It made Nick feel even more alone, even more scared.

"Jesus, are you all right?"

Charles hardly ever swore but he was a constant blasphemer. He had no belief in any god that would put his wife through as much suffering as she had encountered before death. Religion – that to him was swearing; religion and gods were hate and death.

Beltran intercepted him by blocking access to the bed.

"He's fine, Mr Stuart. Could I have a word with you?"

Charles looked up at the attractive black woman who stood in front of his son's sickbed, her face twisted to face him. Nick watched his dad calculating who she could possibly be – doctor, friend, work colleague, possible replacement girlfriend.

"Police business," she added to help him out.

"Of course." His face was set into a mask of concern as he glanced over at Nick's recumbent form.

"You don't mind, do you?" he asked of his son, the knowledge that a police request was something you obeyed but desperate to reach out and help his own child evident in his eyes.

Nick waved them away.

Beltran led Charles down to the end of the ward. Nick watched them standing next to each other discussing his frail form. Beltran was lithe and somewhat taller than his dad, who seemed even smaller than usual. Squat almost. It seemed the older his father got, the smaller he became, as if he were shrinking in on himself. He didn't seem to stoop; rather he was collapsing inwards, disappearing into his own body.

Beltran did most of the talking, leaving Nick's father to nod in agreement or shake his head when he disagreed. When he did speak it was mostly to confirm details that the detective wanted to corroborate.

They finished talking. Beltran placed an arm on the top of Charles's shoulder and tapped him lightly as if he were infirm. She appeared to hesitate, then opened her notebook and retrieved a neatly folded sheet of paper which she passed to him before moving off down the hall.

Nick noticed that his dad's face was grey as he walked back, his skin pinched and drawn downwards. He sat slowly in the seat freed up by Beltran before asking Nick how he was.

"I'm OK, just feeling a bit shit. What did she want?"

Charles answered but he seemed preoccupied with other thoughts.

"Just a few questions about Natalie. I told her I wouldn't be much help. You gave me a nasty scare."

"Sorry. Were you asleep?"

He looked down at his crumpled pyjama top. Nick noticed there were stains down the front that looked like egg yolk. His father pulled at the offending shirt as if noticing it for the first time. He chuckled.

"Jesus, I must look an escapee from the asylum."

He went silent before handing over the sheet of paper.

"She told me to give you this. The police artist made several copies."

It was the picture of Natalie. Nick looked at it briefly before folding it and passing it back to his father.

"You look after it for me."

His father nodded.

"Let's get you out of here."

Charles went to find those in charge and spoke gently with the doctors and nurses. They wanted Nick to stay in overnight so that his condition could be monitored but Charles, ever resourceful, eventually persuaded them to let his son go as long as he was released into his own care.

Nick was helped down to his father's car and bundled into the back with a blanket to keep him warm. Tess barked in excitement at being joined on the back seat of the car. She licked at Nick's face in recognition before slumping down heavily onto the leather, her weighty head wallowing on his lap as she stared up at him.

Nick remembered going on a childhood holiday. The cool of the interior of the car as they were whisked from the warmth of their beds, the morning still dark, the grass on the lawn wet with emerging dew. The duvet, from one of the beds, was picked up with the children still in it, allowing them to remain half asleep as their father drove the car south to pick up the early morning ferry to France. Wendy and Nick would snuggle up under the duvet until the first rays of dawn pierced the inside of the car and the heating warmed their sleep-tired limbs. As they waited for the boat to pull in their mother would produce breakfast and dress them ready for the holiday ahead.

Charles put Radio 4 on low and turned to look at his son.

"We'll go back to mine for today. Do you need to pick anything up on the way?"

No. There was nothing. With his father here Nick had no desire to go back to an empty flat. This time he wouldn't hide in the darkness; he would pull himself out of the depression with the help of his dad.

It was meant to be their night. They made a point of it, always had. Even when Abeni had been small they would take time out once a week, put the child to bed early and cook good food, not the frozen meals that they often ate during the week, but wholesome cooked food with plenty of spice. They would open a bottle of red wine and sit down together, with the music on, the television off, and talk. If they were both not too tired they would take a bath together and later, if Abeni was well and truly asleep, they would have sex.

They took it in turns to cook, tonight was meant to have been Bonita's turn. After her visit to the headmaster, they had meant to discuss what they thought best for their daughter. Abeni had sat sullenly throughout the episode as the headmaster spoke about how she was a bright and clever child but needed to push herself a little more. He had gone through a long list of current misdemeanours that the girl had taken a part in, to which Abeni would scowl and twist her lips in teenage insolence. But she had eventually agreed, somewhat begrudgingly, to start acting in a more mature manner.

Bonita had wanted Miles's advice. She had wanted to sit down over a green curry and make a decision. Choose a new path for their errant daughter, perhaps get her to change schools, but that had all altered as soon as she had got stuck with Nick Stuart.

"I'm sorry, I'm sorry..." she grumbled as she came into the kitchen, noting the washing up on the side and Miles sitting slumped in front of the television, the sound turned down low so as not to wake Maman or Abeni.

He stood as she bustled in and smiled.

"It's OK. Work?"

He knew as well as anyone that their jobs got in the way of life. That's why so many on the force either chose to be single or ended up divorced. But they were a little different. From the outset they had both realised and discussed the immense pressure their relationship would be under and that if they were going to make a go of it they had to act as a team. Their night had been set aside to act as a pressure valve for when the times got tough. Once a week they could get together to just be with each other, but work had a terrible way of intruding.

Miles stood and moved over to his wife, giving her a long kiss before moving over to reheat the meal he had made.

"Some guy fainted on me and we had to rush him to hospital."

As the food was warmed through, Miles turned his attention to pouring out a glass of wine for them both and then washing the dishes.

"All right, I hope?"

Bonita sat on a stool, her bag thrown into a corner out of the way.

"Yeah, fine physically. Not sure about his mental state though. I think he might have gone a little funny in the head, either that or he's been like that all the time and no one noticed. Reminds me of an old case. Perhaps they're linked somehow?" She spoke out loud, more to run the day through her own mind than expecting any help from Miles. "His father turned up and mentioned that his son suffered from depression, bouts that came and went, but he'd never seen anything like this before."

"We live in a fucked up world," Miles replied flippantly and indicated a brown file that lay on the kitchen table in front of Bonita.

"Toxicology caught up with me as I left. They passed on those."

Bonita looked down at the file. She didn't really want to look at it tonight but she could not help herself. She picked it up and let the contents slip out.

"That was quick, but it hardly seems worthwhile now. I think the disappearance I've been investigating was the loss of someone's mind rather than a real living person."

"Is this the missing Hope woman?"

She nodded, surprised that Miles had heard of the case, what with his own work pile being so large. He was part of a team investigating 'The Missing Man' abductions for which there still seemed no leads, plus he also had jurisdiction over some of the worst areas of Nottingham. Inner-city suburbs and estates seemed to be collapsing into chaos as the heat of the summer pressure cooked the gangs into acts of mindless violence to property, people and to each other.

Miles caught the look of surprise and explained.

"All missing women in the profile sixteen to thirty-five have to pass my desk. According to Jones yours didn't match."

Bonita looked down at the report. The results of the blood identification caught her attention. Miles dished up the food while looking over her shoulder.

"We found blood at the scene. Not much, but I thought it was worth taking a sample; that was before I realised the woman never existed."

"Probably the results of a bit of DIY gone wrong," commented Miles.

She read the small print, ignoring the multi-syllable chemical equations. "Seems someone had tried cleaning away the marks with a heavy-duty stain remover but was unsuccessful."

"Well, you don't want blood splattered across your floor. Very unsightly when visitors call."

Something didn't hang right. Bonita had been prepared to ditch the case, but now she felt unease spread through her.

"Not sure anyone really cares that much; the apartment block's in a terrible mess. No one's cleaned that hall in months. I checked with the building owners. They don't have a set of cleaners at the moment. I think they're trying to force the tenants out by giving them a meagre service, hoping they'll get annoyed enough to leave." She turned the page and read the blood results. "That's interesting – the blood is quite rare. AB negative."

Miles was about to top up the wine glasses when he stopped. He put the bottle down slowly.

"Jones said there was no match. One of the girls I'm looking for, she's AB negative. Can I have a look?"

She handed over the file.

"You think it's 'The Missing Man'? It could just be coincidence."

"Less than one per cent of the population has that blood type, plus I don't believe in coincidence. Where was this found?"

"It was outside the front door to Nick Stuart's flat. It's down in the Lace Market. Old grotty building that needs pulling down if you ask me."

"All the women were abducted from within the city centre; the Lace Market falls into that area."

Bonita shook her head.

"I don't think Nick is a killer. He's not the type. I think he just needs help. His mother died recently and I don't think he's come to terms with that. I think he created this Natalie as a substitute. He's just getting over the loss."

"Have you ever seen Psycho?"

"What, you think he's got them embalmed in his flat? I've looked the place over. There's nothing there. No sign of a struggle, not even a trace of hair. The place is empty. If he was involved he didn't bring anyone back to the flat."

There was a noise behind them as Maman shuffled in the room. She wore her thick dressing gown done up to her throat even though the night was stiflingly warm. Her feet made a soft hush across the kitchen floor as she pushed each foot forward, making every step a struggle.

"Hello, Maman. Can we get you anything?" Bonita enquired of her elderly mother.

Maman would get up several times during the night, finding it difficult to sleep for too long, her bed uncomfortable and her bladder weak. But she was still fiercely independent and even though her movements were curtailed by age, she still attempted to do everything herself.

"No, no," she muttered, her watery eyes taking in the work spread out on the kitchen table and the full wine glasses.

"I's all right, my dear, just need a glass of water."

Miles got a glass down from the tall cupboard and let the water run until it was cold enough to drink.

Maman turned to her daughter and took on the mantle of the matriarch.

"You'se been at work too long, it's not good to be working so much. Abeni needs a mother at home to look after her."

Bonita smiled. "I know." It was an old argument and one for which no answer would satisfy her mother. She came from a different time, before two incomes and convenience food were a necessity.

"Heard you'se talking shop from the stairs, plenty of peoples disappeared in the old country. Stories of whole villages vanished; we had our own 'Missing Man' as well."

Miles held out the glass for his mother-in-law and grinned.

"I don't think this is anything from there, it's just a seriously disturbed man. We'll catch him." He sounded confident.

"Don't mock me, the old stories haven't gone away; they're still here, they've got nowhere else to go."

Bonita knew her mother's love for the tales of her homeland. Myths and fables she would recount late at night, stories of witches and genies, mystical castles and hidden places. Stories set in windswept deserts where the sun burned and in high mountains, the very peaks of which were made from diamond. Bonita had enjoyed them as a child, they had evoked a rich imagery and history and though she had outgrown them with time, every now and again she would persuade Maman to recount a tale. She had hoped Abeni would be just as taken with the stories, but she seemed to despise them. Perhaps times had irrevocably changed and the young didn't have the time to dwell on such old-fashioned ideas. Their daughter didn't have the patience or the will to listen and with Maman's passing a lot of the old stories would be lost forever.

"I wasn't mocking you. I've heard your stories and they're good."

Maman nodded as if this was a given.

"Think you should check for the Ifreet, that's the one who grabs the children and makes the people disappear. That's a real 'Missing Man'."

The old woman took her glass and turned back to the stairs, shuffling slowly away, the sound of her feet muffled on the carpet. They remained quiet until Maman closed her bedroom door. Miles turned back to his wife.

"Ifreet?"

Bonita shrugged, she had heard Maman speak of them but wasn't quite sure they had anything similar in Britain.

"Deamons, kind of like a genie."

Miles laughed and turned back to the kitchen sink.

The desert was cold, when he had always expected it to be hot. The sun had disappeared from the sky; sinking away, the ball of golden fire painted the world in contrasting shadows that rippled away towards the horizon. This was followed with the deep scarlet of a sunset and then the inky darkness of night. The moon replaced the sun, silver and luminous, the desert monochrome. A breeze started to shift the sands, making them rasp like a serpent's tail as the land re-formed itself around him. He could feel the wind on his body and what little warmth was left inside him disappeared. He felt dead, a corpse alone in the wilderness.

Time was impossible to judge and before long he could not remember if he had been here one night or a thousand. The sun did not reappear so he assumed time itself must have stopped.

He was not walking and yet the desert moved past him, pushed on by the wind that was growing in intensity and power. The sand stung his skin so much so that he worried it would rip the very flesh from his bones and leave only a smooth bleached skeleton behind.

He waited.

Stars in the sky changed position; constellations that he was sure he knew moved slowly to the east and were replaced. Was this the march of eons or the simple passage of a night sky? He tried to concentrate on one bright star, the most dazzling in the sky. He watched as it shifted from above his head to the horizon, where it disappeared behind far-off mountains, only for it to reappear behind him. The sky held no clues to where he was as it did not seem to obey natural laws.

Still he waited.

The wind increased in strength again. It howled out into the night as a scream of rage. He watched as, far off in the distance, the sand formed itself into a column that thrust itself up from the desert floor. A dust devil that careered wildly across the open ground, spinning and lurching like a drunk – he knew it would eventually turn towards him. It came close but veered away at the last moment, the flying sand scything past his face. It mounted a dune, reshaping it into a mountainous peak but on reaching the summit, it turned and headed towards him again. This time it did not deviate and he was pulled within the vortex; the desert grated through him, filling all his senses and entering his body. He fell to the floor, foetal, desperate to protect himself from the abuse. He curled himself up into a tight ball as the desert claimed him.

The wind stopped.

He took a deep breath and opened eyes that had been screwed tight shut. It was still night, the moon hung menacingly in the night sky flanked by a carpet of stars but now all was still and silent. He could hear himself breathing; the steady rise and fall of his ribcage soothed him. He stood slowly. The desert was new, born again, a different land, reshaped and vital.

He looked out and saw the tent erected some way off. It was made from a dark fabric that glittered in the moonlight as if it were made from sleek and healthy hair. The tent had been richly decorated with strange swoops and whirls that imitated the night sky while the ruaq, the entrance flap, stood open, enticing him to enter.

Taking a step forward he staggered, unable to lift his left foot. He looked down and noticed the sands sucking at his ankle. The ground shifted and opened, pulling him in deeper, its hold strengthening. He tried to gain purchase and pull with his other leg, but now that too had sunk under the desert.

He bent forward and scratched with his hand at the changing sands. It felt like silk, slipping through his fingers as if a liquid. He sank deeper. He pulled back as both knees vanished below the ground. He knew he should keep still and shout out for help but his body refused to be drowned without a fight. He struggled as if possessed by a daemon. He pulled and twisted and grabbed at the ground, desperate for any purchase. He sank deeper, the speed of his descent increased by his rapid movements. His fingers started to bleed as his nails cracked and splintered, his muscles tightened as the vice of the ground pushed the air from him. There was no escape and he watched terrified and yet curious as his waist then his chest sank and vanished from sight.

He held his head up, straining, his chin thrust up into the sky. He felt the sands tickle as they slipped to enshroud his shoulders. He waved his hands above his head. Signalling for any help, though he knew there was little point. This desert was to be his tomb, a mausoleum far below the earth, where his bones would be crushed and ground to dust until such time that he was deemed worthy to become a part of the vast wilderness, at last at one with the desert.

The sand scorched his throat and filled his nostrils, filling him slowly. He was choking and without thinking, opened his mouth.

The sand moved in where no air was available. It slipped down into his lungs and coated his windpipe as his head disappeared below the desert.

A hand grabbed his and pulled. It was strong and determined, refusing to let him disappear forever. His descent stopped and in the darkness he felt his body move upwards. He tried to help, to squirm in search of the night sky and air. He pushed and wiggled and stretched and with a last thrust he was out.

It was a bedroom. The duvet was tucked about him, covering him from head to toe in feathered warmth that was suffocating in its heat. He sat up and looked about. It wasn't dark, but neither was it daylight. The curtains were open but there was nothing outside. No land, no sky, no horizon. Nothing.

He pushed aside the bed covers and realised for the first time he was not alone. He looked down at the end of the bed and was able to discern a shape, a human form that triggered a memory. He knew this person, this woman. She was looking away as he stretched out an arm desperate to touch her, not believing she was real.

She turned and smiled and he knew at once that he was dreaming.

"What are you doing here?" he asked.

She didn't reply, just shook her head as if what he had asked had been the wrong question.

"This is a dream, isn't it?"

She stood and moved over to the window. He feared she would open it and fly away into the nothingness but on reaching it she turned to him and spoke.

"Sometimes we're better off where we are. We don't want to be found. There is nothing to look for."

Her voice was softer than he remembered, clear and concise; her diction perfect, as if she wanted him to understand fully what she was saying. This was a rehearsed speech, one she had to give before the moment was over.

"I need to know if you're happy."

She nodded and then was gone. He had blinked and in that instant she had ceased to be, nothing remained. He held out a hand as if he might touch her essence, to feel it fading from the ether, but there was no magical spark to remind him of her presence.

"Mother?"

She didn't reply.

Nick woke up with someone in bed with him. They were snuggled up close and snoring lightly, a rising ribcage pushed against him for warmth. He stirred and Tess grunted before waking and shuffling off the bed ready for her lunch.

He felt bruised and his muscles ached, though he had done little in the way of exercise in the last twenty-four hours. His body seemed to have stored up all the anxiety of the last few days and used it to manifest aches and pains in parts of his body he had not known existed, until now. He tried to flex, stretching until the sinews snapped and readjusted themselves. The back of his hand was a dark mess where the drip line had been fed in. There was a scab forming over the top of a dark bruise. There was the distinct smell of hospital disinfectant about his body and he felt damp and unclean in the crevices of his body.

He pulled back the covers and sat on the edge of the bed. There were no curtains on a window that looked out over open country. The sun was high in a blue sky more akin to the Mediterranean coast than that normally hanging above a Lincolnshire potato field. He watched birds swoop in large numbers on to the patches of green that had not been parched to an insipid yellow by the hot sun. He could smell the heat and knew that outside it would already be unbearable. Somehow he still shivered.

So that was a breakdown. He had seen it acted out on the television, lots of blubbing and tears, the tearing of hair and gnashing of teeth. The screams of those sent terribly insane by their own inability to cope. He'd had bouts of depression before; he'd even been advised to see a doctor but had never gone. The moods came and went, but not so often as to be much of an issue in his life. Prior to living with Natalie he had just taken a few days off work and moped about the house, watched old films on the television or spent hours in bed alone with his dark, miserable thoughts. The rest of the time he felt fine, sometimes better than fine. On the good days he felt amazing, confidence bubbling out of him and infecting all those he came into contact with. It had never been a real issue. Sure, the bouts had been a little more regular since his mother's death, but that was bound to get anyone down; death was not the most affirming of life events. But he knew what he had just experienced had been different. He had sunk to a place he never wanted to visit again, a place of sucking sands, searing heat and a crushing darkness that was all-pervasive. It was a place of shadows, loss and hate.

He remembered the dream. It had felt so real. He could taste it, smell it, almost touch it. He knew real fear and he knew that if he had allowed the dream to swallow him entirely it would have resulted in death, both in this world and the other place. It was as if his mind wanted to punish him for a crime, some act that he had committed and was guilty of, that had started that night in the bar with the black-skinned man with eyes of fire.

He knew now that it was no good going out to search for Natalie. She could not be found. Natalie was more than missing, more than merely absent. That meant she was unlikely to come back. He knew that was not going to happen. She had vanished, she was extinct. It was no good looking for further clues; what few existed had been exhausted and would in time fade and vanish from this world. Apart from the single booking at a hairdresser's and a half-remembered face there was nothing else, no missing piece of the jigsaw puzzle. Perhaps in time she would even fade from his own memory, and then she might never have existed at all.

The only thing left was to hunt down his tormentor. He knew now what he had to do, who was the cause of all his problems. He would search this man out and he would in turn tell Nick what happened and the dreams would cease and he would no longer have to fear the darkness.

Nick moved downstairs where he could hear his father speaking to someone on the telephone. The house was a small cottage that must have been built for some past agricultural worker. It had been modernised in so far as it now had electricity and the toilet was not in a shed down the end of the garden – but that was about it. Charles was not that fussed about anything modern. The house he had owned with his wife had been a 1970s monstrosity with strangely shaped rooms and corridors that did not go anywhere. Whoever had designed it must have been suffering from a kind of schizophrenia as they tried desperately to include every type of design style from the last fifty years into one immense pile. It had been the family home and Nick remembered fondly the parties his mum would put on, the music in the living room to which people danced, the smiling faces of the adults, his parents' friends, as he and his sister appeared downstairs to pinch some of the food and wave at the dancing couples.

When his mum died, Nick's father had sold the house, complaining it was too large for him, which in truth it was. He had kept a few bits of the furniture and put them in his new petite cottage, but everything looked too big, ungainly and slightly out of place.

Charles replaced the receiver before coming over to his son's shuffling form. He seemed younger this morning, now dressed in jeans and a shirt open at the top to reveal tanned skin and a mass of hair. Nick always thought of his dad as dressed, and seeing him last night in his pyjama top had for the first time brought home to him how old he was getting.

"Sleep all right?" he asked.

Nick had always been an excellent sleeper, a trait he got from his mother. Charles was the complete opposite – always up early, even at weekends. Tess was in many ways his perfect partner as she never complained about the time and was always eager to be up with her owner.

Nick nodded that sleep had not been a problem.

"Who was that on the phone?" His voice sounded cracked, disjointed.

"It was that detective from last night. She was just checking on you."

Nick wondered if she was a bit more interested in the case now that he had gone a little crazy, or whether she would drop the whole thing. Call the case closed.

"She wants to have a look around your flat again and talk to the neighbours. I said we'd be at your place in a couple of hours. Is that OK?"

He nodded. Nick wanted a cup of coffee and started to search the kitchen for it. He could feel his father following him around and behind Charles, wagging her tail, trailed the dog. It was if they were doing the conga around the kitchen.

"You sure you're all right?"

"Yes. I'm fine."

His voice sounded whiney, like a disgruntled teenager forced to get out of bed. He knew he wasn't fine though, and his father had concern etched into every corner of his face.

"Where's the coffee?"

"Top cupboard. I want to talk to you. About Natalie."

Nick turned and looked at him. He had never seen him look so serious.

"What's the matter?"

"Will you sit down? I'll make you a coffee."

He sat as Charles busied himself with an old kettle that needed to be heated on top of the stove. Eventually after much fussing he sat down heavily next to his son and let out an involuntary sigh. Nick had a feeling his father was building up to something.

"Are you sure you're feeling one hundred per cent?"

Nick knew it was his father's logical way to think of a person being split up into individual units, some of which could be working fine while others were malfunctioning or on the blink. Everything compartmentalised, broken down into its constitutional parts, to be reassembled when required. His mum used to say it was like living with an android sometimes, but Nick accepted that it was just his father's way of dealing with the problems that life threw at him. He was methodical.

How did he feel? Was he eighty per cent, eighty-three, ninety-one per cent fine? He couldn't think in such mathematical terms. Nick thought of himself as more of a colour person. He liked words and art, raw emotion expressed through a shrug or the turn of a head, a lilt of the voice. When he thought about it, he felt grey and black, monochrome at best.

"I think this Natalie has affected you in ways you don't really understand and I think you need help. I want you to go and see a doctor."

He was sombre in his tone. He looked at Nick, his son, full in the face, testing him for a response, hoping that he would understand the seriousness with which he took his role as father.

"I'm fine. It's just that she's gone and left no clues; that's the problem. I want to know what's happened to her. I'm confused."

"That's where professional help is needed. I'm not the sort of person who can work this out with you. I've made an appointment for tomorrow morning."

Charles was troubled; concern oozed from his pores. Nick knew he wanted to help; he wanted to care and look after his son. Stand in for the mother no longer present in his life. He was trying to be two parents at once.

"I'm not sure they'll be much help, I don't need a doctor. I just miss her – Natalie."

He nodded as if that was a given.

"Nick, you may have to face the fact she's not coming back."

"I know – it's just that I have to do something first. It's all my fault and I need to be forgiven."

"Will you go?"

Nick thought about it briefly but knew he couldn't face being prodded and poked by men in white jackets or sitting on a couch recounting his childhood, looking for the hidden clues, where it all went wrong. He already knew he had an issue with his moods, the violent blacks and high whites that come upon him at any time. He didn't need a doctor to reconfirm that.

"No."

His father nodded, accepting his son's choice. His 'talk' over, he stood and kicked the chair neatly under the table. Nick drank his coffee and waited for his father to leave the room. Eventually Charles stepped outside to play with Tess. Nick snatched at the phone and dialled Munch at work. His friend picked up after leaving it for the maximum number of rings but just before the answer phone kicked in.

"Where you been, mate? I've had to make all sorts of lies up for you. I've told them you've broke your wrist so you're going to have to come into work bandaged tomorrow." Munch was whispering, his hand held close to the mouthpiece to further quieten his voice, but it only made it sound muffled and no doubt made him look guilty in the office.

"I'm not coming back yet, but I want you to meet me tonight."

"Why?"

"That bar we went to last Friday. We're going back. I want you to come round straight from work."

Munch sniffed as if considering his options.

"Midweek drinking? I like it."

"No. I want to find that guy who we were with the other night."

"OK, but you know that place is meant to be a bit rough. Weekends it's busy but I've no idea who hangs there midweek."

Munch actually sounded concerned, his usual bravado melting away now that he was sober. Nick gave him no option.

"I'll see you after work. My place."

He hung up and looked out of the window. His dad was halfway down the drive throwing a stuffed toy in the air for Tess to catch.

He dialled again. This time the call was to his agent. The man sounded concerned and yet relieved that Nick was all right. He repeated his request from the production company. Nick wanted to hear it spelt out again so that he could fully comprehend what was being offered. It was the chance of a lifetime and not something Nick had ever expected to really happen. It was somewhat strange that they did not require him to formally try out for the part, to jump through the hoops of an interview and a meeting with the producers, but he supposed he must have really impressed them with his audition tape. He volunteered to go to London the following day but was told not to worry. The producer was coming up to Nottingham. They were to meet tomorrow to discuss the role.

"He must really like you, Nick. This guy would never leave London. It's been offered to you on a silver platter. See, I told you, if you commit yourself, dreams do come true."

As he replaced the receiver Nick briefly deliberated on his agent's glib comment and realised that if dreams came true then, equally, nightmares could as well. The idea made him shudder.

"We should go over to your place. The police are expecting us," said Charles coming into the kitchen and slightly out of breath.

Nick agreed.

The drive back to Nottingham was pitted with a little conversation but nothing that related to 'his problem'. Nick welcomed the silence.

There were two officers waiting for them when they returned to Nick's flat. Beltran almost smiled at seeing him, but the look soon faded as another officer, a tall thin man with greying, closely-cropped hair pushed himself forward.

"Detective Miles Borrail. Thank you for agreeing to speak to us again."

He held out a hand which both Charles and Nick shook. Despite his slight frame the man was strong; determination oozed from his heavily pumping arm. The detective turned and looked toward Beltran who smiled warmly at them.

Nick noticed the look. They were obviously involved, there was a connection between them that said more than just colleague; it spoke of sex and trust. He wondered whether they were allowed to be a real couple or whether that was something their roles forbade, the joining of two officers ripe for manipulation.

Charles led the way inside and got everyone settled in the living room. Nick remained standing. "What do you need to know now?" he asked.

Miles stood up and started to pace the room.

"The blood found outside your door is of a very rare type. I'm investigating an enquiry into the abduction of three young women, one of whom had the same blood type. Do you know what blood type your missing girlfriend was?"

"No idea. I didn't even know it was blood, not until you confirmed it. You're talking about the 'Missing Man' case, aren't you?"

"I'm not at liberty to say."

There was no need. Nick knew; he'd read the stories and seen it on the news. The police were getting desperate.

"Do you think it's this girl's blood or Natalie's?"

"We don't know yet. How long have the marks been there?"

"I really can't help you. As I explained to your wife, I normally don't bother with the lights and only noticed them when they were pointed out to me, by her. They could have been there since the day I moved in or been made in the last week."

Miles fished in a black folder and handed over three photos. Nick took them and looked at each in turn. They were of women, all young, smiling and happy when the photos were taken. One girl was winking at the camera while her friends gathered around her, out on a birthday or hen night. Another was wearing the gown of a graduate, her face done up for the occasion. Nick imagined her parents looking on from behind the cameraman's back, a look of pride in their eyes. He wondered what had happened to them. Were they lying somewhere, dead in this world, all life snuffed from their bodies as they rotted down to nothing? Or could they still be alive, scared and alone, waiting for the sound of footsteps that would herald either death or release? Counting the moments and wishing they had never gone out that fateful evening?

At least they could be found. Whatever state they were in, eventually something would be discovered. Natalie however was different; she no longer existed at all, only his memories of a woman who was disappearing with each passing day, every extending hour, his memories her only lasting testament.

"What about others in this apartment block? Any strange noises? Have you heard anyone outside your door – that sort of thing?"

Nick shook his head in despair as he handed the photos back.

"This old place makes all kinds of strange noises. On this floor you have my delightful neighbour who wages war against anyone who steps onto the landing. As for the others, I've seen a few of them but that's all. There was a sound outside my door earlier in the week but it could have been my imagination. I haven't been sleeping well."

Bonita interjected.

"The man across from you. How long has he lived here?"

"As long as I have. He keeps to himself mostly. I assume he's retired as he doesn't appear to go out much. To be honest, I stay away from him."

Miles turned to Beltran.

"You did a full sweep in here, including the loft."

Beltran nodded as Charles interjected.

"You can't possibly believe that Nick was involved in these women's disappearances, can you?"

"We're not ruling out anything yet, Mr Stuart. Three women have disappeared without trace. We take that very seriously. Until they turn up unharmed everyone is a suspect."

"Four."

Miles turned on Nick's comment.

"Four have gone missing if you include Natalie."

"And you think her disappearance is related?"

"No," he said quietly.

"You seem quite sure about that."

Nick remained silent. He didn't like the way the questioning was going. It sounded to him as if the detective was attempting to lead him down a blind alley. He could see the desperation in the man's eyes. He wanted someone for the crimes against these women and he thought that Nick was a prime candidate.

"I really don't think I can help. I'm sorry."

Miles turned to Bonita.

"Shall we go and knock on a few doors?"

They hurried out of the apartment, the door closing swiftly behind them as they exited. Bonita knocked on the door opposite. There was no answer.

"I thought our friend Nick said his neighbour never went out?"

She knocked again, harder.

"Police. Will you come and open the door?"

Still it remained silent.

"He was returning home when I first made his acquaintance. He must have to go out for food, for shopping."

"Let's try downstairs."

The two officers spent the next hour going from door to door asking questions and showing photos. Everyone played dumb. No one had seen any of the women. They even added Natalie's drawing but again everyone shook their heads. They had drawn a blank.

Back on the street they walked away from the building, turned a corner and sidled over to a car that was parked down one of the dark cobbled roads. The window was wound down and a bald-headed police officer stopped chatting with his colleague and looked out.

"Any luck?"

Miles shook his head.

"His neighbour is out though, so we still need to question him. Detective Beltran will call in again when he turns up but I want you two sat outside monitoring any movement. Tell us when the neighbour comes back and if Nick goes out."

There was a park before you got to the street. The council had attempted to clean it up, turn it into a child friendly area with chipped bark for them to fall on without hurting themselves, and basketball courts on which to practise. The flower beds had been redesigned and a water feature added to tempt those who wished to linger; a haven in the city. Perhaps they expected people would bring their children and sit on the grass idly gossiping, or perhaps have a family picnic on the greens. But the swings and slide remained unused and the only people who sat on the benches more often than not spent the night there, pissing behind them in the well groomed shrubbery. This was a park for the drug dependent and homeless, they colonised it many years ago, moving into the area as the police forced them from the streets, and a lick of paint by the council was not going to persuade them to move on.

Nick and Munch skirted the park. The street they wanted lay on the other side and while it made sense to go through the park's centre, they did not want to wander around the place in the dimming light. The streets were bad enough, but in the park anyone could have jumped them. Inside they moved in packs, it was like a human game reserve.

Nick was wearing jeans and a dark hooded top – trying to fit in. He hoped that with a bit of luck he would look like a local and most people would ignore him. He was wearing trainers in case he needed to do any running. Munch on the other hand had turned up from work in his cheap suit with his nylon shirt hanging out of the back of his trousers. He carried a plastic carrier bag in which an empty lunch box clattered noisily against a drinks bottle. He stuck out like a sore thumb.

The road was busy with traffic; the route linked the city centre with the east end of the growing conurbation. Car owners drove with the doors locked. This was not the part of town to stop at junctions for too long or a place to ask for directions. It was a through route and nothing else – the business men secure in their company cars, the parents looking down on the inhabitants from their deluxe four by fours and expensive people carriers.

The presence of the traffic made Nick feel a little more relaxed. If anything did happen on the street he hoped that at least if someone would not stop to help, they would call for assistance. But then they might just drive on and do nothing, the crime acknowledged as further proof of the city's descent into hell.

The area was run down, the buildings decayed and rotting; in some places fire had been allowed to burn unopposed, the building and trade removed by insurance scam. Those businesses that remained looked tired. They clung to the rock face of respectability but were already losing their grip. Few people wanted to shop here; those that did, did so because it was all they could afford or it was as far as they could walk. The population looked scared, frightened of what lay in the rubbish-strewn alleyways and vacant lots. They grouped together for comfort, only looking up when a siren alerted them to the presence of the law. They hated where they lived, who they were, what they had been born into – but there seemed little chance of ever escaping.

They walked past the bar the first time. It blended into the background with all the other shabby refits, as if hiding from the world that drove past them. The building must have been a factory at one time, but any clues as to what was produced had long been removed and the walls covered up with chipped stucco and several layers of flaking paint. There were no windows at street level; the building seemed to consist of one long dirty wall punctuated with badly spelled graffiti. The windows further up the building were blanked out. Something black had been painted onto them, either to stop the sunlight from entering or to conceal whatever was going on inside.

It was only a small plaque screwed to the wall that gave any hint to the fact the building was even occupied. Behind a sheet of cracked Perspex was the name of the place: 'Jerrod's Meeting Hall featuring The Bar'. It gave no other indication as to what the place was. No mention of drink or music, telephone numbers or occupancy levels. It looked like the sort of place that functioned on whatever was needed at the time – the sort of place that people would ignore forever until it was raided or a body was discovered inside.

The main door they had used on their first visit was closed. Nick worried that the place was shut for the night, but Munch pointed out a small side alley that led to a door of reinforced glass. There was a bell fixed to the wall. A piece of paper had been stuck underneath it, yellow and partly peeling away. On the paper was written in large capitals 'BELL', just in case visitors needed help in identifying it.

Nick gave the door handle a try but it was locked. He could hear the bass line of music being played somewhere beyond the door. Someone was in.

It appeared to be some kind of private members' bar, a hidden club for some of the less-than-savoury inhabitants of the area. There had been several private clubs open in the city recently. They used to be the reserve of the rich and powerful or for families where Dad worked and Mum looked after the screaming children; the sort of place that advertised bad comedians and karaoke nights. Now they seemed to be springing up all over the place. Clubs for every type of disenfranchised member of society who did not want to mix with the rest of humanity. Clubs for those that smoked and wanted to be left to do so; clubs for those who were not prepared to toe the line; clubs for men and clubs for women, clubs for black and white.

Nick pushed the bell. He had the feeling he was going to stick out like a sore thumb in this place. It made a far-off ringing noise which was followed by the door buzzing as the electronic lock opened. He pushed at the door and entered. Munch followed, checking over his shoulder for anyone watching.

Drunk, the place had seemed exotic, dangerous and thrilling, but in sober reality it was nothing other than ugly. The carpet was covered in cigarette burns and spilled drink marks plus whole pieces of chewing gum that had been mashed into the weave. The walls were a lurid pink colour; the colour of old-fashioned school toilet paper. There was a framed picture on the wall of some tropical island that had been taken years before mass tourism covered it in beach villas. It was old and discoloured; the sea too turquoise, the palm trees an unsightly shade of lime.

A black man sat behind a partition that had been hastily rigged up. Large six-inch nails had been half hammered into the brick and held a curtain in place, the rough red fabric moth-eaten and covered in drink spills. The whole partition wobbled as the door shut behind them, locking out the remainder of the daylight.

He stood as they entered, quizzically looking them up and down. The man was tall, very tall, and carrying somewhat too much weight around his middle. He resembled a fat nursery rhyme character. His hair was cut short, though in places he was bald, which made his head look mangy. He cocked his head on one side and spoke in a deep Jamaican accent.

"All right?"

Nick nodded.

"It's ten pounds for non-members."

The man seemed to be acting as some kind of host until the bouncers arrived. He held out his hand for payment. Nick only had ten pounds and a little loose change in his pocket. There was a sign on the wall saying they accepted cards. He thought about it but then decided it was not the sort of place he was going to hand over a credit card. He turned to Munch.

"Do you have any money?"

Munch looked sheepish.

"I haven't got enough for the both of us," Nick added.

Munch tutted but eventually relented and dug out his wallet. He handed over the money which the host checked against a naked light bulb. Once the money was safely placed in a hip pocket the man pointed at a curtain.

"You'se can go in."

Munch stepped forward as Nick turned to the black man.

"I'm looking for someone."

He raised his eyebrows in anticipation of the demand, as if this were a common enough request.

"We were in here last week and got talking to a man. He's thin, with scarred cheeks and he has these eyes that..." Nick was unsure how to finish.

The host looked Nick over again. He pointed to Nick's head and waggled his finger in irritation. Nick obliged and pulled down the hood that was obliterating his features. The guy was in his early fifties at least but Nick was in no doubt that he could kick the shit out of him if required. He probably had some weapon behind the rickety wall as well.

There was a look on the large man's face that made it obvious he knew who Nick was talking about.

"What's your name?"

Nick ignored the question, not sure if he should go into his life history with such an intimidating-looking individual. By giving away such information he worried that they would come looking for him. Nick didn't want to chance that.

"He took something from me. I want it back."

The host nodded slowly as if that was a given fact before picking up the telephone and ringing a number. He moved away and hid behind the wall so that Nick could not hear what was said. He mumbled into the phone before putting it back again as if it had burnt him.

"You'se wait here. Someone'll be out in a minute."

Nick was glad he didn't have to go into the bar. It reeked of a refuge for the dispossessed and dangerous; the music now floating from behind the curtain had a distinct hard rhythm. He had also started to notice a sweet smell in the air that caught at the back of his throat, causing it to tickle. Someone was smoking quite heavily and, whatever it was, it was not tobacco.

Munch tried to peek behind the curtain, the music turned down low and the intoxicating smell of alcohol drawing him in, regardless of the evident danger. He looked over at Nick, an expression of want in his eyes. Nick had seen that look one too many times but chose this time to ignore it. He didn't want to get stuck here; he didn't want to risk letting his guard down and letting this place into his life.

The big man sat back down and looked at a monitor. It showed the door they had used to come in, the camera fixed into the round light that hung above the door. Looking back, Nick noticed that, as well as the electronic lock, the front door had several large bolts. The club did not like uninvited guests, and was well prepared for when they turned up.

There was something sordid about the place. Something foreign and alien that did not sit well with Nick. Natalie liked to dance. She was never more alive than when she was on the dance floor moving to the beats being played out. She almost went into some kind of trance, moving her body in ways that many would think indecent. He didn't like to think of her in this place, moving slowly to the music as large men watched her from the bar or even worse, joined in, rubbing themselves against her, their hips thrusting against her arse, a noticeable bulge evident in their tight trousers.

As Munch took one last look through the curtain that led to the bar, it was roughly pushed aside leaving a clatter of music and light to spill from the briefly created opening as if desperate to escape. It was dragged back and muffled as the curtain swung closed.

A gangly black guy with a thin goatee beard twisted into a point that had been grown to cover disfigured cheeks grinned at Nick, a single gold tooth reflecting what little light there was. He wore a lurid orange shirt that was half open, revealing a smooth emaciated chest adorned with gold jewellery. His trousers were tight, hugging his thin hips that could be seen as knotted points above the waistband. He wore shoes that came to a sharp end; they had been carefully cleaned to reveal a deep gleam. Nick noticed for the first time that he had a tattoo covering one arm. An intricate pattern of swirls and clouds that disappeared into his rolled shirtsleeve. He looked like a pimp.

"You'se looking for me?" he asked in that familiar soft voice, more acknowledged at the back of the head than heard.

Nick felt suddenly afraid. The man stood before him, half hidden in the darkness, as if not daring to step out of the shadows. His stare never left Nick but everyone present could feel the power coming off him. It was as if something far darker was hidden by that mask, a small glimmer of which could be caught in the eyes of flame that even now seemed to dance and cavort. To Nick it looked briefly like an eye defect, a mist that glanced over the outer membrane, or perhaps the reflection of a naked light bulb. He blinked and the light dissipated.

"I'm looking for Natalie. She's not come home."

He shrugged as if to say that was none of his concern.

"Do you know where she could have gone?"

"What you saying?"

Nick could tell the man did not like him. He never raised his voice but the threat of violence was defiantly imminent.

"Nothing. I'm not implying anything. I just want to find her."

He pursed his lips, an act of contemplation. There was something familiar about the man – that movement, those eyes, orbs of white that were tinged almost blue that seemed to pull him into their scorched centres, down deep into cores that ended in a pinprick of darkness. He seemed more like an animal than a human, something feral and wild.

"The bitch is gone."

Bitch seemed to be an endearing term. Nick wasn't very good at the gangster talk. He didn't listen to rap and never tried to take any parts that required him to act it. It just never sounded right coming out of his mouth.

"Gone where?"

He shrugged.

"Does it matter? She's no longer anyone's concern."

Nick didn't like the way he kept talking about Natalie in the past tense.

Munch, noticing for the first time that Nick and this strange man had some common history, at last recognised him from the previous weekend.

"You were the rum man."

He nodded.

"Cool. Let's all go in and have a drink. We can discuss this inside."

Munch made to move but the man held up an arm, barring entry to the inner sanctum.

"You should leave. This ain't no place for you two. What's done is done, nuffin' you'se can do about it."

He addressed the last remark to Nick.

"Go back wherever you came from and forget the bitch. Don't worry about her. She'll be fine where she is."

He turned to leave, while nodding at the man behind the counter. The large man stood up. Their interview was over.

"The police are looking for her."

The man turned back suddenly, knocking Munch away from the

door. There was a look of anger in his face, a look that frightened Nick, causing him to step back, away from the danger. He had wanted to rile the man, to get more from him than just mystification, but now he was afraid he might have overstepped some invisible boundary. The light in his eyes flickered while the snarl came from deep within him. He seemed transformed into something inhuman, a brutal creature ready to strike out.

"You don't tell them about this place. We never spoke. I don't want no tangle with them. You hear me?"

He was close to Nick, so close that he could smell his breath. Nick had expected it to be foul, but it smelt pleasantly of rum and ozone, a clean, pure smell. His breath was hot against Nick's cheek.

"I need to find Natalie."

"Forget everything about her."

"But if she's still alive, I need to know she's all right."

He stopped and pulled himself backwards slowly. He put one hand out to part the curtain, ready to leave them behind.

"Don't mess with stuff you don't understand. You go back home and forget her, little actor man."

He moved back through the curtain, the light and sound once more reaching out and dragging him back into the darkness, returning him to the fold. That was it. Nick had no desire to follow. Whatever was on the other side of that door, it was not the sort of place that would welcome him now, plus the lingering host had unsaid orders to get rid of them quickly.

Munch squared his shoulders, bravado evident now that all danger had passed. He pursed his lips and folded his arms across his chest.

"You gonna let him talk to you like that?"

Nick thought that his friend was at first going to follow the man into the darkness. He held up an arm to bar the way but felt no real resistance. As usual with Munch it was all talk and no action.

"I don't think we're wanted here."

Munch looked deflated before turning to the large host who still hovered behind them.

"Well, I want my money back then. We never went in."

The man pointed to a sign that stated 'No Refunds' in capital letters.

Munch's face crumpled as he realised he'd been done. "Aww, fuck off!"

Perhaps thinking that Munch was about to get violent, the man reached down and picked up a baseball bat that must have been hidden behind the counter. On cue, three men stepped from behind the curtain and advanced towards them.

Nick grabbed Munch by the arm and led him backwards out of the door. His friend seemed unfazed by the danger and more concerned about his lost cash, but Nick understood that this was no show of bluster. These men were willing to use force if required; they would relish the chance to hurt.

They left and moved out onto the street. The door swung closed behind them. Faces could still be seen at the glass staring out; looks that said 'leave now or pay the consequences'. The deep thud of the music dwindled as they walked quickly away, growing quieter, until nothing more than a whisper could be heard, a whisper that was eventually taken up and blown away into the hum of the city.

The evening was still warm but outside felt cooler than inside. Nick had been sweating heavily in the bar and he could now feel it drying on his skin. His clothes felt damp and clammy while his heartbeat rapped out a tattoo on the inside of his chest. Munch seemed unfazed, but Nick knew different.

He wondered whether or not to inform the police about the bar. It was true that he now blamed only himself for the loss of Natalie, but it did seem from that last encounter that she was still alive. He hadn't contradicted Nick when he had said as much. Was he the 'Missing Man'? If so, then perhaps the other girls were still alive.

It would explain why no bodies and no ransom had been received by the police. All four of them could be in that building. Locked away, hidden deep inside, never knowing whether they would see daylight again. The men inside could do anything to them, unspeakable acts of degradation and violence, rape and mutilation, all hidden away from the world in a dingy bar basement, their screams muffled and gagged.

The man's voice echoed inside his head: 'actor man'. Nick had given away too much that night. He was being toyed with because he had gambled and lost. He got out his phone and started to dial Beltran's number.

"What are you doing?" asked Munch.

"I need to let the police know what happened in there. He's the one responsible for all of this. He's probably the 'Missing Man' for all we know."

Munch grabbed the phone and held it at arm's length away from Nick.

"Don't be an idiot. If you ring them and the police turn up and start asking questions, who do think they're going to come looking for?"

Beltran was already aware of the places that Nick visited. The call had come in seconds after he had left the flat. They had followed at a discreet distance. They shadowed the pair across the park and down into the rough part of the city. The officer had watched the pair go in the club and reported back.

"Don't know what they're up to. It's not the sort of place you'd go for a midweek drink, if you're a nice rich boy. Not unless you're slumming it."

He listened to Beltran's response. Wait and see what happens, if necessary call for back-up, but under no circumstances was he to go into the bar himself. They would be able to smell police from a mile off.

He waited. Eventually the men re-emerged, looking troubled but in the main unharmed. Whatever they had gone in for, it wasn't a drink, the time was far too short, but they also had not been asked to leave immediately. Something had happened inside.

The officer waited an acceptable period before he followed. As he moved from the shadows across the street a second person stepped out from the darkness and joined the chase, all following the prey as they snaked their way back to the city.

Five

She was concerned; concerned that she had unwittingly discovered something more than a simple shout for help. "Just follow it up" was what the Superintendent had said when she had made her concerns known to him. She had enough to 'follow up' without getting involved in yet another family dispute issue. There were real crimes happening out on the streets that required time and effort, thorough investigation and interpretation, but as usual they ended up getting shunted down the pile as these little 'follow ups' landed on her desk.

The public more than ever wanted a police force that was vigilant to the point of hand holding; they wanted a police force that prevented crime before it happened, recorded it while it happened and apprehended those who committed it after it happened, while at the same time walking the streets to remain a presence, pointing tourists in the right direction, looking for lost pets, lecturing children on bicycle awareness, helping old people to hospital and moving on drunks on a Saturday night. The more they were asked to do, the less time they had to complete the job.

This was meant to be a form-filling exercise. She had been prepared to establish that Nick's girlfriend had run off with a friend, allowing her to get back to some real work – but as the case had developed, the lack of a victim or evidence and the out-right concern Nick had for someone who did not seem to exist had interested her. The blood had led the trail back to her husband's case and something far more sinister, the 'Missing Man'.

She no longer knew what to believe. Was Nick a worried boyfriend, a pawn in some elaborate game or a suspect? After last night's call from the police tail, a new name had come up, a name which made Bonita concerned that things were spiralling out of control.

Imamu Ferreira. The name had been mentioned to her in the past. The name always came up. He was a drifter, moving from one city to another, from one gang to the next. Involved in everything from drugs to prostitution to murder, but he had never spent a night in custody. There was never enough evidence to bring him in; it was always circumstantial, hearsay; witnesses' details always clashed, and the more the man was investigated the more he seemed to disappear, to become less substantial. Facts and truths melted around him until he vanished, only to reappear months later involved in some other criminal act. She was sure that the name was a front, a plausible moniker for a phantom. That was how he worked; everything sounded solid until investigated and then, then the whole earth shifted and ran through your fingers like sand.

But if Ferreira was involved then Bonita feared that something serious was going on. If Nick had become entangled with this man, then perhaps his fears were substantiated. His missing girlfriend might not just be a cry for help, but a real crime statistic. The only way to know was to investigate; a full, time-consuming, expensive investigation with both Miles and herself at the helm. It would mean late nights, missed appointments at the gym and less time spent with Abeni who would in turn play up for attention.

Bonita's stomach growled, hunger gnawing at her. The investigation would start in earnest in a few short hours. She reached for her mug of coffee, hoping it would settle her nerves.

"This is how it stands…"

Miles and Bonita stood before the assembled team. They had called them in early, the sun had barely risen and a few of the faces looked tired, still in need of morning caffeine and some form of breakfast. They had been lucky, a break in a case that up until now seemed impossible to investigate, a link to the unknown person who struck in the heart of the city on busy weeknights, leaving no clues and no witnesses – the 'Missing Man'. No bodies had been found and no ransoms received. They believed he was male but what he wanted with these women – what he had planned to do to them – was still unknown.

Miles liked to hope that the victims were still alive somewhere but the look he received from the other officers when he mentioned this bordered on pity. Everyone had expected the bodies to turn up; hoping that when they did the case could really begin. Except they never had. Two months and nothing.

"We've been lucky. A missing person case run by Detective Beltran has thrown up a possible blood match for our second missing girl, Trudy Grasson. The amount found is significant but not enough to claim a crime scene. We have a blood type match and it's my belief we'll get a DNA match as well. Toxicology reports state that someone at some point has made an attempt to wash away these stains with a kitchen cleaner. Detective Beltran will elucidate."

Miles stepped back as Bonita opened her notebook.

"The disappearance of Natalie Hope was reported by her boyfriend. He claimed that she had gone missing and had not done so of her own accord even though the pair had argued the previous evening. On further investigation the team's conclusion was that Natalie Hope never existed."

There was a murmur of surprise amongst the seated, some even going so far as to start taking notes.

"Background checks could reveal no person of that name and birth date ever being recorded, plus Mr Stuart, the boyfriend, could give no credible evidence of individuals who knew her. A forensics team was sent into the property and no trace of Natalie could be found. It was this that led us to the belief that Mr Stuart had made this woman up to compensate for the loss of his mother or other mental issue and perhaps as a way of garnering police attention.

"It was during the forensic search that the spots of blood were discovered outside the apartment door of Mr Stuart's flat. He is to be considered a suspect in the 'Missing Man' case."

Bonita returned to her seat. The next surprise would have to come from Miles.

He stood and cleared his throat before approaching the stand.

"Normal police procedure would require us to do a full sweep of the suspect's flat but this was completed as part of the missing person investigation and nothing was discovered. However, last evening our suspect made an unexpected stop at a club off the St Ann's Well Road. A place known to be frequented by one Mr Imamu Ferreira, an individual known to be attached to a number of possible criminal groups and several ongoing investigations. We've never been able to get anything to stick on him before but if he is involved it would be..." he paused for effect, "...most fortunate.

"This club is the area in which we wish to concentrate our investigations. Any questions?"

Amongst the assembled officers hands shot up and Bonita joined her husband.

"Yes, John?"

"Sir, why don't we just raid the place? There must be a hundred ways to get a warrant for that shit hole."

"True. But it's known as a place where weapons have been traded in the past; it's also believed that Mr Ferreira is considered dangerous to approach. It's believed any direct interference could be considered ill-advised at this time."

Bonita picked up the answer and continued.

"We also want something that sticks. If we rush in there and find nothing it could be seen as harassment in an area of the city that does not have the best relationship with the force."

They had discussed this already and decided that a strategy of review was still necessary. While many would want to maximise the potential of the situation, both of them knew the consequences of rushing in before the facts were undeniable.

A further selection of questions was rattled through before they were able to direct the meeting around to duties. A rotating watch was placed on the club and Nick Stuart, with all movement to be reported. It was now a waiting game.

Nick entered the hotel lobby whilst slipping the sunglasses from his nose and placing them inside a pocket. He had only ever been here once, many years ago, to celebrate his mother's sixtieth birthday. It had the sort of restaurant attached that was well out of his price range, but on that occasion he had gone halves with his father. It had been a good night.

They had renovated since he had last been in, making it look more modern with the addition of mirrors and upholstered leather. Nick hesitated a moment, the expense of the place overwhelming him briefly, before he turned to the receptionist who gave him a broad, highly paid smile.

"Can I help you, sir?"

Nick asked for the bar and was directed past the restaurant, half empty at this time of day, through an arch and into a large room decorated in black and gold leaf. He looked about and spotted his agent with a tall elegantly dressed man who Nick remembered from his brief visit to Television House in London.

The agent, dressed in a ridiculous canary yellow shirt and green tie, beamed on spotting Nick and waved him over.

"Nick, Nick, my good boy. How are you?"

He wondered briefly about whether or not to tell them that his life was a complete and utter mess since his girlfriend had been magically removed from it and erased from the memories of all who knew her, but thought better of it.

He was directed to sit and the producer was introduced. As

wine – which was ordered from the expensive section of the menu, Nick noted – was sorted by the bar staff, the producer wasted no time and got down to the detail.

"Nick, we were impressed with your audition tape, very impressed. To be honest, supporting actor tapes very rarely make much of an impression on me. I'm far too busy to watch them, but I saw yours and you sparkle. You've got talent. It's a shame we've lost Richie; he was good, he was a name, but accidents happen and there is nothing we can do to stop them. But I think you can hold your own. I know this is a gamble, but I believe you have star appeal. I want you for the lead."

It was laid out that simply. The sort of miracle that should never happen in reality. They were offering him the lead role in a pilot on the BBC. No messing, no further auditions or interviews. From this point forward Nick knew that his whole life would be different, and for some unknown reason he felt as guilty as hell because of it. He had expected to feel elated: this was the moment he had always waited for, but now he just felt wrong. He put it down to the issues of the moment and tried to listen to what was being said.

His agent prattled on about his previous work, which sounded small and mundane, while the producer smiled and nodded sagely; but Nick's mind kept wandering to the events of the last week and the man in the bar.

Documents were placed in front of him. Crisp, white and freshly printed, they listed the role and his remuneration. It was a lot, more than he had ever earned working with Munch. He was passed a pen, the lock depressed for him and the correct line indicated for his signature.

He looked at the space next to his name, typed out and spelt correctly. He thought of Natalie and it briefly crossed his mind that with this contract his whole life would change. He would have to move south, leave Nottingham and his old life behind. Would he forget about her, would she become some dark echo in his past, a shadow that would slip between his dreams, forever locked away as an ugly reminder of what he once was and how he became what he would be?

He signed the document in a hand that shook and left behind a slight smudge – a dark mark against his name.

More wine was ordered to celebrate as the men slapped each other on the back before returning to work. He was to report for a run through in two weeks' time. Then he was left alone; stunned and silent, a signed contract on the table.

Nick finished his wine. For the first time since he arrived he noticed the black man sitting at the bar. He seemed to be watching him in the mirror which hung suspended above the bottles of spirits, far more interested in what was going on at the table than the newspaper spread before him. He was alone, while everyone else, apart from Nick, seemed to be with friends or colleagues. Nick judged him to be out of place. Was it one of the men from the club? A message from his tormentor, a warning to back off? Nick stared back. The man blinked and looked away.

Nick stood and grabbed the contract. The man was far too well dressed to come from that end of town. He worried that he was becoming paranoid and perhaps just a little racist, jumping at every coincidence and anomaly. But then he realised that if the man from the bar had taken Natalie, he would know where Nick lived. He knew everything about the 'actor man'. Until Nick moved he would be forever looking over his shoulder, listening for the creak of a foot on a step, his front door opening to let in the stranger. Munch had warned him off telling the police about the club, but he felt that he owed it to Beltran. If he was going to be leaving soon then she could follow it up. He doubted they would tell her anything but he wanted to send out his own warning.

As he walked away from the hotel he took out his mobile and punched in her number. He let it ring while checking he was not being pursued by the guy from the hotel. The only person behind him was a slightly dishevelled man in an overcoat – too warm for a day like this.

Beltran answered after only a few rings.

"I think I've found something."

"Really?"

Beltran sounded cautious; her words deliberate, as if she was talking for someone else's benefit.

"The night Natalie disappeared we went to a club outside the city centre. Some kind of private members' bar that's seen better days."

"You didn't mention this in your statement."

Nick didn't like the inference. She seemed cold, less open to any pieces of information he could give her than previously.

"I only just remembered." He had no time to get involved in a debate about whether or not he had been right to withhold this information. "I went back last night. There's a guy there who I think knows what happened to Natalie."

"Where is this place?"

"It's towards St Ann's, past the bingo hall."

"That's not a nice part of town to be drinking in, Nick."

Beltran's voice still sounded strained but the mention of the club had pricked her interest. She seemed to know where he was talking about.

"You know it?"

"We're aware of the place."

"Well?"

Nick didn't understand. Before, she had been desperate for any kind of information, any shred of detail that would push the case forward, but now she seemed to be shrugging him off.

"You have no intention of following this up, have you?"

"I'll look into it, Nick."

The phone went dead as she hung up.

Bonita looked across at Miles and smiled. He shook his head, already well aware what it was she was thinking.

"No way. It's too dangerous."

"You're only saying that because you're married to me. If it was you, you'd be in there like a shot. This is the perfect opportunity. I can just go in and claim I'm following up a lead."

Miles stood and moved over to the window. He didn't like the idea one bit, but they had spent all morning trying to find a way into the place. The car sitting outside monitored the comings and goings from the club but it didn't tell them what, if anything, was going on inside. Bonita was correct in what she said: if it was him he'd already be on his way.

"We need to know if he's inside. Chances are they've already spotted the car. He isn't going to walk out and let us follow him just like that."

He knew she was right.

"OK, but I'm coming with you."

"Can't risk me taking all the glory, I suppose."

A man stood on Nick's doorstep. Nick had not heard him approach the door; he must have gained access to the building and come up the stairs quietly. As Nick looked at him through the spy hole, the man furtively looked back down the stairs, his face a mixture of anxiety and concern. He was middle-aged and unshaven, his thinning hair scraped back with sweat. Nick thought at first that he had been discovered talking to the police and this was his comeuppance, but the man had knocked. The 'Missing Man' could come in whenever he wanted to. Door and walls seemed to be no barrier to him. He had already done it once; knocking was not his style.

Nick opened the door a crack and was about to ask for some identification when the man pushed, sending Nick sprawling to the floor with a shout.

The man stepped inside and looked about quickly before shutting the door behind him.

"Shut up," he muttered. "You trying to wake up the whole building?"

From his prone position Nick rounded a kick at the man's ankle.

If anyone was going to rob or murder him he decided he was not going down without a fight.

"Fuck off."

The man kicked back but made no further advance.

"You on your own?"

Nick wanted to lie but he knew the man would soon check and it might result in yet another kick.

He stood above Nick; a dirty raincoat flapped open revealing jeans and a scruffy white shirt. He must have been hot and appeared to be breathing heavily. He was a parody of a private detective, all tobacco smoke and whisky-drinking bluff. The only thing missing was the fedora. He sniffed the air before stepping over Nick and heading down the corridor.

Nick lay on the floor and watched him go. The man seemed intent on leaving him to his own devices and he pondered briefly whether to run away or at least try calling for help. He heard a tap running in the kitchen. Throwing caution to the wind he pulled himself up and followed the sound.

He stood in the middle of the living room taking a long slow drink from a glass of water he had helped himself to. Assuming he was not a private eye who had got lost, the only other explanation was that he was a homeless person who used the unorthodox method of housebreaking to get some loose change. Nick felt in his hip pocket for what money he had and pulled it out. He proffered it to the man.

"What's that?" he asked, placing the glass on a table and squinting at the hand holding the coins.

"It's all I have. You can take the DVD player as well."

The man scoffed.

"Put your money away; I'm not here to rob you. The name's Michael."

He held out a hand and took a couple of steps forward. Nick shied away, unsure what the crazy man might do next.

He let out a sigh before getting closer and grabbing hold of

Nick's hand.

"It's called shaking. I'm Michael, you're Nick. Introductions complete. Do you know there's an unmarked police car parked outside your front door?"

Nick didn't. Beltran had not mentioned leaving behind a watch. He wondered if he could get downstairs and alert them to the intruder.

The man moved over to the window and nodded at the street below. He beckoned for Nick to join him. Looking down, the man pointed to a dark blue saloon car.

"They're watching you, which means they probably suspect you of getting rid of your girlfriend."

Nick stepped back, weary of the stranger who already knew more about him than he had been prepared to tell.

"Who are you?"

Michael didn't turn, keeping his back to Nick while he looked out over the street.

"I'm the man who's gonna explain to you what in hell's name's been going on."

He turned slowly and grinned. It was wide and slightly dangerous-looking, too full of crazy knowledge.

"Now, if I've got this right I'd say your girlfriend's disappeared, only now no one can remember you having a girlfriend. All trace of her has vanished, leaving you not knowing whether you've gone mad or not. You feel like you've entered some kind of other world where everything you thought was correct has suddenly stopped making sense. Stop me if any of this rings even the slightest bit true."

"You know where she is?"

"No." Michael went quiet as if really sorry that he could not give this information. The fact that he did not know the answer pained him. He shook his head as if coming to terms with the fact for the very first time. "No, I don't know where she is, but I know she's alive."

"How? How can you know?"

Michael looked up, as if knocked out of his reverie by the demand.

"All in good time. What I want you to know is that you're not alone. You're far from alone."

Nick moved away from the window and sat down. He looked at the man, who continued to smile but now less aggressively; he now looked only tired. Tired and drawn, as if coming here and getting inside the flat had taken all his energy and now his quest was at last over.

Now that Nick really looked at the intruder he noted that he was not quite so frightening. He was a little rotund around the middle and his face, though covered by a day's growth of stubble, was homely, worn down, a lived-in face. He had kind eyes, a little small, but kind.

"How do you know?"

Nick heard his voice wobble, the knowledge that Natalie was still alive overwhelming him.

"Because, wherever she is, my daughter is with her. A daughter that my wife says was never born, but I know she's mistaken, because I watched that little girl grow up day after day, year after year. You don't get those memories from a bump on the head or from the diagnosis of some psychologist. You have them because they are real and these things happened."

"What was her name?"

"Deborah."

Nick made a drink and put out some food for Michael who ate with gusto. He drank tea, thick and strong, with only a spot of milk, a leftover he said from his days driving trucks. Between biscuits that were popped into his mouth almost whole, Michael explained his loss and his quest to find others like himself.

"How did you find me?"

"I read the papers, I check the internet, I listen to police 'chatter'.

Your missing person investigation has created quite a bit of noise on the radio. Seems the police thought at first you were just a nutter, but now you've been linked with these 'Missing Man' murders. You're very popular at the moment. I don't think the police outside are for your protection. I think more likely they're there to make sure you don't disappear."

"They suspect me?"

"Yes. The police have a bit of a problem with these cases. You're being labelled a murderer, you think that's bad? You should have heard what they called me. Look, you're not alone and I want you to meet with someone."

"Who?"

"A doctor."

"I thought you said you didn't believe in all that."

"I don't, but there's a woman at the uni who's been looking into all these disappearances. She wants to meet with you."

The way he asked it became more of a plea than a request. As if Nick's visit would accomplish something of great importance to him.

"You make it sound like there have been lots of these events."

"There's been a few. In time you might get to meet the others."

"What does this doctor want?"

"She just wants to talk to you, that's all."

He fished inside his coat and pulled out a scrap of paper. It held a name and a telephone number.

"It's up to you to call, but believe me it'll be worth it. If you do, maybe we can talk some more."

He stood up and looked about the flat.

"I don't suppose there's a back way out of here?"

"You could go down to the car park and out that way."

Michael nodded. "We'll speak again."

He left. Nick didn't show him to the door. He knew his way out.

Hearing the door shut, Nick let out a sigh of relief. The danger past, he felt he could breathe again. Not that Michael had given any indication of being a threat. He was a little unorthodox in his way of approaching people and only put the boot in after Nick had attempted to stop him. There was something almost sad about him, as if it were him reaching out for Nick's help rather than the other way around. He had sounded desperate, but then if it led to information about Natalie, all the better. Time was becoming short.

He looked at the piece of paper and the number before picking up the phone and dialling.

Miles had tried several times to talk her out of going and letting him follow up the lead on his own. She knew he was just being protective, but it had eventually begun to annoy her until she had snapped and retaliated by calling him a sexist pig. He had apologised, but the air between them in the car remained silent until they had arrived at their destination. She knew he was just trying to be protective, but sometimes she found his caring nature grated on her. She knew she had made mistakes in the past, become too personally involved, but she had learned the difference and Miles needed to accept that.

They had decided to go during daylight, before the bar opened up for the day, on the understanding that the club would be empty of customers and so they would be less likely to risk an incident. They hoped that a manager or member of staff would understand the circumstances and perhaps give something away. A gesture was all that was required and a few hints about the revoking of licences would probably be more than enough of a push to get the management talking.

They drove through the early afternoon traffic, thinned out now that the lunch hour was over. Crowds still covered the pavements, a wave of humanity that appeared listless with no place to go, the heat of the day already beginning to irritate them to distraction. There were too many people, the multitude swollen by those who had phoned in to work faking sick or had bunked off school.

They swung past Nick Stuart's flat and spoke briefly to the officer on watch. There had been little action with Nick keeping to his apartment, since the interview with his agent and a producer at a hotel earlier that day. It seemed that a job offer had come his way. Perhaps he was still unaware of the seriousness of the situation he was in, certainly it looked as if he was trying to find a way out of his mess and leave the city behind. If he decided to run they would have to arrest him.

Miles noted that from Nick's flat to the club would probably take less than ten minutes on foot. The two places were close to each other, worlds apart as neighbourhoods, the haves and have-nots sitting side by side, rich and poor coexisting. They wanted to ignore each other, but each area impacted on the next, so they tolerated each other as much as possible. Had Nick decided to take a wrong turn into the other world that coexisted with his own? Perhaps the missing girls had paid the price for that transgression.

Returning to the car they drove the remaining distance and passed the club at a slow crawl. No lights were on and little movement could be seen. They parked on a side street. Stepping out of the car, glass crunched underneath Bonita's shoe; it looked like windscreen material. Miles looked up and down the street; it was empty but he noted a curtain twitch at a house across from them. The car with its clean lines and highly polished body looked out of place in this neighbourhood. It was too new, too big and looked powerful next to the late models and rusting buckets that had been left by the curb. Miles pulled out a police card to place in the window but Bonita shook her head at his decision. That might only provoke a bad reaction here.

They made their way back to the road and the building that contained the club. Litter had blown up tight against its dirty white walls, smashed beer bottles and rusting cans sought shelter in the shadow of the decaying building. This place had been used by many businesses in the past. There had been a window that faced out onto the street, a shopfront perhaps, back when the area had not fallen on such hard times, a local shop saving people the walk into the city. It had long ago been bricked in and the wall was now covered in thick, sharp concrete, once bright but now ingrained with dirt, the only suggestion of its original function a slight indentation where the window sill had once been. There was further evidence of a plumber having used the place, a tatty sign up on a wall, too high for anyone to bother removing.

They ignored the front door which was closed, a snaking chain linking the handles and protected with an oversized padlock. Walking through a gate and down a side passage, some of the factory history was still visible with pipes and covered chutes in the wall. They reached a smaller glass door and tried the bell. Bonita didn't expect anyone to answer and thought they might have to knock and show their badges to gain access, so was surprised when she heard bolts being pulled back and the door being opened by an old woman who looked at her with a quizzical expression.

Bonita dug in her pocket and pulled out identification. Miles had his ready.

"Police. We're investigating a missing person case. Can we come in and look around?"

The woman's face turned into a scowl as she examined the badges closely and carefully compared the photos with the faces above.

"S'pose," she added, and shuffled into the dim interior.

They stepped inside. The dual use of the building seemed to be continuing. There was a definite smell of alcohol in the air accompanied by nicotine, plus she noticed several sticky glass marks on a Formica table top. But this contrasted with the obvious sound of an exercise class going on in the background; music and the rhythmic thud of feet moving in time, making the floor shake.

The old woman, white hair incongruous against her dark wrinkled skin, had picked up a broom and was attempting to clean the tatty floor. It was having little effect. Assuming that the woman had no desire to be interrupted and would be unable to give them much in the way of information, they passed her and the little booth that had been turned into a reception area and entered through a door into the main part of the building.

Miles moved over to a set of doors and looked in, but found nothing more shocking than a couple of toilets that smelt of bleach and a room used as a store cupboard for cleaning products.

Bonita entered the small hall. At the far end was a raised stage above which a large wooden crucifix had been screwed. In front of a class of about ten pensioners, done up in baggy trousers and sweatshirts, a young girl in a leotard attempted to conduct a slow exercise class. No one could keep up with her, resulting in much laughter and encouraging grimaces on the old faces of those taking part.

The building seemed to be used as a day centre; there was a long pin board down one wall to which had been stuck posters advertising all sorts of activities and days out. There was a hatch in the wall, behind which was a kitchen area. Above the hatch she could just make out the licence permitting the place the right to sell alcohol.

She could see someone moving about inside the kitchen and moved over as the pensioners finished their energetic shuffling.

The kitchen was sparse, a tea urn and a few glass-fronted fridges, which a skinny guy was filling with bottles of beer, a row of optics above his head. The fire escape was open and a van was drawn up, its back doors open, revealing boxes of branded drink. A man leaned against the van puffing on a cigarette and nodding his head in time to the music, but unwilling to help in the unloading.

The skinny guy, realising someone was behind him, turned and grinned up at Beltran. He had a thin face with the beginnings of a ragged ginger beard on his chin.

She flashed her badge again and the guy's face fell through

the floor.

He looked round at the van owner, who noticed the look of concern and quickly bolted the back doors of the van, sat in the driving seat and started the engine. As it pulled away Bonita noted the number plate. It seemed that whatever was inside, police scrutiny was not welcome.

"Can I help you?" Ginger man asked as he stood up, his grin having vanished.

"I'm looking for Imamu Ferreira."

He shook his head like the name meant nothing.

"He drinks here at night."

"Lots of people come here."

Bonita could tell the man had no desire to talk with the police. He tried to look everywhere but at her face. He resumed stocking the fridge but was careful to turn the name of the beer away from her.

She thought briefly about getting a little heavy with him but at this stage she didn't want Ferreira making a run for it. He had a habit of disappearing when the police came calling. She was sure that, by just being here, her presence would be reported to him sooner rather than later.

"Tell him I'm looking for him," she added as she placed a card with a contact number down on the bar. She didn't expect he would ring, she didn't even expect the card to get to him.

The man nodded.

Miles joined her by the hatch and gave the man by the fridge a hard stare.

"The woman running the class says she just rents space from the management. She doesn't know our man."

He turned to Ginger, who was now even more of a jitter, his hands visibly shaking as he continued to stack the bottles. They clinked as he touched them.

"Have you heard of a man called Nick Stuart?"

He shook his head, his voice too quiet to be heard.

"Who's the manager of this place? Who's in charge?"

"I dunno. I just look after the bar. The society pays me in cash."

"The society?"

"Yeah, the group who look after the place – the Reverend."

"You'll need to get him to contact us."

The man nodded.

They returned to looking around the place but found nothing of interest. Any hopes of finding hidden basements or locked rooms were dashed. The place just appeared to be a slightly run-down community centre that at night hosted a bar for the more disenfranchised in the community. While they were convinced drugs, weapons and illicit goods probably came through the place, that had more to do with the individuals than the building. Close this place down and the trouble would just hide better next time; it would dig further into the dirt of the city.

"There's nothing here," commented Miles.

"What were you expecting?"

"I don't know. Anything, something."

Bonita's mobile began to chirrup. She answered, listening to the voice that sounded excited.

"We'll be back as soon as we can."

She closed the mobile, her face a mask of concern.

"This just gets weirder. An old face has turned up at Nick Stuart's. Seems he's hanging out with a known paedophile now."

He had only ever seen inside a psychologist's office on television, normally on American shows. It seemed to be a mark of success; the actor dropping the name of his shrink into everyday conversation, obsessing over the effects the mind can have on their actions and health, their neurosis. It was funny, always done for a joke or a quick laugh, but that was not the reality of twisted minds and disillusionment.

To his father, going to the doctor's was seen as a weakness; a shrink, therefore implying some Achilles' heel of the brain. Mental illness was not an affliction to boast about; state the name of your shrink on a bus and the rest of society edges surreptitiously away. Protecting themselves in case the 'nutter' has just been released back into society, damaged goods waiting for a cure to take hold.

However with Nick's ideas being limited to both the little and big screens, he was disillusioned enough to expect plush offices with lots of books and mahogany furniture. What he got was a crappy little workplace in a hidden part of the university complex that smelt of damp and dirty ashtrays. Backing onto the incinerators, there was a distinct burnt smell in the air that had permeated into the fabric of the waiting area. The room was nothing more than a small antechamber, cramped, with a plastic chair and a potted fern that was yellow with age. A small occasional table had the words 'Are you lost?' carved into its top, a statement made in jest by a past patient who had never been found.

He sat reading the local paper. It was not something he normally looked at, but now he read any paper he could find, scanning the headlines for any mention of a body or a sighting of his lost love. But as usual there was no news, just the continual scare stories of a city descending into violence and the increasing petty crimes of the disenfranchised. The editorial commented on the police's inability to cope with the task and their lack of direction, particularly in the investigation of the 'Missing Man', the real life horror story that infected the street.

Someone was pacing down the corridor towards him. He could hear the shuffle of their sensible shoes on the polished floor, a rasp of air followed by the crunch of a heel. A large woman dressed from head to toe in purple came into view. She looked down on him as he sat in the chair, his knees braced in front of him as if he were taking a crap. Her arms were full of papers which she shifted slightly as she tried to examine a wristwatch.

"Mr Stuart? Shit – I forgot. Sorry."

The voice was a warm Scottish accent that made her sound better suited to running a small boarding house and offering up afternoon tea than to probing into the minds and unconscious of the slightly disturbed.

She pushed past him, her bulk brushing against his knees as she kicked a door open and walked into the office.

"Doctor Muldoon?" he asked as she moved out of the way and allowed him to stand.

"Call me Anne. I don't go in for all that title stuff, unlike others in this place."

She indicated that he should go into the office and pointed towards a chair at an angle to her own desk.

"Just shove that stuff on the floor. You don't mind if I have a fag, do you? I'm gasping."

She had already lit up by this point so asking was irrelevant. Opening a small window she blew her first drag outside, the cloud billowing from her in an exaggerated exhalation.

"It's fine to smoke in here as long as the cigarette Nazis don't catch you."

"I don't smoke."

She turned to look at him and shrugged, her neck briefly disappearing into her double chin.

"Whatever floats your boat."

She took another long draw.

With her back turned, Nick took a chance to look her over. She was dressed in a skirt that seemed tired of life, a leftover from the seventies that she had probably kept in the hope it would come back into fashion. Her clothes were faded in places, the top cut into gypsy lines, the material cheap tie-dye bought at an open air festival. Her messy yellow hair was pulled back and tied into a bun; the few stray hairs that escaped were grey and frizzy. They stood on end and floated in the light breeze.

"I know your dad, of course."

She said the last part to herself as she flicked out some ash from the end of her cigarette. Taking a couple more drags she blunted it on the windowsill before throwing the butt out onto a patch of gravel that, hidden from the view of the cleaners, was full of similar dog ends. She turned and sat.

"My father will be pleased I came, if nothing else. He wanted me to see a specialist. I guess you're one of those."

Anne shrugged as if the compliment meant nothing. "I'm a psychiatrist by training. Missing persons is something of a hobby of mine."

She looked at him, a gaze of surprising intensity that left him feeling like a prize exhibit in a cheap raffle. Her lips were screwed up and pursed as she made a funny slurping noise. Nick couldn't tell whether she was mulling over an opening gambit or she had a bad case of wind. Her face finally relaxed and she spoke, her voice deeper as she took on the mantle of her chosen profession.

"So why are you here? What do you hope to get out of this session?"

He didn't know how to answer. What did he hope to get from being here, from opening up to a stranger and admitting that his life was descending into madness? How could this overweight middle-aged woman begin to find a person who never existed, restore her to life and then help to patch up their relationship?

"Answers; I just want some answers to what has happened."

She nodded as if that was obvious.

"Michael has filled me in on the details and I've spoken to Charles. Sort of. He finds it hard to talk about such things. He's such a rational man."

She spoke as if she knew him in a more profound way than just a work colleague. He had never thought of his dad having relationships other than that with his mother, his deceased wife. He never spoke of anyone outside his close circle of old friends and immediate family. Nick briefly had an image of his dad, nestling his head between this fat woman's large breasts. The idea slightly repulsed him.

"Dad's not the problem. The police don't believe me. The officer in charge, Beltran, she thinks I made Natalie up."

"Really?"

She seemed honestly shocked by the idea that the police would give him such short shrift. Nick assumed she was playing to his better instincts, opening him up, permitting him to crack apart his chest and bare his heart so that she might examine its numerous scars.

"And did you make her up?"

Nick looked at her full in the face. He wanted her to believe him.

"Of course not!"

The idea made him angry.

"But you came to see me anyway?"

"This man, Michael, said I should. But I don't see how you can help."

He wanted to make her understand that he was beginning to tire of the whole episode. Though he was careful, he didn't want to completely alienate her, aware that if he could make Anne believe then she could work on Beltran. If he could get a doctor's note proving he was not mad then perhaps the police would have to take him a little more seriously.

"I know the story sounds crazy but I didn't just make up the last six months of my life or the fact that I was living with Natalie. I can describe her in perfect detail. She either left in the night or..."

Anne grabbed at a pile of papers from a buff folder and pretended to read.

"It's not that I don't believe you, it's just that as a mind doctor I can only operate within certain definite rules. I imagine the police have the same problems. I think your missing person's case falls outside of that quarter. There's not much in the way of clues. The police like clues and their only lead is you. Did you kill her?"

She said it calmly. Almost as a matter of fact, as if Nick being a murderer was of little consequence to her. It simply meant she could dismiss him and get on with some other work. The case would have been solved. Nick didn't know how to respond and sat, shamefaced that he could not think of a suitable riposte.

"Did you chop her into bits and get rid of the body? Because that's what most people will think happened to her. It rarely does, but people like to believe it anyway. Nothing like a grisly murder to get the locals interested."

"She just vanished." His response sounded vacant and dull.

"I thought so. You don't look the type to own a hatchet, never mind know how to use one."

Nick supposed that was a compliment.

"Michael thinks you're like him. He's been following your story closely but even after all this time he still loves the black and white approach. Sometimes black and white doesn't tell you what's going on. When I take off my doctor's hat I much prefer the grey bits. I want you to tell me about Natalie and the morning you woke up."

Nick recounted the story as best as he could. He wanted to recapture the past and bring the events to life. Anne asked the sort of questions the police were not interested in. The colour of the curtains, the height of the bed, how soft the pillows were, did the room smell. He told her everything, the fact that he was naked and sweaty, the feeling of scorched alcohol in his head, the room smelling of lavender.

After he had finished she sat back in her chair, her hands forming a steeple over her ample chest. Her face set into a mask of concentration as she assimilated the details of his story.

"Michael came to me with a similar tale several years ago. A loved one that disappears leaving no trace but in the mind of the people who knew her. He lost his daughter. The police investigated and branded him a lunatic with paedophilic tendencies. It nearly crushed him. If it was not for his firm belief that his daughter was still very much alive I think he would have killed himself. I can't say I have all the answers, but you are not alone in this. I want you to meet with some friends of mine; a group of people who have had similar experiences. Are you free this evening?"

"What sort of group?"

He had a vision, a collection of seriously disturbed individuals who sat rocking slightly in their seats before partaking of a group hug. He didn't want to get too close to the seriously disturbed, their presence clawing at him, dragging him down deeper, bringing him home to the fold.

"All of them have had loved ones disappear and like you they all have the problem that no one believes these missing people existed. It's an, as of yet, unexplained phenomenon. They come from all over the country once a month to discuss any issues and help each other. It's kind of a support network, kind of a social gathering. I normally supply the wine and come along for a chat. I enjoy their company."

The fact that there were people who had experienced the same as him was in many ways a disappointment. It made his problem seem almost common; a casual happening that did not warrant the police's time or energy. It made him feel less unique.

"Phenomenon? I don't believe in UFOs or anything like that."

"I don't think anyone's brought up little green men. I just use the term for the want of anything better. I'm sure there's some logical explanation. There normally is. We just don't know what it is yet."

That seemed a good rationalization to Nick. "Perhaps we're all a little bit disturbed?"

"No." She dismissed the idea with surprising intensity, her double chin wobbling slightly as she shook her head vehemently. "I've interviewed all of these people and had fellow psychologists submit similar reports. They all believe these loved ones are real, in the same way you think of Natalie as part of your life. None of them are what we would term disturbed or prone to psychotic episodes – except for Eric, bless him."

Anne seemed adamant in her beliefs. Nick could tell she didn't like him referring to her work in the same vein as the sort of people who saw angels or fairies. This was serious to her.

"Obviously it's up to you if you come or not. I won't force you, but I think you'll find it useful."

Nick knew he was going to go and meet with them. She didn't need to ask. Anything was better than the feelings of displacement that currently plagued him. Maybe a member of the group would offer up a nugget of detail that he could use in his own search. What he didn't want to do was meet with individuals who had 'given up' – that would be too depressing. If they were going to help, then fine; if not, he could leave them behind. He needed to stay focused.

"Will you come?"

"Yes."

"Good. We're meeting in the student bar, they have a room upstairs that we can use afterwards. Can you be there about nine?"

"Of course. What about us?"

"Us?"

"I need the police to carry on looking for Natalie. They have no choice if you say I'm sane."

Anne bit her bottom lip and looked bashful.

"Our meeting isn't official – I imagine the police are still looking into your case. They probably think you're hiding something or even that you got rid of Natalie, but they would never stop looking. It's not in their nature."

"Detective Beltran wants to believe me but I think her colleagues are telling her to stay away."

Anne continued to gnaw at her bottom lip before sitting back in her chair. Something concerned her. She paused before continuing.

"I've met this Bonita Beltran before; she's tenacious and clever. I'm sure she's doing all she can to help. But be careful – she has a nasty habit of making assumptions. They all do."

Nick was surprised.

"What do you know about her?"

"I met her several years ago. She was investigating the

disappearance of Michael's daughter, Deborah Wheen. The police had given up on the case but reopened it with gusto after the body of a child was found in woodland near the Wheens's home. She led the original investigation and so was heavily involved when the body was found. The problem was that according to Wheen's wife, family and friends, they never had a child called Deborah. Beltran got it into her head that Wheen was perhaps a paedophile who had murdered a child and transposed the idea onto the imaginary daughter. A cry for help that she exploited to try and get a confession out of Michael."

"You can't hide having a daughter from your own wife – that's impossible."

Anne raised an eyebrow as Nick realised that what he had just said placed his own mystery on an equal footing.

"He's convinced his daughter exists. You can make up your own mind tonight; he'll be coming. He never misses one of our little gatherings."

Nick thought about Michael trying to prove to his own family that he had a daughter, the anguish and pain that must have caused him. The horror of a child disappeared was bad enough, but for his own wife to deny her existence ensuring that his grief was not shared, that would have been terrible.

"But there would be photos to prove she existed, surely?"

Nick winced again as he heard the naivety of his question.

"There were no photos in the house, though Wheen was convinced his wife had taken plenty over the years. Sound familiar?"

"Does Beltran only do missing persons?"

"Bonita? She sort of got fascinated by them back in New Zealand. Something to do with a body that she was trying to find a home for. I don't think she ever found out who that was. It's become a bit of a personal crusade of hers ever since. She finds the subjects in the group as fascinating as I do, the few searching for their lost souls."

Lost souls. The term resonated.

It had taken fewer than three hours' work with a couple of methadone addicted informers, the ripping up of two arrest warrants and one black eye to work out the reason the ginger man from the bar had been so shaken by the appearance of two detectives. The beer he had been loading into the fridges had been identified as hooky, stolen goods that had disappeared from another city bar a few weeks earlier. Their superior wanted to go in and arrest the manager but Miles had requested that they hang back or at least wait until Ferreira put in another appearance. With a bit of luck the stolen goods might come in handy as a tool of leverage. If not, if nothing came to pass, they could always arrest the manager and shut the place down for a while.

A packet was thrown onto Bonita's desk, a Manila envelope. She opened it but was already sure she knew what it would hold. It was the photos from that day's surveillance. Three pictures, in slightly fuzzy black and white, showed a man in a brown overcoat walking quickly with his head bent forward and his collar pulled up. On one photo he stopped and looked about, perhaps conscious that he was being watched, which allowed the concealed photographer to capture his features full on.

There was no mistaking him. He might have aged since she had last set eyes on him, his face puffy and lined from bad living and poor diet, but it was undeniably Michael Wheen. She had been wrong to dismiss the similarities to the Wheen case earlier in her investigation; there were too many comparisons for her not to have gone back to the case notes and reread the tawdry affair. She hadn't wanted to be reminded of her past failure and that had probably stayed her hand.

She felt a presence behind her as a shadow passed over the picture. She spoke.

"Nick, Michael and Ferreira, a stranger trio you could not invent. They come from three completely different demographics that in theory should mix like oil and water. So what have they got in common?"

Miles looked over her shoulder. He was well aware of who Michael was, his wife having explained the case to him a thousand times. He didn't think she had been wrong in her assumptions; they would have been the same ones he made but he thought she had approached the case from the wrong angle. If he had been in charge, Michael Wheen would now be in the serious offenders' wing of some jail getting a rough time from his fellow inmates. He had not of course made this known to Bonita.

"Perhaps we've been approaching this having made a wrong assumption. Perhaps it's not one man we're after, but a gang. It would explain how this 'Missing Man' disappears so successfully. One of them causes a distraction while the girl is snatched. Two men working together could easily overpower an intended victim. One could look after the transportation while another silences the girl in the back."

"But why? There's no motive."

"There doesn't have to be. You thought previously that Michael might be a paedophile. The victims would just be satisfying a want. Perhaps he's moved on from little kids and is some kind of young female predator now."

"Then why would Nick make up the abduction of his own girlfriend?"

Miles shrugged. "A cry for help?"

"It all seems so implausible."

Miles agreed.

Bonita looked over the information again. The club seemed to be a dead end. There were no hidden bodies in there. The place was too public, their hope of finding a den of iniquity had been dashed when she saw the exercise class. It was nothing more than a community centre, and far too busy for anyone to use it as a possible hiding place.

The 'Missing Man' had to have some kind of holding area for the girls. It would be too risky driving around all night with an unwilling victim in a van; someone might hear something or report it in as suspicious. As soon as the girls were taken he must have taken them to a place of seclusion, somewhere remote or soundproof that would allow him to indulge in whatever his fantasies consisted of. If they could find this scene of captivity, the place used by the 'Missing Man' for the detention of the girls, then they might find some clue that would shed light on his identity and perhaps link these men.

Ferreira had still not raised his pock-marked head into view and it remained highly improbable that he would simply step out into the daylight for all to see. The club would remain under surveillance until he reappeared, but she was certain that it was not a crime scene. Michael would need to be followed; perhaps that might provide some clues. He probably still lived in the city and she assumed he had a place close by. If he was the missing link they would soon have the chance to delve deeper into his life. That only left Nick, and his apartment had been searched twice and nothing found but the small bloodstains outside his front door.

She considered the dank building he lived in with its ramshackle central staircase and the decrepit lift shaft that screamed as if in pain. The smell of the place filled her senses as she pondered its shadows and mysteries.

"Nick's apartment block is old and in a bit of a mess. The management group appears to have given up looking after the place, probably hoping it will fall down. I wouldn't be surprised if it contained buried places in which you could hide things."

Miles nodded, encouraged by the idea.

"I'll arrange the paperwork."

Friday 16th September 2005

The car hummed lazily to itself, a purr of power drummed out of the cylinders with maximum ease. The car had been a perk of the new job, one of the many things that had attracted her, that and the stock options, pension rights and yearly bonus. She had never had a decent car in her life; everything prior to this one had been second-hand or bought off her mum. They were small engine vehicles with just enough care left in them to pass an MOT. She had owned several, all similar shades of mottled brown or faded red. This car was something different. It was powerful; it took only the slightest twitch of her foot to make it lurch forward as if she were on an uncontrollable fairground ride. She knew it was fast as she had once opened the car up on a quiet stretch of road. She had to stop for a few minutes afterwards to get her breath back; she'd been holding onto it for the whole exhilarating ride. She never told any of her friends or Eric about her desire for speed. It was her secret – one of many. The car was British racing green and she loved it.

She had stayed off the motorway on the way back home. She was not expected back in the office today and she wanted to be hard to find. She manoeuvred the car towards the quiet road that criss-crossed the moor; it would take her longer this way, but she wanted to drive. The low hum and empty view helped to calm her mind as she mulled over her predicament and what manoeuvre she was likely to make next.

That was how she thought of things now, the language of her career permeating into her everyday life. She put plans into action, monitored her goals and made damn sure that all possible risk was mitigated. Of course it hadn't always been like that. She had given up on a promising degree course when she met Eric, happy to stay at home and get a job at the local cash and carry. They had moved in together; he already owned a small new build on a scrubby plot of land in the suburbs. He had been everything to her back then, and she had never thought to question her life or the restrictions he imposed on her.

It had been small things to start with: asking her not to go out with her friends quite so much; money, he assured her, being the reason. Then he stopped allowing her access to his beaten-up old Ford, restricting her visits to see family or to get out of town. Soon after, the holidays to Cornwall ended and he refused to replace her mobile phone when the old one broke. Could she help herself that, despite it all, she had still loved him and wanted to be with him? And it could have been so much worse. He never beat her, or shouted (he was too small himself to cause any real harm), he never refused her small amounts of money and he did most of the housework, as he preferred it done in a distinct way.

Now she found it all creepy. The way he never said anything but just watched her with those dull, deep-set piggy eyes, that slack jaw, and that hangdog expression. She hated it when he came up behind her and, unaware of his presence, she would suddenly feel a hand stroking her hair or slipping round her waist. She didn't like it that she found her clothes and underwear neatly arranged in piles, folded and smoothed by his hands, but worst of all was the sex, and the way he asked her not to look at him, to turn her head away, keep still and close her eyes.

Luckily her career, as she now thought of it, had changed her life. The cash and carry had closed down, forcing her to get a new job. She had joined a temping agency and soon found herself working for a large insurance company. She had spent the first year filling in the same form with claim information but found that she enjoyed the work and was a natural at picking up the language of the office and the politics of the company, and she remembered the names of the bosses. Someone higher up must have been watching because within a year she had a permanent contract and was moved on to more demanding tasks, a role in which she excelled. Only last year a job had come up as an analyst, and she had been urged to put her name forward, shocked and surprised when she was offered the position.

Things started to change in quick succession from then on. With the job came a package and a need to be out on the road, meeting clients and sometimes staying away. She became part of team of men and women who respected her thoughts and input. The women became friends and took her out for cocktails or dinner in expensive restaurants. The men flirted with her, inviting her after work to the pub, eager to sit next to her in meetings.

Eric responded badly, but she found that she didn't want to spend so much time with him anymore. She wanted to be out and, since her salary far outstripped his, there was little he could say or demand. This man, her husband, became a shadow haunting her life. She started to despise him, wishing that he would leave her alone and stay away. He didn't suit her anymore. He was old-fashioned, shabby in his badly cut trousers and thin white shirt bought cheap from a supermarket. He was unable to communicate with others, petty and sad. She had outgrown him.

The final straw had been when she met Adiel. He worked the bar at a nightclub she had visited with the girls from work. He was sleek and handsome, with a winning smile and an infectious laugh. She had spoken to him and he had responded to her, nodding in agreement while he poured her drink, his voice deep and seeming to resonate within her. She found herself looking on this well toned black man in a way that made her blush. She thought of him touching her in places that made her itch in a most pleasing way.

He had looked at her with eyes deep and as unfathomable as the darkest of hidden pools. She had almost flinched away but was drawn forth to a flicker of light, a flame within their centre and she saw within them the knowledge of what could be, what was missing from her life, what she most desired.

She found herself returning the following week, his face etched into her mind. She longed to see him and it was as if he was waiting for her. They had spoken at length, her propped up on a bar stool, ignoring her friends on the dance floor, him serving at the bar but talking, always talking. She found herself telling him things, personal details about her life, to which he nodded solemnly. She knew he understood and before she could stop herself, she had started to dream and he had encouraged her, telling her it was possible, all was possible; all she had to do was ask.

So that was her dilemma – she wanted out of her marriage with Eric. She wanted to leave him far behind and move on and up. She needed a new life, a new beginning, excitement and a love that was all-encompassing. She remembered leaning into Adiel and asking for it all and she remembered his whispered breath against her ear, hot and lush.

"All you have to do is ask. You can have it all if you so wish."

The sun was hanging low in the sky but she was heading east so it did not cause too much discomfort unless she looked in the rear-view mirror. The shadow of her car gambolled in front of her, always a fraction of a second ahead, a ghost car that raced and dared her to go faster.

The foliage was dark and matted from this morning's rain. Where the sun played across it the bracken became copper in colour. She could smell the gorse coming through the air-conditioning system; it smelt sweet, unsullied. The road twisted in wide arcs through the rusty landscape, a man-made sliver of reclaimed earth that snaked towards civilisation. She liked the road; you could see what was coming but there were still enough hidden dips to make it interesting.

The car nosed around a bend, slipping onto the wrong side of the white line as she refused to apply the brakes too much and risk slowing. Safely round, she slipped the car up a gear and returned to her careful cruise. Up ahead she could see another vehicle parked by the side of the road. She slowed in case it was the police.

Getting closer she noticed it was a van, white in colour, the sort used for setting speed traps. She applied the brakes even further and dropped a notch below the speed limit, anxious not to end up with any speeding fine or points on her licence. The last thing she wanted was to get her licence revoked, stopping her from doing her job and, even worse, marooning her at home before she had time to get out.

A man stepped from behind the vehicle into the middle of the road and held up his hand. The road was not very wide and unless she ran him over there was no way around. She slowed the car and eyed him cautiously. She left the motor running but made a grab for her mobile, placing it in her lap with a finger hovering over the call button just in case.

He was squat, small; his limbs looked diminutive in relation to his body, as if a child had drawn him, and he had been brought to life by some spell. He wore a uniform of dark blue. It was similar to that worn by the police, but without the epaulettes, without any markings. He waved at her and smiled. She felt nervous.

She hit the button and let the electric window down halfway.

"What's the matter?"

He moved out of the road and came round to her side. He was the same height as the car so didn't need to bend.

"Sorry to have stopped you, but I've got a flat and need to change the tyre."

He had an American accent, a soft twang to his words. He came from the southern states.

She wondered what to do. He didn't look threatening; in truth even despite his deformity she felt some kind of attraction to him. It was as if she could see beyond his appearance. She knew he was a good man. Yet, something at the back of her mind told her to be careful. She looked in the rear-view mirror; the road was empty.

She indicated she needed to pull the car to the side of the road. He stood back and let her. Getting out she kept hold of her mobile, slipping it into an easy-to-reach pocket.

"I don't know how much use I'll be to you. I've never changed a wheel," she admitted as he rolled a tyre from the back of the van, leaving one of the doors wide open.

"That's OK; I only need to borrow your spanner."

Did she have a spanner? She wasn't sure. There was a tool kit that came with the car but she had never looked inside it. If anything was ever wrong with the machine she took it into the garage and they fixed it.

He moved over to the back of the car.

"Would ya pop the trunk?" he asked in his singsong accent.

She pressed the key fob and the lock of the boot clunked. The lid slid open smoothly. The man looked inside and opened the tool box.

"Nice car," he added as he selected a large tool from the set.

She watched in mute fascination as he moved back to the van and started to work on the nuts of a tyre.

Did she know him? He was terribly familiar to her. She felt completely relaxed in his company, safe even. She liked watching him work. His short arms bulged with muscles. He might be small but he was strong and masculine, protective and reassuring.

She moved over to help and passed the back of the van. The inside was done up for living in. There was a stove and fridge, a small television and two cots. On the smaller of the two makeshift beds lay a sleeping child.

As the man placed a jack under the car and started to pump, the small girl woke up. She yawned and looked about as if in a daze. She had the same awkward features as the man, her head was too large and her limbs too small. She smiled at Janice when she saw her – a great big toothy grin. Janice thought she was the most beautiful child she had ever seen.

"Could you hold Arlene for me while I take the tyre off?" said the man, who now stood by her side looking inside the van. She had not heard him approach.

"I don't want her to rock the van while I'm changing it."

At his voice the child got down off the cot awkwardly and moved over to Janice. She held out her arms to be picked up. Janice took hold of the little girl and folded her into her arms. She was light.

The man returned to changing the wheel.

Eric felt cold. He sat staring at the television set with disinterest.

It was on but held no appeal. Nothing held any appeal any more. He had not eaten for two days. He had been given food but he ignored it until it congealed on the tray and went cold. He drank only a few sips of water, enough to keep him alive, and he only slept when his body permitted it. The rest of time he just stared at the television.

They had tried to bring him round but he was still in the early stage, still prone to hallucinations and mental imaginings which affected his personality. He was still unsure as to what was reality and what was part of the fantasy world, the little life he had created for himself. It was only four days since the incident.

The programme finished and the television station announced that the news would follow. Eric's eyes flickered and focused.

A nurse looked up from where she was ensuring another patient took their pills. The doctor had told her to be diligent when the news came on, as that was the only time they got any response from their newest inmate.

Eric pulled himself upright in the chair and leant forward. He was thin, the bones of his neck stood out, his thinning hair sat at odd angles. His slack jaw firmed up as he heard the familiar tune and the chimes of Big Ben.

It was always the same article that started the fit and rage. For such a small thin creature he could pack quite a punch. Something just bubbled up from inside him and had to be unleashed. Yesterday he had knocked an orderly's tooth out with a well placed kick. The nurse rang for assistance. She hoped they would be here in time.

Eric watched the national news with interest, but it had already been bumped down to the local broadcast. Already they had reduced his plight to second billing. The rest of the country no longer cared about him, about his loss.

He pushed himself out of his chair. He felt weak, his bones hurt from the inside. He glanced over his shoulder at the woman who watched him with hawk-like precision. The rest of them would be running now, ready to hold him down and inflict the suffering they called compassion.

The local news started and the picture flashed up onto the screen. It was always the same one. The car sat by the side of the road, its door and windows shut tight. The morning sun was bouncing off the bonnet and forming a visual halo on the film. It gleamed as if it was more than a car. For him it held all the answers.

He started to mumble as the nurse came forward.

"Janice? It's her car…why can't they find her. My Janice?"

The nurse put a comforting hand on his shoulder. Perhaps today he would not get so agitated. Perhaps she would be able to soothe away whatever inner turmoil was eating away at him.

"Sit down now, Eric," she whispered soothingly into his ear.

The newsreader was talking now, with a picture of the car over his left shoulder. Eric was starting to get more agitated, more frustrated with what he was hearing.

"It's Janice's…it belongs to Janice."

The picture of a large black woman was now shown, below which was a foreign-sounding name in bold white writing. Eric went quiet and closed in on the television.

The nurse approached cautiously. She didn't want to alarm him.

Eric tapped the screen. That wasn't right. That was not his Janice. She wasn't black. She had dark hair, cut short and spiky. That woman looked completely different. That was not her name. It was spelt wrong. Too many letters. Why didn't they understand? That car belonged to his wife, not this other person. Where was she? Why was no one looking for his Janice?

As the nurse laid her hand once more on the poor creature he started to whine. It was animal in origin, a deep rumble that started low down inside of him and erupted from his mouth on a wave of spittle. Sheer frustration built up within his fists that clenched tight, the bones of his knuckles pricking at the underside of his grey skin.

The help came through the door as Eric turned and lashed out. He smashed a fist into the back of her turned head sending the woman slewing to the ground. They ran forward, over the prone body of the nurse, and grabbed at Eric's flailing limbs. He was crying and sobbing, snot and mucus flying into the air in great stringy knots as they pulled him back from the television. He fought back. Legs flew out and fists started to fly. The tangle of bodies became one.

Eric didn't feel the pain. He was beyond that. He just wanted to get rid of the people who wanted to remove the image. That was his link. That's how he held on to her memory. Once that was gone she would vanish from this world forever.

He was pulled backwards until he lost sight of the news report. His foot lashed out violently and caught something soft that yielded in pain before it crashed into the set. The television tottered backwards on its trolley, tipped and smashed to the ground. Sparks leapt up briefly as the set exploded. It fizzed and died.

The noise briefly stopped the struggling mass as they turned to witness the destruction. Eric was shocked. He had not wanted to do that. He was lost without the television.

The orderlies turned from the wreckage and smiled. Eric flinched as the first of the ugly blows bit into his weak body.

She looked down at the small child. She had large brown eyes just like her own. The child grinned, a lopsided mess of teeth that needed a good clean. Her breath was artificially sweet. She must have been eating candies.

"Give me a kiss, Ma," said Arlene while puckering her lips up towards her mother.

Janice gave the child a big wet one on her cheek, followed by a raspberry blown on her fat soft flesh. She giggled and wriggled in her arms.

"Eurgh, Ma!"

Her husband came back round, the flat tyre bouncing in front of him.

"She awake?"

Janice put Arlene down and watched as she moved over to the edge of the road and picked up a stick that she threw out into the dry desert bush.

"You be careful now, Arlene. There's bad things out there."

She turned back to her husband who was stowing the broken wheel in the back of van.

"How much further?"

He turned and looked down the long straight road that stretched into the distance.

"Two – maybe three hours, I guess. We should hit the city by nightfall."

They got into the cab. Arlene snuggled between the middle of them and promptly went back to sleep. The van started first time. Gravel crunched under the new tyre as they pulled away.

"You OK, princess?" said her husband from his driving seat.

"Yeah fine," she drawled.

"It's goin' to be fine. We can start afresh," he added.

Start afresh, she thought. Yes – that would be good. To leave the old life behind, the debt collectors and suspicious neighbours, the interfering do-gooders and a family that insisted they knew right or better than she did, people who poked fun at her husband and child, people who called them names. The life of small-town America would be behind them, they were going to the city. She was sure that this was what she had always wanted, what she had always wished for.

Six

It was almost dark when Nick arrived for the second time at the university campus. There were a few families and teenagers making the most of the sculptured park and small lake that fronted the grey buildings. They came from the red-brick housing estates that surrounded the park, heading for the greenery, the ice cream van, a little feeling of country in the built-up sprawl of the city.

A Frisbee skimmed low across the lawn as a youth threw it for his dog to retrieve. A couple sat on a blanket with the remains of a picnic scattered about the parched grass. Somewhere someone was listening to a radio. There was a squeal of laughter from the lake as a girl tried to stand up in one of the boats; it rocked from side to side as the keeper shouted for her to sit down and bring the boat back in.

Nick walked through the happy groups towards the grey buildings on the top of the hill. The main building, which stood proud and austere with just enough columns and windows for passers-by to know it was important, looked more like a stately home than a university. Nick headed for the small squat ugly buildings that had sprung up around this grand construction, hunkered to its side like distorted limpets.

The Students' Union was a collection of buildings from different eras that were connected through a series of winding passageways. On entering, Nick received funny looks from some of the younger members who had stayed on during the summer break, but the older students now outnumbered them two to one.

The halls would not be filled with young minds for another month and the university felt half deserted without them.

It was darker inside than out; even with the lights on the bar seemed grungy and unclean. The dark walls seemed to suck up the light and refuse to give it back. His feet stuck to the linoleum tiles; it felt like walking across molten tarmac, spilt lager acting as glue. A bar erected in one corner of the room, poorly stocked and managed, sat squat with the rest of the room, which was taken up with a hodgepodge of differing tables and chairs.

Nick spotted the group straightaway. There were not many people in the bar on such a warm day, and those that were inside sat in couples. He watched them nervously and decided to get a drink before approaching. As the barman poured a thin-looking lager from a can into a pint glass a voice piped up from the group.

"This is the gentleman I've been telling you about. Nick, Nick...Mr Stuart!"

Anne was standing up at the centre of the assembly and waving at him from across the room. He smiled weakly and moved over while taking a sip of the too warm drink.

"Everyone – this is Nick, our newest member."

Five faces looked up from their conversations and gave Nick a series of smiles and grimaces. One of them he recognised instantly. Michael smiled warily, as if ashamed to be seen in his natural habitat.

"Here, sit down, mate." He indicated to a seat next to him.

"Thanks."

Nick sat as Michael leant forward, his face entering the pool of thin light that streamed through a dirty window set high in the wall. He was wearing a cheap white shirt that allowed his hairy chest, pot belly and the tattoo on his forearm to be seen through the synthetic weave. He wore discounted grey trousers that, like his overcoat of earlier, looked much too warm for a day like this.

Michael noticed him watching and shrugged.

"I don't get time to do much shopping, not now."

Nick was introduced to them one by one. A series of names and faces. A thin man with hair grown long to cover up his bald patch gripped onto his coffee cup and gave a weak smile at the mention of his name – Eric Kimble. Nick thought he looked ill and though it was obvious he was listening to what was said his mind appeared to be elsewhere, as if he sat between two worlds and was unable to decide which way to turn.

Next to Eric sat two women. One was old yet still very elegant, her skin dark brown from a recent holiday while her hair was white and cut short to show a youthful-looking face with large green eyes. She was introduced as Rebecca Bowles and waved while she sat in conversation with a woman who was almost her complete opposite. Small and dumpy with glasses perched on her nose, she peered over the top of them and nodded hello as her name was announced: Margaret Bryson, wife of the man sitting next to her who was also large, his fat cheeks resting on a larger neck, gingery tufts of hair and pink skin – Terry Bryson.

"You've met Michael already." Anne gestured at the man by Nick's side.

He remembered his earlier conversation with Anne about how Michael, according to Beltran, was a suspected paedophile and murderer. He didn't look like a child killer as he inspected his pint of bitter and fished out a floating crumb. He looked more like the sort of man you would find propping up any public bar in the country. Opinionated, but never a threat, more interested in keeping company than offending outright, the sort who would describe themselves as 'honest'.

"Right, now that we're all here shall we move upstairs?"

The group were in agreement and chairs were pushed back as Anne picked up a bag that clinked with wine bottles.

Upstairs consisted of a small room set out ready to receive them with chairs in a circle, a small table with plastic beakers and a bottle opener. Everyone sat in seats that seemed to be their regular spots, leaving Nick a free chair between Anne and Rebecca.

Michael opened the bottles and poured red wine into plastic cups before handing them around. Nick took a quick swig; it tasted cheap and was not improved by the sharp ridge of the cup that bit into his lip.

"Right, as Nick is new I thought we'd just have a quick recap and give him a little bit of our backgrounds before he tells us what happened to him. Is that all right, Nick?"

He nodded at Anne, unsure as to what he was going to say, but decided to worry about that when it got around to his turn. He felt like he was auditioning for a bad play and wondered if later they would commence with a trust exercise, falling back into the waiting arms of a 'new friend'.

"Who wants to go first?"

Michael coughed to announce he would go first which the rest of the group also seemed to expect. He was that sort. Eager. Nick thought that as the initiator of the group it was only fair, though he seemed to rely on Anne for the organising, preferring to take a back seat.

"I'm divorced now, but used to be married, lived over in Mansfield. We had two kids, Robert and Deborah. It was coming up to my wife's birthday and we were planning to have a few people round for dinner that Saturday. I wasn't working shifts back then so got the weekend off. Deborah had been hassling her mum all week for some jeans with a swanky name – you know how kids are when they're thirteen, they want anything their mates have got. Anyway to get her out from under her mum's feet I said I'd take her into town and buy the jeans while she cleaned up.

"It was busy in town but we eventually got to the shop and found the sort she was after. Fifty quid for a pair of tatty-looking things with frayed edges. I could've got two pair of jeans for that price, but Debs had set her heart set on them." Michael raised his eyes to emphasise the point, which was met with muted encouragement to continue.

"She wanted to just buy them there and then, but for that price I wanted her to try them on and make sure they fit so I got one of the staff to show her to the changing rooms.

"I remember she turned round just before going behind the curtain, looked at me and said, 'I want you to be the first to see me in them.' That was the last thing she ever said to me."

Michael stopped briefly as if what his lost daughter had said was of importance, the words imbuing a meaning to him that was just as obvious to the rest of them. "While she was in there I had a quick look at some of the sale clothes. I thought I might be able to get her to buy a cheaper pair. When I came back she was gone."

There was a pause. Nick expected him to go on, but he just looked down at his feet and pursed his lips, his words still hanging in the air. It was all he had to say. He looked back up at the group and grinned as if embarrassed.

"Thanks, Michael. Rebecca, would you tell Nick why you are here?"

The older lady nodded her head and turned slowly to face Nick. She smiled. She looked like an old film star, perhaps Bacall – she had similar bone structure, strong yet feminine.

"I lost my husband sixteen years ago. It was just a normal workday in the summer. The weather was hot, like today, and Lawrence had to work a little later than usual. We were living in Haywards Heath at the time, my husband worked in the city, commuting the distance every morning and evening. He liked the train; it meant he could catch up on work and spend more time in the garden when he got home.

"He said he would be back on the ten past eight train and, as it was a nice evening, I walked to the station to meet him. It was something I liked to do, meet him from the train.

"Anyway the train arrived, only he didn't get off. At first I thought that perhaps he had simply missed it and would be on a later one, which was unlike him, but as this was before the days of mobile phones there was no way to contact him. I went home to wait and everything was different. I never saw him again."

She went quiet and smiled at Nick. He thought at first she was going to add more details but, similar to Michael, that was it: the story ended abruptly. Like his own story, the loved one simply vanished. No conclusion, no follow-up. They were gone and all the other person could do was carry on with their life.

Next to speak was the married couple, Terry and Margaret Bryson, not that Terry had much to say and when he did his wife constantly corrected him on the detail.

"Our Juliet was beautiful. She was quiet and not that good at school, but to look at her would brighten up anyone's day. She had won a couple of competitions in the local paper – they run a Miss Spring every year. She wanted to be a model and we encouraged her. It was her dream.

"She had seen an advert in the paper for models and asked us if she could go along and be interviewed. We of course said yes but were a little nervous because there's a lot of weirdos around nowadays and you never know what some people could be up to."

She looked at her husband who tried to carry on the story.

"I said I would accompany her…"

"No, I asked you to go with her, but she didn't want us to come in with her. She said it looked unprofessional turning up with your dad."

"I wanted to go but she made me park around the corner. A man had given us an interview time, said she would only be half an hour."

"But you waited for over an hour."

The husband lapsed into silence as an old argument reared its head. One to which he had no answer.

"Terry finally gets out the car and goes around to the address; only the people there don't know anything about a modelling agency even though we wrote the address down for her properly. No one had seen Juliet or knows who we are talking about."

"The doctors said we have created her because Margaret can't have kids…" added Terry unnecessarily, though his distress was pronounced.

"OK, thank you, Terry," interrupted Anne as Margaret turned on her husband, her face flushed with an erupting outburst. She calmed down as her husband turned to look at the floor, his head bent forward, resting his chin on his chest.

The last to speak was Eric. Nick could tell he was not that comfortable around people and found the storytelling hard going. He stuttered throughout and lapsed into silence in places. It was if he were pulling the story from somewhere deep inside of him, a dark, terrible place that it pained him to visit.

"My wife disappeared while she was all on her own. She...she was on her way back from work. She was a manager and so she....she had to do lots of driving. They found her car parked up on the road on the moor. The handbrake was on and all her things were inside, nice and neat, just how she liked them...but she was gone. They...they said the car belonged to some other woman though, that it wasn't hers at all. They never found her, though they...they searched the moor for several miles. Nothing, they found nothing, not a trace. They took me away after that...said I'd had a fit or something."

He lapsed back into silence and looked down at his knees, shaking his head as he muttered the final sentence over and over again to himself.

"OK, Nick has recently lost Natalie." Anne indicated their newest member. "Can you tell the group what happened?"

He looked at the eager faces all ready to get into the new story. A little more flesh to add to the bones of their own tales, expected clues maybe hidden in the telling which would match their own loss. They needed to hear these stories again and again; as if by being told, the missing people were being kept alive.

He told them. They nodded and looked at one another. Agreement spread throughout them. Here was a similar story to their own. Another disappearance that mirrored their loss. Their suffering was being replicated and passed on to others. They were no longer as alone. They listened intently, not prepared to interrupt him once he was in the flow. Nick tried his best with the material, added emotion at the right point, emphasised his loss. To an outsider they must have resembled a storytelling group. Weird fables and frightening myths told around a campfire – the people who disappeared, never to return.

"It's early days yet, though," he finished. "The police might still find her."

The fat couple smiled in pity as Michael let out a short burst of laughter.

"Sorry, mate, but if you're one of us then the police will have already given up. Because Natalie doesn't exist, she's never existed according to them – how can they keep the case open when they think you're mad as a hatter and you've made your girlfriend up?"

"It's true, I'm afraid," added Rebecca. "Anne likes to get her interesting subjects together but we have all experienced the same. According to my friends and family my Lawrence never existed. I'm a spinster with no children who lives on my own. According to them Lawrence is a figment of my imagination. Anne thinks we have some kind of hysteria, some experience which has made us create these people and then, for some reason, we've decided to misplace them again. Isn't that right, Anne?"

Anne stood up and grabbed the bottle of wine, pouring a second cup for herself before offering it around.

"I have no such theory. I'm not sure where I sit, yet."

"If it's hysteria, how come we both have memories of our Juliet?" piped up Terry.

"We can't both be mad." The fat man looked to his wife. "Can we?"

"Well, there have been cases where two people have experienced similar sensations. A kind of collective hysteria."

"So you see the problem, Nick. No one can prove or disprove us. We're either a bunch of very good liars, mad people or…"

Michael seemed uncertain how to finish the sentence.

Nick looked at the faces that were all turned his way and felt angry. He could feel rage bubbling up inside of him. How dare they say his Natalie had never been real? He took a deep breath and let the hurt subside before he spoke.

"Well, Natalie existed. I spoke to her only last week. We had been having a bit of a bad time, which makes me thinks she's simply had enough and left, or she's a victim of some crime. There are some bad things going on in this city. Don't try and tell me anything different."

"Really, and all your mates and family have rallied round to find her, have they? Are they missing her as well?"

Michael spoke while the others remained quiet. They already knew the taunts, having heard them used many times before.

"Well, not exactly…"

He didn't let Nick finish. "No, mate, 'cause as far as they're concerned they have only ever heard of Natalie from you. I'm betting none of them can remember ever seeing her. Am I right?"

From his tone of voice it was obvious that Michael already knew the answer to that question.

"Look, I don't want to be rude but you don't know what you're talking about. I know she existed. I refuse to believe that the last six months of my life has been a complete and utter fabrication and only now am I waking up to reality. I have had no reason to go mad, no trauma in my life, no incident that this can all be traced back to. I won't believe it; it can't be true. If you do, then fine, but don't tar me with the same brush."

Nick stood and pushed his chair under the table.

"We're not trying to upset you, Nick. Please sit down." Anne stood and placed a reassuring hand on his arm, but Nick was already pulling away.

"No. This is stupid. If the police aren't interested then I can still make my own enquiries."

"You could listen to my other theory?"

Michael had stood up as well. He grinned over the table, taunting Nick to stay. This was what he had been building up to. It was as if he had wanted to rile the new guest.

"When you hear this one, you'll think I really am mad."

The Bryson couple moaned out loud.

"Not this rubbish again. I thought we told you we were not interested in your stupid ideas."

"It is a little bit outlandish," commented Rebecca.

Nick looked at Michael and noticed his wolfish features. He had too much hair for someone of his age and thin pointed teeth that were slightly yellow from coffee stains and a bad diet.

"What have you got to lose?" he added.

Nick weighed up the response and realised he had nothing that he had not already lost through his own inaction. He pulled the chair back and sat as Anne poured him another glass of wine. He accepted it gratefully while noting that she had yet another glass for herself. He decided she was either a bit of an alcoholic or else enjoyed these sessions just a little too much.

"Go on then. Knock yourself out."

There was a communal groan throughout the group. Whatever Michael was about to describe it did not meet with general approval.

He took in a deep breath and looked Nick steadily in the eye as if what he was about to say would have a profound effect on all of them. He was a master conjurer, calming his audience, gaining their attention before the grand finale.

"What do you know about alternative realities?"

Nick knew nothing, but didn't comment. He just shook his head.

"What if Natalie has not disappeared at all? What if she is exactly where you left her, only you and she now exist in different parts of the universe?"

Nick took a drink and bowed his head, if only to cover up his embarrassment.

"Look, I know it sounds implausible but someone once said that once you remove all the probabilities, whatever you are left with must be the truth."

"I think he's talking about Sherlock Holmes," interrupted Rebecca.

He thanked her for her help before continuing.

"All of us here have experienced the loss of someone we love, someone who we know to the nth degree. We are convinced that these people are living, breathing individuals, yet as far as the rest of the world is concerned they never existed. So what if they existed for us but not for the rest of the world? What if every so often alternative worlds cross and a person or an object suddenly gets caught in the new universe?"

Nick smiled. He had enough of a problem dealing with his own reality at the moment, never mind having to worry about another him existing elsewhere.

"So who exists in this other place? Am I now in the alternative reality or is Natalie? And why us? What's so special about us for this to have happened?"

"I don't know. I haven't got all the answers yet, but it's something I'm working on."

The others spoke up now.

"It's ridiculous; the whole idea has no merit," said Eric speaking up for the first time, his face twisted with anger. He had heard Michael's comments before and he resented the man just for voicing such an idea. "People do not just vanish off the face of the Earth. My wife is still very much in this world I…I just can't locate her at the moment."

That spoke of some truth. Nick felt that Natalie was still very much part of him; whether others thought of her as fictitious or she had in truth run away, she was part of his life, part of the sum of his parts. Even if the majority of people thought that he had created her as an imaginary girlfriend.

"I know what you mean," replied Rebecca. "Just because no one believes these people exist, does not mean that for us, they don't. These people are very real."

They all responded to that idea. The fact that no matter what the hidden answer was, to them these missing people were very real.

"There are times at night when I think I can hear Janice calling for me. You know that time when you're not quite asleep and not quite awake, that's when I hear her. It's like she's next to me in bed just talking about her day, what she's been doing and such like. All that stuff she used to do, she's still doing in my dreams."

Eric's story made the rest of the group go quiet as they remembered their own tales of the vanished.

"That's what I'm trying to say. Somewhere your life is just going on as normal. You are sitting in bed with Janice talking about whatever, it's just that in this here and now there is no such thing as a Janice. Here, there is just you, but out there…" Michael waved his hand around his head as if indicating some far-off world, "…somewhere, she still exists."

They lapsed into silence as Anne took a noisy gulp of wine. Nick could see them recounting the precious moments of their lives with these people. Replaying their own home movies inside their minds, the leftovers of lives lived. Nick hated to break their reverie but he had to speak.

"I can't believe that. For me it doesn't make any sense. I think there is something more. I think I caused it. I think it's my fault Natalie vanished."

It was the first time Nick had admitted the guilt to an audience. He felt like a recovering drug addict. Admitting the problem is the road to recovery.

"Something happened on the night she vanished. Something I did."

He kept having the recurring image of the bar, the shadowy drinking den that he knew he had frequented, Munch laughing into his beer and…and…and then the man with the burning eyes. If he could only remember what had happened after that, what had been said, discussed. He was missing a vital part of that evening and he knew that it was the key to the whole episode.

"This idea of Michael's doesn't explain why they were here for a bit and then just vanish. What is so different about us to cause the world to make these changes?"

He was given a series of blank stares in response to his question.

"That's what we have to find out," he finished.

Anne was starting to get restless and wanted to change the subject.

"I don't think this is really helping anyone. We are here to support one another and talk about the future, not concoct possible reasons and excuses. You can't change what has happened so we have to look at ways to come to terms with it."

"Perhaps you can change it. If something's happened once, it can happen again," finished Michael before downing his pint.

Anne shot him a look that told him to be quiet.

The rest of the meeting was solemn and less animated than that initial discussion. The group talked about how to move on with their lives and how to cope with the feelings of emptiness, what to do to stop thinking about the missing. All the belief and emotions that you expect from a counselling session were rehashed and addressed. Nick noticed that Anne always referred to the missing as the 'departed'; as far as she was concerned these people were best considered dead. They all took turns to talk about how they dealt with the issues of just getting on with life, but Nick could tell the group weren't interested; their heart wasn't in it. The initial discussions had given them hope, reasons to recount the mystery and trust that their loved ones were still very much alive – just lost. The rest of the conversation simply accepted they were gone, and none of them wanted to do that.

Nick could not get Michael's final words out of his head. His idea sounded flawed, but if you could reverse the process…the idea was tantalising. He looked over at the man who seemed more interested in getting as much beer down his throat as possible than listening to any more 'coping mechanisms'. When not looking into his pint pot, his eyes sought out the floor, his mind elsewhere. Just once he caught Nick's eye. He smiled and nodded.

The wine was finished which seemed to signal that the meeting was over. Everyone said their goodbyes and agreed to come again, to meet up in another month to go through the 'healing' process again. They were a bunch of junkies that hated the drugs but still relied on the replacement every once in a while. A feeling of 'belonging' mainlined into a vein.

Nick slipped out into the night. Anne had invited some of them back to her house for more wine, but only Rebecca seemed interested, the rest making a dash for the door. It was only ten but most of them had driven to Nottingham and spent several hours on the road. They were all eager to get home.

With it being summer and most of the students away the campus was only partially lit. Nick moved carefully between the parked cars in the darkness heading for the lights of the road that could be seen in the distance. Michael was waiting for him. Nick thought he would be, but didn't see him until the pair almost collided.

"I don't really know why I come anymore," he said.

Nick couldn't see his face in the dark but he could smell his beery breath.

"It seems that I just like to see those who are in a similar position to me. I've ordered a taxi – would you like a lift?"

Nick knew he wanted to talk and realised he had at last found someone who would listen.

Two police cars sat outside, their engines idling, blue lights spinning and lighting up the stone façade of the crumbling building. Lights had gone on inside the many apartments and interested faces now looked out of open windows, dull television shows remaining unwatched as the tension built.

They had entered and secured the lift, taking it briefly out of action to ensure no one used it as a possible route of escape. Officers had already been posted at all four corners of the building and were in the process of directing people away from the site while keeping a keen lookout for any of the three suspects whose descriptions they had been given.

As they moved up the stairs, doors opened and people demanded to know what was happening. Their cries went unheeded as they were asked politely but firmly to stay inside their homes. Some stood in pyjamas, already preparing for bed and the long day at work to come. Others seemed to be relaxing, bottles of cold beer pressed into a hand, delivered pizza boxes on the table. They were told only what was necessary – to not worry, everything was under control.

Bonita had knocked on Nick Stuart's door as a matter of routine but they already knew he was not at home. He had been tailed to the university. They wanted him out of the way; he could be picked up later if required.

The thin wood of the flat door snapped with one blow from the battering ram. The police went in, securing the area for those in charge. Bonita stepped inside. Nothing had changed. It was still clean and sparse, practically empty. The accumulation of one man's possessions, one single individual with no one to share his life or his home. With the door to the loft open there was nowhere to hide and the flat was quickly discounted as a crime scene. If any evidence had been hidden, it had long since been removed.

She stepped back outside to see an officer standing next to a now open fire exit. The sounds of the city flooded into the dirty and mildewed hallway. She stepped through the doorway and on to the flat roof of the building. It was covered in pigeon shit, wet and slippery underfoot. She cursed the mess it was making to her shoes as she looked about. The area was bare apart from a small half-collapsed wooden hut and a metal water tank, now corroding under the elements.

Along the side of the roof ran a small brick wall, a slim protector from the skyline of Nottingham. The city was lit up with the glare and hum of activity. It sloped away from her down towards the canal with its bars and restaurants and then far off in the distance was the river marked by the stadium lights of two football grounds. Over to her right she could see the castle sitting on a sandstone plug that glowed a soft orange while, behind her, the noise of the square could be heard, its location pinpointed by the green copper dome of the Council House.

Miles was already approaching the makeshift hut, two officers flanking him as they closed in. He wore latex gloves and trod carefully, wary of damaging any possible evidence. Bonita watched him as he bent forward and gingerly teased at the ramshackle door.

There was a flurry of noise and a shout of horror as something warm stroked across his face, filling his vision with epidermal damp. He fell backwards as a pigeon, alarmed by the intrusion, flew up and out into the night sky.

"Fucking hell," he murmured, ignoring the snigger of laughter from the officer behind him.

The smell released by the bird's passing was grotesque. A deep suffocation of an odour that filled his nostrils and made his eyes stream with water, it caught at the back of Miles' throat, sending him fishing for a handkerchief. He held it tight against his face as he teased again at the door.

A light was shone inside the dark recesses of the hut. Cobwebs dangled from the pitted ceiling, catching the light and turning the interior into a Christmas decoration. Old shelves, empty of bottles but forming perfect perches, dotted the walls, and on the floor lay years of decaying and aged bird excrement. The smell was heightened by the dead carcass of a pigeon, torn apart by its scavenging neighbours, nestling in the dirt.

Miles turned and stood upright, gulping in clean air and shaking away the permeating stench that seemed even now to have woven itself into the fabric of his clothing. He looked at Bonita, the disappointment obvious on his face.

"Nothing."

"Perhaps we'll find more downstairs. I imagine this place has a large basement – plus there's the car park."

Miles agreed and started to move the officers back inside. Bonita took one last look at the night sky and turned to follow. As she passed she looked down at the rusting water tank. It had long ago been painted black, but was now no longer used. Much of it had corroded; rust flaking through the bubbled paint. Only the bolts affixing the top plate still shone with a metal gleam.

Bonita stopped dead.

She looked closer.

The paint had been scraped away exposing what lay underneath. A tool had torn the edges, knocking away the years of oxidation, the metal remaining fresh due to the lack of rainfall.

"Miles?"

He turned to look at her and followed her gaze to the tank. He saw what had happened and stopped the officers from leaving. Tools were radioed for and once received, the nuts were loosened one by one, each bagged for further investigation.

They stood back as a jimmy was placed under the top plate and pressure applied. It moved easily, scratching its way up the helter-skelter screws. The lid was removed and a new odour leaked out into the evening. It was noisome and rancid, raping the night with its brutality; it was the stench of putrefication that needed to escape its enclosure.

The officers stood back. One gagged, vomit forcing its way up his throat and out through his nostrils. Beltran could feel the bile rising in her own throat but stood firm, desperate not to display any weakness in front of these men.

She grabbed a torch and shone it within the confines of the dark interior. A parody of life was illuminated. Three bodies in varying degrees of early decomposition sat around a small table. They were positioned with their backs against the wall of the tank, slouching, with their legs stretched out in front. One girl, her face distorted and now slightly bloated, lips peeling away to reveal black gums and yellow teeth, had an arm resting on the table, palm upwards as if waiting to receive a gift. A second, her thin summer skirt neatly arranged to keep her modesty, could not hide the dark blemishes of rot that pockmarked her skin. The bodies had not been thrown in and left, they had been carefully arranged, placed inside with forethought and precision. They resembled a corrupt and sinister tea party of the dead; only one side of the table remained free as if awaiting the arrival of a final guest.

The headlamps of the taxi lit them while they stood in the middle of the car park. Michael had given the address of a modern hotel on the edge of the city, the sort of place frequented by men on business, not those who had decided to take a holiday. It was plain but functional, flanked on one side by a small marina full of narrow boats and on the other by a large supermarket with its sprawling car park. The taxi driver was paid and Nick was shown through to a small bar. It was empty and they had to get the bored-looking receptionist, who sat with his feet propped on a chair, to leave his post and pour them a couple of overpriced beers from underused pumps. He did this with an air of reluctance and obvious hatred for the customers who had interrupted his evening.

"What did you think of tonight?" Michael asked as soon as they sat down.

Nick told him he thought it had been interesting, but he did not consider himself a victim and was almost convinced he was not mad. Nick admitted that he didn't see how this sort of low-key therapy could help him or any other of the unfortunates present.

"And what about my idea?"

"I'm open to suggestions, but your idea is no more provable than anyone else's."

"I may have proof. I'm not sure yet. I've been collecting data for years now but it takes a lot of sorting. A lot of the stuff is just the weird imaginings of slightly disturbed people. This phenomenon has happened since records began and it's not located to the UK. It's happened all around the world. Every country seems to have stories of the missing, the earliest going back to the Middle East and Africa."

"People would notice. Scientists, the military – those sorts."

"Why? They're just like us, unable and unwilling to face what is in front of their eyes. We like everything rational and these missing people don't fit into that category. It's as if our minds are unable to accept what has happened. It's just too…" he stumbled for the right word. "It's just too big a concept. I think disappearances happen all the time but normally no one remembers. People don't just vanish; they are erased from history, from the world as we know it. Only once in a while someone who has a deep emotional connection to the person notices they are absent, but normally – nothing."

Nick was silent. He didn't know what to say. He looked at the man opposite him. He was middle-aged; slightly balding at the back, but the hair that remained was still thick and wiry. He earned money and made a living so that he could pursue his never-ending quest for a missing daughter who might not be real. His wife and family had disowned him, the medical profession thought that he was mad and the police considered him a possible paedophile.

Nick was worried. Was this how the world saw him? Had he become a pathetic nobody who would spend the remainder of his days looking for the perfect woman, the dream girl who gave him great sex but as far as everyone else was concerned was a figment of his imagination?

"Why are you telling me this? Did you tell the others and they just dismissed you as mad? Am I just another guinea pig?"

He shrugged the accusation off.

"I just thought you seemed a little different. A bit more open to the possibilities. Perhaps I was wrong."

He looked away and signalled to the hotel staff that he wanted another drink. The receptionist scowled at the request.

"You said you had some proof. What is it?"

"It's outside."

Nick considered his options. This man, this stranger, was either going to lure him out to the car and try and commit some perverse lewd act upon him or he was the genuine article. He figured the receptionist had seen him enter with Michael so if the police did find a ravished corpse at least they would know who to pull in for 'routine questioning'.

"If I'm wasting your time you'll be out of here in five minutes. What's five minutes?"

Nick agreed, leaving Michael to pay the bill and head for the lobby. Nick followed, but made sure the hotel receptionist saw him. He watched them from behind his desk with a look of disgust etched into his pallid features.

Back outside Nick expected Michael to head for a car in the partially lit car park, but instead he made for the warren of apartment blocks that ringed the marina. Once across the road they stepped quietly past the large plate glass windows, some lit up from the television sets inside, the light of the many screens playing across the pulled blinds.

In the centre of the compound was a metal gate which led out onto a criss-cross of boardwalk. Michael opened it with a key and pushed; it screeched into the night. Stepping through, Nick followed the man down the wooden walkway which swayed ever so slightly from their combined weight. A number of small sailing boats were moored close by, their bright fibreglass hulls lapped by the sluggish canal water.

Reaching the end, Michael pointed out a small narrow boat that had seen better days, its paint chipped and mottled, a window to the cabin smashed and replaced with a piece of thin cardboard. The only recent refurbishment to the wreck was the freshly painted name on the side: 'Deborah'.

Michael stepped aboard and snapped open the folding door. A light had been left on and it lit up his face as he looked in.

"It's not much but it's better than sleeping rough. A bit damp in winter, but you get used to it, given time."

He vanished inside as Nick stepped over the threshold. The boat tipped slightly and then righted itself as Michael moved through its slender confines. Nick looked down the three steps to see a room that was simple but functional. Cupboards had been built into every conceivable space and what little mildew-covered furniture there was seemed sensibly bolted to the floor. A battered brown suitcase sat in one corner of the boat. It was open, a pile of clothes hanging out of one side. Michael did not appear to spend a lot of time choosing his clothes; they were all of a similar shape and design. They served a function, nothing more. There were a couple of books on the side of the small day bed, heavy reading, psychological works by the look of them, the one on top entitled 'Exploring Perception'. Not the sort of books designed to help you sleep at night.

The only other piece of Michael's life was a box. It was solid looking, with large strips of tape where someone had attempted to reinforce it. The contents lay spaced evenly across the bed in neat piles. He took more care of these items than his clothes. Piles of folders and orderly papers were lined up side by side. Carefully typed or with red pen used to highlight paragraphs or drawings, they were accompanied by photos, quick shots, blurred reportage. The work was held together by multi-coloured rubber bands.

Michael looked at Nick, studying his new acquaintance as he took in the sight.

"I use the rubber bands to identify the folders – red for old cases, blue for hoaxes – that sort of thing."

Nick made a noise to say that he understood.

Michael started to rummage through a pile marked with a yellow band as Nick moved inside, careful to leave the door open. The file chosen was the only one with that colour band. Eventually he stopped and held up a photo. He passed it to Nick, indicating that he should take it.

Nick looked down at a photo of what appeared to be the top landing of a house, a family home. There were several doors leading off the hall, and at the far end was a cabinet with a large ornate mirror on top. It was quite difficult to see, as the photo was in partial darkness. Either it had been lit badly or had been taken at night. He turned it over to check if there was anything on the back. There was nothing. Whatever this was meant to prove was initially beyond him.

"I don't understand."

Michael looked anxious.

"It's quite difficult to see, I'm afraid. Here – I've got a magnifying glass somewhere."

He returned to the box and pulled out a large brass eyeglass that he must have bought from an antique shop.

"Look at the mirror," he said as he handed it over.

Nick fixed his view where Michael had indicated. In it was reflected a set of stairs that must have been behind the photographer. They led downwards to a hidden part of the house. There were a couple of pictures on a wall to the left, framed family photos. There was also a doorway that must have led off to yet another bedroom. The door had been left slightly ajar but it was too dark to see inside.

"I still don't understand what I'm looking at."

"I took that picture in our family home just before me and Deborah's mum split up. I had been sitting at home when I thought I heard Deborah calling from upstairs. She'd been gone two weeks. I ran upstairs as quickly as I could. I never found her but in the hallway I could feel all this...this..." He stumbled with the meaning, stammering as he attempted to find the perfect example. "Stuff like when you pull on a jumper straight from a dryer."

"Static electricity?"

"Yes that's it, but it was more intense. I went back downstairs and took my camera up to take a photo and got that."

He pointed at the photo.

"A photo of your landing?"

"You're missing the point. I took the photo from the middle of the hall, from the top of the stairs."

"Yes?"

"Where's my reflection?"

Nick looked back down at the photo. It was well thumbed; the colours had yellowed with age. It was true that the only way in which a photo could have been produced was for the camera to have been placed in the middle of the hall. All the lines were straight and due to the mirror's position both ends of the hallway could be seen. The reflected image showed the background in slightly fuzzy detail; the subject however was missing. There was nothing there.

"I took photos all around the house as I was so convinced that it was Deborah that I had heard. I kept looking at them for weeks when they returned from the printers, as if she was somewhere in them – trapped. I must have looked at that picture a hundred times before I noticed."

He could of course have simply made it up. Nick was no photo expert but he knew that they were open to manipulation and change. He had sat in the dark of the cinema and seen all sorts of weird stuff – all of it false. But he could tell Michael believed in this little scrap of glossy paper. This was his hidden clue, the treasure map that would lead him to his Holy Grail.

"But what does it prove?"

Nick handed it back to him, he took it almost reverentially.

"It shows reality – I think. For that brief moment of time the camera was able to see two realities. I was in one and the reflection that was in another. I know Deborah existed, she was my daughter – I loved her. She still does exist but not in this now. Not here. I'm trying to find a way to bring her back but I don't have all the pieces yet. The jigsaw is a little over halfway complete."

"That still doesn't explain why Deborah, or why Natalie? Why were they the ones to get lost, to vanish from our lives? What's special about them?"

"Like I said, I don't have all the pieces."

It was late by the time the bodies were removed. A forensics team had been on standby just in case anything was found so the officers on site had wasted little time in bringing them in. They recorded the scene in minute detail, photographing the party of death, recording the deeds of the 'Missing Man' for posterity.

Due to the cramped conditions of the water tank only one person could get into it at any one time, though it was hoped that due to the site remaining undisturbed, forensic evidence would be easy to record, traces of whatever demented piece of humanity had created such an evil tableau, left behind for a conviction. Bonita, however, was not so sure. She suspected that the 'Missing Man' would not be stupid enough to contaminate the scene.

A call was immediately put out for all three suspects. One, or all of them, was the murderer. Bonita was unsure as to whether they were dealing with an individual with a disturbed mind or a group of unhinged predators, but she knew that only a corrupt and dysfunctional intelligence could have carried out such macabre work.

It would only be a matter of time before Nick and Michael were brought in; their whereabouts were already noted and under surveillance. She wished she could be there when they were taken. She wanted to see their eyes, the knowledge dawning that, whatever it was they had planned, it was now at an end.

Her radio crackled as an officer called for support back inside. The neighbours were alarmed by the sudden intrusion into their world by such diabolical evil. Though none had been given details of what had been found, the arrival of the forensics team and the morgue van soon set tongues wagging and a look of fright entered their eyes. They knew something terrible had occurred in the apartment block, its dark interior with its crumbling masonry and unexplained sounds had finally given up its ghosts. The inherent mood of unease had finally been proven correct.

The police called in reinforcements who now went from floor to floor, assuring those who spilled out into the corridors that all was well. They were to remain inside; details would be passed to them as soon as the police were satisfied that the crime scene was secure.

An old woman stood in her dressing grown sobbing for the unknown, a large man – all beer belly and sweating brow – bellowed that he had a right to know what was happening, while a small child crawled around the black boots of the police.

The officer who had radioed in for help was having trouble back on the top floor. The obnoxious neighbour was causing an issue, cursing those who blocked his way. Bonita joined the argument that was already heated.

"I don't give a rat's fuck what you've been told – I'm going out."

"Sir, we've been asked to keep all residents inside. Please return to your home."

The young police officer was holding up an arm, a barrier of resistance that even now the scrawny man pushed at with his bony fingers.

Bonita was not surprised at who was causing such a disturbance and came up behind the officer, her badge on show.

"Oh, I might have fucking known," the man shouted on spotting her.

The officer turned.

"He won't go back inside, ma'am. He's been asked several

times, but claims he has a train to catch."

"I'm on my way to see my sister in Derby and this fuckwit says I have to stop indoors."

The man was dressed in dark trousers, the fabric thin and shiny where it had been worn down, and a T-shirt that was slightly too large for him. He had shoved a red cap on his head to hide the mess that constituted his scalp, the peak shadowing his eyes. He held a brown leather bag stuffed to overflowing with clothes that he dropped out of sight as Bonita scrutinised it.

"You're not going anywhere tonight. We need to take a statement off everyone in the building. You can go tomorrow to see your sister."

"What right do you have to stop me? She's expecting me."

"Go inside, sir."

The man looked at the two imposing figures and realised they were not going to let him pass. He turned before shouting over his shoulder.

"Bastard pigs."

The officer thanked Bonita for her assistance. She noted his youth but knew his face from around the station – a new recruit. He had been mentioned in a circular. PC Ben something. She could not remember his surname.

"Give him time to simmer down before you get a statement. His flat is next to the fire escape; he might have heard something that could help us."

Once the crime scene had been correctly detailed and all the statements recorded, they would have to switch to interview mode. Nick and Michael would be brought in and interrogated; their responses would define the direction of the investigation. Tonight was going to be long and arduous.

They were waiting for Nick to make a move. Having arrived quietly, the police had manoeuvred slowly through the undergrowth and around the well-tended flower beds. In single file they had crept across the wooden walkway, listening with intent to the low hum of conversation that came from the inside of the narrow boat, timing their steps to the period of talk. Two more officers stood on the far bank of the canal, blocking off any escape route should they decide to jump. The trap was set.

Inside Nick still fingered the old photo as Michael brewed up coffee. It was getting late and he was tired. He wanted to go home but felt impelled to stay, to talk to this man who understood his situation, their shared situation. He didn't think he could help in any constructive way, but just knowing that someone believed him made him breathe that little easier.

Outside, the boardwalk creaked as someone moved. Michael came over and placed the mugs on the small Formica table. He bent and looked out of the window, but it was too dark to make out anything clearly.

The boards creaked again as Nick picked up the drink, thankful the smell of coffee removed the taint of damp in the air.

Interested by the noise outside, Michael put his head through the door, only to receive a sudden blow to his face. He fell backwards with alarm, blood pumping from a cut across his nose; he collapsed to the floor, screaming. Nick's coffee flew from his hand, spilling scalding liquid across his lap. Figures in black body armour stormed the boat, leaping through the space vacated by Michael who struggled to roll away from the descending steel toecapped boots.

He was thrust to the floor, a foot heavy on the back of his neck as his arms were pulled and secured behind him. The boat rocked dangerously and underneath the hull Nick could hear the disturbed water lapping and buffeting the small vessel.

He was pulled to his feet and at last got a view of his captors. He had been expecting a gang from the club, his appearance the other night having ruffled too many feathers, but the people in front of him wore uniforms. One of the officers leant forward.

"Mr Nicholas Stuart, you're under arrest on the suspicion of kidnap, false imprisonment and murder."

He was read his rights but Nick was not listening anymore. This was not right. There had been some sort of awful mistake; it was he who had gone to the police for their help. They were meant to be investigating and arresting those who had aggrieved him, not the other way around.

He tried to splutter his innocence, to get Beltran down here, but he was interrupted by a roar of anguish and was pushed from behind. Michael rushed the officer in charge sending him crashing backwards, cracking the soft frame of the walls. The man staggered and pushed back.

"Fuck off, I ain't going back," Michael shouted before kicking at the prone officer, his foot connecting with the man's chin.

Two more officers descended to plug the widening gap. They filled the tiny space of the cabin. They brought truncheons down heavily on Michael's knees and back, but he acted like a man possessed. Nick called out for him to stop.

Finally, one of the officers, tired of the confined struggle, pulled out his pepper spray and released it with full force into Michael's screwed-up face. This was followed by a punch to the back of the head ensuring that his evening ended in unconsciousness.

The pepper spray lingered in the air, caught in the back of Nick's throat and pained his eyes. He was grabbed roughly and pushed up the stairs and across onto the walkway. Through tear-stained eyes he could make out more officers surrounded by an audience of curious onlookers, some enjoying the action from the comfort of their balconies, glasses of wine in hand.

He was marched forward as a police van rounded the corner. The back was opened up and a cage made ready for him. He was handcuffed to the mesh and the door was closed. If he had not already been crying from the pain of the spray he would now have broken down and wept.

Bonita was at home. It had been decided to interview the men early the following morning. A night in the cells might soften them up, make them more pliable for the next day's discussion. She had left at three in the morning, tired and exhausted, the faces of dead women tattooed to the inside of her eyelids. She wanted so much to sleep but knew it was not going to happen. The best she could hope for was a warm bath to ease her aches and some food to replenish her energy.

Miles had overseen the delivery of Nick and Michael into the cells. He had signed the detention order and then followed her home. The night shift didn't need him hanging around.

The pair of them sat in the living room with the television turned down low, a late-night Chinese spread out on the table. They picked at the food, too tired to eat and too tired to speak.

The door to the living room creaked and Abeni looked in. Her eyes shone from the darkness of the hall, lit by the light of the flickering television screen.

"Abeni, what are you doing up?" enquired Miles, who noticed their daughter first.

Bonita screwed round in her seat.

"Sorry, darling, did we wake you?" she whispered.

She came into the room and shrugged.

"I was worried; you'd been gone so long."

"We got stuck at work."

Abeni moved around the sofa and snuggled up close to her mother. Bonita could not remember the last time she had craved so much affection; in her tiredness she seemed to return to a state of childlike innocence.

"Maman made me go to bed but I wanted to stay up and wait for you."

"Is everything OK at school?"

She nodded dumbly, her head burrowed into her mother's side.

Miles sat closer, his eyes now heavy with sleep. He kicked off his shoes as the final member of the family joined them.

Maman came into the room, shuffling and silent on her bare

feet. She held a glass of milk in one hand and sat down heavily in the chair opposite. She smiled at them.

"You work too hard."

Bonita nodded, she didn't want to argue. She wanted to carry on enjoying this moment. The delicate touch of those she cared for, those she loved, around her, keeping her warm and secure. She wanted to lock out the death, the evil that she knew lurked outside the house, the unnamed things that wanted to rip and destroy everything that was real. She wanted to bathe in this golden moment and not think about the last minutes of those girls, all alone, hoping someone would come and save them but knowing that they had been forever deserted.

Her mother smiled from the other side of the room, making Bonita feel like a child again. She remembered being at home on cold nights in New Zealand, a fire crackling in the hearth as her family spent time sharing their warmth.

"Tell us a story, Maman. Tell me where the missing people go."

The old woman took a slow drink of her milk leaving a small white moustache on her top lip before carefully putting the glass down. She seemed to think for a moment before smiling and starting the story.

"The times had been hard in the village because the rains had not come and a drought had set in. Kakudra went every day to tend his field and pray to the gods that the rains would come but the gods did not listen, and little by little the fields wilted until they returned only enough for him to feed his family of seven children." Maman's voice was calm and deep. Bonita felt her eyes closing as the story washed over her.

"One morning Kakudra, his stomach growling and his throat parched, was scratching through the dust of his field and unearthed a small bottle with a lead stopper. Hoping it might contain water he opened the bottle releasing a jet of fire that danced into the air before dying. So stunned was Kakudra that he fell back on to the soil and threw the bottle far away from him.

"When the flame had died he stood and approached the bottle carefully, only to find it had vanished and in its stead stood a dark-skinned man who smelt of flames.

"'You seem very busy,' said the man.

"Kakudra looked at his field.

"'I am, but no matter how hard I work I will remain forever poor. My family grows and so I must harvest more and more to feed and clothe them.'

"'Can they not help you?'

"'They are still young and too small to carry water. Maybe one day they will help but not now.'

"'Then you have much to look forward to,' finished the strange burning man, turning to take his leave.

"'But I do not wish to wait that long.'

"The dark-skinned man stopped and turned. He held his head on one side as if thinking.

"'I could help you. I am a powerful Djinn and in need of company. Give me one of your children and I'll ensure you have a great harvest so that you may earn more gold this year.'

"Now Kakudra loved his family but he loved gold even more and so he agreed. One child out of seven was not going to make any difference and he would at last be a little richer. The bargain was struck.

"Returning home that night Kakudra found his youngest son had vanished and no matter how many times he mentioned his name, his wife knew not of whom he spoke.

"That summer Kakudra had a good harvest and with the extra gold bought himself a bigger house, though it was very expensive and he could not fill all the rooms.

"The following harvest Kakudra was visited by the man again and the bargain was repeated. Again Kakudra lost a child and in return he became just a little bit richer.

"When he had run out of children Kakudra bargained his wife away, leaving him the richest man in the village.

"Kakudra sat in his big house full of gold and cried when the Djinn appeared before him.

"'Why do you cry when you have all that you have wished for?'

"'I have no one to speak to and no one to love. Grant me a wish and I'll give you all this wealth in return for my family.'

"The Djinn replied, 'What need would I have for wealth when I have a growing family who one day will help me to earn more riches than you can ever imagine? I am willing to wait.'

"And with that he vanished to the sound of seven children laughing."

Maman finished and looked at the family but they were already asleep. She crossed to the couch and pulled a blanket from the back of the sofa, covering them to keep them warm. She then mounted the stairs slowly and returned to her own bed to dreams of the old country and myths half remembered.

Seven

The outside light was fitted to a timer and it chose that precise moment to turn itself off, plunging him into shadows. He blasphemed under his breath as he lost sight of the inside of the car boot. He felt tepid rank breath on the side of his face as Tess shifted her weight to lean briefly against him. She let out a little whine of displeasure.

"It's all right, girl," he whispered in the hope of calming her down before they moved out onto the roads. Like him, Tess didn't like to be moved from her place on the couch once they had curled up for the night. But he had no option. It was time to sort this affair out. He had no idea how long he could expect to be away from home and so had to take Tess with him. It would only prey on his mind if he left her alone in the house.

He shut the car boot carefully, talking to her all the time.

"We're just going to see Nick. It won't take long."

It sounded as if he was attempting to reassure himself rather than the dog.

The small gravel of the driveway crunched and shifted under his feet, causing him to keep hold of the edge of the car as he moved his way around to the driver's door.

While searching in his numerous pockets for the car keys he looked up at the sky. There was no moon tonight and few clouds to hide the stars that seemed to be out in abundance. He searched out his wife's, a pinprick of light that he had christened after her in one of his sentimental moments. He felt relieved when he identified it with ease.

He fumbled with his keys in the dark and thought about stumbling back up toward the house to reactivate the light when the door unlocked. The internal light came on.

"All right, girl?"

He would continue the narration to Tess all the way into the city. She liked the sound of his voice and if she remained calm then he would remain calm.

The car started and he reversed out of his drive carefully. He nosed the car towards the orange smudge of artificial light on the horizon.

As the car gathered speed he worried about his son. Nick was the last thing in his life that really caused him grave concern. To everything else in life he now had a *laissez-faire* attitude. It had not always been like that. Perhaps it came with age?

He slowed the car as he moved from the side road and into a quiet village. He had no parents to worry about – they were long dead. He had few, if any, work worries – the university liked to keep him around because he had been there for so long they felt in some small way indebted. He still worked, but it was more on a casual basis than an actual necessity and he only assigned himself something taxing if he thought the work was likely to stimulate him. He had more than enough money tucked away and since the sale of the old house he had no mortgage to swamp him.

His wife had died ten months ago and it was her death that had freed him up more than anything else. It was not that her death was in any way wished for; on the contrary, he would rather have her here than anything else in the world. It was just that after her death he found that things he always considered important were no longer worth worrying about. Life no longer appeared so precious. Mortality had scored against him and he knew there was little point in contesting the result. Once he accepted her death and accepted his new life he felt freer than at any other time in all his years.

Only Nick gave him cause to reflect in a sober light. He had never thought that his son would react in such a delayed manner to his mother's death. Nick had stoically remained calm and appeared to accept the inevitable when she had gone into hospital for the final time, but now it seemed that a small wound was festering in the boy's heart and he had ignored it. Now, it appeared, that wound had gone bad and poisoned his son.

Nick had been dutiful, never overbearing, visiting every couple of days to sit with his mother. His trips became increasingly frequent closer to the end and yet he appeared to take her death as if it was the natural closing of a chapter. He cried at the funeral but after all the condolences had been read, he seemed to rally and get on with his life. He had problems adjusting – they both did – but he had never appeared to be suffering from the torment that now seemed so apparent.

Afterwards Nick had dutifully stayed in contact. He had helped his father to move house when the one they had always lived in was sold. Charles had ensured his son got a bit of money from the sale as he still thought of it as the family home – Nick's as much as his. Nick used the money to pay off part of his mortgage on the apartment in the Lace Market. He had appeared content; he went to work as usual and even though he moaned about the fact it was not what he wanted from life, he seemed to be making headway.

He had always thought that his son was made of the same metal as himself, a chip off the old block. He considered himself an emotionally stable person. That was not to say events had no impact, and like anyone else from one day to the next he could ride the complete gamut of emotions from ecstasy to depression. But those emotions were always moderated to the external world. He was known as a calm and relaxed individual who would cast a cool eye across any problem and turn it into a solution. 'Rational' was one of his favourite terms.

But his son had been starting to act a little differently; his actions had been decidedly odd over the last few weeks, with more talk of wanting to leave work and then talk of a girlfriend that had gone missing. From the first telephone conversation he had thought that perhaps Nick was referring to some recent young girl who had caught his fancy and then gone off without so much as a thank you, but when he met his son he realised something was seriously wrong. He spoke about the woman as if they had been together for a long time, soul mates ripped apart, and the pain he was displaying was evident. He spoke as if she had been abducted rather than merely leaving of her own free will, as if stolen away in the night by some mysterious thief.

Charles knew that any such person would have been introduced to him by his son. They were still very close and Nick would have wanted his father to see her and approve of his choice. He had calmed his son with talk of being forgetful but he knew that no such woman existed, not now and probably never.

Nick was becoming manic; he was full of anxious energy that was spilling out and obvious for all to see. He had mood swings that sent him from the soaring heights to pitiful lows and his eyes seem to dart about the room as if constantly searching for this lost girl or those that he held responsible for her disappearance. Something was not right with him.

The police had soon realised there was an issue here other than the real disappearance of a woman. The state of the apartment had a decidedly male tone; there were none of the small feminine articles that would slip into a place once a woman came on the scene. His wife had always been keen on lace doilies and every piece of stout solid furniture would receive its own lip of lace on which she would stand a vase or other *objet d'art*. Every piece of furniture that they had owned in the old house looked as if it was wearing a pretty cap, as if dressed for an impending wedding. They didn't do anything, these *froufrous*; they just cluttered up the place and made it difficult to keep the rooms free of dust. There was nothing like that in Nick's flat. He had a pile of books in one corner sitting on plain shelves, and a large collection of music CDs, DVDs and old, slightly yellowed film magazines. There appeared to be no feminine touches; come to think of it he never even saw any lotions or potions in the bathroom. What happened to all the bottles of shampoo, make-up and sanitary products that women collected? Once, just briefly, he had experienced the aroma of lavender when entering the flat. Was this her perfume of choice? Or simply the smell of air freshener?

He knew there were many contributing factors to the decline of a person's mental stability. He had spoken to colleagues at the university, people who had studied this issue for years, and the diagnosis did not seem good. They spoke of acute loss and its effects and the understanding that he was hypersensitive and prone to mood swings – and all of them came back with a similar response. Bipolar disorder, manic depression – though of course they all declined to make an official prognosis until he came in for analysis.

From the outset the police had wanted to know about the loss of Nick's mother. It seemed immediately apparent that the lead officer was thinking along similar lines. Beltran was sympathetic and had mentioned to him her real concerns about his son. There was little she could do, as it was not really a police matter, but having the foresight after Nick's little episode to contact him was appreciated. They were powerless in matters of missing imaginary friends. She had made it known that only if Nick became a threat to himself or to the public could they then intervene. Up to that point, apart from wasting police time, he had only come across as confused.

But now it appeared the police had deceived him; they had put all this detail together and in their desperation to keep the streets safe they had fixed on Nick's enfeebled mind and come up with something far too sinister for words. They had put two and two together and come up with five.

The phone that morning had rung several times before he had

managed to pick it up. The loud intrusive noise in the calm of his house woke him from his sluggish repose, at first confusing him as to where he was, in which house he now lived. The voice of his son was panicked, a tumble of words and snivels punctuated in staccato confusion down the phone. He thought at first Nick must have had another turn, an episode that was threatening to overrun his troubled personality, but the real reason soon became all too evident. He had been arrested.

He had rushed around the house getting ready, locking it up for his time away and putting in a call of help to a solicitor friend. Now moving towards the city he took stock, in the hope that a clear mind would be able to cope with the impending arguments and recriminations that needed to be heard.

Bonita had decided to interview Nick. She felt she had a history with both men but the knowledge of what Michael Wheen could be, plus the shelved Natalie investigation, had made her decision clear. She felt she could reason with Nick; that somewhere within that damaged persona there was an individual crying out for her help. She felt she could draw him out and at the same time get a conviction against the other man.

At six in the morning Nick was removed from his cell. He had not slept and his eyes were ringed with red. Whether this was from tiredness or weeping she was unsure, but he looked depressed, wretched, as if he had been through the very pit of hell and returned with the images drawn large on his memory. He had been given a cup of black coffee and now sat alone in an interview room.

His father had turned up an hour earlier but was told to wait by the desk sergeant. Though his mouth was set into a grim line of determination he had sat down, but Bonita knew his patience would be short and would fritter to nothing once his solicitor arrived. She had at best a few hours to get something of worth from Nick.

She entered the interview room accompanied by a young detective. Upon seeing her Nick's face turned from one of abject misery to recognition and hope. He forced out a smile but she remained po-faced, causing his smile to falter and then fade.

"What's going on?" he asked, concern spreading through him like a cancer.

Bonita sat and placed a tape into the recorder. She started it running and turned to Nick.

"Wednesday the thirteenth of September, the time is six ten. Nicholas Stuart, you have been accused of the crime of abduction, false imprisonment and the murder of Nikki Syms, Tracy O'Connell and Meta Purves. Do you understand the crimes you are accused of?"

Nick's face dropped. He looked from Bonita to the other detective and back again, gulping in air in the hope of calming himself. He appeared to shrink away from them, to disappear into himself.

"This is a mistake. I've never done anything to harm anyone."

His skin was ashen, fear and panic goading him to stutter while speaking. Bonita was impressed. She knew he was an actor and if this was his way of presenting a face of innocence, it was good. He resembled a poor panicked animal, desperate for help, for some kind of escape. He would probably chew his right arm off in front of her if it meant he was free.

"Do you live in Flat Eighteen, Hollowstone House, Nottingham?"

"You know I do."

"We found the bodies in your building. They had been there for some time, hidden close to your flat."

He felt numb as the seriousness of his situation started to seep into his mind. The bodies of three women had been found in his apartment block. The idea repulsed him but he was not surprised. The building had always felt haunted, crowded out with suffering souls. He had heard of places which absorbed all the pain and anguish committed in the place into its very fabric, dark emotions oozing between the building's mortar and stone, the dying essence of the victims soaking deep into the foundations.

"Can you explain to me why blood from one of the victims was discovered in the communal hallway, outside your front door?"

He shook his head.

Bonita pointed to the tape recorder. "You have to speak."

"I've no idea. I never noticed it until you pointed it out."

A reasonable answer, she supposed.

"Have you ever been onto the roof of your building?"

"No, never."

"Why not?"

"Why would I want to? Besides, the door is locked. There's no way out."

"The building managers claim they have never locked that door. Who has the key?"

"I don't know."

This didn't seem to be getting anywhere. Bonita decided to change her attack.

"How do you know Michael Wheen?"

Nick looked up.

"He found me. I opened my door yesterday and there he was. He said the same thing that had happened to Natalie had happened to his daughter. It's got nothing to do with these dead women. He introduced me to other people who have experienced it as well. That's what we were discussing on the boat."

"You do realise that Michael Wheen is a suspected paedophile?"

"He explained that. He said you accused him of the crime when a girl was found near his house. Kind of like how you're now blaming me for murders I have absolutely nothing to do with."

Nick felt resentment at the idea that anyone would even think him capable of committing any crime, never mind something as heinous as killing a girl.

"Like before, you're trying to fit up the wrong person. I had nothing to do with these deaths. It was me who came to you for help. Christ, can't you see this is ridiculous?"

"We have you on camera going into a club in St Ann's to meet with Imamu Ferreira, a man known to the police. Care to comment?"

Nick understood that he must have been under surveillance for some time now. Michael had been correct. They had been gathering evidence against him, building a case from circumstantial evidence and misunderstanding.

"I don't know his name, but I went there to find Natalie. I met with a man who I had seen the night she went missing. I thought he could help."

"And did he?"

"No. He spoke some kind of mumbo-jumbo and then started to get nasty so I left."

"And where is he now? No one has seen him for several days."

"I've no idea. I don't even know if we're talking about the same guy."

The questions continued for another hour. Going backwards and forwards over the same ground. It seemed to Nick that no matter how many times he denied something, the accusation was not going to be lifted. He tried to answer what questions he could but he knew nothing. He could see the frustration on her face, the anger starting to rise but being controlled, even though he knew she wanted to grab at him and shake him until something she liked was uttered from his lips.

Bonita let out a long sigh. Nick sounded confused and frightened. If he was involved with these other men his current mental state seemed to stop him from acknowledging the danger they posed. She hit the pause button on the tape recorder and turned to her colleague who had been silently transcribing notes.

"Can you leave us alone a moment?"

"Ma'am?"

The detective looked confused at the breach of protocol but Bonita gave him a look that told him not to argue. He gathered up his things and left.

"I'll be just outside, ma'am."

The door closed behind him with a satisfying thud. Bonita turned and looked at the shaking man before her.

"Nick, you're in trouble, deep, deep trouble. If you don't give me something you're going to go away for a very long time. You've been seen in the company of two men, both of whom have priors with the police. The bodies were found in your apartment block and blood was found outside your front door. You claim a girlfriend who doesn't exist has magically disappeared and personally you seem to be having some sort of breakdown. Now if you're trying to get away with an insanity plea then I can guarantee you'll get it, as long as you tell me how the three of you are involved and help me put the other two behind bars."

He shook his head, disgusted at her simple plea bargaining. He hated her. How dare she try and set him up for this crime. He had nothing to do with it.

"Natalie is real and I did not kill those girls."

Bonita turned the tape back on.

"Interview halted at seven fifteen."

After that they had to let the solicitors in to see their clients. Two men in serious suits with proper haircuts, both of them angry at the interviews having started so early, livid that they had not been included and wondering how best to bill their customers for the lost time. Nick's father was also permitted to see his son. They kept the video surveillance cameras running just in case he confessed under parental pressure.

Just like Bonita, Miles had also been unsuccessful at extracting any information, though Michael had proved far more obstinate that Nick, having refused to speak altogether and turning to face the wall. He had ignored all the questions and sat with a look of resigned hatred on his face. Miles had spun him around in his seat and screamed at the man, spit landing on the suspect's forehead and running down the side of his nose. Michael had hardly blinked.

"Seems to be a conspiracy of silence," commented Miles as he filled their coffee cups with too much instant coffee.

"Nick's talking; I'm just not sure how much he really knows. I think something has happened but he doesn't understand what the ramifications are."

"And that's stopping him from making any rational sense?"

Bonita agreed. "Plus it means any chance of a conviction might be in jeopardy. He could claim mental instability."

Miles listened to his wife and noticed the despondency in the timbre of her voice.

"You sound like you think he's innocent."

She was confused. What had seemed straightforward yesterday seemed more tangled and messy in the new light.

"I think we're only going to find out what happened when we speak to Mr Ferreira. Did Michael indicate whether or not he knew the man?"

"No, nothing. He's like a blank canvas, that one."

Down the hall one of the solicitors slipped out of the interview room and started a call on his mobile. He was nodding furiously and in some state of agitation. Miles watched the man and scowled.

"They're going to make us let them go if we don't get something concrete."

"I think that might be for the best. I think Nick might lead us back to Ferreira. If we were to follow, we could bring him in for questioning. He's the one I really want, anyway."

Miles sipped his coffee; it was still too hot and hurt his lips but he liked Bonita's idea.

The solicitor stepped back into the room and smiled a wide hyena grin at Nick who sat speaking quietly with his father.

"Looks like they might have to drop the charges," he said. "I think they've realised that all the evidence is circumstantial. It seems Michael isn't talking and you've not admitted to anything. I wouldn't be surprised if they let you out this evening."

The solicitor sat as Charles thanked him for his help before turning to his son. He touched him lightly on the back of his hand, partly to comfort him, partly to gain his attention.

"I told you, Nick, this is all a big mistake. I suggest you go back home, get some stuff together and come and live with me. Soon you'll move down to London and all of this nightmare will be over. You've got a career to think about now. This will all blow over when they find the real killer."

Nick turned slowly to look at his tired father. During his time in the cells, throughout the questioning and accusations, only one thing had been running through his mind. He kept coming back to his new contract and role, the idea of which now felt sour, sullied by recent events. He hated himself. This was the worst of times. Someone he loved had disappeared forever and all he could think about was his own acting career.

"If the press find out I'll be dropped from the show."

The solicitor bent forward to sweep papers into his case and snorted.

"The police aren't going to leak this to the press. Arresting innocent people is not something they like to admit. Makes them seem somewhat inept. I'd be surprised if it makes the papers and if it does, it'll be buried."

The solicitor must have had prior information because it was not too long before a uniformed officer entered the room and asked the men to leave. The solicitor protested but he was informed that Nick was being returned to the cells. Charles put his hand on his son's shoulder and gave it a squeeze before he was escorted from the room.

Back in his cell, which smelt of piss and disinfectant, he was given breakfast and a bottle of water. He ate merely for something to do rather than nourishing any hunger. He kept trying to take stock of the events, the meeting with Michael, the talk of unknown powers at large in a world that had always seemed benign yet dull, and his sudden arrest. He was more convinced than ever that the police were simply trying to pin the murders on him and Michael, but the fact that the fire-eyed man was known to the police had raised the hair on the back of his neck. They had called him Mr Ferreira. If this was same man that Nick had met with then he could indeed be the 'Missing Man'. He was violent and unstable. Perhaps it was just coincidence that he had chosen Nick's apartment block for storing the women's bodies, but by using that place he would have come into contact with Natalie; he could have seen her and marked her out as a possible target.

He remembered now, a brush against his arm in the darkness of a forgotten hallway. He had been climbing the stairs, unsteady from drink, his hands held out in the enclosing darkness. Something had lashed out from that gloom and sent him to the floor. Had that been Ferreira? Had he already been to Nick's apartment and removed Natalie, storing her body in the soul-tortured building until he was able to return?

Ferreira was still the key that needed to be addressed. Nick decided at once that he would seek out the man tonight. Whether he was the 'Missing Man' or an innocent bystander, this could be his last chance to put paid to the demons that plagued his own mind.

Nick was let out at six in the evening. His personal items were returned to him and the doors of his cage left open. He noticed that Bonita and the other detectives were conspicuous by their absence.

His father wanted to drive Nick straight to the flat but Nick declined with an excuse. "I need to walk, to get some fresh air and mull things over. Meet me back at the flat."

Charles was not at first convinced but a bark from Tess reminded him that his son was not the only one who needed to walk, and so he begrudgingly agreed.

It was, as ever, a warm night and Nick strode through the city, desperate to put as much space between himself and the police cells as he possibly could. He felt slightly light-headed but he put that down to lack of sleep and the intoxication he felt at just being free.

Reaching the apartment block he noted the police car pulled up outside and the uniformed officer walking part of his beat past the front door. He didn't acknowledge Nick as he passed, and whether or not the man knew that Nick had up until half an hour ago been held as a suspect was unclear. Nick assumed that not all of the police in Nottingham would know who he was.

The phone was ringing off the hook by the time he got in. He picked it up, expecting his father. It was Michael. He had expected him to be waiting outside the station but had been informed that he had been released an hour earlier. He made no comment about the arrest, as if it were just a regular occurrence.

"I took a copy of the photo. Can I come round?"

"I don't think that's wise, considering, do you?"

Michael paused.

"You know you're still a suspect; I'm still a suspect. The only reason they released us was because they don't have enough evidence. Right now they are watching you and me for any signs of alarm, any sign of us doing something stupid."

"Isn't that an even better reason not to be seen together?"

"No. We have to carry on as normal."

Nick agreed on that point and soon relented. Michael must have been calling from close by as it was only a couple of minutes before the buzzer went and Nick let him in. Standing at his half mangled door, Michael appeared sheepish. He was wearing the same clothes as last night.

"I made a copy."

He handed over the photo. Nick looked at it, his only clue – a photo of nothing.

"Thanks, do I owe you anything?"

"Nah." He seemed at a loss for what to say.

"Are you going home?"

"Maybe. The police will be watching the place but it's all I have. I'll need to get the door fixed. Are you staying here the night?"

No. Nick could not face being here, not now.

"You feel dislocated after one of these events. It's probably best if you get away for a bit."

"My father's coming to take me to his later but I've got something to do first. Did the police mention to you a man called Ferreira?"

Michael agreed that they had.

"He's behind all of this. I met him the night she vanished; I don't know if he's someone who Natalie might have known or if he found out about this place because of something I let slip, or whether he is really the 'Missing Man', but he knows something and I want to find out what it is."

"I'd stay away. He doesn't sound like the sort of person to be messing with. You've got a good life ahead of you. Don't end up like me."

Nick noted how dishevelled and pitiful Michael looked – the crumpled clothes, the bad smell, the ravished features, but he ignored the comment.

"I went to see him at the club after Nat disappeared; it's a place for the black community, a place they've set up themselves. He's a strange guy, all quiet and kind of intense, but you know there is something more going on. He has these eyes that sort of look inside you."

His companion suddenly looked interested.

"A black guy, with a thin face?"

"Yeah, do you know him?"

He started to rummage inside his jacket, pulling out a small pile of photos held together with an elastic band and a black notebook full of tiny scrawled handwritten statements and numbered diagrams.

"I've been investigating the claims of the others. Some of them don't mind, Rebecca for instance. She wants to help. The others were less than accommodating. However, something I noticed was that in all of their lives at some point a black man makes an appearance."

"That could just be a coincidence."

He shook his head furiously, the excitement building within him.

"I don't think so; you and me live in the city, but the rest of them, they live in the sort of demographic areas that just don't have a high black population."

Nick was impressed – when it came to research he'd checked out every possible angle. Or was it that he was so desperate he clutched at any straw?

He passed over a wad of photos, seven or eight in all.

"I'm nothing if not thorough."

He looked down at the selection of pictures. They were all different in composition. Some must have been taken furtively, a quick sideways movement of the camera and a rapid trigger of the lens. Another was taken with a telephoto lens from some great distance; the people looked small and insignificant, dark outlines against a lighter pavement. One example was a reflection, the photo of a shop window, the people behind Michael caught in midstep on a busy city street. All of them had one thing in common. They all showed a man in his late thirties with a thin face and deep-set eyes. In some instances he was dressed as if on his way to work, in others he wore street clothes, in yet another it appeared that he was wearing a uniform of some sort. In all of them he was watching. His glances may have been discreet but he was looking directly into the camera. It was intimidating. A face in the crowd that was forever there, forever studying.

"I think he's stalking me. I don't know why, I can never get close to him to ask. I've tried laying all sorts of traps – hidden in doorways and all that stuff – but he has the knack of getting away from me. It's a canny trick. Is it him?"

Nick looked at the face, the eyes; he studied the posture and demeanour. He cast his mind back to the meeting in the club. He was wearing different clothes and his hair was cut in different styles but there was no denying it. It was the same man.

"Those pictures were taken in all of the localities of the missing people. He's always there. Look, he's even in this one."

He helped Nick to find a photo of a road that cut through a soggy looking moor. There was a car driving along the centre line having gone around a bend rather too fast. Looking out of the passenger window was the same face. The same eyes staring defiantly.

Nick took the photo and sat down. His hand moved over the shiny surface. In the dark recesses of the car, hidden almost from view was the clue. A pair of eyes that was watching them, looking out from the darkness, someone who was making sure no clues were ever found, hiding away the missing. But what were his motives? What was this man trying to hide from them? He tried to distinguish the faces of the others in the cars but they were hidden or too blurred to make out. Were they involved, were they part of a bigger plot?

He returned to the other photos. All the time Michael watched him, his breathing quick, his eyes lit up with the knowledge that he might at last have a convert to his ideas.

"The 'Missing Man' is meant to be able to disappear on a whim, the same as this man."

Nick checked the photos for any other similar faces, others who appeared in more than one of the photos. People who could back up this lone man, who acted with him, part of a gang or a cartel, a group who would act as one in the snatching of innocents. There was no one else.

"You sought him out?" Michael asked almost reverentially.

The words stung. That was not right. If anything it had been the other way around. He had not been looking for this man; this man had sought him out.

"He found me."

"But you know where he is now?"

"What do you think he has to do with all this?"

He shrugged. "I don't know…all I know is that he's always there. Always."

Nick looked at the eyes again. They were the eyes of an arrogant man, a man who knew more than others, a holder of dark secrets. Nick could imagine that he was into some sort of crime – drugs, kidnapping, slave trade. Whatever, crime required an innocent to feed it.

"I've been told to stay away from him. He's dangerous."

Nick thought about what Beltran had told him. She had been giving him a warning based on experience. Whoever this man was they should stay away or else…he didn't want to think about 'or else'.

"If he's that dangerous then why has he never tried to stop me? I've seen him but not once has he spoken to me or warned me off. He just taunts me from afar."

Michael had a point. On numerous occasions he could have intervened. Turned Michael into one of the disappeared, or simply beaten him up. But not once had he put his life in danger.

"I want to take this to the police. Beltran, she could help. It could clear our names. They would have to take you seriously if you give them this evidence."

He looked appalled at the idea and took a step back.

"No way. No police. They will just slow things down. We have to act fast. If you're not coming then fine, but tell me where I can find this 'Missing Man'. I'll go alone if necessary."

Nick tried to think of the all the awful things that could happen to Michael, a lone man in the sort of neighbourhood that was best to avoid, meeting a known criminal in a seedy bar. He couldn't let anything happen to him. He had given more clues in the last day than the police had managed since Natalie disappeared. He needed this man and he knew his conscience could not take the loss of another.

"I'll show you where the place is, but I need to speak to my father first. He's expecting to find me here."

Charles did not like it. He had begged with his son to stay in the flat until he arrived but the boy was adamant. He had been curt and to the point in his argument, explaining he would be back by nine and not to worry. He had hung up, leaving Charles angry and feeling hopeless. Nick was going to destroy himself; he was manic, his condition making him act like a rash fool. He knew when Nick was like this there was no reasoning with him so he called Beltran out of sheer desperation.

She picked up after only two rings.

"Nick's going to see this Ferreira man. I want you to stop him."

"I don't think I'm going to have any influence. If he wants to meet with him he will."

"He's going there now."

He didn't know why he said it. Nick had been determined that the police should be left out of this but he wanted to shock her, drum her into some kind of action. The words were out in the open before he had time to think about the consequences.

"What's does he think that'll achieve? The place will be closed this early in the evening. He'll just wind up on a breaking and entering charge."

"Michael wants to talk to Ferreira. They're desperate to find out what he knows. I said to wait until I got there, but they've already gone."

He left the implicit idea hanging on the wire between them, hoping that Beltran would pick it up and run.

"I could get a car to drive past. See what they are up to."

"I doubt they would see anything, or else it could provoke them into doing something stupid. It would be better if you went."

He could tell she didn't want to; she didn't want to get too involved or too close to them in case things got unpleasant later on, but he wanted to leave her with no option. She must go. He was sure she would be able to solve any possible issues that were more than likely to arise. He wanted to mitigate any chance of his son being hurt. She was his insurance.

"I'll go. Chances are they'll just go back to the flat afterwards anyway. I'll wait with them until you arrive."

She hung up the phone. He was left listening to nothing for a moment before he switched off the handset.

Would she go? He was sure she would. She wanted to know about his son. There had been a flicker of interest in her voice. A small tremble that made him think she was concerned.

Bonita was already more than aware where the suspects were going. A listening device in the flat had caught the whole conversation and an officer had already called in the couple's departure with Miles relaying the data to her. She had been on her way home, close to the location of the bar that the watch outside had noted as quiet tonight. She turned on a red light to the screeching of brakes, and headed in the new direction.

The officers were waiting for her when she arrived, parked under a tree, all lights off, blending into the background. They got out as she walked towards their car, tall men retrieving helmets and readjusting batons, pepper spray clipped into belts. They nodded a hello; she knew one of them, the young man named Ben from the raid. She hoped nothing kicked off that was going to test them. She knew it was an overreaction but she wanted to feel safe inside.

They followed at a respectful distance once she explained. It was just an enquiry. A polite police follow-up. They were not to get heavy, not to force the issue. If necessary she could always come back with a warrant. The stolen goods would permit that.

The door was opened before they even knocked by someone

watching the relayed images of the camera, someone who didn't want trouble.

She flashed her badge at the man on the door and explained. He nodded his assent.

"Yes, he's here. Came in an hour ago. Do you want me to get him?"

Give him time to get away. No. She didn't want that. She would go herself. She didn't want him leaving by the fire escape.

She swept into the darkness of the bar, her escorts following nervously behind. Dark eyes turned to face her. A few women and men locked in a slow grinding dance on the floor, bottles of beer hanging from hips or thrown over shoulders, music a deep Reggae beat, a sexy mishmash of vocals, smoke hanging in the air. Drinking started early in this place, the artificial night made it always seem late. It was always just after midnight.

The police officers behind her looked very much out of place.

She spotted him leaning against the bar. He was thin, too thin, a ragged yellow shirt, casually open to reveal a skinny torso, a gold crucifix around his neck hanging over his sweaty gleaming chest. Blue light from the dance floor played over him, lighting him up. He knew they were here for him. He turned his back to her, an insult, a jeer, saying that he didn't care.

She started to walk towards the bar, taking the quickest route across the dance floor. Couples got in her way, blocking her view. Behind her she heard one of the officers curse as someone stepped on his foot or kicked him in the shin. She lost sight of Ferreira when a woman, looking over the shoulder of a man, blew a gum bubble at her; it popped and stuck back to her lips.

She moved aside. He had left the bar; she scanned the room and spotted him heading around the floor, back towards the door.

She turned, colliding with the officers behind her. The music had started playing louder this time, faster. Couples parted and became single dancers, each jumping and moving, shaking and pulsing in time to the beat. By parting, the dance floor had doubled its population and now seemed even more crowded than before. It was too loud to shout. She pointed back the way they had come, the officers turning as one and starting to push their way through the crowds.

She could not see her prey at all, just the backs of the officers as they tried desperately to make a path through the bobbing and weaving sea of humanity. Someone took the opportunity to pinch her arse. It stung her flesh. Normally she would have grabbed the man but she didn't have time. She could feel impatience rising as she pushed the offending arm away.

They broke through the last of the dancers as she saw the yellow shirt of Ferreira duck through a door and into the toilets. They were right behind him. The door slammed shut.

The first officer went straight in, Ben following. Bonita hesitated. But then she changed her mind and moved in after them. She wanted to be there when they grabbed him. She wanted to look into those eyes she had heard so much about.

It was cramped inside and smelt of piss and shit. It reminded her of the toilets in a school she had attended back in New Zealand. The officers were gathered around a person, she pushed them apart, desperate to view the catch.

The old cleaning woman blinked at her from dull watery eyes. A little mouse surrounded by lions. She smiled at seeing Bonita, a big toothy grin accompanied with a shrug.

Bonita didn't understand. They had seen Ferreira enter the toilets. They all had. She had quizzed the officers before she released them, before she allowed them to return to the streets. They both said the same. They had seen the suspect enter through the door and go into the toilets.

They had been mere seconds behind him and there was no other way out. No windows, no doors, no hidden cupboard, the ceiling was solid. There was no possible way for him to leave. And the cleaner, she had just chuckled and clucked, shaking her head.

No…no man had come in, not while she was cleaning the place, it wouldn't be right. It would be indecent.

Her phone started to chirrup. The night was not over yet. Nick and Michael were close. It was time to fall back and see if their presence would be enough to flush out the 'Missing Man'.

Once they were out of the Lace Market, away from the pubs and bars, the streets became quiet. The bright lights were replaced with boarded up windows and large deserted warehouses shrouded in silhouette. Nick could hear the shouts of the drunks in the park as they argued over whose turn it was to buy some more cider. They were lost in the shadowy overhanging trees. Disembodied voices that floated over the iron railings as the world hurried past. They headed for the park now, feeling brave in their companionship. Away from the road they could stalk up on the bar and watch. Examine their options before they went inside.

Sitting behind a wall in the long grass they waited in silence. The club's ground floor was lit in part, the main hall in use while the further outreaches of the building remained in darkness. There was music to accompany the lights; the rhythmic punch hitting out into the night, the bass tones evident from their hiding place.

They waited, watching the clock and the sun. Waiting for one to hide behind the buildings and cast the city back into darkness and the other to count off the minutes before they returned to their united quest.

"What do you do when you're not searching for your daughter?" Michael looked around from his vigil.

"Nothing. I work if I can, in one town or another, until I hear something, and then I leave."

"What about family, friends? Don't they worry about you?"

He shook his head, now just visible in the growing darkness.

"It took a long time to get used to, but eventually you realise what it is they see. You and me, we're just the disturbed to them, and they think it's catching. You'll notice after a time people stop touching you and when you touch them they flinch. It's like being a leper."

"But they still care about you?"

"Probably. But they don't believe what you're saying. It's like being a child again. I left normal living behind a long time ago – it's better this way."

Nick couldn't face that happening to him. To be so alone, to always be the outsider, the person that no one wanted to know. Perhaps they were worse off than those who had gone missing. Few would weep for them as they were forgotten, obliterated from existence, while Michael was a ghoulish creature left to haunt memories only he had.

"Don't you want your old life back?"

"Sometimes I go back to the house where we lived – where we played happy families – and see my ex-wife with her new family. She looks so content. My son, he no longer speaks to me." He paused, as if the idea pained him. "But I can never get it all back. I just want to know Deborah is OK, that's she safe and happy."

Nick wasn't sure anymore that he wanted his old life back. He wanted her, or the idea of her, but he also wanted so much more. He wanted the tantalising life that was just within his grasp and that made him feel as guilty as hell. Like Michael, if he knew that she was all right then perhaps that would be enough, perhaps then he could move on and in time forget about this.

Michael stood up, the conversation spurring him into action.

"Let's go."

Nick looked over the road.

"It's busy. Last time they wouldn't let me through into the main club. They want to take your money but as soon as it came to asking questions the doors are kept closed."

"I don't plan to go through the front door," was Michael's reply.

After waiting for a gap in the traffic they crossed, ignoring the main entrance and heading down a side alley. There were bins blocking the way, overflowing with rubbish heated from the day's sun, the smell ripe and rotten. They squeezed past, small dark shadows flitting away as they moved further down into the darkness. The passageway led them around the building until it opened up into a rear yard. This too was used as a rubbish dump, with discarded broken chairs and beer crates littering the cracked paving slabs. The building itself revealed more of its old character back here. An ornate window with stained glass, dark and unlit, rose to a point in a wall, the red brickwork exposed and blackened. There was a door recessed into the wall that would not look out of place in a church, a brass knocker sitting at an angle at its centre.

They moved across the shade-filled arena, their panting sounding loud in their minds. Michael tried the door but found it locked.

"Should we knock?" asked Nick, already aware it was a stupid question.

"No need," replied Michael, quite prepared to add breaking and entering to his growing list of misdemeanours.

"What about that?"

Nick pointed up at the camera half concealed in the eaves. There was a small red light that glowed under the circular lens. A sign of intelligence, it resembled a faint pupil in a dulled eye. Someone was watching them. He could feel their presence assessing, weighing them up and evaluating. Nick hoped they would not be found wanting.

"Ignore it."

Michael pulled out a penknife and chose the long thin pick. After only a few seconds there was an almost inaudible click as the door unlocked. Michael pressed down on the handle and pushed his way inside. Nick followed.

"Where did you learn to do that?"

"I didn't know I could. I think the lock clicked back on its own."

Nick didn't like the sound of that. It was if someone was playing with them, teasing them or else luring them onto the rocks that would be their death.

Inside, this part of the building smelt musty and damp. They could hear the all too familiar sound of the pumped up music but it was dulled and echoed around the chamber they found themselves in. It was a large hall, reminiscent of a church, chairs already in rows as if in anticipation of tomorrow's sermon. A lectern had been placed at the front of the hall ready to receive a preacher, a man who would bring the light of the Lord into your life, if you would only listen and pay over a small fee.

There was no one present.

"Someone opened the door," whispered Michael, scanning the scene. "Whatever happens, stick together."

He had nothing to worry about. Nick didn't plan to look around the place on his own.

They moved about the room cautiously. There was a curtain at the far end but all it concealed were more stacked chairs and a couple of tables. Apart from the entrance they had used there was only one other way into the room.

"They must be through there," muttered Michael.

He turned to the door and approached it wearily. There was a cough from behind them, a clearing of a throat that had spent years smoking too much strong tobacco.

Spinning around they saw a small old woman shuffling between the chairs. She was bent double and wore an apron around her middle. She held a can of furniture polish in her hand. She looked frail and made a brief effort to dust the back of the chairs.

Where she had been hiding Nick had not a clue. She could have been in some antechamber that they were unaware of, though she was so small she could have been hidden behind some tall piece of furniture. One thing was for sure: her sudden appearance had alarmed them both. So intent was she on moving silently around the room that she resembled a ghost, a silent wraith forever having to clean the inside of the dim hovel.

She didn't seem to think they were any threat to her and

seemed intent on ignoring them until they made some approach.

"Excuse me; we're looking for a man named Ferreira. He comes here to the club. Do you know if he is in tonight?"

She stopped shuffling forward and looked up at them for the first time. Her face was a map of life. Every event was recorded in the wrinkles that formed folds and valleys in her skin. She had a slight moustache that was darker in colour than her skin – which was pale even though she was of West Indian decent. The hair on her head was sparse and it was possible to see a scalp that resembled dark Stilton cheese. It was a disgrace that she still had to work and that the club had even considered employing her at such a late hour.

Her eyes, dark and watery, regarded them with interest.

"We is closed. Come back tomorrow."

She had either not heard them or decided the question was not worth answering. She pouted her lips and waited for them to leave.

"Do you know Ferreira?" Nick asked, assuming she had not heard them the first time.

She turned her attention to him. He felt the full weight of her look, an intensity that yet again made him feel as if he was being examined.

"What you'se wants with him?"

Nick was not convinced she knew who they were talking about; he was not even sure if the woman was on the same wavelength as them, her mind befuddled with age.

"You know him?"

She shrugged and came a little closer. She didn't seem at all scared at being alone in a room with two men who had come in off the street. Perhaps she thought her age guarded against anything untoward happening.

"I knows lotta people."

Michael stepped up to her.

"This man is tall, kind of thin in the face with marks on his skin, scars. He comes in here sometimes. Do you know him?"

She seemed to mull over the description.

"And what would you be wanting with him?" She sounded insistent, as if she would not part with her carefully held information until they replied to her questions.

"We just want to talk. I'm looking for someone and need his help. I think he knows where she is."

The woman came slightly closer again. It was as if she were stalking them, as if they were the prey and she some cunning hunter getting closer bit by bit in anticipation of the fateful final leap. She suddenly stopped her shuffling and sat down in a chair with much expelling of air.

"A girlfriend? He knows lotta girls."

"This was my girlfriend."

"Ahh." She smiled knowledgeably as if this was a regular occurrence. Whether it was over some private joke or the thought of Ferreira turning another man into a cuckold it was hard to tell. Whatever it was, it seemed to be giving her great satisfaction.

"Can you help us?" Michael sounded more forceful this time and it jolted her out of her reverie.

She grunted a non-committal sound. Nick was starting to think that she was not all there and was simply using the conversation as a way to take some time away from the mundane task of polishing the room.

"Finding him won't do you any good. If he runs off with your girl you might as well kiss her goodbye. Do you really want her back after he's had her? Is it worth it?"

She looked up at Nick. Her eyes were dark and hooded. Great wells of inky darkness that didn't appear to have any end. She didn't blink, just stared. Her eyes reminded Nick of Natalie's, lush and mysterious. Eyes that were able to probe deep within you and pull out your innermost secret, expose your most intimate of desires. The old woman had the eyes of a much younger person but they were also eyes that knew of many hidden secrets.

"I want her back. I didn't treat her right. I never really knew who she was and how I treated her was wrong. I need at least to say sorry."

The thoughts and feelings seemed to come out of nowhere. They welled up and broke out of his mind; the words were forming on his lips before he knew what he was going to say.

"I should have been…I would give her anything she wanted, go anywhere and do anything only if I can see her again and explain. I need to know I'm forgiven."

She held out her hand. Nick took it. Her skin felt like dry autumn leaves that appeared to crack and break under his much firmer touch.

"She didn't deserve me. She wanted so little and I gave her nothing. I was selfish."

He felt tears prick at his eyes and knew he was about to cry in front of this stranger. He felt himself kneel down as she wrapped an arm around his head and pulled him close. He could smell her sweat and dirt, the fat she cooked with, the washing powder she used, the cats she kept, the smell of the rain and the wind and the sun that she walked through. All of it mingled and enveloped him. She smelt like a mother, she smelt like his mother.

"There, there," she cooed, her breath hot on the back of his neck.

Nick pulled back from her and looked around at Michael who was standing still, his face in a state of anguish as he attempted to understand what impact this woman could have on the loss of his daughter.

"Who is he?" he asked in voice that was almost a whisper. "Why does he do these things?"

The old woman ignored Michael as Nick got back to his feet and wiped his face.

"Who is he?"

This time Michael shouted the words and stepped forward. The old woman stood her ground and looked at him. She ignored what he asked and simply shook her head as if he were a disgrace.

"I need to know."

Nick put out a hand to stop Michael from getting any closer. He had seen him have an outburst before and knew he was capable of violence. All the frustration of the hunt seemed to boil up in him and explode all at once. He wanted answers and he wanted them now.

"Calm down," Nick said, putting a hand on his arm. He feared Michael would turn and hit the woman in his anger.

He pushed the arm away, his eyes barely alighting upon Nick who now realised that this man never had any intention of helping him. This had always been about him, about his loss and his search. He had merely used Nick to get to this point and now he wanted answers.

"I will not calm down. I want to know."

He pushed past, causing Nick to stumble backwards and collide with a set of chairs. The noise of them clattering on the polished floor reverberated around the room. He put a hand down to steady himself as Michael leapt forward and gathered up the old woman in a tight grip.

The veins in his neck were engorged with blood as he thrust his face close up against her and screamed.

"Tell me where my Deborah is!"

He shook her violently. She was nothing more than a pathetic rag doll in his arms, too weak to push him away or struggle out of his vice-like grip.

"I swear to God I'll kill you if you don't tell me!"

Nick grabbed as his arm and attempted to wrench him away from the defenceless woman.

"Michael, you're hurting her. Stop it."

He let go and turned to look at Nick. His eyes were glazed over, a madman's stare made of nothing but ice. He shook his head as if to dispel some wild thought.

"Sorry, I don't know…"

He seemed to have calmed down as Nick turned his attention back to the old woman. With Nick's eyes averted from him for a second, Michael balled his right hand into a fist and punched Nick in the side of the head. Nick being no fighter and not prepared for any kind of violence was caught unawares, the blow spinning him around. He lurched and smashed into the fake pews. The chairs scattered beneath his weight, plastic mouldings and metal legs sprang up, jabbing him in the ribs and thighs as he landed awkwardly amongst them.

Nick could hear Michael screaming as if suddenly demented, but whatever he said was lost in the sound of the chairs and the crunch of his body. Nick kicked at the open ground and tried to get to his feet as Michael turned and kicked him sharply in the thigh, sending Nick skidding across the polished floor.

"Don't you dare get in my way, you fuck!"

He advanced on Nick again as he scrambled desperately to get to his feet. Nick knew he was bigger and stronger than him and this pent-up aggression now appeared as brute strength. Nick slipped again and only managed to get onto his back as Michael stood over him.

"I need to know what happened to her..." His face was red; spittle erupted from his mouth, disgust was etched into his features.

Nick looked around for any chance of escape. There was none. He was worried that he was about to get the beating of his life and, even if at some point he fainted away from the pain and knocking of his brain against his skull, he knew that Michael would continue to rain blows down upon him. He wanted to close his eyes but he could not look away from the distorted face of his assailant even though he knew it was a hopeless task to stop him.

A voice behind Michael said one word.

"Stop."

Nick thought at first it must have been the old woman but the voice was strong and commanding; it was a voice that had to be listened to, a voice that had to be obeyed.

Michael half turned as if aware for the first time that they were not alone. As he turned something hit him. Something far more powerful than himself. He was lifted for a brief moment from the ground before he crashed back down with a sickening thud and slid along the polished floor scattering chairs through his momentum. He didn't get up.

Standing where Michael had towered above Nick was Imamu Ferreira. He rubbed at a hand ornamented with large gold rings, any one of which could act as a sizeable knuckleduster. He clenched his fist once or twice to check no bones had been broken before looking down at Nick.

"The Lord examines the righteous, but the wicked and those that love violence his soul hates."

He held out an arm for Nick to grasp and pulled him to his feet with little effort on his part. Nick looked about. There was no sign of the old woman who in all the excitement must have gone to get Ferreira. She must have moved quickly as there was only one way out of the hall and he had never seen her leave. Nick had not seen Ferreira arrive either. It was as if he had suddenly appeared behind Michael.

Nick looked over at Michael's slumped form. He lay quiet, not moving, but he was still breathing.

"I'm sorry; I would never have brought him if I'd known he would get like that."

He shrugged as if the apology meant nothing.

Nick expected Ferreira to now start on him. The man was all muscle and bone and he must have had several willing accomplices waiting in the wings. It would not take much to give Nick the thrashing of his life. Only his father knew where he was and he doubted he would be of much use. He watched with large brown eyes as Nick stepped back, out of his reach, a distance of respect. He neither smiled nor said a word. He looked inquisitive as if Nick was something new, some strange and exotic creature. Something he had never seen before.

What should Nick say to him? Here he was at last. Standing

alone and defenceless. Nick pondered whether to run at him, pick him up from the floor, dash him down and beat the living daylights out of him until he told him what had really happened. Told him where Natalie was. But in his heart of hearts he knew it would be useless. Ferreira could be as inconsistent as the air if he wanted and one false move from him would result in him disappearing. Perhaps this time he would fade away forever and Nick would end up like Michael, eternally searching for a ghost.

Ferreira tapped at his hip pocket and brought out a packet of cigarettes. He lit one from an old matchbox and took a hard drag before speaking.

"Why do you search? Don't you know your task will be fruitless?"

This was not what Nick wanted to hear. The only wish he had right now was to get Natalie back, apologise and return to his new life. Ferreira spoke as if she were dead.

"Did you kill her? Is that why I'll never find her because you're this 'Missing Man'? You're the person the police are looking for, the one abducting all the girls?"

He looked amused at the idea as if the mere thought of such a thing were impossible.

"Missin' Man? Yes, I suppose I am a missin' man. I've been called many things over the years and that's as good a name as any, but I have nothin' to do with the abductin' of young women from the streets. I'm far more subtle than that. I offer only what I'm asked to provide."

He took another long slow drag on his fag, gulping at the nicotine and smoke. He blew it out slowly, forming the last little breath into a ring that grew as it departed his lips, becoming more indistinct as it floated up into the air.

"What happened to her? That's all I want to know," Nick pleaded.

Ferreira stretched like a languid cat in the full day sun and smiled. It was a grin that stretched across his face until it hid all other features.

"Even I don't know that. She no longer exists as far as you are concerned. But you wished it and because of it your life will be better, perhaps hers will too. It's never just what you say, man, it's a thousand little things. Perhaps you would always have ended up seekin' me out. People often do, comin' to me before they've even thought about it prop'ly. Don't blame yourself, man, it's the way you're made."

"She is still alive though."

He turned his lip up in a non-committal way.

"I'se can't say. I just help them on the way."

"What are you?"

He moved his head from side to side making the bones crack while he yawned.

"What's it matter? I am what I am; I was put here to help. It's not my fault that after all this time you lot can't even ask for a simple wish. I would not exist if your race had not created me in the first place. You spend so much time dreamin' and wishin' and hopin' for somethin' better that the universe had to fill in the gap. I'm what it created. Just look on me as your 'fairy godmother'."

He smiled another Cheshire cat grin.

"So what d'ya want from me?"

Nick thought about the myriad possibilities he could ask of this man but when it came down to it there was only one thing.

"I just want her back. I want to apologise."

"She can't come back. It's a one-way ticket."

"Then send me after her."

He regarded Nick as he sucked on his teeth.

"I can't. One request, that's all you get. Three little wishes don't wash with me. You should be careful what you wish for, that's what they always say. It's not my fault that none of you listen. What about your life here?"

"I don't care." Nick said it but knew he was lying to the man.

"You would never find her and even if you did she might not

want you. She doesn't even know who you are anymore. She could be livin' a million different lives by now."

"I'll search her out."

He seemed to examine this proposal and then decided.

"Take what you've got, what you're goin' to have, what you've wished for and enjoy it. You lot are only here once and for you, if you're careful and take what I've given you, you get to be famous and rich. Be content. In time, if you let it, this'll all seem like a dream."

He pushed past Nick who followed him to the outside door. He turned and faced Nick for the last time.

"Perhaps you'll learn from this. If you find someone that's more important than your own dreams, never let them go. It was you who said the magic word; now you have got to live with the consequences. I know it's hard for your lot to cope, but in life you have choices. Sometimes you make the right ones and sometimes you don't. Whatever happens you have to live with that. 'I wish' is a powerful idea."

Nick was shocked at what this creature was suggesting. He had willed it to happen and by doing so had to understand that his action had consequences. But he had not meant for it to come true, he had not really wanted it like that, it had been an off-the-cuff remark, he had been angry, he had been drunk. But it all made sense. He had been a fraud as an actor; it was a dream he entertained, nothing else. This week all that had changed dramatically. He had got the dream job in a way that was not normal, his life had shifted and everything he had wanted was now coming true.

And then he remembered, he remembered the bar and his spoken command...

"I just wish things were different."

"I just wish things were different."

"I just wish things were different."

He had condemned Natalie without a moment's thought.

He looked around at the slumped form of Michael.

"What about him?"

Ferreira looked over at the body and seemed to consider what to do.

"I'd leave him here. He'll wake with a sore head. You should never get involved in another man's quest."

"But what did he want? What did he wish for? Because I don't believe it's what he got."

The creature grunted. "He didn't ask for anything. Someone else did. His wife."

Ferreira opened the door to the backyard and looked outside. He sniffed the air. "I think it's time I left this city," he said, almost to himself.

There was a commotion from the bar. The music which had been playing continually since they had arrived suddenly stopped dead. It was replaced by the shouts and curses of those angry at being interrupted. Nick thought he could hear fighting coming from the bar, the sound of tables being overturned and the dramatic sound of glass breaking.

Ferreira stood in the doorway, the warm darkness of the night outside and the dim interior of the hall casting him in shadow. He turned to look at Nick.

"Friends of yours?" was all he said before beams of flashlight lit him like fireflies playing over his body.

"Stop, police!" came the cry from some unseen officer.

Ferreira grinned at Nick before shaking his head solemnly, the beams from the torches causing his features to warp him into some mythic gargoyle, a creature of darkness, his eyes lit from the inside by the heat of long forgotten deserts.

"Time to go," he whispered, as he stepped back into the shadows and vanished.

Later Nick was unable to believe what he had seen and the account he gave to Bonita was garbled, a mishmash of disbelief, but from where he had stood Ferreira had simply disappeared. He had been there one moment and then…nothing. No slow fade or flash of light – he had just gone, melted into the shadows and vanished. If it was not for the fact that two armed officers also claimed that they had had Ferreira in their sights and had experienced the same thing, Nick would have blamed it all on some mental imbalance and the stress of the last week.

Michael had been woken with some less than gentle prodding from the police and now sat in the space where he had previously lain sprawled. He was stunned, and as the police officers moved about he ignored them. Sitting like a baby with legs bent out in front of him, he was shaking his head from side to side accompanied by a low mumbling from trembling lips.

Nick looked over from his place next to a standing Bonita.

"He went berserk," he muttered, still not fully able to conceive how the man who had been helping him had changed with such ferocity into the mindless thug who had attempted to hit a defenceless old woman.

Bonita eyed him with a look of hatred.

"He's a violent man. I suggest you stay away from him and from Ferreira."

"He's gone."

Bonita looked back and got out a small notepad.

"Where? We still need to bring him in for questioning."

Nick knew that they would never be able to find him. Whatever he was, whatever his powers and abilities, he was not accountable to this world. If he wanted to stay hidden he could.

"You won't find him. He's gone."

"That leaves you two in a bit of a predicament."

"There's nothing I can do about that. One thing I do know, Ferreira, if that is even his real name, never killed those women. He's not the 'Missing Man'. I don't know what he is, but he's no murderer."

"I don't think you vouching for him is really going to help."

The police had stood Michael upright and were busy applying handcuffs. He still seemed dazed and confused and let them help him to his feet; he let them treat him as fragile, breakable. Nick watched as they manoeuvred him towards them, Michael's face never leaving the floor.

"Am I under arrest again?"

Bonita looked up.

"No, but you'll have to come in for questioning."

She followed Nick's gaze to the shackled Michael and understood his concern.

"We won't need the cuffs."

The officers understood and the handcuffs came off.

"Are you all right?" Nick asked Michael, worried that perhaps Ferreira had hit him too hard and caused some kind of brain trauma.

He looked up at the voice and whispered, "Where's my Deborah?"

His face took on the look of a simpleton, a blank mask of misapprehension and tortured knowledge that he didn't want to admit.

Beltran was unsure how to respond. She decided on sympathy as her best bet. "She's all right, wherever she is, she's all right."

"But why?"

It was a simple question, deep-rooted to the very notion of who Michael was. He had spent so much of his life in pursuit of the answer and to be thwarted at the last moment must have been agonising for him. He was so convinced that by tonight he would have had his answer.

Nick was not sure Michael could cope with the truth but found himself blurting it out.

"It's our own fault. Ferreira said we were to blame for daring to wish and giving up what was most precious to us."

The man's face shattered into a thousand lines as tears welled in his eyes.

"But I never wished. I never wanted for anything…"

He began to sob as the police led him away.

"What was that?" asked Bonita.

"The truth," he replied.

The policewoman shook her head as if believing the whole world had gone mad. She was about to reply when a commotion back outside made her dart for the exit. Nick followed, closely watched by a couple of uniformed officers.

Back out in the yard, the police were making for the narrow alleyway that led back out onto the street. Nick was pushed and jostled forward. Something was happening out on the road. Exploding out of the gap, the crackle of a police radio in his ear, Nick just had time to watch as Michael disappeared into the now dark park followed by three running officers. A fourth officer, his nose a bloody mess, lay on the floor, his hand clamped to the offending gushing appendage.

Bonita was screaming at more officers to get after him as Nick felt a hand on his shoulder. He was not going anywhere. She marched back over and in a voice barely concealing her anger told his escort to take Nick back to the station.

Within an hour Nick found himself in yet another interview room; his father had arrived and was sitting at his side. He was not under arrest but they were angry and desperate to know where Michael was going.

They had lost him in the dark of the park, disappearing into the thick bushes and, they assumed, scaling a wall into the back garden of an adjoining house. Whatever he had done to escape, by the time a police helicopter was in place with a powerful spotlight, no trace of Michael could be found.

"Where's he going?" asked Bonita.

"I don't know. Back to his boat, away from here. I have no idea."

"Did he say anything to you to suggest where he might go next?"

"Nothing. His daughter won't be coming back, he knows that

now. He's probably gone somewhere quiet to come to terms with it."

He knew she was angry but he didn't have any answers for her anymore. Michael had gone, Ferreira had gone, Natalie had gone. That was the end of it.

"What did you mean when you said to him that it was your own fault?"

"That's what Ferreira meant. It was my own fault that Natalie disappeared. I brought it on myself and there's nothing I can do to change that. She's gone forever. Michael's the same; all of them are the same. We dared to risk everything when we wished and this time someone was listening."

Bonita had run out of questions. She looked tired and drained. She felt even worse. They had been so sure that these three men would lead them to the end of this investigation, that one of them would turn out to be the killer, but instead the whole investigation was falling to bits as the suspects seemed to vanish into thin air.

The whole case was becoming as intangible as one of her mother's stories. People who vanished never to be seen again, it was all too inexplicable for words. It did not belong to her world of procedure, cause and effect.

Her phone went, a text from Miles asking her to come up to the office. Perhaps he had some good news.

"I'll be back," she mumbled as she left Nick talking to his dad in an almost relieved and excited manner.

Back upstairs Miles was sitting next to one of the uniformed PCs and listening intently. He was nodding, his eyes gleamed with excitement.

Bonita entered the room.

"Nick doesn't know anything. I think we're going to have to let him go again."

"No problem. I don't think it's him we want anyway. I've been going through the reports made from the interviews of the residents at Hollowstone House. Nick's neighbour tried to leave on the night the bodies were found, saying he had a train to catch."

Bonita sat; she knew the story, she had been there and suffered the tirade of racist abuse he had spat at her.

"Well, PC Sharpe here, on his own initiative, checked the rail timetable." He pointed to the officer she knew as Ben who smiled sheepishly. "And there were no trains to Derby that time of night."

Bonita nodded.

"So he's a cantankerous old git who likes wasting police time. So what?"

Ben turned around in his seat and carried on the story.

"I went in that evening and took his interview. He claims he never saw or heard anything, just like all the other residents. He had nothing to say of any use but I noticed his rooms were decorated with puppets, you know the sort that they use in the theatre or in Punch and Judy shows. Hundreds of them, all staring out from the walls, some looked quite old. It was creepy."

Bonita imagined their faces looking with blank unseeing stares into the room, aware of the decrepit figure of the old man watching them in their individual niches. Empty faces, sightless eyes, sitting and waiting in the semi-darkness. The idea brought to mind another image. Dead bodies arranged in anticipation of his return, women done up like dolls sitting in the darkness, waiting for a vicious killer to come home and play, their eyes glassy and blind, all hidden away in the night. She thought of a hidden room, where a puppeteer could sit amongst his dead brides, his creations mere playthings, now that life had been drained from their bodies.

"Oh God…" she muttered to herself. He had been there all the time, watching and listening as the investigation unfolded around him, her attempt to link Nick to the crime and find the one missing body he had nothing to do with. She remembered him touching her, the repulsion she had felt as his skinny finger had jabbed into her, how it had lingered slightly too long, how beneath the thin lace of her blouse he would have been able to feel her skin, her flesh.

She had discounted him too early, perhaps worried that she was only considering him because of his serious skin ailment. She didn't want to be seen as prejudiced, accusing just because he seemed to inhabit a corrupt body.

"He would have tried to get rid of the blood; the marks were right outside his door. He must have had trouble with Trudy Grasson's corpse as he dragged her out onto the roof."

Miles nodded.

"It also explains why no one has seen anything. Once he had got them back to his flat he could have dispatched them quickly and then taken them out on to the roof. No one overlooks the building and it saves him going back out onto the street. His only possible witness would have been our friend Nick, and let's face it, his mind was elsewhere."

Bonita felt ill as she wondered whether the 'Missing Man' had been sizing her up, thinking of placing her half naked amongst his growing party of corpse dolls. How many times had she been upstairs as he had watched her through his door spy hole?

Miles picked up the phone and ordered two cars to meet them at the apartment building. He stood and moved out towards the car.

"PC Sharpe, come with us. I don't suppose he will put up much of a fight but you never know what he's got hidden in that place."

Beltran followed, Nick and his father forgotten in her excitement to bring the case to an end.

"They're not coming back, are they?" Nick felt tired and wanted to leave. It was all over and now all he wanted to do was get back to living his life. He had things to do; a career to start that would require all of his energies and resources. Somehow this felt like the end. The events that had unfolded in the old chapel building were now a bit of blur. He was no longer quite sure what he had seen and whether any of it was really true.

"They're busy. I'm sure someone will be along before too long."

His father was as pragmatic as ever: if you waited long enough you got an answer, you just had to be prepared to wait out your time. Nick spent the next five minutes mentally ticking off the things he had to do to get his life back into order. He was only interrupted when a police officer, stuffing his face with a canteen sandwich, looked in and said they could go. Beltran was not coming back; she was too busy to see him. This was the end; he was no longer needed.

The door was tougher than it looked and it took the officer three attempts with the ram to bring it down with a brutal crash that sent dust and dirt from the floor high into the air where it was breathed in and stung at Bonita's throat. It smelt old, corrupt, the air of a discovered tomb that had not been touched for centuries. She was almost too scared to enter, fearful of the horrors she would find lurking inside. She was a child again, looking deep inside the darkest of caves. Evil lurked inside, dark matter that did not deserve a place on this Earth, something ancient and primordial that brought only terror to the real world.

She entered on a wave of police officers, their blue uniforms and fluorescent jackets, screaming radios and powerful torches reminding her where she was. This was not some prehistoric creature. This was a man, and men could be stopped, they could be brought to justice and silenced.

With her first step inside she became aware that they were right. They had found the 'Missing Man', this was his lair. It was from here he had planned and from here that he brutally murdered women. All this time she had been so close, and yet she had been so wrapped up in Nick that she had not read the signs. She was fallible; she had failed in her job.

The officers, led by Miles, fanned out into the different rooms; they moved with brutal assertion. They had come to reclaim this place from the darkness. The curtains at the windows were ripped down, light switches were snapped on and furniture was overturned in their eagerness to annex the flat. They opened cupboards and ripped beds from the floor, bookcases were moved and the loft space interrogated but the flat was empty of life. They were alone, the 'Missing Man' had already moved on. He had left behind his old life, left behind the decaying apartment in a dying building, in a city gone mad. His time was over.

Bonita joined her husband in the living room. A single armchair sat in the centre of the floor, the stage surrounded by his adoring spectators. Around the walls sat the dolls. All shapes and sizes, theatre puppets, mannequins, a child's rag doll, Barbie, even a sex doll, all done up in their best with ruby red lips and staring eyes. An audience of mute still women, forever alive and yet forever dead, waiting for the return of their master.

Bonita felt a shudder pass through her and looked to her husband. He was looking at the walls, disgust etched into his features.

"He's gone," she said, the words coming out as a whisper. Her voice was hoarse from the thick dust.

"We have to find him."

They would scour the country for the 'Missing Man' and with the help of other forces he would in time be caught, but his escape would always be on their conscience.

"We will," was all she could say.

Eight

Nick was packing up the remaining items of his life, piles of which lay on the floor of the living room, into crates. He had thrown a lot of things out. He wanted to travel light, start afresh with as little to bind him to his old life as possible. He needed to make this change but the nagging memory of Natalie was slowing him down. This would be his last night in the flat; he knew already he would not miss the place. The studio was putting him up in a hotel until he found somewhere in London to live.

He had not so much quit his job as just not bothered going back. Munch didn't seem to mind. He said he was bored with the whole set-up as well and planned to move down to London perhaps early next year. He'd had enough of Nottingham and wanted to try somewhere different – new bars, new clubs, new people – a completely new life.

There was a knock at the door. Nick had not been expecting anybody. It was already dark outside and far too late for his father to be calling. He moved to the new front door and opened it.

Bonita stood with her back to him; her overcoat was wet from the torrential rain which had started that evening, cleaning the now empty streets of the summer debris. She was looking at the doorway across the hall, the frame smashed and broken, a piece of hardboard screwed into place where the entrance should have been. It was covered in police stickers warning people to stay away. Most people would not need to be warned, the rooms beyond seemed to radiate some dark message, easily picked up by those who knew what had happened inside.

She turned and smiled at him.

"Sorry it's late; I was just in the neighbourhood."

Nick knew that was not really true. If she had come it was because she had something left to say. He wondered about inviting her in but decided against it. He had an early start in the morning.

She slipped her hand inside her coat and handed over a paper. It was dated today, a local newspaper from the city of Derby, a town close to Nottingham but far enough away to spark animosity and distrust between inhabitants, resulting in regular fighting at football matches and name-calling between kids. She pointed to the headline. Nick read it and felt a pang of guilt.

"He was arrested for beating up his ex-wife. Took a claw hammer to her. It's touch and go as to whether she will live."

"Why?" It was all he could think to ask.

"Kept saying something about how she gave Deborah away, that it was all her fault, not his. He kept speaking about daemons, a pact with the devil."

Nick looked at the grainy black and white image of Michael being led into a police station. He seemed to have slipped back into a state of quiet resignation. His head was slumped against his chest and his whole body seemed to have collapsed in on itself.

"He won't talk. Won't say anything. Looks like he hasn't eaten for several days; he must have been hiding out somewhere because he stinks. He was just waiting for the right time to strike. The doctors are calling it a serious mental breakdown."

"What'll happen to him?"

She shrugged.

"He'll be charged but will probably end up in a high dependency unit. The doctors say he has a form of bipolar disorder, the same as you, which is interesting, don't you think?"

Nick understood what she was trying to say. How she was attempting to rationalise away the 'missing'. His supposed disorder was a nice tight box into which she could place all the unanswered questions; it was convenient and, to her logical mind, welcome.

"Do you want the paper?" she asked as he refolded it.

He handed it back. "No, thanks."

Turning to leave she stepped back into the shadows of the crumbling hallway. She halted and spoke again, her voice quiet as she kept her back to him.

"Do you know what an Ifreet is?"

Nick was about to close the door. He stopped and let it rest open, a crack of light from his hall spilling out as a single shaft across the filthy communal carpet.

"No. What's one of them?"

"Something my mother talks about, a creature from the old country that can make loved ones disappear."

Nick hesitated. He mulled over the possibility of such ancient things existing today, living within Nottingham, a myth made real, a creature from foreign nightmares. He shook his head before replying.

"Never heard of them," he said dismissively and closed the door.

He listed to her feet retreat as she headed back down the stairs. They faded into muffled footsteps before they vanished completely.

Nick moved into the bedroom. In the darkness, the rain pitting against the window, he took off all his clothes. The bed was still unmade from the morning he had awoken to find her gone. The sheets felt cool. The first time in weeks. He slipped between them and closed his eyes and thought of Natalie. From somewhere he could smell lavender and it comforted him. He hoped the smell would remain ingrained into the sheets of the bed, the pillowcases and his clothes, but he knew that when he washed them it would slowly disappear, fading away until nothing remained, forgotten with time until it became nothing more than a dream of a period that might never have happened.

Tomorrow

It was raining in New York City. It had started that afternoon, thick black clouds that blew in from the sea, dark and bruised blotches that blocked out the sunlight and made it feel as if night had already drawn a blanket over the State. The pressure had grown as the street grew quiet; the wind died to almost nothing, litter falling to the sidewalk while the withered tree leaves stopped their rasping. A single crack of thunder announced the rain. An explosion of lightning bounced off the tall glass offices, making many think a new attack had begun, but it was merely the herald of change.

Fat, greasy globules fell from the sky, splattering off awnings and fire escapes. They were slow at first but soon built in momentum, filling up the dry spaces until the smell of dust was lost and the pedestrians were forced to seek shelter from the torrent.

Sara watched as a hobo, pushing a cart laden with trash, made for the underpass. He shuffled forward, his rags darkening in colour as the rain was soaked deep within his mishmash of clothes. He didn't seem to be too bothered, keeping his head bent and continuing his slow walk down the street to the intersection. He reached the end, stopped and looked up at the sky, acknowledging the weather for the first time. He shook his head and laughed at a private joke before turning the corner and disappearing from view.

Cars slowed as visibility shortened. A cab sent an arc of water, dirty from a pothole, high up against a chain link fence, drenching the billboard behind. Somewhere a dog howled to be let in and far off in the distance a fire truck blared into life.

The few customers that had sat huddled together down one end of the diner departed over the next few hours. Some waited, sipping freshly brewed coffee, for the worst of the weather to pass. When it didn't they hailed cabs or ran down the street under dampening sheets of the New York Post and made for the subway.

The short order cook left early, putting up a sign that read 'No Food', even though he still had two hours of his shift left. He gave Sara instructions to lock up before his bus rounded the corner and he dashed out into the evening.

Alone, she read a magazine a customer had left in one of the booths, a lurid tabloid that contained nothing but short articles on worldwide conspiracies and diet fads or else sensationalised the pain and anguish of others. She tried the crossword but discovered she had finished it in twenty minutes and the remaining quizzes were too easy to even bother with.

She turned to the first of the coffee machines and turned it off. She cleaned down the sandwich bay and took the trash out the back. She wiped down the Formica tables and swept the floor clean of the day's debris; she even threw some bleach down the toilets in the rancid washrooms.

With the place now empty, she finally decided to lock up early and moved over to the door. As she did so a shadow crossed her path and the bell to the door chimed. She cursed herself for being too slow and placed her foot against the bottom of the door.

"I'm afraid we're closing for the night, sir."

She wanted to go home, she wanted to slip out of her uniform that smelt of grease and had a large ketchup stain down the front; she wanted to bathe and wash away today. She wanted to sit on the couch and watch the TV and she wanted to forget all about what had happened.

She pushed herself forward trying to close the door but somehow the customer got inside the premises and stood behind her, dripping onto the newly mopped floor. She had been convinced that the gap would be too narrow to allow entry, but the man had slipped past her with ease, like a cat through a picket fence.

She turned to him and scowled.

"Just a cup of coffee?"

His voice had an accent, strange and exotic, that matched his thin dark face, pockmarks on his skin. He smiled and white teeth flashed before he turned and removed his overcoat.

Sara didn't normally care to be on her own in the diner with just male customers. She had heard stories and she worried. Even with the illegal pistol her boss kept in the office, she still felt vulnerable. But she felt relaxed with this stranger. He felt more like a family member or a long-lost friend than someone who had just barged their way into her life. She shrugged and went behind the counter to get the coffee. One cup wouldn't make any difference; she would still be home earlier than usual.

"Don't talk much, do you?" he said as she poured the coffee out in front of him. He took the cup with both hands and took a swig, even though it must have been far too hot to taste.

"Just how's I like it. Thick and strong and sweet. Reminds me of the coffee we used to get back home."

Sara studied his face. He was handsome yet at the same time forgettable, a face with no age. He could have been thirty or eighty or somewhere in between. Only his eyes gave away a gleam that could be put down to youthful mischief, they seemed to almost glow with a hidden heat. They were eyes that hid a tantalising mystery, but she didn't feel afraid.

"Where's home?" she asked.

He looked at her, a fire haze seeming to pass across his stare, a reflection from the metal counter she assumed.

"Faraway," he seemed to sigh. "Faraway and a long time ago."

Sara didn't really understand what he meant. How could anyone be from a long time ago? She put it down to a mistranslation; perhaps his English was not too hot.

He smiled again, making her relax even further, drawing her closer to him.

"But enough about me. Tell me about you. What's an intelligent, pretty girl doing working in a place like this?"

And to Sara's surprise she told him. She told him everything, about the college course she wanted to do, the crap apartment she rented with her friend, her father whom she hadn't seen for ten years and the man who was married and said he loved her but lived uptown with his wife and his family and house and his sports car and she wished how everything could be different, how it could all change and how she wanted a new life.

The mysterious man smiled, his eyes widening as he grinned and nodded his head. He understood change; it was what they always wanted. It was what they always asked for. It was why he existed, those wishes, whispered with casual abandon when they thought no one was listening. Well, he was listening, he was always listening.

"Good," was his simple reply, his eyes flashing with a flame born from a forgotten desert, and his smile widening. "Very good indeed."

And for a second the world skipped a heartbeat, the rain increased in tempo and a life shifted.